Telling the Truth about Jerusalem

For D

ANN OAKLEY

Telling the Truth about Jerusalem

A Collection of Essays and Poems

Basil Blackwell

© this collection Ann Oakley 1986

First published 1986

Basil Blackwell Ltd
108 Cowley Road, Oxford OX4 1JF, UK

Basil Blackwell Inc.
432 Park Avenue South, Suite 1503,
New York, NY 10016, USA

BRITISH LIBRARY CATALOGUING IN PUBLICATION DATA
Oakley, Ann
   Telling the truth about Jerusalem: a
   collection of essays and poems.
   1. Women — — Social conditions
   I. Title
   305.4′2   HQ1121

   ISBN 0-631-14773-X
   ISBN 0-631-14951-1 Pbk

LIBRARY OF CONGRESS CATALOGING IN PUBLICATION DATA
Oakley, Ann.
   Telling the truth about Jerusalem.

   Includes index.
   1. Feminism—Literary collections.   I. Title
PR6065.A44T4 1986   828′.91409   86-11764
ISBN 0-631-14773-X
ISBN 0-631-14951-1 (pbk.)

Typeset by System 4 Associates, Gerrards Cross, Buckinghamshire
Printed in Great Britain by T J Press Ltd, Padstow

Contents

Note about the Title

The title of this book is not intended to refer to any real or imagined goings-on in the city located in the Israel of either Biblical or modern times. The 'Jerusalem' of the book's title signifies a land we aspire to live in, regardless of the fact that we're unlikely ever to make it.

Another historical referent of Jerusalem is described on p. 29. It's no accident that women in British Women's Institutes sing a setting of William Blake's poem of that name. Blake's Jerusalem displaces the reality of grimy, industrializing England with a (w)hol(l)y rural idyll. A man demands all sorts of militaristic equipment ('a bow of burning gold', 'arrows of desire', a 'chariot of fire', etc.) in order to make his country the green and pleasant place it ought to be. Women demand all sorts of ideological and social equipment in order to do the same for their own sex. Telling the truth is important in this endeavour. We need to tell the truth about all cultural accretions, including symbols. We need to tell each other what it's like to live in time, and understand that people in the future (if there is one) may read into our experiences all kinds of meanings we don't know are there.

Part 1

Living in the Present, While Still Having Dreams

'Mummy, what are those steps going down off the pavement?'
'What steps?'
'The steps going down from the pavement, over there.'
'They go down to the Underground, to the trains that go under London.'
'No they don't. They go down to the Queen's palace and to the country where the fairies live. That's what I dream about. I think that's much nicer.'

Child (aged four)
Mother (aged thirty-seven)

1

Introduction:
the Snows of Seinäjoki

Seinäjoki is a medium-sized town (population 25,000) in the flattest part of Finland – a region called Ostrobothnia, lying east of the Gulf of Bothnia which divides Finland from Sweden. At Seinäjoki, five railways meet: it is a provincial centre of some importance. Its inhabitants are proud of the localized prosperity of Seinäjoki and look inwards to their own culture and history with an attitude of infantile indifference to the world beyond. Moreover, as the town brochures boastfully proselytize, Seinäjoki is itself world-famous because it is the homeland and workplace of the Finnish architect, Alvar Aalto. Aalto designed the town's Administrative and Cultural Centre, which includes a town hall, a library, the state office building and a church, 'Lakenden Risti', consecrated the year Seinäjoki became a town (1960). The church has a cubic volume of 20,680 metres and seats 1,374 people. It could be a cathedral. Its pews of North Karelian red pine hide loudspeakers in their backs: acoustics were not Alvar Aalto's strong point, and the priest at first could not be heard. But the church's marvellous undulating white ceiling, geometric brass candelabras and stark wooden cross undoubtedly sooth a European eye accustomed to the architectural excesses of Chartres, St Peter's, St Mark's and St Paul's. This is a cleaner way of feeling closer to heaven – if there is a heaven. The air is not even cold, despite the minus 25 outside; it is warmed not by the Holy Spirit but by underfloor heating. The Finns do not think suffering ennobles the soul.

In the morning the sky has a metallic cast of blue. It shines, sunless, moonless and starless, like the glossy prints of Christmas cards so hungrily bought by the rain-drenched English, who lust after the symbol of a white Christmas. In England it snows at Christmas only once or twice in a decade. The snow when it finally descends is apt to be disappointing, glancing off the pavements into a nothingness of water.

But the snows of Seinäjoki are different. Uniting home and institution, road and river, railway and telegraph line, their sanitariness is efficiently convincing: this is a good world. We need the snow to cover our tracks, our mistakes. Here it does so. Thus we are saved.

I think the Finns take this view of the snow. At least, such a view is reflected in the way in which they deal with it. For the Finns walk confidently, placing the various bits of their feet down in a different order from that required in summertime. They wear sensible, well-cut boots with ridged non-slip soles, so there can be no danger of unintentionally sliding on the snow (intentional sliding being, of course, another matter). Even the men wear fur hats with earmuffs like wings. You know they're not really taking off because of the rooted seriousness of their expressions. There is no danger that these Finns will fly. They don't even try any funny business in their cars, though one learns not to trust in anyone's brakes when crossing the road. The fact that a few car bonnets are open and emitting long leads under windows signals the occasional failure of the system: everyone needs their batteries recharged occasionally. At night, when only an idiot would be on the streets, the snow ploughs take over; huge, irreverent ETs. It isn't nice (so unromantic) to see the natural environment thus ineluctably preserved by mechanical aids.

The other side of the snow is the setting of each twig of every tree in diamons effervescent like champagne; rainbows underfoot, breaking and remaking themselves in the sharp noises of frozen snowflakes; plains with their cushioned acreages under a wide silver moon. It's the moon at teatime brushing great blackbirds into the sky; rivers masquerading as roads; Seinäjoki's only hill, an upturned lilywhite Anglo-Saxon breast; cold air in shotgun bursts down the lungs, filling the warm pink spaces with a warning of natural hazards to be overcome.

Snow is kind, but also cruel. It doesn't want us wholly to be taken in by its appearance of benevolence, for it knows that the inhabitants of a snow-bound world are forever changed by their uncomfortable purifications.

I went to Seinäjoki in 1983 to work, to talk about how to do medical sociology in an inhospitable climate – although I'm not sure whose climate I'm talking about now. The course to which I contributed aimed to teach a variety of health-care professionals a greater understanding of the causes

and social context of health and illness than their professional training
was likely to have given them. It was also designed to help them with
that activity called research. Perhaps the cultural difference made this
seem less of an uphill struggle than I would have found it in my own
country. Perhaps the Finns are simply rather polite to strangers, or
perhaps the power gap between scientists and social scientists is less of
a chasm there. At any rate, I enjoyed both the teaching and the learning
that went on in Seinäjoki. Amongst the mini-research projects presented
for discussion by the dentists, obstetricians, psychiatrists, and so forth,
was one on the effect of smoking on pregnancy – or on the pregnancies
of the 288 pregnant women in Tampere, Finland, known to be smoking
in 1980. According to another survey, in Oulu and Turku 66.3 per cent
of a randomly sampled community of persons were classified as psychotic,
neurotic or bedevilled by character disturbances in 1969–72; five years
later the women had become slightly less neurotic and the men slightly
more so. We also had a very interesting discussion about how to research
adolescents' perceptions of the threat of nuclear war, and the possible
impact of the atomic threat on what is inaccurately described as health
behaviour. In the end a nationwide postal survey was done, of 6,851
Finnish twelve to eighteen year-olds. The response rate was 81 per cent;
one in four of the young people thought about the threat of nuclear war
two or more times a week.[1]

Seinäjoki stands as a metaphor for many of the themes in this book.
First of all, many of the pieces included in it were originally written or
presented in international settings. Secondly, there is the symbolism of
the snow. When I came back to London from Seinäjoki, I hung above
my bed a local landscape. The snow in the picture is pale blue touched
with pink, and it is heaped softly around the roots of black lace trees.
In the middle of the picture, lines of fir trees intercept the blue of the
snow and the blue–red of the sky; it is sunrise or sunset and a white
button sun is hanging there in the sky just off-centre like a UFO (the
best things on earth attract a science fiction language). The sun is
balanced in a line of red–pink colour stretching above the fir trees and
from one side of the picture to the other. Its presence makes the sky
bleed but the sun doesn't care. The only other items in the picture are
a few farmhouses, brown-walled and snow-roofed. In them one supposes
lie sleeping Finns enclosed in pine, heavy-duty duvets and many centuries
of learning one-up-personship on the Eskimos' laughably sophisticated
answer of using the snow to live in as an answer to the problems of living
in the snow.

Rural snow-bound landscapes, such as one finds in Scandinavia, have always been a potent cultural symbol for me. The other day I met at a party a woman who is an expert on Chinese ceramics, and she said she had always been fascinated by China, but she hadn't the slightest idea why. She even said that as a child she had found Chinese easier to learn than English, because she couldn't spell, and the Chinese use a pictorial language. But this is really not an explanation of why China had this meaning for her. Nor do I have an explanation of why snows such as one finds in Scandinavia have had a special place in my head.

So far as travel is concerned, there are many appropriate philosophies. 'Travel broadens the mind.' 'It's better to travel than to arrive.' 'Travelling makes you appreciate home.' Fanny Burney said that 'Travelling is the ruin of all happiness'; once you've seen the Acropolis in the early morning, or St Mark's in Venice wrapped in yellow autumn mists, there's not much love left for St Pancras station and even less for the Saturday trip to Tesco's or Sainsbury's. Travel can reduce sane, organized people to a mere semblance of their former selves. (I once paid an excess baggage charge only to find the cause was an unemptied hot water bottle.) A few days or weeks trying to survive inhospitable foreign plumbing will lead most of us to substitute a steaming hot bath for our more usual intimate fantasies. I've seen normally sensible people become quite deranged when chasing the all-elusive bath plug in Russian hotels – a misery which clearly divides the sexes, women being much more disturbed by it. On a visit to China with 18 European 'experts' on maternal and infant health care, I remember a trip outside Beijing to see two rural communes. It's the habit of the Chinese to ply their foreign visitors with endless pots of tea during meetings and then with an infinite supply of Chinese beer during meals: one is therefore driven, sooner or later, to find a way of emptying one's bladder. But the communes, being communal places, neither believe this should be a solitary act nor have any plumbing at all – simply dug-out earthen pits with wooden covers in buildings that look like cowsheds. In this situation the European 'experts' reacted in one of three ways: (1) they developed a condition called acute retention of urine; (2) they invented all sorts of complex strategies for being alone in the cowshed ('I'm just popping out to have another look at that laboratory'/'I think I left my notebook/camera/glasses down the corridor'); (3) they made the best of it. Both gender and nationality were good predictors of these reactions, Norwegian men being especially prone to the first reaction, while Danish women excelled at the third (and English women came somewhere in between).

One may, of course, travel far to learn things about oneself that could have been learnt at home. Lecturing in Beijing or Birmingham, in

Seinäjoki or Shanghai, I am able to focus my energy single-mindedly on work and myself, which I cannot do at home – even though I know it's good for me. I suppose this is one of the things Fanny Burney had in mind when she said travel ruined happiness. In *Travels with a Donkey* R. L. Stevenson put forward the idea that the reason for travelling is travelling. I don't think this is quite right. The seasoned traveller's worst nightmare is of the journey that is never over. Yet, on the other hand, perhaps the habit of our culture *is* too much to pursue the moment of arrival. Savour the peace of the train journey along the Rhine, the red sun hung over the Oslo fjord early in the morning, and the wonderful curiosity on the faces of the Shanghai Chinese, because these are moments of being alive which enable us to break out of our normal channels of thought and activity. They give us intimations of a world beyond ourselves.

The title of this book, *Telling the Truth about Jerusalem*, comes from an article I wrote for the magazine *New Society* in 1984. It refers to the origins of Sir Hubert Parry's setting of William Blake's poem 'Jerusalem'. The musical setting was written for the suffragette victory of 1918, but is more usually acknowledged as a celebration of British nationalism, not to mention colonialism. Truth is always relative and always subjective. There is always more than one truth. For the same reason, I am not going to apologize for certain features of this book. As one of those who read the manuscript 'anonymously' for the publishers put it: 'the fact that she's been to all those fancy places will get up some people's noses.' Of course. Allergy to privilege and elitism is quite rightly rife among those who identify with the underprivileged. I can only say that my travels abroad, without a donkey, have mostly been hardworking ones, and they've been undertaken because I believe a parochial vision is one reason why our planet's in such a mess, and because, having long ago given up hopes of a revolution, I now concentrate on the finer and smaller-scale question of how to alter the world by changing the attitudes and behaviour of just a few of its inhabitants.

I don't know what price has to be paid for this choice of strategy, but there's always a price for everything. It's not reassuring (but it is logical) to discover that 'professional' people have more than their fair share of brain tumours.[2] No assumption is worth having unless it can be challenged. For example, accidents are a main cause of death in many countries, and when it comes to the question of prevention, it's essential to know the culture. In Papua New Guinea, 48 per cent of burn cases admitted to hospital are due to grass skirt burns:

...grass skirts, made from dried coconut or banana leaves, and often stained with natural or artificial dyes, are a popular, traditional and economical mode of dress worn by females of all ages and by some males too. But their use is not without risk, since open fires are used commonly for cooking and warmth, and are mainly tended by the women.[3]

Before the advent of *in vitro* fertilization and embryo transfer, not all conceptions were by copulation:

On 12th May 1863, a bullet fired in the American Civil War by the Confederates is said to have hit and carried away the left testis of one of Grant's soldiers. The same bullet went on to penetrate the left side of a young woman who was ministering to the wounds of the injured. Two hundred and seventy eight days later, she, firmly insisting on her virginity, gave birth to an 8lb boy.

Yet even such bizarre conjunctions may have the starry endings of a Dallas soap opera:

[The doctor] approached the soldier and related the story, later introducing him to the mother. The two formed an attachment and married, later producing three more children by conventional means.[4]

The themes covered in this book do not range as widely as I would have liked them to have done. The material in the book comes mostly from one distinct period in my life, governed by particular preoccupations. The book's four sections deal with living in the present, motherhood, health, and the possibility of a feminist sociology. Feminism, whatever it is, has inspired all of them. But the concerns within feminism that are taken up in this book reflect, not unnaturally, my own concerns: motherhood and heterosexuality rather than non-motherhood and lesbianism, for example. By talking about what I know about rather than what I don't, I wouldn't, of course, in any way want to belittle other people's options. Yet within the themes covered in this book there *are* some more all-embracing orchestrations: technology and its social control, the mind-body divide, conditions of health and illness in the individual and the community, that admixture of personal statement and public reflection called for by the insistently intimate politics of feminism itself.

Some of the pieces are marred by a certain repetition; the difficult relationship between fewer deaths and more doctors cited in Peebles and Helsinki is one example. I have edited the lectures to cut out many of these repetitions, but some refuse to be removed. A further obstinacy in the book is the way in which poems appear from time to time. Just as *Taking it Like a Woman*[5] was a combination of fact and fantasy, so *Telling the Truth about Jerusalem* is a mixture of scientific fastidiousness and poetic licence. Within both literature and science, the last 20 years have seen a growing recognition of how knowledge and its literary representation are socially constructed. Whatever is produced, whether a compilation of scientific data or a simple story, we are sticking to a quite arbitrary collection of rules. As every good feminist and every good revolutionary knows, rules are meant to be broken. But there is another consideration here: the set of a culture becomes like concrete aspic unless some people sometimes start to do some things differently.

There are many different ways to tell stories about science and about life. *Telling the Truth about Jerusalem* suggests some of them – but it is in no way a definitive statement. It's more in the nature of a peace offering.

2

From This Moment On
Making the Most of It
Sanctus

These three poems are all in different ways about time, about the desirability of getting the most out of the present, and understanding that neither the very best of our experiences nor the very worst are likely to last. 'From This Moment On' was written during the course of a rather difficult year in my life, when it felt as though dreadful events kept happening, and it wasn't easy to cling on to the knowledge that most human beings are survivors. The second poem, 'Making the Most of It', was written after a concert at the Royal Festival Hall in London in 1979, where I went with a friend. I was impressed by the tragedies around me, but determined to brush them on one side; going out on the town wouldn't get rid of the tragedies, but would allow the experience of present pleasure to overlay that of past misery. More than that, it represented an ethical choice about a better way to live.

In 1977 I had a malignant growth on my tongue, and the piece that follows the poems, 'Minor Intimations of Mortality', is an account of aspects of that experience. The third poem, 'Sanctus' belongs in this context, since it affirms the immediacy and vitality of our everyday environment – qualities which are lost when we are tempted to brood endlessly on the fatal possibilities around and inside us. In her famous essay, 'The Moment', Virginia Woolf asks what constitutes the present moment:

If you are young, the future lies upon the present, like a piece of glass, making it tremble and quiver. If you are old, the past lies upon the present, like a thick glass, making it waver, distorting it. All the same, everybody believes that the present is something, seeks out the different elements in this situation in order to compose the truth of it, the whole of it.[6]

From This Moment On

the tree stands in a milkfield
bland without looking
green summer is gone with its harvest
of flowers, on stiff stalks unbending

now only the wind blows
hard through the glass
and dark rain drops unbelieving

in a vast silence
when feet straddling pine needles
sit at odd angles wondering
where they are pointing

things that have happened
seep in round the doorposts
pour liquid light through holes
chased forgotten into clean white ceilings

old events insinuate cheap credit
across the midnight blue of plastic skies
held up by angels

angels denying their satanic past
when halos were crowns of thorns
and hearts bled in the garden of Eden
under moons of cross men

so although we might stand naked in some innocence
trying to think purely of time present
yet still all the rest of it

is with us and around us, like a dirty overcoat
dragging pockets full of coal and pebbles
along difficult pavements
defeating even the luck of the black cat

12

all time is beyond a joke
but now especially in our middle age
(the middle age of time, as well as our lined faces)
we cannot help but crack a winning smile

finding small emeralds in our pockets
there instead of cats' eyes
flashing us on our way

Making the Most of It

the whole world's a cripple

the violinist with his wasted legs
the man over there with his foot on a chair
you with your questionable ego
me with my malignant tongue

oh dear the president's got piles
the gp's heart went out like a light
during a busy surgery one night
I know a man who no legs at all
and he's forty this fall

my aunt had holes in her face
from eating grass they said
my granny's brain clogged up with blood
it isn't nice to see the dead

the whole world's a cripple

but you don't need legs to make music
you can dream if you can't shit
those who pride themselves on being fit
aren't – and anyway what the hell
as the man said the bell

tolls

life is a gift
to celebrate
what's your tipple
mine's a cripple

just hold my hand
and we'll paint the world gold

Sanctus

sometime ago, I believe last week only
it seemed to me that life was holy

flowers opened in the sunshine
people smiled showing white teeth
tadpoles turned triumphantly into frogs
nothing too dangerous fell from the sky

a pacific mood governed the universe
all was well with the world and its people
no wars would happen; little confrontations
might melt in the sunshine, becoming instead
litanies of mild affection

calm like custard covered me
nothing moved inside me
except the word 'sanctus'

I saw power only in dewdrops
lust lived quietly in white butterflies
anger floated as an unborn cloud
at the end of an endless road

but this should have warned me
of the imminent moment when
sacred would become profane
being unable any longer to hold within it
old blood, dry tears, and a broken lightbulb

3

Minor Intimations of Mortality

Looking in the mirror, I could see that the side of my tongue was lumpy and irregular. For some time I had been bothered by a slight soreness on that side, especially when eating apples. Trying hard to disregard and 'normalize' the symptom, I had in any case little time to pursue it, having just had my third baby in the midst of an uncompleted research project. I then went for a routine dental appointment, and showed the mysterious area to my dentist; I said gaily, and somewhat unthinkingly, 'It's not cancer, is it?' He arranged for a biopsy to be done. The consultant who told me the result used the strange, euphemistic language that I have since recognized as the dominant mode of communication with patients with cancer. 'Most of the area we biopsied was all right', he said, 'but a little bit in the middle was invasive.'

THREAT TO HAPPINESS

I was thirty-three, had never smoked or consumed undue amounts of alcohol, was not a curry addict, and had never encountered syphilis in an oral (or any other) manner. It seemed unfair, to put it mildly. That night I lay awake until the baby's 6 a.m. feed, frozen (literally, despite a warm spring night and two hot-water bottles) by the knowledge that I had cancer. I knew little about the disease, but assumed that it was always systemic and terminal. I had watched my father die painfully

Source: Originally published as 'Living in the Present: a confrontation with cancer' in the *British Medical Journal* (1979) 1, pp. 861–2.

of bronchial carcinoma some four years earlier, and I was now under the same consultant at the same hospital as he had been. What seemed particularly outrageous was the contradiction between malignant disease and the benignancy of birth; this third baby had been especially welcome, and was (is) an exceptionally beautiful, calm, and responsive child. My illness threatened this postnatal euphoria and the happiness of our entire family. It was a concrete threat to the baby, since I was breastfeeding and was told to wean her immediately. But most shattering of all was the realization of my own mortality – like the dying man in Tolstoy's *The Death of Ivan Illich*,[7] most of us 'know' that life is temporary, but few of us apply this perception to ourselves unless we have to.

My treatment consisted of an iridium wire implant, preceded by a nasty dental extraction (five heavily filled teeth and one impacted wisdom tooth). Against considerable opposition, but encouraged by a sympathetic lady registrar, I refused to wean the baby, which is why I had the dental extraction as an outpatient, and I felt a quite disproportionate sense of achievement at negotiating hospital admission for the iridium implant on the morning of the operation (so I could give the baby a couple of extra feeds) instead of on the more usual day before. My four radioactive days were spent in relative isolation; friends could visit for 10 minutes each, and some nobly did, one bearing a half bottle of champagne which I sipped through a straw. My older children (then nine and ten) were allowed to rush in and hold my hand and rush out again, and the baby was held up for me to see through the glass wall of the cubicle. This I found especially distressing. I got through the four days mostly by defining the expression of breast milk as my main occupation; I threw the milk down the basin, but the object was to keep up the supply. The trials of obtaining a breast pump on a cancer ward would have been funny in any other context, and I'm sure I was seen as a 'difficult' patient.

Attitudes to Malignant Disease

That was getting on for two years ago. After six weeks of not being able to eat, talk, or sleep (these doctors never tell you enough about side effects) I recovered sufficiently to move house, finish my research project, and write two books. The baby went back to the breast after four slightly difficult days on SMA administered by a devoted father, and stayed there (on and off) till she was 14 months old. Every three months I go back to the hospital for a check-up, during which I stick out my tongue and have to remember not to wear polo-necked jerseys so that the doctor can feel my neck. I have graduated down from consultants and registrars, and am now seen by whoever happens to be around, which I count as progress.

I cannot say that I ever forget that I have had cancer. But it is amazing what people learn to live with. It has been an eye-opener in many ways. Firstly, I am impressed by the need for research in communication between medical staff and patients with cancer. I was never offered any information about my illness, and although my questions were certainly answered, I know (by checking with my medical colleagues) that some of them were answered dishonestly. Most doctors seem to be unable to confront their own feelings about cancer.

Secondly, anyone with cancer has to come face to face with society's attitudes to malignant disease and these are extremely fatalistic. I'm sure that some of my friends expected me to drop dead almost immediately – or at least to *look* different – and when I didn't they didn't know where to look. Susan Sontag has written about all this in her excellent book *Illness as Metaphor*,[8] which I advise anyone concerned with the treatment of patients with cancer to read. Children, as always, go to the heart of the matter. I remember explaining to my ten year-old son what it was that I had on my tongue, using suitably childlike expressions. 'You mean you've got cancer', he said. The biggest bane of my life as a patient with cancer is the lady in the pink overall (a voluntary helper, I imagine) who weighs people in the out-patients clinic. 'Oh good', she says, 'you've put on weight' – when I am still desperately trying to lose my post-baby bulge.

LEARNING TO LIVE IN THE PRESENT

While I definitely could have done without the experience of having cancer, there is no doubt that it has permanently altered my attitudes to the conduct of my own life. I have learnt to live in the present, which seems by far the best way to live. I have ceased to be impressed by the ephemera of academic life, and am interested only in doing the work I want to do as well as I can. I reckon that if people have unfulfilled ambitions they ought to fulfil them, so this year I am going to write a novel, not start another research project. All those tortuous wranglings with conscience about work versus motherhood suddenly seem very clear to me. Children are precious and lovely and, although they do not 'need' their mothers as our cultural ideology of motherhood suggests, I, as a mother, certainly need them.

Oddest of all is the fact that only this confrontation with death has enabled me to realize how happy I am. That, I'm sure, must be a poignant reflection on the kind of society in which we live.

4

Millicent Fawcett and her 73 Reasons

Histories of British feminism are not complete without the struggle for the vote, and among the names synonymous with this is that of Millicent Fawcett. The official story of Millicent Fawcett's character and role is somewhat dull, but, as usual, the truth, when probed, is considerably more interesting. I wrote the piece that follows in response to a request for a chapter to be included in a book on feminist theorists – both known and unknown. To write it I spent a delightful week at a cluttered desk in the Fawcett library in east London. What was delightful about the week was both the excursion into Millicent's intimate affairs (cupboards full of letters and assorted papers), and the chance to escape from the standard routines of life: telephones don't ring much in libraries, and the life of a historian, when only briefly experienced, seems happily bereft of those immediately painful decisions and choices that have to be made all the time in other disciplines.

At the end of the week spent in the Fawcett library, I did not much like Millicent Fawcett. Her sense of duty and honour reminded me of my grandmother, who had devoted herself during much of my childhood to trying to get me to behave properly. But on the other hand, I could see that Millicent could laugh at herself (a golden quality), and was possessed of an imagination that pushed her on to achieve and experience things other people would die merely thinking about.

Source: Originally published under the title 'Millicent Garrett Fawcett: duty and determination' in D. Spender (ed.) *Feminist Theorists*, London, The Women's Press and Pantheon (USA), 1983.

Her memorial in Westminster Abbey describes her as having 'won citizenship for women'; her obituaries call her 'the Mother of Women's Suffrage' (*Oxford Mail*, 5 August 1929) and 'a great reformer' (*Manchester Guardian*, 6 August 1929); it is certainly part of that amputated history of women most of us encounter during our formal education, that British women owe their enfranchisement to some unanswerable combination of Millicent Fawcett's sweet reason and the Pankhursts window-smashing activities.

There is no doubt that by far the greatest part of Millicent Fawcett's life and energy *was* devoted to the cause of the vote. But for 61 of her 82 years she worked for an objective – the enfranchisement of women – that she herself always believed would be achieved eventually because of widespread social change rather than because of the activities of a single political movement – or, indeed, her own (or anybody else's) as an individual. In 1886, 16 years after her first public speech on the subject, and 32 years before women obtained the vote on equal terms with men, she wrote: 'Women's suffrage will not come, when it does come, as an isolated phenomenon, it will come as a necessary corollary of the other changes which have been gradually and steadily modifying . . . the social history of our country.'[9] She compared progress towards the vote with 'the gradual triumph of Christianity'[10] and with 'the movement of a glacier. . . like a glacier. . . ceaseless and irresistible'.[11] Denial of the importance of her own role as leader of this 'ceaseless and irresistible' movement was a motif of her speeches and writings throughout her life; 'I am always troubled' she once wrote 'by the knowledge that I get so much more praise than I deserve.'[12] In her Introduction to the 1891 edition of Mary Wollstonecraft's *A Vindication of the Rights of Woman* she stated (partly, no doubt, in order to console herself that such a morally questionable figure as Mary Wollstonecraft should have been associated with the same cause as herself), 'There is no truer or more consolatory observation concerning the great movements of thought which change the social history of the world than that no individual is indispensable to their growth.'[13]

So, the two largest unanswered questions about Millicent Fawcett have to concern what the vote meant to her (why was it important?) and how she managed to pursue with such apparently unfailing determination and optimism a goal that took so long to reach and which she did not see as within her power to win anyway. The paradox of the second question provokes two possible answers. Either Millicent Fawcett's relation to the enfranchisement of women must have been akin to the irrational fervour of a religious crusade (God/good will triumph in the end and I believe in him/her), or there must have existed in her character strong qualities of dogged persistence and an unrevolutionary lack of imagination. Both answers appear, in some measure, to carry some weight.

Millicent Fawcett was born Millicent Garrett, either the seventh or eighth child of Newson Garrett, an East Anglian shipowner, and his wife,[14] an intensely religious woman who worshipped her husband and was a domestic superwoman, organizing her large household of ten children with such methodicalness as would have qualified her, according to Millicent, for a role in big business. Millicent was fond of saying that she was born in the year of the Irish famine and the repeal of the Corn Laws (1847), and that the following year saw the downfall of half the old autocratic governments in Europe. In her autobiography, *What I Remember* (1924), her mother is scarcely mentioned, but the close relationship that existed between her and her father gets a good deal of attention, and it was undoubtedly very important in moulding her outlook on life. Through her father, the political events of the day and their importance were communicated to her. She recalled at the age of six holding her father's hand while he persuaded men to volunteer for the navy at the start of the Crimean War; and some time later him 'coming in at breakfast-time with a newspaper in his hand, looking gay and handsome, and calling out to all his little brood, "Heads up, shoulders down; Sebastopol is taken."'[15]

Important events in the emancipation of women had a habit of happening on Millicent's birthdays: Queen's College, the first institution for the higher education of women, opened on her first birthday in 1848; on her ninth in 1856 came the first petition for the removal of the disqualification to the holding of property by married women; on her eighteenth in 1865 her sister Elizabeth (later Elizabeth Garrett Anderson) qualified as the first woman doctor; and on her seventy-first birthday in 1918 the Representation of the People Bill, giving women their first right to the franchise, became law. She claimed to have been a woman suffragist 'from my cradle', a deeply held sentiment which was reflected in her biography of one of the historical figures she most admired, Joan of Arc: 'Someone in the crowd called out to ask if she were not afraid. Her reply was "I was born for this."'[16] The apocryphal story of how Millicent first explicitly appropriated the fight for the vote as her own is recounted by Ray Strachey in *The Cause* (1928, 1978). It tells how she, her sister Elizabeth and Emily Davies, Elizabeth's friend and pioneer of women's education, were sitting together one night in the Garretts' house in Aldeburgh:

After going over all the great causes they saw about them, and in
particular the women's cause, to which they were burning to devote their
lives, Emily summed the matter up. 'Well, Elizabeth', she said, 'it's quite
clear what has to be done. I must devote myself to securing higher education, while you open the medical profession to women. After these things
are done', she added, 'we must see about getting the vote.' And then she
turned to the little girl who was still sitting quietly on her stool and said,
'You are younger than we are, Millie, so you must attend to that.'[17]

Growing up in such a household taught Millicent the lesson that there
was nothing odd about the ambition to improve the lot of women; such
an ambition was, in fact, expected of her. In particular it was expected
of her by her father, who was also instrumental in encouraging her sister
Elizabeth, through a series of vicissitudes, to enter the medical profession. A streak of feminism ran through the extended family: her sister
Agnes and her cousin Rhoda trained as home-decorators, an occupation as unfeminine at the time as that of doctoring; various women in
the family supported Josephine Butler's campaign against the 1866 and
1868 Contagious Diseases Acts, and allied themselves with one branch
or another of the suffrage movement. It was her sister Louie who took
Millicent to one of J. S. Mill's election meetings in 1865 – the first public
occasion on which women's suffrage was brought before the English
electors as a practical question. Mill's example, personality and con-
victions 'kindled tenfold' Millicent's own nascent enthusiasms.

Girls in the Garrett household were encouraged to non-domestic
achievement, but they were also expected to marry. This Millicent did
at the age of twenty. The man she married was a blind thirty-three
year-old Cambridge academic and liberal politician, Henry Fawcett,
best known for his career as Postmaster-General in Gladstone's 1880
Government (a position in which he made substantial improvement in
the employment conditions of women post office workers). The proposed
marriage created a rift between Millicent and her sister Elizabeth – not
the only one they were to experience; Elizabeth opposed the marriage,
and Millicent's biographer, her lifelong friend Ray Strachey, does not
say why. However, according to Josephine Kamm (1966), Elizabeth
herself had been invited to marry Henry Fawcett some years earlier,
and remained especially fond of him. Such complications in Millicent's
life are hard to uncover, partly because, in commissioning Ray Strachey
to be her official biographer, Millicent almost certainly made clear that
there were a number of things she wished to be omitted; and partly
because with absolutely proper Victorian reserve, she herself was not

given to committing her feelings to paper or, indeed, indulging in them
publicly at all.

Millicent was quite obviously devoted to her husband. For some years
she acted as his secretary, a function that served her own advantage as
well, in that it marked what she called the beginning of her true political
education; 'naturally I had to read and write for my husband. I grappled
with newspapers and blue books, and learned more or less to convey
their import to him. He took care that I should hear important debates
in the House of Commons.'[18] But, most significant from the point of
view of Millicent's own development as a public figure, was not the
marriage but the subsequent death of her husband in 1884 at the early
age of fifty-one when Millicent herself was thirty-seven. It was after this
that she took up in earnest her work for women's suffrage (the parallel
with her competitor–collaborator Emmeline Pankhurst, is striking;
Emmeline was widowed in 1898 at the age of forty).

Millicent's only child Philippa was sixteen when her father died. There
is every reason to believe that Millicent was a devoted mother according
to the fashion of the time (she knitted baby clothes and attended to
Philippa's early education herself), but by the age of sixteen it was evident
that Philippa herself was a help rather than a hindrance to the noble
cause her mother had chosen to pursue. In 1887 she went to Newnham
College, Cambridge, the college that was founded in her parents' drawing
room when she was only old enough 'to toddle about in her white frock
and blue sash among the guests'.[19] In 1890 Philippa Fawcett was placed
first in the mathematical tripos – far above that honour oddly entitled
'senior wrangler' which could only be awarded to a man. This was a
most significant 'first' for women as a class, proving, as the *Westminster
Gazette* put it, 'their intellectual . . . sinew . . . sheer mental strength and
staying power'[20] – qualities which had hitherto been regarded as
entirely foreign to women. So far as her mother was concerned, Philippa
did not sustain this early brilliance. She was unmoved by any of her
mother's suggestions as to appropriate careers – as an astronomer,
physicist, lighthouse designer or engineer. Instead she returned to
Newnham to teach mathematics, until her mother dug her out of this
rut by applying on Philippa's behalf for an assistantship to the Director
of Education in the London County Council, a job never held before
by a woman. Philippa got the job, and stayed with the LCC until her
retirement in 1934, during which time she did manage to achieve the
appropriate goal of establishing equal pay for men and women in that
employment.

It is too simple to say that, having got marriage and motherhood behind her, Millicent could turn her energies outwards to the world. After Henry's death, she did have more time on her hands to pursue political activities of her own, yet she had never really regarded women as being in need of confinement to the home. It was under her husband's auspices that she first began her career as a political writer and campaigner. Her first article, on lectures for women in Cambridge, was published in 1868, and she gave her £7 fee towards J. S. Mill's election expenses. In 1870 she completed *Political Economy for Beginners*, which was immediately successful and went rapidly through ten editions, and two years later she wrote with her husband a volume called *Essays and Lectures on Social and Political Subjects*. In the year of her marriage she joined the newly formed London Women's Suffrage Committee and it was at the second public meeting of this committee that she made her first speech. In 1870, in Brighton, her husband's constituency, she took the platform again (a vote of thanks was passed to her husband for 'allowing his wife to lecture').

Another measure of the degree to which Millicent had already become a public figure before her husband's death, and before her best known suffrage work, was the fate of another of her enterprises, novel-writing. In 1874 a fall from a horse kept her at home for six months and during this period she wrote her novel *Janet Doncaster*, the heroine of the title bearing a marked resemblance to herself, and the whole adding up to a tract against the evils of alcoholism. The book did well, but Millicent suspected that its success was due merely to her own reputation. To test her suspicion, and with characteristic determination and shrewdness, she wrote a second novel, published it under a pseudonym, and watched it fall completely flat.

It was in the 1870s that Millicent Fawcett emerged as the leader of the women's suffrage movement. One of the members of that first committee wrote to Millicent years later: 'I sometimes tell my children how when you first came to our Women's Suffrage Committee. . .you looked like a schoolgirl rather than a married woman, and how you listened to opinions and suggestions as they fell from different members, and would then throw in your own counsel, which always seemed the right thing for us to adopt'.[21] In the same year that widowhood released Millicent for a wider public role, she was offered the post of Mistress of Girton, which she refused on the grounds that she was incapable of 'thinking about any subject but one'.[22]

Although nothing during her early adult years dissuaded Millicent from a belief in the rightness of the fight for women's suffrage, in her autobiography she notes that a number of seemingly trivial episodes etched on her conscience the truly appalling situation of women. One day she was in the waiting room at Ipswich station, between two clergymen's wives who were engaged in lace-making for the benefit of their respective parish schools. '"What do you find sells best?" said No. 1 to No. 2, who instantly replied, "Oh! Things that are really useful, such as butterflies for the hair!"'[23] On another occasion, she had her purse stolen. The thief was apprehended and charged, and on the charge sheet Millicent saw that the alleged offence was described as 'stealing from the person of Millicent Fawcett a purse containing £1 18s 6d, the property of Henry Fawcett'. 'I felt as if I had been charged with theft myself', she commented.[24]

The suffrage question was relatively quiescent from 1870 to 1884, when it re-emerged with Gladstone's Reform Bill. One particular change since 1870 necessitated a reappraisal on the part of the suffragists of their strategy, which had hitherto been to argue for the enfranchisement of single women only. Since the basis of the franchise at that time was a property qualification, this was the only plausible case to argue before the Married Women's Property Act came into force in 1882. Millicent herself had contended this: 'We find in practice,' she wrote to her cousin Edmund Garrett as late as 1885, 'That where there are ten men who favour single women having votes there is only one who is in favour of married women having it; this is what makes the women's suffrage workers as a body rather keep back on the claim on the part of married women. Half a loaf is better than no bread.'[25] The Married Women's Property Act enabled married women to hold property in their own right, and therefore made it possible in theory for the franchise to be claimed on their behalf as well. Millicent decided in due course to back this claim. Gladstone's refusal to consider the women's suffrage amendment when the Reform Bill came before the House had deeply angered her, and indeed his decision fuelled a growing sense of disillusionment among members of the suffrage movement with the ability of the British party political system to deliver the goods – a disillusionment that was in no way altered by the events of the succeeding 30 years. The passage in 1883 of the Corrupt Practices Act, which outlawed paid canvassing at elections, created further difficulties for the suffrage movement, difficulties through which Millicent again steered it on a straight course. Following the 1883 Act, women's usefulness as unpaid canvassers was obvious; the Liberal party even issued printed instructions directing its agents to 'make all possible use of every available woman in your locality', but Millicent saw clearly that women would not (at least at that stage) win the vote by allying themselves as unpaid political handmaidens to men.

Lydia Becker, who had co-ordinated the work of the women's suffrage societies from their inception, died in 1890. Millicent took over the leadership of the organization, in 1897 renamed the National Union of Women's Suffrage Societies (NUWSS), and she maintained that position until 1919. Those years were years of drama for women, for Britain and for the world. Yet the outstanding impression one gains from surveying Millicent Fawcett's life was that it was marked by monotony and by great tranquillity of spirit, and by no detectable change or development in her moral philosophy or political attitudes. The central question of her life, why she espoused the cause of women's suffrage with such steadfast determination, is partly answered by the biographical circumstances of her childhood; yet it also has to be seen as part of the general view on political affairs and human values to which she held throughout her life.

Without the complication of women's suffrage, Millicent Fawcett would have been a staunch liberal supporter. She followed the philosophical individualism of her mentor and her husband's friend J. S. Mill, and took the view that a sound and sane society can only rest on the foundation of self-help. Accordingly, she eschewed the demand for free education: 'On moral grounds there are many reasons for believing that its influence would be pernicious,' she wrote, 'many a father may have overcome the temptations of a public house, through the ambition to give education to his children.'[26] Free education would raise the birth- and alcoholism-rates. Poverty, she contended, does not call for such remedies as cheap food or lowered taxes, but for the imposition by the state on parents of their full responsibility for maintaining themselves and their children. To this end she disagreed profoundly with Eleanor Rathbone on the matter of mothers' pensions and family allowances, which she saw as the ruin of family life, and a nail in the coffin of Britain's greatness rather than as the road to women's economic freedom. Indeed, it was on this issue that she found herself finally alone, and eventually renounced her personal membership of the NUWSS altogether.

Millicent Fawcett may have put the vote first, but she seems to have had a limited view of women's role. Writing on 'The Electoral Disabilities of Women' in 1872, she said: 'surely the wife and mother of a family ought to be something more than a housekeeper or a nurse – how will she be able to minister to the mental wants of her husband and children if she makes the care of their physical comfort the only object of her life?'[27] In a speech she made in Manchester she asserted that 'We want the electoral franchise not because we are angels oppressed by the wickedness of "the base wretch man" but because we want women to have the ennobling influence of national responsibility brought into their lives.'[28] And, looking back in 1920 in her book *The Woman's Victory – and After*, she reminded the reader that the 50-year struggle had not been fought for women but for the benefit of the entire community: 'this is what we meant when we called our paper the Common Cause...It was the cause of men, women and children. We believe that men cannot be truly free so long as women are held in political subjection.'[29]

She always recognized that her work for women's suffrage was simply one aspect of a many-sided movement – the three main other sides were education, morals and employment. On these aspects too she contended that women's emancipation was principally for the good of society as a whole. Discussing the Report of the Schools Inquiry Commission referring to Girls' Education (the Taunton Commission, 1864) she observed that 'Women cannot really be good wives and mothers if charming accomplishments and domestic tasks are to be considered their highest virtues...The likelihood of a girl becoming a mother ought to be to her parents one of the strongest inducements to cultivate her mind in such a manner as to bring out its utmost strength, for upon every mother devolves the most important educational duties; from her...are derived the child's first notions of duty, of right and wrong, of happiness, of a supreme Being, of immortality...how vastly important for national welfare it is that mothers of children should be persons of large, liberal and cultured minds. Such women as the one Wordsworth speaks of:

> The reason firm, the temperate will,
> Endurance, foresight, strength and skill;
> A perfect woman, nobly planned
> To warn, to comfort and command.'[30]

She said that people with inferior and ill-developed capacities were no good as wives, either.

This most traditional line of reasoning was no doubt partly a response to the atmosphere and attitudes of the time. The objection that educating or enfranchising women would destroy the family had to be met with the answer that, on the contrary, educated and enfranchised women were just what the family needed. In her speeches, Millicent Fawcett displayed what was obviously a talent for anticipating and countering in a highly spirited and often amusing way the common objections to women's emancipation. For example: 'It was sometimes put forward as an argument that home was the best place for a woman. She did not object to that argument, in fact she heartily concurred in it – but, on the other hand, if they accepted this view, home was surely the best place for a man also [laughter].' On the constitutional unseriousness of women, she observed that: 'She once heard a couple of gentlemen discussing the respective merits of the candidates for a North Country borough, and one of them strongly recommended a gentleman on the ground that his brother's dog had won the Waterloo Cup [loud laughter].'[31]

This was all splendid fighting stuff, but delivered in tones and in words which never suggested any antagonism towards men as a class. Millicent Fawcett seemed always able to maintain a belief in the inherent goodness of men towards women. There are occasional undertones of disapproval, as in a letter she wrote in 1892 to a colleague supporting the inclusion of women on Hospital Boards: 'Don't you remember...what the old waiting maid in *Felix Holt* says: "It mayn't be good luck to be a woman. But one begins with it from a baby; one gets used to it. And I shouldn't like to be a man – to cough so loud, and stand straddling about on a wet day, and be so wasteful with meat and drink."'[32] And in her book *Women's Suffrage*, she was quite clear what the basic problem was: 'However benevolent men may be in their intentions', she observed, 'they cannot know what women want and what suits the necessities of women's lives as well as women know these things themselves.'[33]

An intrinsic element in Millicent Fawcett's campaign for the emancipation of women was an improvement of their moral status, an issue to which the question of men's moral habits was directly relevant. Millicent entirely approved of Josephine Butler's crusade for the repeal of the Contagious Diseases Acts, and although at the time (the 1870s) she took a firm decision not to express her support in public lest the cause of women's suffrage be damaged, she undertook to write with E. M. Turner a biography of Josephine Butler for the centenary of her birth. (The book was written when Millicent herself was eighty.) In this she called Josephine Butler 'the most distinguished Englishwoman of the nineteenth century' and could find no fault with her apart from 'the one with which Mary Magdalene was also charged when she broke the precious box of spikenards over the Saviour's feet. Mrs Butler was recklessly generous to those whom the perverseness of men's laws and also of men's lawlessness had brought very low in the world's esteem.'[34] In particular she filled the coffin of a young prostitute she had befriended with camelias. Millicent's response to this was to cite Judas, 'to what purpose this waste?' and to ask what camelias cost in March in Liverpool.

The moral values that motivated Millicent Fawcett are the least accessible side of her character. However, there are a few pointers. One is the very obvious distaste with which she viewed, in her introduction to the *Vindication*, the personal side of Mary Wollstonecraft's life (although she did feel herself able to argue that Mary Wollstonecraft 'in her writings, as well as in her life, with its sorrows and errors, is the essential womanly woman'[35]). Another clue is a letter from Thomas Hardy in reply to one of hers (not surviving) in which she apparently expressed an appreciation of his novel *Tess of the D'Urbevilles*:

> With regard to your idea of a short story showing how the trifling with the physical element in love leads to corruption; I do not see that much more can be done by fiction in that direction than has been done already. . . . The other day I read a story entitled 'The Wages of Sin' by Lucas Malet, expecting to find something of the sort therein. But the wages are that the young man falls over a cliff, and the young woman dies of consumption – not very consequent, as I told the author.[36]

But the oddest (least known and certainly least understood) episode in Millicent Fawcett's life concerns a one-woman campaign she launched in 1894 against an MP, Henry Cust, who was at the time standing for the Conservative candidature in the constituency of North Manchester. She had heard ('on good authority') that the previous summer Cust had seduced a Miss Nina Welby, 'a young girl of good Lincolnshire family' who subsequently became pregnant. Cust deserted her and offered marriage to someone else. Nina Welby wrote Cust an imploring letter which he 'showed to other men at the country house where he was staying, with odious remarks intended to be facetious'.[37] Millicent sent these details to the Honorary Secretary of the Women's Liberal Unionist Association in Manchester, because she considered that Cust's conduct threatened the sanctity of marriage and the family and that such a man ought not to be in a position of public responsibility. When no action was taken, Millicent persevered, indeed seems to have gone to extraordinary lengths to persecute Cust. Cust had given up his candidature, and had married Miss Welby (who had lost her baby and began pleading with Millicent to leave her husband alone). By the spring of 1895, Millicent's friends were beseeching her to stop, telling her that they had heard people say that a woman who was behaving as she was behaving did not deserve the suffrage (and that they themselves would withdraw their own support for women's suffrage).

This was perhaps the only exception to the rule of Millicent's utterly single-minded and lifelong devotion to the suffrage cause. The ennobling of women by the vote was for Millicent itself almost a moral, rather than political, objective – although she was also keen to point out that a whole host of other freedoms were not likely to be obtained without this fundamental human right.

Such feminism as there was in Millicent Fawcett's thinking tended to be overruled by another set of values – those to do with defence of, and love for, her country. Millicent was a nationalist and an imperialist. She was a 'worshipper at the inner shrine, the holy of holies, all that England stands for to her children, and to the world'.[38]

Admiration for English institutions has to be seen as the most potent determining factor in Millicent's ability to campaign for the vote *in a constitutional manner* over a period of many years. 'We have a peculiar skill for inserting the graft of new ideas into the stem of old institutions', she wrote in a women's suffrage speech of 1899:

> . . . this has given a continuity to our political history which has frequently received the tribute of respect and admiration from foreign observers. It has enabled us to achieve progress without revolution, to avoid all breaks with our past, while stretching forward to the new ideas and new life of the future. It is because an extension of the parliamentary franchise to women householders is in distinct accord with these national traditions that I urge its acceptance on you. . . . All that we need to obtain this goal are the commonplace English qualities of courage, patience and tenacity; if we have these, we shall make way with the task we have in hand.[39]

It consequently probably came as no surprise to her that, as she often pointed out, it took a mere two years less to obtain the vote for women than it took for men to win household suffrage for themselves (and they started with the advantage of already having 2 million voters).

Again, there was nothing out of line about Millicent's nationalism. Many of her colleagues on the suffrage committees were strong nationalists, and Blake's poem 'Jerusalem' was the suffrage hymn, although it lacked a suitable musical setting until Millicent and a friend, Kathleen Lyttleton, asked Sir Hubert Parry to compose one for the celebration of the suffrage victory in 1918 (this is the setting that is used today). But Millicent was more inclined to put her country first than many other suffragists. In 1901 she became a member of an all-women commission selected by the Government to investigate conditions in the Boer War concentration camps in South Africa. The overall function of this commission and certainly Millicent's own part in it was seen in some quarters as 'whitewashing', that is, implicitly approving of the concentration camp system and of the political principle and practice of persecuting the Boer people. The eventual report produced by the commission restricts itself almost entirely to a discussion of the living conditions of the camps and the steps necessary to ameliorate them. Yet it definitely does not indicate any sympathy on the part of commission members with the world-view of the camp inmates; the inmates were, for example, blamed for the high death-rates obtaining in the camps, the cause of which was said 'to be found in their extraordinary notions regarding the treatment of disease. Bathing the person is not, in health, commonly practised . . . in illness they regard the washing of the patient as next door to a miracle.'[40]

Millicent's nationalism also made her a primary instigator of the move, adopted by the NUWSS at the outbreak of the First World War, entirely to suspend the suffrage campaign for the duration of the war, and carry out such work as was necessary to relieve war distress and sustain 'the vital forces of the nation'. Her message to her followers was clear: 'Women, your country needs you. . . . Let us show ourselves worthy of citizenship, whether our claim to it be recognised or not.'[41] She called it the 'supreme sacrifice' and there are signs that she was truly depressed at what the war might mean – indefinite postponement for women's freedom. Nevertheless, her attitude to pacificism in the case of inter-national war was curiously at odds with her attitude to militancy in the intranational war of women to obtain the vote. Many leaders of the NUWSS wanted women to do more than sustain the vital forces of the nation while men got on with the war; they wanted an international women's peace movement. Millicent was very strongly opposed to this, believing that national loyalties had to be put first (accordingly, she was also very much against conscientious objectors). In 1915 there was an internal struggle for leadership within the NUWSS between Millicent and the pacifists: Millicent won. This was the second period of great personal difficulty she had met during her allegiance to the suffrage cause. The first occurred with the emergence of the militant campaign orchestrated by the Pankhursts some years earlier.

There is little direct evidence available as to what Millicent Fawcett thought of the Pankhursts, or they of her. Sylvia Pankhurst's account of the movement contains a number of asides pertaining to her view of Millicent's character and contribution to the cause: 'always strictly temperate in her observations',[42] 'a trim, prim little figure',[43] she recalls the abrupt change of attitude on Millicent's part that occurred between 1906 and 1907. In 1906 Millicent gave a banquet at the Savoy hotel for the first suffragette prisoners. 'Some comment was made on the fact that the invitation was not extended to me', Sylvia could not refrain from observing. 'The reason given was that though I had gone to prison on the same day my sentence had been shorter. It was clear, however, that the name Pankhurst savoured a shade too strongly of militancy for the non-militants, even in that expansive moment.'[44] A year later the expansive moments were no longer in evidence, and Millicent was issuing statements explicitly opposing the strategy of the militants.

Yet she remained, to some degree, ambivalent in private, and the public front she turned to militancy was, like so much else in her life, a decision taken on the basis of political expediency. In 1909 she wrote to her friend Lady Frances Balfour, of the militants' activities: 'The physical courage of it all is intensely moving. I don't feel it is the right thing and yet the spectacle of so much self-sacrifice moves people to activity who would otherwise sit still and do nothing till the suffrage dropped into their mouths like a ripe fruit.'[45] When Lloyd George argued that the Government could not possibly support women's franchise while the militant campaign continued, she responded that it was not within her power to stop it, but only within his: if he gave women the vote the militancy would stop. He replied by repeating the same point, namely that militancy was losing the suffrage campaign support. Millicent then drew his attention to a recent case in his own constituency when his supporters savaged the Conservative Club and were let off by the magistrate on the grounds 'that allowance must be made for political excitement'. 'Why', asked Millicent, 'is allowance made for political excitement in the case of men who can and do express their feelings at the ballot-box, but no allowance is made in the case of women when they are excited by political injustice and are driven to express their indignation by acts of violence? Of course there was no answer to this inquiry', she added uncompromisingly, 'but Mr Lloyd George deftly turned the subject and said he wished to introduce me to his wife.'[46]

But, so far as the militant campaign was concerned, Millicent could not, she said, in the end support a *revolutionary* movement, nor was she able (she noted, somewhat contradictorily) in good faith to support a movement that was ruled 'autocratically at first by a small group of four persons, and latterly by one person only'.[47] There is a nice anecdote which expresses the conflict between her desire for unity and the distaste she felt for violent tactics: '"Why can't we all be united?" a militant suffragist once asked her. "Yes", she replied breezily, "shall we all break windows, or shall we all not break windows? The Gadarene herd was very united."'[48]

In setting herself up as leader of the constitutional movement against the alternative of militancy, Millicent constantly needed to remind herself of, and draw courage from, a quotation from Morley's life of Gladstone:

'No reformer is fit for his [sic] task who suffers himself to be frightened off by the excesses of an extreme wing.'[49]

These conflicts did depress Millicent a good deal, not least because they were associated with a division of opinion and action within her own family. From 1908–11 her sister Elizabeth supported the militants and at over seventy took part in one of the raids on Parliament. It is a measure of the solid upper-class standing of the suffragists (not to mention some of the militant suffragettes as well) that in the face of Millicent's distress at the danger Elizabeth might be in, a promise was secured behind the scenes from the Home Secretary by Millicent's friend Lady Frances Balfour that Elizabeth would not be arrested. However, the internal dissension in the family could not be dissipated so easily; Elizabeth's daughter, Dr Louisa Garrett Anderson, continued to support the militants and was herself arrested in 1912, thus providing Millicent with a continuing uncomfortable prod to her conscience: people whom she loved, trusted and respected could, and did, hold very different opinions to her own on matters which were literally those of life and death.

Temperamentally, Millicent Fawcett was a different person in private from her public image. Although, like of Joan of Arc 'born' to, or for, her particular struggle, she detested most of the activities this struggle foisted upon her. She disliked public functions and speech-making terrified her. 'No one knows how speaking takes it out of me', she wrote in 1884. 'Before that last [meeting]...I was downright ill, but I know I don't show it, and I believe people think I rather like making speeches.'[50] (She is reported to have welcomed the vote when it eventually came precisely because she would not have to make any more speeches.) Her speeches were always prepared personally in extensive handwritten notes, and in the same vein she refused ever to employ a secretary, or have a telephone installed in her home. Her friend Ray Strachey recalls the elaborate process of speech preparation:

> It was her habit, when she had an important speech to make, first to work over it at her desk, taking notes and arranging her ideas, and then to sit down somewhere else with a piece of needlework in her hands and and go over it again carefully in her head. In that way, she said, she stitched the outlines firmly into her mind, so that there was no danger of losing them.[51]

The effect of these carefully prepared products, however much anxiety they engendered in the speaker, was 'clear, logical, self-possessed, and pre-eminently "ladylike"'.[52] She was not, according to those who heard her, especially eloquent, nor did she appeal to the emotions. Indeed, she was said to be obsessively afraid of showing emotion, and maintained a rigid self-control in the face of all personal and professional disasters. When asked to sign a petition for women's suffrage which stated that she 'passionately desired' it, she responded with '*Must* I be passionate?' Then: 'Oh, very well'.[53] It was probably this very lack of passion that accounted for her appeal as the very model of the kind of woman who proved that women would use the vote well. Her physical appearance aided this impression. Very small, with a lovely complexion and a lot of shiny brown hair, she was undoubtedly an attractive example of femininity, and was always beautifully dressed, usually in a dark silk gown with a large lace collar. *Time and Tide* argued that her unemotional style of argument ideally suited her to the pioneer role, but worked, particularly, because 'she looked nice, dressed becomingly, was married to a heroic blind politician and was to him the perfect wife. . . .'[54] 'If only for her triumph as a wife', added the *Northern Mail*, 'Millicent Fawcett's career was an inspiration.'[55] Such lack of deviation from the accepted path for women was no accident. It was Millicent's self-consciously chosen direction. 'She meant to spell revolution without the "r"', she wrote of Emily Davies, writing at the same time about herself: 'She did not want any violence either of speech or action. She remained always the quiet, demure little rector's daughter, and she meant to bring about all the changes she advocated by processes as gradual and unceasing as the progress of a child from infancy to manhood [*sic*].'[56]

People *liked* Millicent, and they were particularly drawn by her sense of humour. 'I think it quite delightful', she wrote to a friend in 1929, 'that now everyone takes the woman voter as if she had existed from the time of Adam and Eve.'[57] In 1887, when asked by an American lady, who took the view that women professionals must be incompetent (and unsexed) by definition, whether she knew of any woman doctor at whose hands she would be willing to undergo an operation, Millicent replied, 'Yes, there's one woman doctor by whom I would rather have my head cut off than by anyone else.'[58]

The series of events that finally led up to the Representation of the People Act 1918 has been described in detail elsewhere.[59] Before the war brought about a suspension of the campaign, Millicent had experienced a difficult time with an issue on which she had always felt strongly – namely that the best chance for women's suffrage was to be secured by supporting individual MPs who espoused the cause, rather than by attempting to secure the backing of one party as a whole. The defeat of the 1913 Reform Bill led her to reverse this opinion and to pledge the loyalty of the NUWSS to the only party – the Labour party – which had declared a relatively unequivocal demand for female suffrage. It may well be that on this matter Millicent's judgement was erroneous and that, had the policy been adopted earlier by the NUWSS, the vote would have been won sooner than it was. But that, of course, raises the question of how it was that in the end the Government of the day saw fit to enfranchise women after more than half a century of broken pledges and parliamentary disappointments. The *Manchester Guardian* in its obituary presented what was then and is still now a balanced view of the case:

> There were three stages in the emancipation of women. The first was the long campaign of propaganda and organisation, at the centre of which, patient, unwearying and always hopeful, stood Dame Millicent. The second was the campaign of the militants, which, since it depended on sensation, brought to the movement the enthusiastic attention of the popular press and made it a live political issue. The third was the war. Had there been no militancy and no war, the emancipation of women would still have come, although more slowly. But without the faithful preparation of the ground over many years by Dame Millicent Fawcett and her colleagues neither militancy nor the war could have produced the crop.[60]

Or, in the words of the *Daily Telegraph*:

> The names of the militants who broke windows, chained themselves to pillars, or went on hungerstrike in gaol, are sometimes quoted by the unthinking as the leaders to victory, but in reality it was the woman of sweet reasonableness, womanly manner, quiet dress, and cultured style who did more than any other in the cause of emancipation.[61]

Her 'sweet reasonableness' was the quality which has condemned Millicent Fawcett to the reputation of having won citizenship for women, and has detracted from a proper consideration of other factors, individuals and organizations that were essential to this goal. Yet whatever the answer to the question of how the vote was won (and it is not likely to be a simple one), Millicent Fawcett must surely be admired for her early and public adoption of a cause that was at the time both marginal and sensational; for her refusal ever seriously to be distracted from the central ambition of enfranchising women; and for her adamant insistence on not being the cult figure public opinion inclined to make her, especially in the years after the 1918 Act (a mark of which was her conversion into a Dame Grand Cross of the British Empire in 1924).

Millicent Fawcett retired from active political work in 1919. When asked, in that year, why she would not stand for Parliament, she said she had 73 reasons: 72 were her age, and the seventy-third was that she did not want to. Nancy Astor, the first woman MP, said she felt almost ashamed to take that place instead of Millicent Fawcett. However, retirement did not mean the end of Millicent's work for sex equality; between 1919 and 1929 she continued to participate in the affairs of the London and National Society for Women's Service, and in particular helped to secure the opening of the legal profession to women. At the age of seventy-four with her sister Agnes she visited Palestine for the first time, returning on three further occasions, becoming quite involved in the work of the British Administration there, and recording some of her reflections on the subject in a book (1926). It was in Jerusalem that she heard of the final victory in 1928, when the basis of women's enfranchisement became the same as that of men. 'It is almost exactly sixty-one years ago since I heard John Stuart Mill introduce his suffrage amendment to the Reform Bill on May 20, 1867 . . . I have had extraordinary good luck in having seen the struggle from the beginning', she said.[62]

In that year she was still busy writing, and in 1929, her eighty-third year, she and Agnes set off to see the Far East. On 18 August 1929 she was guest of honour at a public luncheon given by the National Union of Societies for Equal Citizenship (as the NUWSS was suitably retitled) to celebrate the first woman Cabinet minister and the return to Parliament of 14 women MPs. Three days later she went to bed with a cold, and died of double pneumonia two weeks later with her sister, daughter and old friend Dr Jane Walker by her side. At her memorial service in Westminster Abbey some months later, the Dean read the passage from Ecclesiastes 'Let us now praise famous men [sic]' – and of course they sang 'Jerusalem'. The woman with whom she did not always agree, and to whom she handed over the Presidency of the NUWSS, Eleanor Rathbone, said of her that practical wisdom was her outstanding feature:

It was this quality which looked out of her grave clear eyes with the lids slightly drooping at the outer corners, and the humorous twinkle in them, which was like the gleam of sunshine on a dark pool. . . . She saw the end from the beginning and the unity which transcended all our differences.[63]

5

At the Heel Bar
The Truth of the Matter
The Poverty of Love
The End of the Affair

A friend, who lives in an extremely healthy country, and is herself a doctor, leading an extremely healthy life, wrote to me that a year ago she was diagnosed and treated for a cervical dysplasia, a precursor of cancer of the cervix. She says the disease does not fit her image of herself. She has a perfect reproductive history, three wonderful children, no history of illness. So she has totally suppressed the knowledge that she did have the disease. 'The whole thing is outside me.'

The next poem signals another kind of ideological discomfort; I wrote it standing in line in a suburban department store waiting to have my shoes mended. Looking at the women around me I became, suddenly, terribly angry. I hated them for their devotion to domesticity, their implicit support for an economic system built on financial profit rather than peace, love and values of emotional connectedness. But I knew that this was not the right feeling to have about my co-*soeurs* in the heel bar line; for we were all women, all caught up in a wheel of fortune we had had no chance to design for ourselves. And living in it did not mean we agreed with it.

Does personal misfortune really give people insights into the human condition? Does it give them more of a right to criticize their fellow humans? Are ideological mismatches between disease and self-concept, between mood and social role, actually the worst disasters of all time?

The next five poems, 'The Truth of the Matter', the 'Poverty of Love' sequence, and 'The End of the Affair' speak to a different theme: the problematic relationships between men and women.

In these relationships, and however much we wish to dwell in the present, we find ourselves constantly turned both to the past and to the future. As Francesco Alberoni says in his powerful book *Falling in Love*,[64] the early stages of passion are marked by oblivion to past and future: the lovers are entirely caught up in each other, are steeped in the breathtaking vigour of the present moment. But later on it is these monsters, history and time ahead, that appear from the wings in a frenzy of anger that they've been forgotten; their presence takes over, breathing fire over our innocent lovers, they force awareness of what has happened and what will to dominate present experience. Loss and disappointment colour the present, not so much in their reality but because of the expectation of their inevitability.

At the Heel Bar

anaemic women with scarves on
this is your life
to stand in line waiting
as clocks mark out coffee hours
grey rain hides windows
the windows of your listless eyes

lumps of bread and red meat
cower in polythene
reside in plastic-coated shopping bags
waiting for their valediction
whitely labelled
as you do

you think these effete palaces
your natural home
bred by checkout tills and showy packages
reared on a diet of profit
to an obsession with comfort
as you are

if you knew as much about time
as I do
this would be the time of your life
cast off from your shop moorings
rid of your baggage
would you thus apportion yourselves?

The Truth of the Matter

well you can't say I didn't look

I looked hard and everywhere
at all those white faces
and brooding eyes with blood at their corners
I looked into all those heads
saw all those pasty thoughts
circulating like busy flies buzzing

and up a mountain one evening
(up any mountain any evening)
I could take my pick

lined up like a police parade shoes shining
they looked at me
rapacious blank voracious

here we go again
primeval hunt perpetual pain

I've had enough of it I said
to the one I ended up with
there's nothing in this for me or you
take my false smile as a bad hint
go

the truth of the matter is

I want to forget history
cut the future off without a penny
live in the back of a broken clock
singing an alarm from time to time

The Poverty of Love (1)

I grow old scarred with paint traces
my arms give birth to red spots burning at midnight
my eyes are hung with a careful veil, cheap gauze
a lover would say only the heart remembers

remembers a zany beating on a sterile screen
hard sheets, white eyes, hands lashed down
stay there, where else? the night is over
now is the cold wet day

the leaves on the trees curl up and die
brown crescents tumble into dark sewers
are eaten alive by a street cleaning machine
machine, machine, if only we could be

I grow old, I who remember
an anger as violent as the Lapland sky
a peace as magic as young angels singing
love, the world's poverty
and lullaby

The Poverty of Love (2)

city of red polystyrene hearts
do you remember

there I was happy
though not in my right mind

there I felt whole
while sitting in a hardrimmed sieve
earnestly gazing at the bright red hearts

I was bound to fall out into a pothole

so I decided to get out of this life altogether

but here I am again
like a rubber plunger, springing back
a battered carbody resisting the claws of the compressor
indestructible and still fancying destruction
at the claws, in the bed, of my steeleyed oppressor

I feel you remember
that's why there are these hearts
strung about horribly bleeding
and if you sugar the pill
by dotting the odd pine tree here and there
that's your business

The Poverty of Love (3)

out of the window
the grey world waits
like a Lowry painting

twigs angled depressed
trees bare passionless
silence the mould of unsavoury tears

a blackbird stands
with a white breast
still on a branchtop

looking around it sees
what hell this place is
hell and damnation, silence and stagnation
every dark shoot in the garden dies on its way to the sky
every worm crumbles in its stony grave
every yellow flower moans with the mixed weight of earth and snow
too oppressed
to give a damn about the life inside it

oh daffodil
where art thou?
fantasies and phantasies
lie together in their coffin
and are buried in an iceberg
ice, the arctic's only answer

looked at sideways with light from the pole star
one can see how the ice traps everything
bits of fluff, dead cats, truth from the garden
moths, fallen aeroplanes, a bleeding heart or two
seeds from last year's summer, a pair of white boots
even pickled roses stiff with sentiment
and here and there an opal dumbly flashing messages from nowhere

to peer into the ice
is not nice, it reminds us
of our cringing confusion
here crystallized in cold discomfort

black ice
greasing the whole globe
nothing sticks any more
even gravity has given up
the apple was simply a joke

out of this awfulness
one is supposed to gather peace
for the hurt soul, the tired mind
the collapsed ego darkened from within
and not insignificantly weakened by hailstones from the north
bits of the iceberg breaking off and finding their real home

peace, proper peace
with the butterflies dancing and clouds humming
with the earth moving, with the flowers turning
with my hand in yours, and love in our faces
the sun streaming banners over ghastly fields
to make a radiance eternal out of midnight

this peace, not passion
man's only true gift to woman

most unfortunately tells us
how meaningless the past is
having a value only in the way
it casts a shadow
over every possible fine day
seen through a window darkly

The End of the Affair

meant as it was to go on
time suffered more than we intended
from a collision of sentiments, an

abbreviation of vision
and in our contracted wisdom
love had no more reason than

babies playing in a graveyard, a
kitten stiff with ice, cherries bleeding
through a wedding veil of white

years we tried and wetly gazed
across prodigal distances waiting
for stars to return to their own skies

moments took us to eternal places
touch burnt us out where
others feared ever to be

love for each other took us
through nights of temptation
was comfort enough in the desert

this world was our world only, and
I would have loved you forever my
friend
world without end

6

A History Lesson:
Ultrasound in Obstetrics

In April 1985 a conference on the use of ultrasound in obstetrics was held in London, at the Royal Society of Medicine. Ultrasound appears later in this book, and does so here not so much because of its character as a medical intervention in motherhood, but because the history of its appearance in this scenario indexes various important lessons of history. Living in the present does not mean forgetting history: on the contrary, it means being aware of the value of the present, and so learning the lessons of history in order to avoid making the same human errors in the future.

In one of his novels, the Irish writer James Joyce said that 'History is a nightmare from which I am trying to awake.'[65] Thomas Carlyle said that 'The history of the world is but the biography of great men.'[66] Edward Gibbon complained that history is 'little more than the register of the crimes, follies and misfortunes of mankind'.[67] The industrialist Henry Ford, being a practical soul, simply described history as 'bunk',[68] while the German philosopher Hegel is said sensibly to have reflected that 'what experience and history teach is this – that people and governments never have learnt anything from history, or acted on principles deduced from it.'[69]

These quotations do not adequately reflect the value of historical work, although I am more in sympathy with Hegel's than Henry Ford's view of what history is able to teach us. I do not think history is bunk. But it is

Source: Originally given at the Royal Society of Medicine Forum on Maternity and the Newborn, Ultrasonography in Obstetrics, 17 April 1985, under the title 'The History of Ultrasonography in Obstetrics'.

apparent that people frequently fail to benefit from its lessons, because in their excitement for what is happening now, they lose sight of the need for a scientific approach to the evaluation of human experience. In what follows I am going to tackle two questions about the use of ultrasound in obstetrics: first, and specifically, why and how did obstetric ultrasound develop? Second, and more generally, what does the development of obstetric ultrasound tell us about the nature of technical developments within medicine (and the nature of technical developments in society more broadly)? What lessons can we learn, despite Hegel, from this?

My own view of history is that there is no single 'right' way to 'do' it. While one may, and must, attempt to be fair to all perspectives, in the end certain choices have to be made about the important questions and about the most appropriate way to approach these. My background as a social scientist leads me to focus on questions to do with the social relations of medicine. Histories written from within the profession are concerned rather more narrowly with medical 'achievements'.[70] This is a difference of emphasis with, of course, quite a number of implications. Secondly, reverting to Carlyle's remark about history being the same thing as biography, I take the view that the development of such medical techniques as ultrasound cannot be explained without understanding the pioneer work of key individuals. Yet at the same time this individual endeavour must be set in a context, that is, we need to know how this work fits in with other developments, including those in the social field.

OBSTETRIC ULTRASOUND: BEGINNINGS

The basic technique of ultrasound does not have its roots in obstetrics nor in medicine, but in warfare.[71] During the First World War detection by sound waves of underwater objects developed as a useful way of identifying underwater submarines. After the war the technique of ultrasonic echo sounding was applied to mapping the ocean floor for the shipping and navigation industry and for locating deep-sea herring shoals. The pioneer medical work on soft tissue ultrasonography was carried out in the USA in the late 1940s and early 1950s, and the translation into obstetrics occurred in the mid-1950s, with much of the original work being done by (Professor) Ian Donald and his colleagues in Glasgow.

The original clinical task spurring Donald and his team to apply ultrasound to the female abdomen was not the surveillance of pregnancy but the diagnosis of abdominal tumours, particularly the diagnostic separation into benign and malignant tumours. Glasgow was a city with heavy engineering commitments where ultrasound was already used in the metal industry. Donald was familiar with this work and it occurred to him to try on human tumours the industrial ultrasound equipment used for detecting flaws in metals. The technique worked, and from the summer of 1955 women patients presenting obscure abdominal complaints were liable to find the doctor putting transformer oil on their tummies as an acoustic coupling medium for an industrial metal flaw detector. Since with one of these detectors nothing showed up within 8 cm of penetration, women had water tanks with flexible latex bottoms balanced on their stomachs. The many resulting wet beds led Donald to think of contraceptive condoms as a solution to the problem. However, being rather reticent himself, he sent a professor colleague from Cape Town into a surgical rubber goods store in a disreputable area of Glasgow, to buy some. The professor was asked if he wanted teat-ended or plain, and proceeded to astonish the sales assistant by saying he would go back to his friend and ask.

Every technical development has its lighter side, but if the new role of the metal flaw detector seemed bizarre, one has only to reflect on that well-known obstetrical saying that 'the commonest abdominal tumour in women is pregnancy' and also, perhaps, on the fact that the fetus hidden in its amniotic fluid behind the surface of the maternal abdomen is not unlike the submarine skulking in obscurity on the ocean floor.

By 1965, the technique of fetal biparietal diameter measurement had been worked out, pregnancy had shown up on ultrasound as early as seven weeks, and early, blighted ova were being recognized, although other obstetric challenges such as the localization of the placenta had not yet been successfully taken up. Other teams of research workers in the USA were taking further this initial experimental work. By 1966 the ultrasound caseload in the Glasgow centre was described as nearly 'unmanageable' with 28 per cent of all that hospital's obstetric patients receiving ultrasound.

Not long after this, ultrasound began to appear in other obstetric departments. Since we do not in this country (or any other) monitor the use of new medical techniques by means of routine data-collection systems, it is hard to find out just when and how use of a new technology escalates. Indeed, this is one of the central problems in constructing the history of ultrasound and other medical techniques. We do not know how many pregnant women and fetuses have been exposed to ultrasound. It is remarkable how unwilling obstetricians are to give information about their use of ultrasound – one postal survey of fellows of the American College of Obstetricians and Gynecologists in 1981 yielded only a 28.2 per cent response rate – nearly 75 per cent of obstetricians would not say how frequently they used it.[72]

Against this lack of evidence we also know that professional contacts and informal social networks promote doctors' adoption of new techniques, so it is not surprising to learn that the first large obstetric ultrasound centre in England was started by a junior member of Donald's Scottish team, Stuart Campbell. Within a year of Campbell's arrival at Queen Charlotte's Maternity Hospital in London in 1968, ultrasound had become a routine method for estimating fetal growth and maturity. Four years later nearly half of Queen Charlotte's patients received ultrasound in pregnancy, and by 1978 ultrasound coverage of the pregnant population attending that hospital was virtually complete.

We cannot understand the history of one technique (ultrasound) applied to one medically defined condition (pregnancy) except by considering it in the context of all such techniques, and in the context of the medical definition of the condition itself. Ultrasound is one technique for acquiring knowledge about what is happening inside the womb. Another such technique is the X-ray, and the use in obstetrics of both X-rays and ultrasound are stages in a long history of clinicians' attempts to secure a better knowledge of what is happening inside the womb than mothers themselves have. Although it has been suggested that the reason for this is obstetricians' ungratified childhood curiosity about where babies come from, the urge to possess superior knowledge is more appropriately explained as an important part of the process of professionalization. Thus, a new technique such as ultrasound rapidly generates a new subspeciality within obstetrics, including diplomas and certification and specialist journals. One other consequence of professionalization is a strong impetus to expand the use of new techniques. By the late 1970s, ultrasound had become a common method of fetal surveillance in many countries, and appears to be used intensively, especially in those countries with insurance-based health care systems. Indeed, commercial motives and interests are an essential area to be considered when we are trying to understand the spread of a new technique – although an area about which it is extremely hard to get reliable information.

SOME HISTORICAL LESSONS

I have deliberately described, in some detail, how ultrasound developed in Britain, because I think this is necessary to abstract the more general lessons. These I would list as follows:

(1) Technical innovation in medicine is usually a serendipitous rather than a rational process. Thus, for example, the obstetric applications of ultrasound developed somewhat incidentally, and the main initial target area for ultrasound was not obstetrics at all.

(2) Scientific evaluation of a new technique is not a necessary pre-condition for the introduction into routine practice of that technique. Or, in other words, ultrasound entered routine use in obstetrics before its effectiveness and possible hazards had been scientifically evaluated. The first controlled trial of obstetric ultrasound was not reported until 1980,[73] which was 14 years after the obstetric ultrasound case-load at the first British centre was described as unmanageable.

(3) The time between the initial experimental use of a new technique, such as ultrasound, and its introduction into routine practice may be very short.

(4) Because techniques such as ultrasound form part of the professional resources of clinicians, the experiences, opinions and consent of childbearing women (and their partners) are rarely considered either necessary or valid data in decisions about on whom the technique should be used, or for what kind of indication.

(5) Those who advocate a new technique are liable to suffer from a strange condition called certainty.

Evaluation

Ultrasound is not the only obstetric technique which has been subjected rather late in its history to the scrutiny of a controlled trial. In fact it is the rule rather than the exception that clinical practice absorbs new techniques on the basis of inadequate evidence as to their effectiveness and safety. The 'seven stages in the career of a medical innovation'[74] run as follows: (1) 'promising reports' begin to appear in the literature; (2) the innovation is adopted by professional organizations; (3) the lay public begins to demand the technique; and (4) the era of routine use or 'standard procedure'. Only next does history expand to include controlled experimental evaluation (5). Finally, we have the last two stages: at which there is professional disbelief in, and denunciation of, the results of scientific evaluation, especially when these challenge the wisdom of routine use (6). This stage merges with one of general discreditation (7) in which a technique hailed earlier in its history as universally applicable comes to be seen as useful only in some cases.

With obstetric ultrasound, I suggest that we are now somewhere between stages 5 and 6. We are beginning to look seriously at routine use of ultrasound, but perhaps not all of us are equally willing to translate the findings of clinical trials into clinical practice.

One of the lessons of history is, of course, that history repeats itself. The development of obstetric ultrasound thus mirrors the application to human pregnancy of diagnostic X-rays: both, within a few years of their 'discovery' were being used to diagnose pregnancy and to measure the growth and normality of the fetus. In 1935 it was said 'that antenatal work without the routine use of X-rays is no more justifiable than would be the treatment of fractures'.[75] In 1978 'It can be stated without qualification that modern obstetrics and gynaecology cannot be practised without the use of diagnostic ultrasound.'[76] And two years later, it was said that 'ultrasound is now no longer a diagnostic test applied to a few pregnancies regarded on clinical grounds as being at risk. It can now be used to screen all pregnancies and should be regarded as an integral part of antenatal care.'[77] On neither of these dates did evidence qualify the speakers to make these assertions. As sociologist J. B. McKinlay has said: 'It is reasonable then to argue that the success of an innovation has little to do with its intrinsic worth (whether it is measurably effective, as determined by controlled experimentation) but is dependent upon the power of the interests that sponsor and maintain it, despite the absence or inadequacy of empirical support.'[78]

On this question of evaluation and ethics, we do not only learn from the history of ultrasound and other similar techniques how rarely and how late the randomized controlled trial has been used for scientific evaluation. Another important question is the uncontrolled use of the technique in experimental research. This is what was said in 1926 about X-rays: 'The use of the X-rays or radium clinically should have been preceded by exhaustive studies, but as a matter of fact the practical application followed promptly upon their discovery and much of the experimental work has been done on human beings.'[79] The same is true of obstetric ultrasound. Amongst a variety of aspects of the fetal life-style, ultrasound has over the last 15 years been used to 'discover' fetal breathing movements and fetal hiccups, monitor fetal eye movements and fetal activity in general, and find out how often fetuses empty their bladders and stomachs. Now this is doubtless fascinating work, but what is its ethical justification? Are the women involved in these experiments (none of whom are getting it because they 'need' it) informed about the unknown long-term effects of ultrasound? What is learnt from all this experimental activity that is likely to be of overall benefit to the welfare of the childbearing population? Selecting one of these studies at random – one focused on fetal movements in pregnancy – I came across the following statements:

> As experience in monitoring fetal movements accumulated, it became obvious that the fetus does not always move in one and the same manner.
>
> Fetal motor behaviour is a complex of spontaneous movements and a motionless period between them.
>
> Strong movements correlate with a high motor rate, while slow movements tend to occur at a lower rate.[80]

This hardly adds up to outstandingly original wisdom justifying the use of a potent technology. Any mother can tell you that fetuses don't always move in the same way, and that sometimes a healthy fetus doesn't move at all, in fact, it sleeps – like the rest of us.

CERTAINTY

When I referred earlier to that stage in the history of a procedure at which people 'fervently believe' it is unethical to withold that procedure, I chose my words carefully. Any historian of techniques for seeing into the womb, or otherwise monitoring the behaviour of people's bodies, cannot fail to be impressed by the *certainty* which is expressed on certain key issues, particularly the *safety* of the technique in question. In 1937, for example, a standard textbook on antenatal care commented that 'It has been frequently asked whether there is any danger to the life of the child by the passage of X-rays through it; it can be said at once that there is none if the examination is carried out by a competent radiologist or radiographer.'[81] But the same textbook declared in a later edition (1960) 'It is now known that the unrestricted use of X-rays may be harmful to mother and child.'[82] The 'knowledge' referred to was of course the report by Alice Stewart and her colleagues in 1956 on fetal X-rays and childhood cancer.[83] It is worth noting that the 1955 edition of the said textbook still carried a section on 'X-rays in Diagnosis of Pregnancy'.

Questions of safety, both in the short- and long-term have also been raised with respect to ultrasound. While the early practitioners of obstetric ultrasound seem to have been reasonably cautious about claiming 'no known harmful effects', what appears to happen is the following: as the technique begins to be used, and as it begins to be used more and more, and as no harmful effects emerge (which generally they do not because no mechanism for finding such effects has been set up), people become more and more certain in their claim that the technique is a safe one. Hence the words of one textbook on *Ultrasound in Gynaecology and Obstetrics* in 1978: 'One of the great virtues of diagnostic ultrasound has been its apparent safety. At present energy levels, diagnostic ultrasound appears to be without any injurious effect...all the available evidence suggests that it *is* a very safe modality'[84] (my italics). Note the leap from 'appears to be' to 'is'.

CONCLUSION

So, to summarize the history lesson:

First of all, in observing the historical parallels between the development of X-rays and ultrasound as components of obstetric practice, I certainly do not intend to suggest that the techniques are likely to be equal in their effects. It is rather that both have been taken up and explored for the potential access to the interior life of the womb they afford obstetricians. What I am saying is that the power of, and behind, the motive helps to explain the extent of their use. I do not think it is mere coincidence that X-rays in obstetrics declined rapidly in the late 1950s – which was also the time at which the pioneering work on obstetric ultrasound was done.

Secondly, while I have drawn out of all this the historical lesson that there is not nearly enough scientific evaluation of techniques that enter clinical practice, I have not commented on the lessons of the evaluation that has been done. One issue is that of *whether* any evaluation of a procedure entering clinical practice has taken place. A second concerns what such evaluation, once it is done, actually demonstrates. Yet a third is whether anyone pays attention to research findings, that is, what kind of relationship exists between evaluative research on the one hand, and what clinicians decide to do, on the other.

Finally, technology brings about a profound shift in the knowledge-base of medicine. Before the present era of medical knowledge, the 'subjective' knowledge of patients about their condition constituted information without which physicians could not practise. The danger of technologies such as ultrasound is that they substitute so-called 'objective' data for the earlier patient-generated kind. But the problem is that this is to substitute one partial view of 'illness' for another. Innovations such as ultrasound have a tendency to transform the social relationships of those who use them. For example, the obstetrician who can view an ultrasound scan, or a chart describing ultrasonically-surveyed fetal growth, has that much less time to spend conversing with the owner of the surveyed fetus – the mother. The machine tells the doctor what the doctor wants to know. For example, too, it has been claimed that ultrasound in pregnancy now enables obstetricians to 'introduce' mothers to their fetuses and facilitate a new phenomenon called prenatal bonding. In exactly the same way, the medical innovation of hospital delivery enabled paediatricians to discover the phenomenon of postnatal bonding. I would suggest that all this is rediscovering-the-wheel activity of a most primitive kind. Mothers and newborn babies bonded before hospitalized delivery disturbed the natural process. Mothers and newborn fetuses were in a relationship with one another before they met on the ultra-sound screen. The implications for social relations of medical innovations are nowhere more important than in the case of pregnancy, which is in itself not an illness condition and is, furthermore, a condition in which social and emotional factors play a profoundly important part, requiring that repertoire of traditional clinical skills that simply cannot be replaced by machines.

I will end with an observation made by obstetric ultrasound's original great enthusiast, Ian Donald. In 1980 Donald said:

> Perhaps the time has now come to stand and stare and to take stock of where we are going and where we are most likely to settle, bearing in mind that sonar, like radiology and biochemistry, must never lose their subservience to the medical art and the paramount importance of the patient who is the clinician's chief concern. Viewed with this sense of proportion sonar comes as a commodity only . . . out of control it can be an obsession . . . sonar is not a new medical religion . . . nor an end in itself.[85]

And, coming back to the definitions of history – with which I started – the following remark of Samuel Taylor Coleridge is unfortunately true: 'If men [sic] could learn from history, what lessons it might teach us! But passion and party blind our eyes, and the light which experience gives us is a lantern on the stern, which shines only on the waves behind us.'[86]

Part 2

Motherhood: its Facts and Fictions

Women and children are always mentioned in the same breath. The special tie women have with children is recognized by everyone. I submit, however, that the nature of this bond is no more than shared oppression. And that moreover this oppression is intertwined and mutually reinforcing in such complex ways that we will be unable to speak of the liberation of women without also discussing the liberation of children...

S. Firestone *The Dialectic of Sex*, London, Paladin, 1972, p. 73

7

The Cries and Smiles of Babies

Centres for research in women's studies, or women, or sex roles, or gender
– the terminology differs – are one of the products of the modern women's
movement. They are intended to convert the masculinist bias of higher
education into a more androgynous perspective, using an emphasis on
the position of women to draw attention to the predicaments of human
beings. Women's studies centres, or courses, do take for granted the value
of education; more than that, they don't directly challenge the conventional tools and approaches of education itself. Readers of esoteric
memoranda on life's real workings may have picked up an item that
appeared some time ago concerning educational graffiti designed to teach
university students the techniques of cardiopulmonary resuscitation. Two
ways of doing this were tried: posters and graffiti on lavatory walls. The
study found that the lavatory wall was an effective means of instruction.[1]

At any rate, for someone who has been battling in a rather solitary
way with the task of doing feminist teaching, writing or research (with
or without the aid of lavatory graffiti), women's studies centres are truly
invigorating places. In 1982 I visited, briefly, one in the USA: the
Women's Studies Research Center at Madison, Wisconsin. The Centre
is housed in a pretty building away from the main university campus
and has been in existence since 1977. I remember cool white attics and
an unhassled atmosphere: women who seemed to know who they were,
and to have found a place in which to be themselves. My own contribution

Source: Originally given as a keynote address to the symposium on the Impact of Children
on Women: *Constructing Mothers*, Women's Studies Research Center, University of
Wisconsin, Madison, USA, 22 April 1982.

was part of a three year effort funded by the Ford Foundation – an 'interdisciplinary study of the institution of motherhood'. Aside from intangible memories, one enduring reminder of my visit is a brightly coloured parrot I bought for my younger daughter while changing planes at Chicago's Le Hare airport, a most dreadful place. The parrot tells me about the fun of feminism, the pleasure accruing from difficult work that may feel like a lonely pursuit although it is, in fact, a collective endeavour.

The piece that follows was given at 3 a.m. (my body time) to a large audience in a glass-walled room overlooking a lake: the usual American hospitality overflowed into champagne afterwards. The piece attempts to draw together some of the most important strands in feminist research on motherhood, and the title, 'The Cries and Smiles of Babies', locates motherhood as both the soft centre and the practical emergency of women's lives.

In her autobiography *Blackberry Winter*, the anthropologist Margaret Mead describes her own struggle to achieve both personhood and motherhood. In 1931, at the age of thirty, she set out for New Guinea with her second husband, Reo Fortune, to work on the question of the extent to which differences in temperament between the genders might be conditioned by culture – work which led eventually to the publication of her famous *Sex and Temperament in Three Primitive Societies*. One of the three cultures she encountered in New Guinea and later wrote about was the Mundugumor. The Mundugumor lived on the banks of the Yuat river in New Guinea and appeared to have set up a particularly unpleasant form of social organization based on head-hunting. The culture was aggressive, rivalrous and exploitative in the extreme. Even so-called 'love-making' was performed deliberately in other people's gardens so as to spoil their yams, and was accompanied by scratching and biting. People committed suicide by getting into a temper tantrum and drifting down the river in a canoe towards the unenviable fate of being captured and eaten by a neighbouring tribe. Such a culture is hardly likely to cherish children, or women as the bearers of children. Indeed, this proved to be the aspect of Mundugumor culture that Margaret Mead found most hard to take. 'Women wanted sons and men wanted daughters', she wrote, 'and babies of the wrong sex were tossed into the river, still alive, wrapped in a bark sheath. Someone might pull the bark container out of the water, inspect the sex of the baby, and cast it away again. I reacted so strongly against the set of the culture', Mead goes on to say, 'that it was here that I decided I would have a child no matter how many miscarriages it meant'. (She had already, at this point in her life, experienced several miscarriages.) 'Further, it seemed clear to me', she observed, 'that a culture that so repudiated children could not be a good culture, and the relationship between the harsh culturally prescribed style and the acts of individuals was only too obvious.'[2] Well, of course, there does have to be some relationship between the broad values of a culture and the acts of individuals. But what is a 'good culture' and should it be a child-orientated one? What happens to women in a child-orientated culture? Can a culture be both child orientated and permit, or foster, the liberation of women as individuals with non-motherhood identities?

Let us think for a moment about the Mundugumor, about the values and practices they espoused which led to Mead's own resolution to become a mother. Are Mundugumor women free from the motherhood-versus-personhood dilemma experienced by Mead and her sisters in Euro-American culture? One striking feature about Mundugumor culture was that the prevailing negative attitude to children meant the application of a similar attitude to women. Everything specifically female about women – their sexuality and capacity to conceive, gestate and lactate – was decried. Any echo of maternity was a vulnerability and a liability. Women as women were hated and hated themselves. Motherhood was quite simply an entirely negative identity.

Leaping unjustifiably from one culture to another, let us now consider one of the laws pertaining to motherhood that operated in New York State when Mead herself achieved motherhood in 1939; newborn babies had by law at that time to be kept in a separate hospital room from their mothers. What does such a law tell us about the values of American culture and the position of women as mothers in it? I suggest that it transmits a message about women which is in many ways not terribly different from the head-hunting Mundugumor.

In both the Mundugumor case and the case of the New York mothers in the 1930s the essential point is that women are alienated from certain aspects of their potential identities as mothers. How they are able to perceive themselves in relation to motherhood is not an open-ended question. One fixed notion *is* given them by their cultures, and that is the notion that being a mother is a problem. In the New Guinea case, biological motherhood itself is bad, while in the New York case, motherhood itself is good, but women are not good enough to do it properly without the expert guidance of the state via its institutional, ideological apparatuses – education, the law and the medical profession. In both cases there is a split between women's concept of themselves and the manner in which they see themselves as mothers.

Biological versus Social Reproduction

In discussing the relationship between women's identities and motherhood, it is, of course, necessary to specify what the term 'mother' means. And it is here that we meet the first difficulty – or the first enlightenment – for what 'mother' means is both the capacity for *biological* reproduction and the exigency of *social* reproduction – childbearing as opposed to childrearing.

Biological Motherhood

Dramatic historical changes in definitions of both biological and social motherhood have occurred quite recently within our own society. Women have been bearing fewer children, have been dying less, and have been subjected to more medical control. Whilst we may presume that unwanted childbearing and unwanted deaths are *not* benefits for women, the increase in medical control which has accompanied (and may even at times have accounted for part of) the improvement, is another matter altogether.

The most profound impact of modern methods of childbirth management on the situation of women is the unfortunate connection between the attitudes and practices of medicalized childbirth, and the psychological constitution of women within patriarchal culture. The relationship between women's psychology and that of men is most easily described as that between a subordinate and dominant social group. The psychological characteristics of subordinate groups form a certain cluster: submissiveness, passivity, docility, dependence, lack of initiative, inability to take decisions, and so forth. Subordinates embody weakness while dominants embody strength. A degree of weakness and dependence is part of the feminine stereotype. 'Real' women obtain their reality by being the very opposite of the assertive, aggressive, empire-building masculine stereotype. And yet these features of femininity (which have been found to characterize actual women in numerous psychological and social studies) are precisely those features which identify the patient in what most doctors consider to be a good doctor-patient relationship and most patients experience to be the *normal* doctor-patient relationship. The doctor tells the patient what is the matter with her or him and the patient believes the doctor. The patient also complies with the doctor's orders in terms of any treatment or change in life style that is thought by the doctor to be required in order to dispel the patient's symptoms. After all, it is said, there wouldn't be any of this nonsense about natural childbirth and delivering babies standing up in the dark and/or underwater, if women understood what is good for them – or, rather, what is good for their *babies*. The naivety of the medical profession in relation to such questions often leads them to pose an artificial conflict of interests between women and their fetuses, to remark on an apparent absence of that effortless altruism which is itself a hallmark of femininity. (This is not to say that the interests of women and of their children always coincide. Clearly, this is not the case. But the point is that it should be women themselves who determine both the circumstances under which their and their children's interests coincide and those in which they do not.)

Social Motherhood

This is the century of the child. It became the century of the child for a number of related reasons: the decline in infant deaths and births, the emergence of child labour into the public limelight of the industrial workplace, the requirements of an industrial economy for specialized and educated labourers. These factors forced the state to take an interest in the protection and preservation of childlife. The population losses brought about by war reinforced this eugenic rationale, for, as one British commentator put it in the early 1900s, 'out of the mouths of babes and sucklings...the strength is ordained which shall still the Enemy and the Avenger'.[3] Not only the British variety of imperialism, but all brands of nationalism, came to be seen as rooted in the home. It is interesting, and most important for our purposes, to note that in the USA, Britain and many other European countries, two strategies were developed absolutely simultaneously for the preservation and improvement of childlife. These strategies were (1) the control of biological reproduction by the medical and midwifery professions; (2) the control of social reproduction by the rise of paediatric 'experts' and the education of mothers for hygienic housewifery and motherhood. The major initial impetus for the medicalization of biological reproduction was not the aim of decreasing infant mortality, but the aim of keeping mothers alive, because, of course, a dead mother could not be educated to be a better mother.

From the start, women were seen as the key to the whole problem. The economic climate and the reaction against feminism combined in the first decades of this century to produce an atmosphere most unfavourable to a vocation for women outside the home. Women had, therefore, to be the child*rearers* – a conclusion supported by the new enlightenment about breast-feeding as the answer to one of the great infant killers – gastro-intestinal infection. As Ellen Key wrote in her 1909 bestseller *The Century of the Child*: 'the transformation of society begins with the unborn child. . . . This transformation requires an entirely new conception of the vocation of mother.'[4] Or as President Roosevelt put it: 'The good mother, the wise mother – you cannot really be a good mother if you are not a wise mother – is more important to the community than even the ablest man. . . . The woman who, whether from cowardice, from selfishness, from having a false and vacuous ideal, shirks her duty as wife and mother, earns the right to our contempt just as does the man who. . .fears to do his duty in battle when the country calls him.'[5]

The battle in the home and the battle outside it: an appropriate gender division. Of course the focus of the experts' advice to mothers has shifted over the years between the early decades of this century and now. *Then* it was on physical aspects of childcare: on the simple mechanistic elimination of 'dirt' from the environment, for example. Now attention is focused on the development of the child's psychology and personality. Rather than a sound body producing a sound mind the formula is reversed, and our modern emphasis on the possibility, if not prevalence, of psychosomatic disturbance, enables us to know absolutely that the basis for a sound body is laid in the mother's creation in her child of a sound mind. It is worth noting that the earlier concentration on the physical side of childcare meant, for women, a total continuity with their function as homemakers. The production of a sanitary environment was the prime goal of both good housewifery and good motherhood. But later on in the century, a discontinuity becomes increasingly evident. What is good for the home is not always good for the child. Charlotte Perkins Gilman was in advance of her time when she called family life neither marriage nor child-culture but 'the running of the commissary and dormitory departments of life, with elaborate lavatory processes', and curtly observed that although 'the mother loves the child, always and always. . .the principal work of her day is the care of her house. . . . Follow the hours in the day of the housewife,' Gilman admonished, 'count the minutes spent in the care and service of the child, as compared with those given to the planning of meals, the purchase of supplies, the labour of. . . cleaning things. . . . In what way', Gilman asked, 'do the meals we so elaborately order and prepare, the daintily furnished home, the much trimmed clothing, contribute to the body-growth, mind-growth and soul-growth of the child?'[6]

To bring Gilman's observations up to date, let us note that, if a market value is assigned to the housewife-mother's domestic services, more than a third of the gross national product in both the USA and Britain is accounted for by housework. The major part of the unpaid work women do at home is not concerned with what the paediatric experts declare to be the most significant function of motherhood.

WHAT DO YOU EXPECT WHEN YOU BECOME A MOTHER?

It is hard to avoid the fact that there is something really depressing about motherhood. In my own study of the transition to motherhood,[7] four out of five mothers experienced a short-term 'blues' reaction to the births of their babies, three-quarters an anxiety state on first assuming responsibility for the baby, a third depressed moods, and a quarter had a more serious symptomatic depression in the early months of motherhood. I looked separately at the women's feelings about the social role of mother and at the relationship the women described with their babies. A third of the women were not satisfied with the social role of mother, and two-thirds expressed negative feelings/ambivalence in their relationship with their babies.

I do not believe that these findings are unrepresentative either of the general situation in Britain or of that elsewhere. The fact that depression is most characteristically a female disorder is well-known. The amount of depression in mothers that is postnatal only in a tautological sense – you have to acquire a child to be called a mother, but mothers can be, and are, depressed at any stage in their motherhood – is enormous. A very carefully done community survey in London found a prevalence rate of 15 per cent in what psychiatrists would call depression.[8] The highest rate was for working-class women with children under six – 42 per cent of these were clinically depressed. But when 'borderline' cases were included, the rate in the commmunity as a whole rose from 15 to 33 per cent. Such statistics provide the background for the very high rates of psychotropic drug prescribing that now characterize the relations between the medical profession and mothers – in some general practices in Britain more than a fifth of all women patients are in receipt of such drugs.[9]

Studies that have examined the factors associated with depression in mothers have shown the importance both of the conditions under which women mother and of past factors in women's lives that appear to make them especially vulnerable to 'depression'. The factors I found to be significantly associated with the outcomes of depression in my own study are a somewhat mixed bag. The medical factors seemingly predictive of depression are those relating to an unsatisfying birth experience in which the mother felt she was not the person delivering the baby, while the social factors relate to the absence of supportive conditions for childrearing and to the lack of previous job experience – that is, little contact with babies before the acquisition of one's own. The community survey I mentioned earlier suggested that four factors in particular predicted women's vulnerability to depression: lack of an intimate relationship, having three or more children under fourteen, loss of one's mother before the age of eleven and not having a job outside the home. In my own study, the occurrence of depression was associated most strongly with four 'vulnerability factors': lack of a job outside the home, housing problems, a segregated role-relationship with the baby's father and little previous experience of babies. In the presence of four vulnerability factors the depression rate was 100 per cent, falling to 20 per cent for those with one factor. It may well be that a relatively simple index of housing conditions, such as tenure, is more predictive of maternal depression than any number of enquiries into mothers' psychological constitutions. Thus, another British survey of motherhood showed a highly significant difference in rates of depression according to housing tenure – from 17 per cent in women who were owner-occupiers to 60 per cent of those living in council accommodation.[10] Clearly, the application of this index to the situation in the USA is not simple – but the basic point is that poverty causes unhappiness, and that motherhood, despite being a morally idealized state, does not guarantee (economic) wealth.

As to possible theoretical pathways between such vulnerability factors and the onset of clinically recognized depression, the theory is that vulnerability factors produce an ongoing state of low self-esteem. When a provoking agent, a life-event or a chronic difficulty occurs, the feeling of hopelessness that is evoked becomes a generalized state of hopelessness which in turn produces the features of clinical depression. Both the factors that make women vulnerable to developing a depressive disorder and the life-events and long-term difficulties that are liable to provoke depression are more prevalent in the lower socio-economic groups: this is but one manifestation of a general phenomenon – the process whereby economic class and gender class are interlocking axes of inequality for women.

According to theorists such as Jean Baker Miller[11] and Nancy Chodorow,[12] everything hinges on the question of self-identity and self-esteem. The fact that women do the mothering in our society accounts for a certain unbroken relationship between mothers and daughters. A consequence of the lack of a daughter's need to repudiate an identification with her mother (which is what a son must do to achieve masculinity) is the difficulty women may have in developing an autonomous sense of self, a certainty about the stable core of qualities one attributes to oneself *through and beyond the circumstances of any particular relationship*. The problem of motherhood for women is that the tendency to seek one's identity in relationships with others is liable to continue, even when the original tie with the mother seems to have been outgrown. Thirdly, an attitude of unreality about the *gratifications*, about the *satisfaction*, of motherhood is bred in women by their earliest experience of the mothering relation.

I think this interpretation helps to explain a number of otherwise puzzling features of motherhood. Perhaps the first question is why do women continue to want children? Between 80 and 90 per cent of adult women in the industrialized world have at least one child, and although fertility has fallen in the sense that there are now more small families, the experience of mothering *at least one child* is now spread more widely across the female population than it was 50 or 100 years ago. Like many questions in this field, this question, why women want children, is impossible to answer on the basis of existing research, since the dominant paradigm has equated biological femaleness and the impulse to maternity: non-achievement of motherhood rather than its achievement has been the problematic of most inquiries. When it *is* asked, the question 'Why did you want a baby?' is usually greeted with some response along the lines of 'I never really thought about it', or 'I always have done.' And this is what would indeed seem to be the case, for as long as women mother, women will always want to *become* mothers in order to recreate the same apparent satisfaction of their relational needs as they experienced as children with *their* mothers.

Another way to put this is to say that what the gender-differentiated nuclear family produces is two classes of people – men and women – who cannot satisfy one another's relational needs. Men want their relational needs to be satisfied in a heterosexual connection with women, while women look, throughout their lives, and in one way or another, back to the original symbiosis of the mother-child relationship. When one compares contemporary industrial society with other non-industrialized cultures, the absence of patterned co-operation and friendship between adult women is one of the most striking differences. Women in many other cultures look to each other for daily help and support and emotional gratification. They did so in our own society before industrialization and before the rise of the nuclear family ethic, according to which the love between man and woman is every woman's salvation. In fact, of course, the promise of this love is every woman's downfall, for as long as women believe in *men* as their saviours they will not be able to find themselves. The nuclear family provides women with only one culturally accepted solution to their own gendered, family-produced needs for intense primary relationships: and that is to invest their emotional futures in their children.

The second puzzling feature of motherhood that is illuminated by this particular interpretation concerns what is *difficult* about mothering. According to Chodorow, those very capacities and needs which create women as mothers lead to potential contradictions in mothering. Mothering involves a dual identification for women, both as mother and as child. Women make good parents because they can take the place of the child, understand the child's needs from the child's point of view. But the mother-child relationship is also marked with inherent conflict, and women run the risk of projecting their own childish needs onto their children, of finding the temperaments, capacities and interests of their children less than satisfying, and of living out problems in their relationships to their own mothers with their own children.

Thirdly, we can see how in turning to the idealised fulfilment of the mother-child relationship women do not begin to solve their basic problem, and that is of an insufficiently individuated sense of self. Nor do they begin to solve this problem for their daughters. This conclusion, which is not intended to be 'victim-blaming' in any sense, helps to identify what may be good for women and their children about women having a job outside the home. There is no doubt that, as we have seen, having another work role that is economically rewarding and publicly valued improves the mental health of mothers, probably because it increases their perception of themselves as individuals and adds to (or provides them with a basis for) self-esteem. At the same time, children of employed mothers, especially daughters, appear to be more independent, more self-reliant, less 'feminine' and less rigid in their conceptions of gender roles.[13] Such findings are slightly curious when one considers that most employed mothers work in low-status, relatively ill-paid jobs which do not themselves appear to be intrinsically rewarding. It would appear to be principally the opportunity for non-domestic identification that is important – for mothers and their daughters. And yet the full exploitation of such an identification may involve short-term hardship, for, as most mothers know, it is still going against the set of the culture to insist that one is oneself first, and somebody's mother second, and extremely difficult for a five, ten or even fifteen year-old to realize that such self-assertion is in her own best long-term interests.

Fourthly, and most fundamental of all, the mother-child relationship is pre-social and in a significant sense 'un-real'. It is the infant's first love experience and it is one in which the infant has little sense of her/his separateness from the mother. The infant attributes to the mother an idealized and sacrificial love and these attributes of motherhood are never entirely lost for either male or female children. The males grow up with a double image of women – as pure and selfless mothers and, on the other hand, as sexy bitches or aggressive careerists. The females grow up possessed of a profoundly unreal fantasy of what it is like to be a mother.

So one of the problems of motherhood in a patriarchal family-oriented culture which assigns childrearing to the female parent, is that women come to motherhood with quite unrealistic expectations of what they will achieve *for themselves* through biological reproduction. *A certain idealization of the state of maternity is itself built into the mothering relation as presently defined.* So long as childrearing continues to be assigned to women, this idealization can be counted as a form of 'transmitted deprivation'. Women are deprived of the chance to understand not only the benefits, but also the hazards that motherhood will pose to their own identities and life-styles.

WHAT KIND OF CHILDREN DO WE NEED?

It was the American sociologist Alice Rossi who, in 1968, drew attention to the fact that the bias in almost all existing research on parenthood within the behavioural sciences is towards finding out the right kind of mothers for children to have.[14] It was assumed that if enough were known about styles of mothering and attitudes of mothers to children, then much of the evident variation among children could be accounted for. As David Levy put it in his much-quoted book *Maternal Overprotection* in 1943, 'It is generally accepted that the most potent of all influences on social behaviour is derived from the primary social experience with the mother... the most important study of man [sic] as a human being is a study of his mother's influence on his early life.'[15] The contrary assumption – that if enough were known about the attitudes of children to mothers and children's impact on maternal identities and lifestyles, then much of the variation among mothers might be explained – was, however, never made. If we shift the emphasis – as research over the past few years has increasingly done, though not by any means sufficiently thoroughly yet – then we can see that the important questions for women include: What is the effect of motherhood on women's lives? What does maternity deprive women of? and, What is the best kind of child for a woman to have if she is to obtain the most gratification and the least deprivation from the status, role and identity of mother?

I do not know that we can really answer this question, given the present state of the art. Margaret Mead, whose initiation into motherhood I referred to earlier, once recalled a letter written by Harriet Beecher Stowe, in which Stowe said that she had in mind to write a novel about slavery, 'but the baby cried too much.' Mead's comment on this was that 'it would have been much more plausible if she had said 'but the baby smiles so much.'[16] The pleasures of motherhood may well be an obstacle to writing books about slavery or being involved more generally in publicly productive activity – but a crying baby is more likely to cause maternal dissatisfaction than a smiling one. An interesting study in Cambridge, England, which followed a group of first-born children from birth to school age, found that children who persisted in waking at night after the first year were those who cried and showed the highest levels of irritability in the early days of life. The only differences in maternal behaviour between the night-wakers and the non-night-wakers were attributable to, rather than causes of, this early difference on the part of the babies.[17]

Given that the sex differences literature demonstrates that is is more usually boys than girls who provide their mothers with such problems, it is not very heartening to discover that according to a number of studies, women more often find mothering a daughter more depressing than mothering a son.[18] One researcher has suggested that female babies are more often depressing to women because they re-enact the initial, unworked out ambivalence of the mother-daughter relationship, and because to have a son is to achieve what our culture continues to hold out as the highest achievement for women. If you can't become a member of the dominant group yourself, I guess the next best thing is to give birth to one.

MOTHERS AND CHILDREN AND THE 'GOOD' SOCIETY

Female parenting is the first and most lasting determinant of women's subordinate group psychology. Daughters are never rid of their mothers – either of their mothers' weaknesses or of their mothers' extraordinarily valuable emotional capacities and sensitivities. Biological motherhood is not the primary problem. Without resorting to a test-tube and artificial womb technology (which, anyway, would not solve the problem because in the present social order this technology would be male-controlled), it *is* possible to see how biological reproduction could be managed so that it did *not* alienate women from their own bodies and identities the way it does at the moment. What is needed is a condition that is at the same time both most simple and most complex, and that is to ensure that women experience themselves as the central actors in the drama of childbirth and motherhood. All the evidence points to this essential requirement: that mother-child relations are severely jeopardized if they begin with the medical infantilization of women, with an insistence that women have to be instructed in the business of childbirth and childrearing by a male-dominated profession of experts and must have their bodies attended to and manipulated like, and indeed, by, machines in order for the child to be safely extracted and set out on the even more hazardous journey to autonomous adulthood. The terms 'control' and 'mastery' – a most telling word in this context – occur often in the literature dealing with what constitutes successful biological reproduction from the mother's point of view. Where a women does not feel that she in some sense directed the course of her own childbirth and is able to direct the course of her own motherhood, she is more liable to come out of it with damaged self-esteem, and with a perception of her baby and herself as strangers produced by strangers. Motherhood as a form of colonial imperialism is something women can do without.

So, it is not too difficult to specify the conditions for biological reproduction that are needed to provide a *positive* self-identity in women and that heightened self-esteem which is the reality behind the cultural myth of maternity's automatic enhancement of all women to a state of grace. But childbearing constitutes but a tiny fragment of time in our total experience of motherhood. Motherhood is not only an experience, it is an institution, and it is with this institution that our greatest problems lie. The strong association between the social and economic circumstances in which women mother and their mental health that is clear from some of the evidence I have quoted, points very firmly to this conclusion. In fact it is *because* of the determination of mother-child relations and the psychology of women by the gender-differentiated family that the element of so-called 'mastery' in childbearing and childrearing is so profoundly important. Can you imagine *men* putting up with the kind of indignities and assaults imposed on mothers by the medical profession over the last 20 years? I can't. The victimization of women is facilitated by their own victimization of themselves. We need to embark on motherhood with strength, assertiveness and a clear sense of ourselves as individuals. But most of us become mothers too early in our own development to have begun to understand that a secure sense of self-esteem is a prerequisite for, and not a consequence of, motherhood.

In order to understand *why* the institution of motherhood takes the form that it does in modern industrialized society, it helps to grasp one other consequence of women's mothering within the family. That consequence I have already obliquely referred to, and it is men's contradictory need both to put mothers on a pedestal and to keep them down – in their place as domesticated, resented, unliberated dependants. It has been observed for a long time by both feminist and non-feminist defenders of motherhood, that motherhood is high in our scale of values – it is a prized and necessary occupation – yet at the same time it is the most socially undervalued occupation of all. Simone de Beauvoir put it well in her classic *The Second Sex* when she said 'There is an extravagant fraudulence in the easy reconciliation made between the common attitude of contempt for women and the respect shown for mothers.' Women who are denied the opportunities and responsibilities of men have babies put into their arms 'without scruple, as in earlier life dolls were given to them to compensate for their inferiority to little boys. They are permitted to play with toys of flesh and blood.'[19] Motherhood is a labour of love. Motherhood is non-work. But more than that, society need not provide for mothers. The pre-social or anti-social character of mother-child relations is reflected in the unflagging determination of our policy-makers to divide the world into two: mothers and others. Mothers do not belong to the public world, but to the private domain of the family in which the state must not intrude to advance mothers' own self-determined needs. One sign of the enormity of the state's failure to take account of the real situation of mothers is the fact that in Britain only some 13 per cent of the under-fives whose mothers have a paid job are in receipt of some sort of state-provided day care, and only about 1 per cent of the total public money devoted to health, education and social services in Britain is used for helping employed mothers (parents) with their childcare responsibilities.[20]

Adrienne Rich has said that 'There has been a basic contradiction throughout patriarchy: between the laws and sanctions designed to keep women essentially powerless, and the attribution to mothers of almost superhuman powers.'[21] The other side of the contradiction is the negation of women who are not mothers, who are woman-identified, or who identify with the woman (person) in themselves. And it is, as Rich points out, immensely ironic that the first and last verbal attack slung at the woman who demonstrates a primary loyalty to herself and other women is 'man-hater'.

Is the experience of motherhood under patriarchy ultimately a radicalizing or a conservative force for women? That is a question Rich asks herself. Does motherhood extract from us an obedience to convention and a social order we know to be morally bankrupt, or does it really put us in touch with the way things are, with the callousness of patriarchy towards women's interests? Either way women tend to be the losers. I think this is one of the things Margaret Mead meant when her excursions into New Guinea forged the conclusion in her own mind that a culture engaged in the repudiation of children and the creativity of motherhood is not a good culture. A good culture in one in which human relationships come first – a good culture is a *humane* culture. Note here that both the words 'human' and 'humane' come from the same root, but that their usage diverged in the eighteenth century so that 'human' meant 'characteristic of man [sic]' and 'humane' came to mean 'kind, benevolent, civil, courteous, obliging'. As men became, linguistically and socially, the standard for human civilization, so kindness and benevolence ceased to be attributes of the human community as a whole. Kindness and benevolence are hardly defining characteristics of men in our society today. But to flourish as mothers and as people, women *require* a kind society. There is nothing intrinsically unfeminist about a culture that is oriented to the needs of children, so long as it is so in more than a superficial, eugenic woman-hating sense, and so long as it is understood that the needs of women are not the same thing as the needs of children, and that the needs of women are not the same as the needs of mothers. We do not, in fact, know what it would be like to be mothers in a society that affirmed and respected women as individuals; nor can we imagine how the situation of women who are not mothers might be transformed by a different social valuation of motherhood. We do not know what it would mean for all of us if children were to be valued sufficiently for men to be truly involved in their care. We have no idea how motherhood might be transformed in a world rid of the extremes of class and race inequality, as well as sex inequality. We can only guess at the effect on motherhood of a culture that affirmed peace and life instead of war and death. But we do most desperately need such a vision if we are to pass on to our daughters more than our own impoverished heritage.

8

February's Child
Terminal 1

The first of these two poems is one of my own small sonatas on motherhood, written to the owner of the Chicago-bought parrot when she (child, not parrot) was not quite two years old. This stage in motherhood was, for me, one of the least problematic and the most pleasurable. The poem expresses my desire to hold on to it, and especially to hold on to the deeply satisfying union between the two of us.

'Terminal 1', leaps 15 years on to another era of motherhood. The simple physical sensuality and caring needed at age two is not what is needed at age seventeen: as a mother one must then stand back and respect difference even if one doesn't approve of it. The woman in Terminal 1 is my elder daughter pictured momentarily as she waited for me at Heathrow airport. There is no doubt that this particular moment had a different meaning for each of us, a fact which can lead to difficulties in such relationships, but is, nevertheless, one to be celebrated.

February's Child

baby, baby
give me your answer do
what is it that looks out of your eyes at me
is it love I see

your face is my silk cushion
your uncut hair like honey dips
across the darkness
it is your laugh that nourishes me

if I could plant love in your head
staked and labelled, guaranteed to last
through nightmares and snowstorms
against all error and unkindness
I might hold back the fracture of this union
you, my benediction

Terminal 1

the woman next to me is trying to eat her dinner
on the top of three shopping bags
she is a purchaser of objects
flitting through the world's cities
picking up a skirt here, a suitcase there
even a sock or a sort of spaghetti
all paid for with a visa card
(a fantastic plastic invention, the words
spit out of her champagne-filled mouth)

in my experience
those who are most lost
spend all their time buying containers
to put themselves in

and then they carry them onto planes
and pack them round their persons
thereby making the rest of us
feel we have mislaid something possibly significant

the shopper drinks
and I sit avoiding the accusing fluffiness of the clouds
watching me through the window
keen to tell me I may crash at any moment
(if you look straight ahead you don't know where you are)
here comes the steward
with his tightly zipped flies
(the brotherhood of the skies)
wanting me to drown my feelings about containers
in a cognac, cointreau or drambuie
as though the foreignness of the words
makes it alright to be comatose

landing on a lucid grey tarmac
the awfulness of airport buildings
replacing the simpering clouds
tells me I am home
home being not where the heart is
but where drabness and disarray of buildings and the
national character
are simply self-criticism of a childhood-embedded sort

I exit briskly
drunk in charge of a trolley with a bent wheel
I do not see her standing there
nor she me, being disguised with a black hat
but returning to search the crowds
her figure springs out at me, is the only thing I see

black, black she stands
black like me
black coat, black legs
black scarf catching copper hair
black eyes laser-lighting the people who aren't me

O beautiful woman of Terminal 1
your birth is my container
you are not lost
and I am someone
who has you to come home to

9

The Limits of the Professional Imagination

In early 1982 a conference was held in Finland on 'Women and Medical Science' – the first of its kind in that country. Although according to various indices, for example the percentage of women in the professions, Finland is near the top of the feminist league table, in other respects it is a backward country. The level of public debate about aspects of women's situation and the tangles both genders get themselves and each other in is not high. There is a curious blandness and distracting seriousness about the way the Finns apply themselves to some of the questions I shall discuss in the essay that follows. I called it 'The Limits of the Professional Imagination': it is a summary of some of my own work on the characterizations of women as mothers developed within different professional disciplines. It is itself a very serious piece, but I did try to make a few jokes, and there was no hint of laughter from the audience. Both the weather and the location – an enormous early nineteenth-century government building – were austere. It wasn't quite as cold as Seinäjoki, but the ritual of removing woolly hats, fur coats and wet boots took time and instilled a permanently damp and unfunny note into the atmosphere.

All human societies have to take into account the fact that only women can bear children. This is both important and unimportant as a biological

Source: Originally presented to the congress on *Women and Medical Science*, Helsinki, 25/26 January 1982.

constraint on the general division of labour between the sexes. It is unimportant because in considering how different societies have responded to the biological fact of women's essential role in reproduction, it is not a question of nature determining culture but of different cultural interpretations of nature. Many examples of this are possible: in certain societies and historical periods people have seen no contradiction between the female labour of growing and producing a child on the one hand, and whatever other labour it is customary for women to do on the other. In yet other times and places it has been contended that women's function of reproduction is entirely threatened by work of any other kind: 'nature' forces on women a life of parasitic idleness in the interest of the preservation of the species.

Women's capacity to reproduce is subject to different interpretations. Biology is not destiny. But its very importance lies in the fact that it must enter in some form into the logic of every social system and every cultural ideology.

PROFESSIONAL PARADIGMS OF WOMEN AS CHILDBEARERS

Some of the most powerful images of women and motherhood are those held by the professional disciplines which lay claim to a special expertise in the field of reproduction – namely, medical science, clinical psychiatry and psychology. In order to review the images of women to be found in each of these professional perspectives, I am going to draw on a wide range of data, from my own observations of work in a London maternity hospital in the mid-1970s and interviews with women having babies, to the assumptions made about women as patients in the medical literature. My basic argument can be simply stated; it is that in the contemporary industrialized world, medical science and allied disciplines, in claiming specialist jurisdiction over all aspects of reproduction, have become the predominant source of social constructs of the culture of childbirth. The professional obstetrical view that childbirth is a pathological process and women are passive objects of clinical attention has become an integral part of the way in which the community as a whole sees childbirth. Science is in this sense itself ideology; it is certainly not a matter of objective 'fact'. However, we cannot let the matter rest there, for there is ample evidence that 'professional' images of motherhood conflict with the experiences of mothers themselves. Most women's experiences of becoming a mother are considerably and uncomfortably out of tune with the expectations they have absorbed from professional advisers to mothers (amongst others) about what the process will be like.

IMAGES OF MOTHERHOOD AND WOMEN IN MEDICAL SCIENCE

The single most important aspect of medical attitudes towards women as mothers is their concealment behind a screen of what are presented as exclusively clinical concerns. The attitude is that there are *no* attitudes: it is purely a question of how medical knowledge determines the 'best' maternity care policy, one that will guarantee the lowest possible mortality rate for mother and child.

There is, in a sense, no answer to this: for what mother does not want to survive childbirth with a healthy child? But the issue is a great deal more complicated. In the first place, obstetricians and other makers of maternity care policy have rarely possessed the evidence necessary to prove that any particular obstetric practice is really 'better' than another (or the alternative of no practice at all) as judged by the objective of the lowest possible mortality. In the second place, the assessment of the 'success' of childbirth in terms of mortality (and to a lesser extent physical morbidity) rates is itself an attitude of extreme, if benign, paternalism. It hides two assumptions: (1) the usual but disputable medical-scientific claim, challenged convincingly by Ivan Illich,[22] Thomas McKeown,[23] and others, that improvements in health-care are due principally to medical treatment (rather than to changes in social and economic conditions); and (2) that all other indices of successful childbirth are irrelevant, or at least of very minor importance. The way in which obstetrics has developed has ensured a preoccupation with the *physical* model of reproduction. Social and emotional measures of reproductive success do not count, although the evidence is that such measures are extremely important to mothers themselves. Such evidence is hardly ever collected by obstetric researchers investigating the efficacy of particular obstetric practices. Maternal attitudes to obstetric practice and maternal assessments of successful reproductive outcome as research topics have been considered by obstetricians to constitute the 'soft', and by implication inferior, material of social-scientific surveys – where, that is, they have been considered at all.

In modern obstetrics, the dominant image of women is a mechanical one: women are seen as reproductive machines. 'To put the matter rather crudely, obstetrics treats a body like a complex machine and uses a series of interventionist techniques to repair faults that may develop in the machine.'[24] The mechanical model is 'man-made' and needs regular servicing to function correctly. Thus antenatal care is maintenance- and malfunction-spotting work. There is a most significant premise here, and that is that any machine can go wrong at any time; there is no distinction between those machines that are in good working order – in other words, the 97 per cent[25] of pregnancies and childbirths that are unproblematic – and those machines with some apparent fault – in other words the small minority of pregnancies and births in which medical intervention does literally save lives. Concretely, as well as ideologically, women appear to become machines. The language of obstetrics itself reflects this – consider such terms as 'uterine dysfunction', 'incompetent cervix' and 'bad reproducer'. Obstetric care in countries such as Britain and the USA is increasingly machine-oriented. In many hospitals all pregnancies are monitored with ultrasound; in some the mechanical assessment of gestation is so important that women are no longer asked for the date of their last menstrual period. Other technological assessments are a routine part of antenatal care. Machines are used to initiate and terminate labour. One machine controls the uterine contractions, while another records them; regional (epidural) analgesia removes the woman's awareness of her contractions so that these do, indeed, have to be read off the machine; and keeping all the machines going becomes what 'looking after' a patient in labour means.

This merging of the pregnant female body with the high-powered technology of modern obstetrics has many implications. But one implication it does *not* have is that obstetricians are merely mechanics to be called in when faults develop, much as one takes a faulty car to the garage to have it repaired. It is usually obvious to a car-owner when her or his car goes wrong, but women cannot be trusted to be experts on their own pregnancies. Thus another prime feature of medical images of motherhood is that women lack the capacity to know what is happening to their own bodies. Doctors are the only experts in the entire symptomatology of childbearing.

This was very clearly demonstrated in the encounters between doctors and patients I observed in a London maternity hospital in the mid-1970s. Perhaps the most striking encounter along these lines was the following:

Doctor: [reading case-notes] to patient: 'Ah, I see you've got a boy and a girl.'
Patient: 'No, two girls.'
Doctor: 'Really, are you sure? I thought it said . . . [checks in case-notes] . . . Oh no, you're quite right, two girls.'

Pregnancy and childbirth in the medical model are medical events. For it is only by an ideological transformation of the 'natural' or 'normal' to the 'cultural' and 'abnormal' that doctors can legitimate reproduction as a medical speciality. Any individual pregnancy or childbirth may be normal but it is only so, according to medical dictate, in retrospect. The mechanical model of motherhood conspires with the model of reproduction as pathology to characterize women having babies as possessing only one role – that of pregnant patients, patients in the delivery room and postpartum ward. Being a patient is separated off from the rest of life. The impact of social, economic and psychological factors is admitted by obstetricians only in so far as it is liable to predict the physical symptomatology or outcome of pregnancy. Hence unmarried patients may receive special medical attention and be referred routinely to the medical social worker, while married patients who experience genuine medical and social problems are not routinely viewed as a 'high-risk' group. Low social class and being unmarried are frequently combined with obstetric factors in medical scoring systems for high-risk pregnancies.

The organization of much obstetric care is based on the assumption that a pregnant or parturient woman has no other responsibilities or interests which conflict with her function of producing a baby. Reproduction is a full-time role. In the antenatal consultations I observed, as well as the medical literature, doctors rarely consider that pregnant women have homes to run, many have other children to look after, a significant proportion are involved in the care of elderly relatives, the majority are married and carry the domestic responsibilities attached to the role of a wife, while most are engaged in addition in some form of paid employment. One example illustrates this point:

Doctor:	'Mrs Carter? How are you getting on?'
Patient:	'Horrible.'
Doctor:	'Why?'
Patient:	'I feel horrible...I feel so depressed.'
Doctor:	'Why?'
Patient:	'I don't know...I feel it's so difficult to walk.'
Doctor:	'You shouldn't be walking much at this stage of pregnancy.'
Patient:	'I don't. But I have my housework to do and I've got the in-laws staying.'
Doctor:	'They should be doing your housework for you, shouldn't they? Isn't that what they're for?'
Patient:	'They're not females...things aren't very good at home at the moment...'
Doctor:	'You do seem to have put on a bit of weight.'

Patient: 'What does that mean?'
Doctor: 'It doesn't necessarily mean anything, but you must take things easy.'
Patient: 'That's what my husband says. It's easy for men to say that.'
Doctor: 'It's your set-up at home. You should have organized things better.'
Patient: 'Well, I've got three children to look after.'

Ninety-three per cent of the questions posed or statements made by patients about social matters and social role obligations in the doctor–patient encounters I observed met with the response of irritation or simple avoidance from the doctor.

Because reproduction is a specialist medical subject, because parenthood is isolated from women's life-circumstances, and because women are typified as essentially ignorant about the process of reproduction, the concept of choice as applied to users of the maternity services is nowhere in sight in the medical model of motherhood. Although many surveys of how women feel about their maternity care show that many wish to be consulted about what kind of medical treatment they receive, the obstetrical claim to unique expertise prevents the exercise of choice by those who have the babies. I am not talking here about those cases in which gross problems in pregnancy or labour clearly necessitate medical intervention, but about the majority of cases in which it is 'policy' in general that determines what proportion of women receive such procedures as ultrasonic monitoring in pregnancy, electronic fetal heart monitoring in labour, and elective induction of labour. Women themselves are often aware that the rules determining their treatment are arbitrary, in the sense that these rules vary from one hospital to another, or from one practitioner to another. Under such circumstances it seems reasonable to mothers that they should have a say in what happens; but it is not reasonable to a medical profession whose claim to jurisdiction over the label of illness and any human life-event to which it may be attached ensures the right (if not the responsibility) to disregard the wishes of the 'patient'.

Those who provide maternity care may see women as walking wombs, but they cannot discount completely the fact that women have heads as well. Thus we come to the second key model of womanhood in medical science – that of the biologically determined 'feminine' female.

In the medical literature, including the advice literature available in Britain and other countries written by medical 'experts' for mothers, there is a clearly set out paradigm of 'normal' motherhood.[26] What is a normal mother? She is a person especially in need of medical care and protection; a person who is essentially childish; but at the same time fundamentally altruistic; she is married; and, lastly, she ought to be happy but is, instead, constantly beset with anxiety and depression.

These typifications of mothers are interrelated and also internally contradictory. Women's imputed need for medical care and control is demanded by the very premise of obstetric science – that women can only be 'delivered of' their babies: childbirth cannot be allowed to be an autonomous act. In turn, the need for medical care requires the imputation of ignorance, unreliability and plain silliness to mothers as immutably feminine characteristics. Women are people who suffer from an inability to remember important facts, like when they last menstruated or when to take iron and vitamin supplements prescribed by their doctors:

> Do remember to take the tablets your doctor has given you. No matter how well you feel, both you and your baby need them and they don't do either of you any good if you leave them sitting around on your dressing-table.[27]

Another instance of such advice is the counsel offered by much of the antenatal literature against moving house in pregnancy. This is described as a piece of idiocy guaranteed to jeopardize the baby's well-being. However, it is widely stated – I don't know whether this observation is to be found in Finnish literature too – that scrubbing the floor and cleaning out the kitchen cupboards constitute 'nest-building' of the type animals engage in, and is a sure sign of the baby's imminent arrival.

In these ways normal mothers in the medical paradigm are not really adults at all. They are like children; and, like children, have to be guided and disciplined into correct modes of behaviour. Yet here we face a profound contradiction: for normal mothers, that is 'good' mothers, do not put their own needs first. They see the world in terms of their children's needs, which they gauge by a mixed and, again, contra-dictory process of listening to the experts, on the one hand, and intuition – the much-famed myth of the 'maternal instinct' – on the other. The stereotype of normal mothers as married refers to a central contradiction in obstetrical/gynaecological work (which reflects the illogicality of the association between the two disciplines) – and that is the conflict between the promotion and prevention of childbirth. The image of the nuclear family as the only valid context for childbirth is still immensely powerful in our society, and the medical profession is hardly renowned for its liberal moral attitudes. Husbands are important possessions for normal mothers because they constitute the sole orthodox channel for mothers' emotional and sexual satisfaction.

The final characteristic of normal mothers in the medical paradigm – their proneness to anxiety and depression – actually comes first in political importance in the social construction of motherhood and womanhood. It does so for three reasons. In the first place, the recognition that it is normal for mothers to be depressed before birth and afterwards proceeds from the recognition that the normal condition of women in general is depression. Secondly, the construction of women as depressed provides a rationale for them to be oppressed also. Thirdly, the prevalence of depression in mothers and women raises the question as to why it occurs and what can be done about it. The standard medical explanation for female depression is a biological one – that mysterious term 'hormones'. The standard medical treatment is pharmacological, for it is by the widespread administration of psychotropic drugs that women are 'adjusted' to their situation. A Canadian study came to the interesting conclusion that women who use psychotropic drugs like valium are consciously aware of taking them in order to cope with the social strains of their daily lives.[28]

PSYCHOLOGICAL CONSTRUCTS OF WOMEN

In an oft-quoted study carried out in the USA in 1970, a group of mental health clinicians was asked to rate the applicability of a range of personal qualities to three different kinds of people: normal adult men, normal adult women, and 'healthy, mature, socially competent' individuals. The results of this study revealed that 'healthy, mature and socially competent' individuals were ascribed masculine characteristics. Normal women were seen as more submissive, less aggressive, less competitive, more excitable, more easily hurt, more emotional, more conceited about their appearance and less objective than the normal men.[29]

In this most significant manner, psychiatry and psychology have tended to reinforce the images of women extant in the medical model. They have underscored three particular aspects of the medical model: the failure to consider the *social* context in which childbearing occurs and women live; the assumption that psychological states (including depression as the normal condition of women) are caused by physiological ones; and the refusal to treat women as human beings because women are a sex apart, 'nature herself'.

The term 'postnatal depression' is part of the language in which women discuss and experience childbirth. But it also exists as a technical concept, which is poorly defined in the literature. However, there is general agreement among the relevant 'experts' that postnatal depression is a form of reactive depression, that is, a response to particular environmental circumstances, in this case the prior circumstance of childbirth. The two main psychiatric theories describe its aetiology as (1) hormones, and (2) some disturbance of femininity. Now, while there are clearly considerable hormonal shifts during pregnancy and after delivery, to prove a causal association between these and the various forms of postnatal depression (from the 'blues' of the early postpartum days to a fully-blown psychosis developing some time later) requires research of the kind that has simply not been done. Those few studies which have examined selected aspects of puerperal biochemistry have done so in relation to early postpartum mood only (because hospitalized women are captive subjects) and, for the most part, their findings have been inconclusive.[30] In other words, the hormonal aetiology of postpartum mental disorder is part of received medical wisdom about motherhood, and it is imported into the domain of commonsense understandings about motherhood where its unscientific basis rests unquestioned. Most importantly, the biological explanation of postnatal depression is frequently taken to disprove the likelihood of this disorder being accounted for by any social influence. We are again back to the mechanical model of women as reproducers.

The second major theme in the psychological construction of maternity assumes that psychological problems result from intrapsychic conflict in the individual as she undergoes the stresses of reproduction. Postnatal depression is the outcome of this internal, individualized conflict. Of course this interpretation also means that women are at the mercy of their bodies. It means in addition that a great deal of medical research has been based on the supposition that reproductive problems in general are caused by women's lack of success in achieving a mature femininity. For example, infertility, habitual abortion and premature delivery have all been analysed as psychosomatic defences, as a result of women's hostile identification with their own mothers, as symptomatic of a general rejection of the feminine role, or as evidence of disturbed sexual relationships with men. The same hypotheses have also been applied to other common complications of pregnancy, such as nausea and vomiting and toxaemia: and the literature is studded with attempts to relate the neonatal condition of the baby to its mother's personality.[31]

In one attempt to relate neonatal condition to maternal mental state, a group of research workers at the London Hospital involved in a longitudinal study of child development decided to begin with pregnancy, and collect a certain amount of 'social' data which they could then relate to pregnancy outcome. There appeared to be a significant difference in mean infant birthweight according to whether or not the mothers suffered from psychiatric illness in pregnancy. However, when factors associated with 'psychiatric illness' and 'non-psychiatric illness' groups were considered, it became apparent that the association of lower birthweight with maternal psychiatric disorder was probably a spurious one: women who were considered psychiatrically ill and had low birthweight babies were also more likely to be smokers, aged under twenty and infrequent antenatal clinic attenders.[32]

Whether or not the 'feminine woman' makes the best reproducer cannot, like so many other professional suppositions about motherhood, in fact be established from existing research. One problem is: what is femininity? Clearly it is something quite different from mere biological femaleness, or there would be no grounds at all for this debate that has raged for many decades in the psychiatric literature.

The first factor that stands out in this literature is that femininity is an ever-changing concept. Pregnancy nausea is taken as evidence of lack of femininity in some studies[33] and of its presence in others.[34] Pain in labour is a denial of femininity,[35] or the absence of pain is.[36] Are real women sick and prone to labour pain or are they not? One investigator, using a masculinity–femininity scale, found that the more 'masculine' women reported fewer pregnancy problems. He was forced to engage in the contortion of concluding that such women, because they wish to appear healthy, simply *deny* their symptoms.[37] For the most part however, and not surprisingly, a feminine woman is defined in the psychiatric literature on reproduction as one who is married, devoted to motherhood and domestic life, unambitious, not highly educated; in short, rather a dull, second-class citizen. Factors such as playing boys' games in childhood, experiencing any kind of sexual problem, and worrying about how to care for the child are predictive of improper femininity[38] – which immediately disqualifies most of us from achieving this label.

The meanings of 'femininity' cannot be derived from the psychiatric literature but rather from the social world. As a final comment on psychological images of maternity, there is the paradox to which I have obliquely referred in mentioning the work of the researcher who was displeased to find 'masculine' women healthier than 'feminine' ones. The paradox is that femininity as conventionally defined is not conducive to problem-free reproduction (nor is the 'normal motherhood' of the medical advice literature). In her study of *The Birth of the First Child*, Dana Breen found that the most feminine women in her sample of 50, were those who encountered a whole range of problems most often. She summed up the situation thus: 'those women who are most adjusted to childbearing are those who are less enslaved by the experience, have more differentiated, more open appraisals of themselves and other people, do not aspire to be the perfect selfless mother. . . and do not experience themselves as passive, the cultural stereotype of femininity.'[39]

It seems to me that the question that should have been asked has not been asked. This question is: Why should it have been considered so important in psychological research on reproduction to demonstrate the link between having a baby and having acquired that particular psychodynamic structure which expresses the socially secondary meaning of womanhood in a patriarchal society? One answer is that there exists a special and mistaken 'psychology of women' which 'implies the need for a special set of laws and theories to account for the behaviour and experience of females.'[40] Another answer is the dominance of the psychoanalytic perspective, according to which much of the sophistication of what Freud actually said has been lost in dogmatic connections between reproductive physiology and female psychology.

SOCIOLOGICAL SURVEYS

Because their subject matter is the social, surely sociological studies of women and reproduction have been able successfully to remove motherhood from its deterministic biological underpinnings? To some extent this is true. But just as there has not been, until recently, even the beginnings of a 'sociology of women' so there has traditionally been no 'sociology of reproduction'. Why is this?

Like most professions, sociology has been male-dominated, although perhaps it has been so in less obvious ways than some. The truth is that the 'agenda' of sociology – its defined subject areas, issues and models of enquiry – has been grounded in the working worlds and social relations of men. The accepted fields of sociology – political sociology, the sociology of occupations, the sociology of deviance, and so forth – have been defined from the vantage point of the professional, managerial and administrative structures of our society. Women have been assigned a special place. Both as subject-matter and as practitioners of sociology women have been overwhelmingly relegated to the domain of marriage and family relations.

The consequence of this for sociological conceptions of maternity is that the psychodynamic structure of the marital relationship replaces the psychodynamic structure of the individual (in the psychological paradigm) as the locus in which the meaning of reproduction is to be found. This 'marital' bias is evidenced in four main ways:

(1)	research on reproductive intentions and practices has been focused on *married* women (much as gynaecologists are concerned to promote childbirth among the married and prevent it among the unmarried);
(2)	the reproductive behaviour of single women has been studied almost exclusively from a 'social problem' perspective, although in many countries 'illegitimate' conceptions are relatively common;
(3)	maternity has been viewed as of primary importance to the development of the marriage relationship, rather than to the development (or otherwise) of mothers themselves;
(4)	the examination of motherhood has been child- and not woman-centred, reflecting a concern with children's needs rather than with those of mothers.

Largely because of the influence of the functionalist school of thought in sociology, its practitioners were for a long time obsessed with the question 'What purpose does the institution of the family (and the category women–wives) serve for society as a whole?' The answer was couched in terms of families being the sole appropriate factories for the production of human personalities – which are, of course, to the sociologist not born but made. Ultimately, biology seeps in within the functionalist model as the fundamental explanation of gender-differentiation within the family. In particular, recourse is had to 'the division of organisms into lactating and nonlactating classes'.[41]

The functionalist paradigm of motherhood has exerted a tremendous influence on marriage and family sociology, and has got in the way of important alternative questions. These include 'what does the family do to women (and men)?' and 'how does the ethic of marriage and the nuclear family constrain the practice of maternity?' In other words, the sociological paradigm of reproduction as the cornerstone of the family has served to distance women from their reproductive experiences, just as medical appeals to biology or psychological constructions of womanhood have done.

The discipline of medical sociology, which has grown enormously in the last five years or so in Britain and the USA, has given more prominence to maternity than sociology in general. The British medical sociologist Sally Macintyre described four types of sociological approach to the management of childbirth, in a paper published in 1977.[42] These four approaches are:

(1) *historical/professional*: an exercise in which the evolution of the professional (and lay) management of childbirth is examined;
(2) *the anthropological approach* – focusing on the relation between the management of childbirth and prevailing belief-systems in different cultures;
(3) *patient-oriented* studies, where the perspectives of those who use the maternity services are articulated; and
(4) studies of *patient-services* interaction, where patterns of communication between users and providers of services are examined.

We now possess a sizeable literature of studies in each of these areas. Most important of all is the fact that the medical paradigm of motherhood has been reconceptualized as a potential influence on the meaning of motherhood to women themselves.

Once the medical paradigm is extracted from its scientific guise it is possible to see it as a cultural project and, as I have already said, it is a cultural product of enormous significance in shaping commonsense understandings of women and motherhood. But we are still left with the problem of the fissure between the actuality of female experience and its dominant ideological expression. Why do professional paradigms of motherhood contain an image of women as, first and foremost, natural maternal creatures devoted to wifehood and housekeeping? Why does the attribution to mothers of the unselfish motive of reproducing the race hide their characterization as childish and incapable of control? Why are mothers seen at the same time as strong and central to the social structure and as weak and essentially marginal to all mainstream public issues? Why are motherhood and childbirth not themselves public political issues akin to, for example, education and the structure of electoral systems?

To answer these questions we have to set the medical care of women within its broader political context. We must consider both medicine as an agency of social control, and the typical forms of social control to which women have historically been subject.

10

Is Breast Best?
Society's Attitudes to Breastfeeding

It is currently possible to talk intensely and endlessly about both the position of women and the welfare of children, without mentioning breastfeeding. Perhaps one reason for this strange state of affairs is that feminists have been interested in breasts but not in breastfeeding. Like natural childbirth, the natural feeding of children poses an incurable dilemma for those asserting the autonomy of women, their right to exist as full members of society. To be social means to repudiate the natural world, where life is governed by animality, and where reason does not exist to tame the disorder of bodies and their secretions. In order to equal men, the argument goes, women must contain their femaleness, and not let it spill out of them as a response to the cries of anyone's child.

The following piece, which was written for a National Childbirth Trust (NCT) conference on the subject of breastfeeding, is about choice; yet choice is precisely the concept that is responsible for most of the mistakes made about breastfeeding. Feminists say women must have choice, and must be able to choose not to give their breasts to babies but to keep them for themselves. The NCT says women must have choice, and so they must be given information, and one of the necessary items of this information is that only breastfeeding is the right strategy for mother and child. When I mentioned at this meeting the notion that the decision not to breastfeed was sometimes the right one, I knew I wouldn't be popular. But I had been

Source: Originally given at National Childbirth Trust Conference, 'The Promotion of Breastfeeding', 8–9 November 1985.

prepared for this. I was not quite so prepared for my own change of position: in the early 1970s I had said in a medical sociology textbook that doctors and other health professionals must do everything in their power to persuade women to breastfeed; this I strongly believed at the time, although I was very much criticized for it by a female medical sociologist of the next generation, whose views I respected. Her criticism upset me, but did not change my mind. Time did that. It seems to me now that it is wrong to be doctrinaire. Who was it who said the trick is not to put yourself into somebody else's shoes, but to know what it feels like to be in those shoes?

The NCT conference was held in the Wembley Conference Centre, a purple and red capitalist place, built for businessmen, and not for women and their babies (expecially those who cry, and whose cries expand to fill the mistaken architecture of the dome of the hall). Somebody made a birthday cake in the shape of two breasts, with nipples as candles. More impressive than that, the Automobile Association put yellow signs up on the North Circular Road pointing the way to the breastfeeding conference, so we all knew where to go, and the day's motorists could see there was something publicly important about breastfeeding.

The instruction to talk about 'society's attitudes to breastfeeding' is somewhat overwhelming, since I have no reason for supposing that I know any more about society's attitudes than anyone else. What I shall talk about instead are three related questions: (1) how and why did breastfeeding become a social and medical problem; (2) who does this problem belong to; and (3) what kind of choice do, or should, mothers have about whether or not to breastfeed?

The most obvious characteristic of society's attitudes to breastfeeding is that society keeps changing its mind. In 1946 a doctor called James Halliday reflected in the pages of the *Lancet*[43] that the psychologies of British people had become a lot more complicated recently, due mainly to profound changes in the upbringing of the British infant. To quote Dr Halliday, in the late nineteenth century:

> Breastfeeding was universal, or almost so. In cases of difficulties wet-nurses were used. The feeding-bottle . . . was used only by the wealthier classes. . . . No special attention was paid to the times of breastfeeding and the occasions of suckling were determined by the desires of the child or the mother. This was facilitated by the prolonged body contact between them, the baby being carried about by the mother in the folds of a shawl or plaid. A wooden-wheeled baby carriage was the prerogative of the wealthy, but . . . its usage was condemned by the doctors of the period on the ground that it denied to the infant the comfort of strong loving arms . . .[44]

It is interesting to find nineteenth-century doctors opposed to the new reproductive technology of the pram, and perhaps we could say it is a pity that twentieth-century doctors haven't followed their precedent a little more closely!

It is clear from Halliday's reflections that initially artificial feeding was a technology beyond the reach of working-class mothers. Nobody in the nineteenth century had invented demand feeding or mother-child bonding because that was what normally happened. Bottle-feeding, prams and hospital deliveries all started out as fashions among the upper classes who then – at least in the case of bottle-feeding and hospital deliveries – passed these habits on to working-class households, and then perversely started to condemn them as dangerous to health.

It is said that, as with natural childbirth, 95 per cent of women are capable of feeding their babies naturally. On a desert island – and as those of you who have had the misfortune to see that amazing film *The Blue Lagoon* will know – under those conditions either the baby will make its way to the breast or the mother will somehow know what to do. It is when we get off the desert island, however, that we run into trouble. The two main troubles that breastfeeding has encountered are the interests of industry and technology on the one hand, and the lack of interest of the medical profession on the other. A third underlying problem, which is perhaps the least amenable to change, has to do with divisions of gender – with the different definitions of masculinity and femininity that are part of every child's conditioning, and therefore part of womanhood and manhood in our culture. Female biology is not the same thing as cultural femininity. It is possible to be good at one and bad at the other. Indeed, research shows over and over again that women who are biologically good at motherhood in the sense of having easy pregnancies, natural labours and following this with breastfeeding, are precisely those who have a strong sense of themselves as people and do not emphasize the more conventional aspects of femininity.

HOW AND WHY DID BREASTFEEDING BECOME A PROBLEM?

The rise of femininity helped to turn breastfeeding into a problem, but there were other factors as well. In industrialized countries, a decline in the incidence of breastfeeding started in the mid-nineteenth century.[45] From being condemned as inferior and harmful, bottle-feeding began to emerge as a genuine alternative to breastfeeding, and the attitudes of doctors reflected this change. By 1890 in this country and many others, the manufacture and sale of proprietary infant foods and bottles had become a substantial industry. By this time there was widespread recognition of the fact that the physical condition of children was something the state needed to be interested in, because the economic and political prosperity of a nation depended on the quality of its population. One speaker at a conference on 'Infantile Mortality' held in London in 1906, recalled Napoleon's complaint about the high quality of English motherhood. The speaker remarked that the complaint was made just after Napoleon had been defeated 'on a celebrated field of battle by soldiers who mostly came from country districts, and who did not know what a comforter was, and who did not know what canned meat was, who played in the open air and were breastfed in the only decent and proper way by their mothers.'[46] The infant welfare movement which started in the early years of the twentieth century was originally rooted in the need to provide clean milk for artificial feeding. The advantages of such feeding were that it was *measureable*: it was possible to know exactly how much and what was going into the mouths and stomachs of babies. Thus, a move away from breastfeeding suited the newly scientific spirit of paediatric medicine. From the early 1900s at least until 1960 it appears that breastfeeding declined in Britain – for example while 77 per cent of three month-old infants in Bristol were breastfed in 1919, only 33 per cent were breastfed in 1939.[47]

Many factors contributed to this decline, and we can only speculate about their relative importance. Changes in the social position of women were important. Along with smoking cigarettes, cutting one's hair, voting and riding a bicycle, the feeding-bottle became a cultural symbol of female emancipation. (We do not know the extent to which women themselves promoted this image, but it does seem as though some women were helped to decide not to breastfeed because bottle-feeding was the modern thing to do.)

Once bottle-feeding had become widespread, the female breast became an embarrassing private object. So private in fact, that when historian Edward Shorter wrote his *History of Women's Bodies*[48] he didn't mention breasts at all. Female breasts don't have a history – they lost it along with their status as organs of nutrition. And of course other factors conspired to bring this about. A society that will not tolerate natural body odours and secretions, particular those of women, who are commercially encouraged to deodorize themselves and all their orifices at every opportunity – such a society is hardly likely to tolerate the messy smells and secretions of the female breast. Unlike bottles, breasts don't have lids, a fact which human babies probably noticed a long time ago.

So much for history. By 1960 society was beginning to change its mind again, and the physical and psychological advantages of breastfeeding over bottle-feeding were being stressed. One reason was the emerging evidence that healthy babies make healthy adults. Another was the growing realization at least in certain social groups, that nature is the best technology for healthy reproduction. However sophisticated the breast milk substitute industry, it remains just that – a substitute for breast milk. A third reason for the new promotion of breastfeeding was the politics of artificial feeding in the Third World. The good nutrition of infants in poor Third World countries is not encouraged by the advertisement and use of artificial feeding, but rather by support for breastfeeding and the breastfeeding mother and moves to improve *her own* nutrition.

In Britain breastfeeding is now on the increase. While 50 per cent of mothers breastfed initially in 1975, 67 per cent did so in 1980. The biggest increase is in mothers of second or subsequent babies, 42 per cent of whom breastfed initially in 1975, while 60 per cent did so in 1980. Breastfeeding also lasts longer now, with two-thirds of mothers continuing beyond six weeks, as compared with less than half in 1975.

Despite these changes, only one in four mothers in this country breastfeed as long as the officially recommended four months. The same social pattern still obtains as was found in earlier surveys – breastfeeding rates are higher among highly educated middle-class mothers aged twenty-five or over and living in London or the South East. For unknown reasons, Scottish mothers are significantly less likely to breastfeed than English or Welsh mothers.[49]

One of the advantages of statistics is, of course, that they can be used to support practically any argument. And one argument derivable from these particular statistics is that better educational and employment opportunities for women are very likely to raise the breastfeeding rate – quite irrespective of whether or not anything else is done about breast-feeding. I think this is true. Indeed, Martin and Monk's 1980 survey of breastfeeding shows that there are now no differences in the incidence of breastfeeding among employed as compared with non-employed mothers.[50] However, returning to the statistics, I don't think that moving all mothers to London and South-East England would have a similar positive effect on breastfeeding. This is a bit like the argument that one way to improve Britain's perinatal mortality rate is to terminate all twin pregnancies (because twins have higher mortality rates than singleton babies).

WHOSE PROBLEM IS BREASTFEEDING?

The whole subject of infant feeding is something of a problem for the medical profession, for the very simple reason that it is beyond their control. These days it is quite easy for doctors to believe that they are somehow personally responsible for conception, pregnancy, labour and delivery. But once the mother gets her hands on the baby the doctor has a problem because babies are fed and looked after by mothers (and to some extent by fathers), and this means that mothers are actually rather powerful. Some of the recent medical swing against bottle-feeding was fuelled by doctors feeling mothers had too much power over that particular technology – for instance, they might load the formula with an extra spoonful of milk powder or leave bottles propped up in cots so they could get on with their other work. (And of course one of the overwhelming images of motherhood – let alone breastfeeding – in our society is that mothers have nothing else to do except be mothers.)

But the medical profession is also very confused in its attitudes to breastfeeding. On the one hand breastfeeding is a good thing for mothers and babies – and the female breast has recently acquired a new status as a means of inducing labour. In a randomized controlled trial of nipple stimulation, this was found to be an effective method of ripening the cervix, and probably one that is a lot safer and undoubtedly cheaper than medical methods such as 'sweeping the membranes' or the use of prostaglandins.[51] (Another natural method for inducing labour which doesn't cost anything but isn't yet popular with doctors, is sexual intercourse.) Yet at the same time as recognizing that nipples and breasts serve useful medical purposes, doctors seem keen to carry out all sorts of manoeuvres which make breastfeeding difficult. The 1975 survey of infant feeding[52] found that women were much less likely to breastfeed after an induced or accelerated labour and following caesarean delivery – 2 per cent of women who had caesareans breastfed, as compared with 53 per cent of women who had spontaneous labours. The most significant perinatal factor associated with a low likelihood of breastfeeding was a delay of 24 hours or more in putting the baby to the breast. In the 1980 survey, 87 per cent of mothers who first breastfed within an hour of delivery were still breastfeeding two weeks later, but this figure fell to 68 per cent for those who first breastfed more than 12 hours after delivery. When the events of labour and delivery were looked at together, three factors had a strong and independent association with early termination of breastfeeding: (1) the baby's birthweight; (2) having a general anaesthetic; and (3) not putting the baby to the breast within four hours of birth. This survey also showed that the longer stays in hospital (more than six days) were associated with giving up breastfeeding by the time the baby was two weeks old, as was feeding at set times other than demand feeding.

Any reasonable interpretation of these statistics would argue that the promotion of breastfeeding requires the prevention of medical intervention. Yet while some things are getting better (there was more demand feeding in hospital in 1980 than in 1975, for example), other things (the use of caesarean section, for instance) are getting demonstrably worse. Some of this confused medical double-think is due to the division between obstetrics on the one hand and paediatrics on the other. This has always served the interests of obstetricians and paediatricians more than it has served the interests of the mother and baby, whose destinies are inextricably linked – and, of course, breastfeeding is *the* prime example of this.

CHOICE IN BREASTFEEDING – SHOULD THERE BE ANY?

Society has changed its mind less on this subject of choice than on some other aspects of infant feeding. For the most part, social attitudes have been unkindly doctrinaire on the subject of how babies ought to be fed. Most surveys of women's attitudes to breastfeeding have asked not why mothers breastfeed, or why they bottle-feed, but why they don't breastfeed. The general message conveyed by this literature is the same as that conveyed by the 'why don't women attend for antenatal care' literature. Breastfeeding and getting antenatal care are the orthodoxies from which any good mother departs at her peril. Or, rather, they are part of the definition of a good mother. This leads to a mystification of the reasons for not breastfeeding – or not going for antenatal care. In 1904, in one of the first surveys of attitudes to breastfeeding, four reasons were found for not breastfeeding: (1) the 'irksomeness' of suckling; (2) lack of knowledge of breastfeeding and its importance; (3) inability to breastfeed because of poor maternal health; and (4) inability to breastfeed because of going back to paid work. The same constellation of reasons, plus a few others, appears three-quarters of a century later in the 1980 survey I have already quoted. In this, one in 20 mothers who chose to bottle-feed did so because they were going back to work – and about the same proportion gave up breastfeeding early for the same reason. Rather more than this stopped because of their own poor health, or because of insufficient milk. One in six gave up because it took too long. One in ten of those mothers who stopped breastfeeding before the baby was a week old did so because they simply didn't like it, and rather more gave up for miscellaneous 'domestic reasons'. Finally, among those who never breastfed, 30 per cent said they didn't like the idea, or 'would be embarrassed to breastfeed'.

Research on women's attitudes to breastfeeding tells us, I think very powerfully, that what need most to be changed are the social and economic factors that make breastfeeding difficult – for example the incompatibility in most cases between breastfeeding and paid employment. In today's economic conditions the choice some women make *not* to breastfeed because they need to go out to work is not a sign of irresponsibility towards the baby, but a sign of responsibility towards their families in general. If breastfeeding rates are to increase in these circumstances there must be provision for breastfeeding mothers at work, rather than simply more pressure on women to breastfeed.

In short, in order to choose breastfeeding, women must have information about it and they must have the right circumstances in which to make that choice and abide by it. Ultimately too they must be free of that attitude which says there is something indecent about the female breast and the function of lactation – an attitude which fortunately babies don't share because they haven't yet been indoctrinated into the habits of their culture. Breasts are best – but only if their owners say so!

11

To Her Uterus
Embryonic Journey
Carnival

The relevance of the first of these poems to a section on motherhood is obvious. At the time the poem was written, I was trying to find out what was going on inside my uterus, which is essentially what obstetricians try to do. However, I was able to talk more directly to it (her) than they were. The poem incorporates an interesting traRnscultural observation about ultrasound scanning. As those of us who have had our uteruses scanned know, one of the penalties we pay is having to sit around for a long time waiting with full bladders because urine helps the technicians with their uterine cartography. In Denmark when pregnant bladders aren't full enough they provide free lager – despite the fact that (at that time) the Carlsberg factories were on strike.

Poem number two in this series uses the metaphor of an embryonic journey to describe a relationship. The phrase 'embryonic journey' is the title of a piece of music to which my son drew my attention when I was trying to find some music for a Channel 4 programme on miscarriage (we ended up, quite appropriately, with Liszt's 'Consolation, No. 3'). The life of an embryo may be short – it often is, given that up to 80 per cent of human conceptions do not result in the birth of a live healthy baby. But every existence is worth having, and every journey, wherever it leads, is one's own.

'Carnival' is a somewhat angry poem about lying in a relationship between a man and a woman. The man wanted to have a good time (which is not all that unusual), and the woman's definition of a good time was different. I know no better documentation of what this poem is about than Lilian Rubin's *Intimate Strangers*[53] which gets at the heart of the emotional incompatibility between men and women and, if carefully read, should lead us all to stop trying.

To Her Uterus

Come on now, I think there's something in there
I can feel a space in the middle probably occupied by something
could it be blood, a fetus or a dream?
Of the three, I think I would prefer the latter
since, following the Greeks,
the uterus is the site of all interesting passion
in women

at least in there it's warm
there are cells to nourish other cells, or nothing
a kind of wonderful sponginess
to absorb and multiply
nature's frequent mistakes

and at this moment
I am inclined to say we are two of them
or made a mistake together
the one that's in there growing quietly
getting on with life
while the rest of us wonder what life is anyway

viewed on any kind of screen life isn't anything much
which is why the lady on the ultrasound machine
gave me a carlsberg to drink
and said nothing can be seen except through a full bladder

the only advantage of a full bladder to its owner
being that it provides some sort of sensation

but, oh dear, when the carlsberg had done the trick
there was nothing to see, just a reaction

are you, my child, merely a response
not to our mutual creativeness
but to our present phase of destruction
for we are surely bent on killing you
and ourselves, in this mad rush to understand the problem

I don't believe in doctors
but now I like the one who said
why don't women have transparent abdomens
so we can see in

I want to see inside my uterus
and know what kind of thing is growing there
whether it will survive to be born
or merely wither away without a murmur

Embryonic Journey

that's what ours was
across the plains of Seinäjoki
marvelling at the fir trees holding snow

that's what ours was
on an island eating strawberries
dreaming the same dream
one black night in Sweden

that's what we thought we were doing
at the first touch, at the moment of entry

that's what we hoped for
at every airport, imagining every destination

that's what we have accomplished now
our own journey is over
oh embryo believe me
even a short journey is one's own

and the man who takes the ticket at its termination
has no right to know what happened on it

Carnival

so you heard the drums on midsummer night, did you?
so your heart beat faster with a waspish will of its own, did it?
so you followed the sound, did you
to a wide messy place without meaning
where big red mouths made sucking noises
and steely fingernails scraped your blonde flesh
and white hair stood on end with surprise
at your beauty, which, as you know, is not your creation

you have no possible excuse
for going into the jungle
and you don't look nice with all that perspiration
falling off your morbid face

but you know all this
that's why you're a professor
however, I have no respect for professors
I lived with one once and he farted
while reading the newspaper
thinking no one would hear

the difference is you know I'm listening

to the sound of silence
the red phone not ringing
a sky empty of its usual planes
the words you say describing
a lie you once lived
and thought I might believe in
but you don't have to be a professor
to know the texture of deception

it's rough like concrete
and dirty, stained with its own constipation
it doesn't even give enlarged midline echoes a chance
or in other words our child, the child of a luxury hotel
is now fated to an existence in
a fetid jungle of unborn souls

perhaps you'll meet in the jungle one day
a grey old man and an angelic little boy
made in your own image
and then one other midsummer night
in the year two thousand in amsterdam
he too will hear the drums beating
and foolishly like his father
run after a big red mouth

12

Social Factors and Pregnancy

In 1979 the World Health Organization's (WHO) European office set up a perinatal study group to examine the state of the maternity services in Europe. I was co-opted onto this group in late 1982: the major part of its deliberations have now been published in a book with the unlikely title of *Having a Baby in Europe*.[54] This sounds a bit like the hitchhiker's guide to the gallaxy, or how to eat in Europe on $5 a day, but is an attempt fairly to describe what is going on in Europe's maternal and child health services. One of the issues in it concerns the technologies appropriate for helping mothers to bear healthy children. On this particular theme a meeting was held in Washington, USA, in 1984 to consider technologies for prenatal care, and this was followed by a meeting in Brazil in 1985 on the topic of birth technology, at which the following piece on social factors and pregnancy was given.

The meeting took place in Fortaleza, the state capital of Ceará in North East Brazil. Brazil contains 137 million of Latin America's 375 million inhabitants, and Fortaleza has 1.5 million of them. The country is extremely poor, with 40 per cent of the population estimated to be living below the poverty line. Eighty per cent of the women are illiterate, and rates of premature death are high: infant mortality averages between 90 and 130 per 1,000 live births (it was 9.5 in the UK in 1984). Small children beg, or more commonly trade an array of trivia, on the streets – chewing gum, shoelaces, plastic hats for unexpected rain. Hotels for the tourists (and the conference-goers) rise up like bad jokes from the

Source: Originally given to WHO/PAHO Working Group on Appropriate Technology in Birth, Fortaleza, Brazil, 22–26 April 1985.

land that fringes the sea: white-golden sands turned out of a paradise into an unhappy money-making jamboree.

Having a baby in Brazil means little or no medical care. Eighty per cent of babies are helped into the world by what WHO has named 'traditional birth attendants' – the granny–midwives and wisewomen who have been motherhood's major medical protectors through the ages. This ancient system coexists in Brazil with one of the menaces of a newer one: women delivering their infants in hospital stand a one in three or, in some places, a one in two chance of having a caesarean section. Some of these operations are associated with sterilization in a predominantly Catholic country, and may even be done partly because sterilization operations can conveniently be performed at the same time. Yet others are undoubtedly due to the financial greed of obstetricians, and the Brazilian cult of beautiful bodies also takes its toll: for in such a culture there can surely be nothing uglier than a female body stretched by the passage of a baby out of it.

Sixty-two people from 21 different countries attended the Fortaleza meeting. No doubt what each of us derived from it differs enormously, but one of the most interesting parts of the agenda for the non-Brazilians was a day of visits to an innovatory health-care programme, which aims to use and improve the community's own health-care resources (instead of importing the usual easy and expensive answer of more doctors and more technology). The traditional birth attendants in the region are given a short basic training, provided with minimal equipment, and given the opportunity to practise in health-care centres – usually small one-storey buildings owned and managed by a village co-operative. Here they help mothers to give birth in the favourite Brazilian way – namely in hammocks – though they have learnt to rehang these so the arriving baby is more accessible to the midwife. The midwife, however, is still paid in kind – with beans, cassava or manioc flour – and the main qualifications for being one are having children oneself, or being called upon by an older village midwife to take up the profession.

We went to look at this health care programme in operation in such proverbially idyllic places as a tiny village called Pecem, where life was lived on the beach, and a donkey and cart took ice down to the fishing boats (a good example of appropriate technology). Here, at least, the children seemed well-fed and everyone had enough to eat. Two other important features of the programme stand out in my memory and my notes. One is the stress on a *practical* education for health. Groups of adolescents are taken through basic biology and hygiene in the classroom, but also in the community, where they are set such pragmatic goals as finding out what people do with their garbage, and then devising healthier ways of disposing of it. Secondly, the programme incorporated the skills not only of the traditional birth attendants but also of the spiritual and religious healers. Use your prayers, and your rituals, the programme-organizers say, and teach us, too, how they work. But sometimes, if you come across, for example, a young child with acute diarrhoea and vomiting, it might be useful for you to know what to do to help the child's body replace its lost fluid. . . . Such combinations of traditional practice and appropriate medical technology are surely the most intelligent way of improving the conditions of motherhood, and allowing us all to emphasize what is normal about childbearing.

One instructive addendum to this, however: talking to the birth attendants (via an interpreter, of course) we asked when the women usually cut the umbilical cord. It is part of the modern alternative orthodoxy that birth attendants should wait for the placenta to be delivered, or at least for the cord to stop pulsating, before doing this, in order to follow traditional 'good practice' in allowing the newborn infant its maximum supply of blood.[55] In Brazil, these midwives said they waited about half an hour for the placenta and didn't cut the cord until after that. So we asked them, was this part of their traditional practice? 'Oh, no', they said, 'we learnt it as part of our training in the hospital. The professor there told us to do it. Before that we used to cut the cord as soon as the baby was born.'

'Social factors and pregnancy' focuses on class inequality in the health of mothers and babies, and reflects the direction of my work over the last two years. Since gender, class and ethnicity are the three main divisions we humans have put amongst ourselves, it is ridiculous to feel comfortable with research that isolates gender at the expense of class, or vice versa, or ignores the fact that the life chances of black people are generally not the same as those of white people. By looking at motherhood and childhood one has a wonderful opportunity to look at all three of these divisions simultaneously. The paper talks about why different social groups of mothers and babies have different chances of living and dying. Within that complex picture it then tries to talk in a technical language about love – described here as social support.

The idea that love is good for people is hardly new. But the argument that healthy babies may be partly secured by social support is not yet one that has got very far in the medical world. In a Third World country such as Brazil, it is more acceptable to make such a statement: the values of the community and of the extended family in helping those who need help have not yet been totally replaced by an ideology of professional 'care'. Of course the reason may be economic – and the ideology of community care in a country such as Britain must be suspect for its thinly veiled oppression of women to an unpaid service role. But, nevertheless, some of the Latin American obstetricians at the Fortaleza meeting in 1985 were impressive for their defence of the idea that human kindness might be as good, or better than, machines in preserving the health and vitality of mothers and babies.

Another theme, a more difficult ethical one, concerns the issue of research on women (or people) as clients of the medical care system. Such research necessitates randomized controlled studies, in order to answer important questions about which forms of care really 'work'. The basis of the method does not allow the client choice – she or he is given a particular treatment according to a table of random numbers. Ethically, therefore, the method is in conflict with humanist and feminist principles. However, I believe that the conflict cannot be resolved by getting rid of the insistence on the need for scientific evaluation. What we need to do is to develop ways of carrying out research and finding answers that are as humane as possible, and do not do violence to the integrity of the subject (which may be considered an everyday occurrence in normal medical practice, where clients are not consulted as to appropriate methods of treatment, and most treatments have not been properly tested for effectiveness and safety).

For many years in many countries social differences between groups of mothers and infants have been shown to be associated with varying risks of mortality and morbidity. There is a consistent pattern of higher reproductive risks for mothers and infants in low socio-economic groups. These increased risks apply to a whole range of outcomes, including spontaneous miscarriage, neural tube malformations, oral clefts, curtailed gestation, low birthweight and perinatal mortality.[56] Longer term psychosocial outcomes such as maternal depression also appear to be more prevalent in working-class women.[57] Although some of the more detailed findings derive from research in industrialized countries such as Britain and North America, the association between low socio-economic status and poor outcome is found worldwide.[58]

In discussions of variations in perinatal outcome 'social class' tends often to be treated as an explanatory concept. However, an association between social class and perinatal outcome is not an explanation. It is itself a problem requiring explanation. We need to know what it is about membership of different social class groups that is responsible for the patterned inequality in perinatal outcome.

EXPLAINING INEQUALITY

Over the years, four different types of explanations of social differences in perinatal outcome have been suggested. These are (1) that the class-outcome associations represent an artefact of measurement; (2) that biological factors are primarily responsible; (3) that differential access to, or provision of, medical services accounts for the different outcomes; and (4) that environmental influences, unevenly distributed throughout the social spectrum, bring about different constellations of pregnancy risk.

Measuring Class

Precisely because social class differences in perinatal mortality are consistently found in different countries and in the same country over a period of many years, it has been suggested that the differences may partly be due to an artefact of measurement. They persist through periods when there have been substantial changes in the definition and status of occupations and in the distribution of the employed population among the different occupations. In some countries, changing fertility patterns have meant changes in the proportions of total births contributed by different social classes. In addition, it has been shown that movement between classes is highly selective. In Britain, women brought up in social classes I and II who marry into social classes IV and V tend to be shorter, have poorer physiques, have dietary intakes lower in protein, calcium, and vitamins A, B and C, leave school earlier, achieve lower scores on IQ tests, enter less prestigious occupations and run a higher risk of perinatal loss than those who marry into their own social class group.[59] The overall contribution of this 'biological drift' must be to maintain the social glass gradient, yet this factor is not likely to provide the whole explanation. There are close links between perinatal mortality and a variety of socio-economic indices both contemporaneously and inter-generationally. Moreover, there is a great deal of evidence (some of which is discussed below) connecting particular social and behavioural factors with perinatal mortality.

It's All in Our Genes

Clearly inborn biological differences between individuals play a role in determining different chances of reproductive success. Like all such questions, we have no way of establishing the relative importance of these factors, for differential social influences begin to operate from the moment of conception on. The effect of diet in infancy and childhood appears to be especially crucial.[60] Biological differences between pregnant women such as parity, maternal and paternal age, and incidental disease during pregnancy also vary between different social groups and have an impact on perinatal outcome.[61]

Medical Care

Use of medical services is often not directly related to 'need'. Thus the question of what has been termed 'the inverse care law'[62] has been noted in Britain and other countries. Poor health is concentrated in lower socio-economic groups, while use of the 'health' services is concentrated in the higher socio-economic groups. There are various possible explanations for this: for example that the poorer health of the socially disadvantaged is due to their 'under-utilization' of medical care, or that currently provided health services are inappropriate to the health-care needs of this segment of the population. However, increasing health service use among working-class people has overwhelmingly been grasped by governmental and medical policy-makers in many countries as the key strategy to improving national health.

In fact, of course, it is extremely hard to establish to what extent high perinatal mortality (for example) is due to inadequate medical care, or whether low perinatal mortality is accomplished because of 'good' medical care. One problem is that it is difficult to disentangle the possible effect of changes in perinatal care from both short- and long-term changes in the health and environment of the childbearing population. Nearly all studies of the associations between perinatal care and outcome are observational ones: there are relatively few controlled experimental studies. Furthermore, controlled trials in perinatal medicine tend to be done on specific component techniques, such as electronic fetal heart-rate monitoring. Underlying organizational structures, such as antenatal care as a mass screening programme or hospitalized birth, have not been experimentally reviewed.

Social and Environmental Factors

No less a body than WHO itself has said that 'There is no clear distinction between social and biological factors.'[63] Among the factors under the 'social' heading which have been shown to be associated with perinatal outcome are the following: paternal occupation ('social class'), maternal employment and household work, maternal and parental education, housing conditions, income, ethnicity, marital status, sexual activity, smoking and alcohol consumption and diet.[64] Some research studies come up with contradictory or unclear findings; this is especially so in the areas of diet and sex. Most of the research does not make it possible to identify independent and dependent/intervening variables in the social factor–outcome relationship. For example, if poor housing conditions are associated with poor perinatal outcome, is this a genuine effect of poor housing, or is it because quality of housing and enhanced risk of poor perinatal outcome are both a reflection of some other influence? This question is perhaps a little easier to answer in the case of postneonatal mortality (deaths from four weeks to one year), since the social class gradient tends to be greatest during this period, and post-neonatal mortality rates are sensitive indicators of general socio-economic conditions.

One underlying explanation for the association between social factors and perinatal outcome is that of stress. The idea that stress affects reproduction receives support from many fields, including experimental work on animals and humans. In recent years, developments in biochemical measurements of 'stress hormones' have made it possible to demonstrate a direct biological effect of social stressors. Low birthweight, preterm labour, the need for obstetric intervention in delivery, and disturbed early mother–child relationships are among those pregnancy outcomes in which stress has been implicated.[65]

Related to this notion of stress affecting pregnancy outcome is the idea that socially supportive relationships in the mother's environment have the potential for mitigating stress and improving outcome.

Social Support

Three relevant studies are those of Nuckolls et al.,[66] Norbeck and Tilden[67] and Berkowitz and Kasl.[68] In the first of these studies, 170 women were questioned early in pregnancy about their social networks and relationships and attitudes to pregnancy, and then late in pregnancy about the occurrence of life stress. When 'psychosocial assets' and life stresses were analysed together, psychosocial assets were found to have a buffering effect on life stress. The study by Norbeck and Tilden also found low social support predictive of pregnancy complications. In their study Berkowitz and Kasl found a significant linear trend between the number of life-events during the first two trimesters of pregnancy and risk of preterm delivery, with the mothers of term infants describing a somewhat higher level of partner support than the mothers of preterm infants.

Apart from these kinds of observational studies, there are also intervention studies which aim to affect perinatal outcome by providing some kind of 'social' intervention during pregnancy or labour. The experimental study by Sosa and colleagues in Guatemala[69] is possibly the best known under this heading. In the Sosa study, women entering hospital for delivery were allocated into either intervention or control groups. The intervention group received constant support from untrained lay women during labour and delivery. This group had a significantly higher incidence of good outcomes, including a lower caesarean section rate and fewer babies delivered with forceps.

The basis of the allocation into intervention and control groups in the Sosa study was random, which is important in evaluating social intervention studies, since many do not use this methodology, and 'matching' of intervention and control groups is often poor. It is then difficult to work out whether the intervention has had a 'true' effect or not. Three intervention studies which suffer from this problem are those of Herron et al.,[70] Peoples et al.,[71] and Sokol et al.[72] These studies claim dramatic benefits of interventions combining such elements as extra clinical care, dietary counselling and home visits. There may, indeed, be dramatic benefits following such interventions, but these studies do not allow us to decide whether or not this is the case.

Other social interventions using a randomized controlled approach, such as that used in the Sosa trial, came out reliably in favour of a beneficial impact on a number of different indices of pregnancy outcome. For example, Runnerstrom[73] showed a decrease in the incidence of low birthweight with a nurse–midwife antenatal care programme, and Sexton and Hebel[74] achieved an increase in mean birthweight with a programme of anti-smoking advice. Other perinatal outcomes shown to be affected by social interventions include medication in labour, patient satisfaction, the health of the baby after birth, and postnatal depression in mothers.[75]

One specific form of social support for childbearing women has been strongly advocated by the alternative childbirth movement – 'education' or 'preparation' for childbirth. Unfortunately, few of these interventions have been introduced in such a way that evaluation of their effects is possible. This does not mean that preparation for childbirth is not a good thing: it means that at the moment we cannot say whether or not this is so. It is perfectly possible, for example, that women who go to preparation classes do better in childbirth because they would have done better anyway, rather than directly because of the classes.

When we come to the evidence relating social support and pregnancy outcome, we confront the question of what social support 'means'. If we take it broadly to mean 'information leading the subject to believe that [she] is cared for, loved, esteemed, and a member of a network of mutual obligations',[76] then a range of interventions that do not *explicitly* aim to provide social support become candidates for scientific scrutiny. One obvious group are dietary intervention studies, many of which do not directly alter diet, but provide some kind of counselling service. What is remarkable about these studies, taken as a whole, is that an effect on birthweight seems to emerge irrespective of whether the mother or the entire family is supplemented/counselled.[77] This suggests that where perinatal outcome is improved by dietary interventions, some of the improvement may be attributable to the mother simply feeling more cared for and supported.

Each new fashion in the childbirth field (as in any other) is liable to breed its own orthodoxy. Thus, an increasing interest in social interventions is often accompanied by the assumption that these attempts to improve perinatal outcome can only be a good thing, that is, it is possible that they do not achieve an effect, but any effect they do achieve is assumed to be a positive one. However, the lesson of the dietary interventions is rather different: some interventions appear to produce a worse outcome.[78] This possibility must be borne in mind in the more general field of social interventions. In a French study by Spira et al.,[79] of routine prenatal care versus routine plus home midwifery care, there was apparently higher perinatal mortality in women receiving extra attention from midwives during pregnancy. In fact the higher mortality was made up of six perinatal deaths, two of which occurred in mothers who had hardly any care. The other four deaths happened to women who had such poor obstetric histories that the authors say they should probably have been hospitalized throughout pregnancy. An important observation comes out of this study: when its authors separated out the women with medical risk-factors from those with 'social' risk-factors, they found that while the intervention of home visits by midwives actually appeared to increase the incidence of preterm delivery in women with medical risks, this same intervention significantly *decreased* the risk of preterm delivery in women with only social risk-factors.

Conclusion

There are other ways to improve perinatal outcome apart from intensi-fying the quality or quantity of medical antenatal care. One flaw in many existing studies is that of small sample size: a pooled analysis of groups of studies is one way of overcoming this, and such an analysis suggests that social interventions may reduce the incidence of an outcome such as non-spontaneous delivery by over 40 per cent.[80]

The extent to which childbearing women are in receipt of social support is one of many social factors with a potential to affect perinatal outcome. Both social support and other social factors are known to affect people's vulnerability to a range of health and illness outcomes: there is no reason why reproduction should be an exception to this general rule, particularly since similar patterns of social inequalities are found in the perinatal field as obtain for other health and illness outcomes. Equally, patterns of relationships between social factors and perinatal outcome may vary between communities and particularly between countries at different stages of development. Yet since we are dealing here with the social substratum of human behaviour, the same kinds of links are likely to emerge in different places. Childbearing is a process bridging the domains of the social and biological; an exceptionally clear example of the close links existing between the individual's existence as a social being on the one hand, and as a biological system on the other; and probably the most convincing evidence of the inability of the modern medico-scientific paradigm satisfactorily to 'explain' the behaviour of bodies in a social world. The terms in which the debate about perinatal outcome and social inequality has been conducted hitherto have not encouraged admission of the 'social' evidence. It is to be hoped that the debate in future will be a more open one, and that the maternity services of the developing world will not lose sight of the 'care' component in the perinatal health services, as has tended to happen in the 'developed' world.

13

Lullabies

Michel Odent is one of the high priests of the alternative childbirth movement. In his work in Pithiviers, France, he demonstrates a determination to respect whatever natural core of the childbirth process is still able to operate beneath layers of cultural and medical conditioning. He shows, too, a touching lack of concern for those 'hard' data so beloved by the policy-makers and epidemiologists. He does not feel it is necessary to prove his approach is safe – this is self-evident. Indeed, he says that the women who need the highest degree of respect for the natural capacity of the female body to give birth are precisely those deemed by the medical establishment to be at highest risk. If there *is* a risk, then you do not add to it by interfering.

This conclusion is at odds with some of the work I quoted in the previous paper, particularly the French study of home midwifery care. More profoundly, Odent's work brings out a paradox at the heart of our model of knowledge. It has been usual to assume that in order to know something you have first to prove it. This immediately confronts the problem of the validity of individual experience. But even if one can get round this, there remains the problem of how to raise the status of forms of knowledge and types of strategy that conventionally have not been counted as important. In the health-care field we tend now to have two opposing types of knowledge/strategy: those emanating from the usual scientific model (for example, perinatal mortality is lowered

Source: Originally published as 'Birth and Power', a review of Michel Odent *Entering the World; the de-medicalization of childbirth* (London, Marion Boyars, 1984) in *Radical Community Medicine*, no. 17, Spring 1984, pp. 39–41.

by more induction of labour); and those deriving from its opposition, the alternative therapy model, which praises other ways of promoting healthy childbirth (for example raspberry leaf tea, evening primrose oil, and Michel Odent). The point I am making in 'Lullabies' is simply that both sides need to talk in the same language about the benefits and hazards of the forms of knowledge they espouse. My own belief is suspended by lack of evidence whether I am confronting an 'experienced' obstetrician with a flower in his buttonhole and a thriving private practice, or a vociferous member of the natural childbirth movement who 'knows' that most childbearing problems can be averted by proper pre-pregnancy diet, or the careful use of expensive substances sold in health food shops. The genders of these two representatives of different forms of knowledge are important; and 'Lullabies' also skirts around the easy and difficult subject of which gender knows most about childbirth.

Entering the World is the English version of Michel Odent's *Bien Naître*, which was published in France in 1976. In a telling section buried somewhere in the middle of the book, Odent quotes his mentor, Frederic Leboyer, on the matter of lullabies. Lullabies, it is said, belong to 'no religion, no culture, no race. They speak the language of a land without frontiers which is called the heart of men. That is why every baby in the world understands them. That is why every woman can sing them.'

Both Odent and Leboyer believe in lullabies. Indeed, the issue of lullabies, their origins and meaning, illustrates what for me are the two central dilemmas of the Odentian position on childbirth (if it is excusable to call it that). The first dilemma is how, or whether, to reconcile lullabies with perinatal mortality statistics. The second dilemma is why women need men to educate them about the purpose of lullabies. Although at first sight it may seem as though these two dilemmas have nothing in common, they are linked at the level of a profound division within the fabric of modern Euro-American culture. On the one hand there is the physicalist world of bodies represented by science, rationality, 'hard' statistical measures, and ideals of masculinity. In contrasting mode is the realm of nature, of art, of emotion and psychology – of femininity. These cultural divisions in ideology and practice can be seen in many different spheres, from social gender relations to the 'consumer' movement in maternity care.

On the matter of lullabies versus perinatal mortality statistics, Odent takes an uneasily shifting and ambivalent stance. He believes in feeling; indeed he credits Leboyer, the 'poet-obstetrician', with a philosophy of love from which sprang the whole 'natural birth' movement. But on the other hand, Odent contends that his objective is to move from feeling through to rational argument 'which will both direct, and be directed by, day-to-day practice' (p. 20). To this end he is prepared to quote the perinatal mortality statistics of his own practice – albeit in such a confused format that it is not easy to make sense of them. It's also strange to find the book prefaced by a 'Tribute' written by the Canadian obstetrician Murray Enkin who, with his colleagues at McMaster University, conducted a controlled clinical trial of the Leboyer technique and found it failed to show any great benefit to mother or baby.

Odent, it seems to me, has here profoundly missed in his work an opportunity for radicalism which the perinatal health services badly need. Death has never been a satisfactory way of measuring the quality of an experience. Love is as measurable as survival – or survival is no more measurable than love. The logic of the alternative way of birth proposed by Leboyer and developed by Odent is a logic that requires, in turn, an alternative way of measuring success.

So far as the gender-relations aspect of Odent's philosophy is concerned, I find myself wallowing in an even deeper mud of confusions. The fact that most obstetricians are male, and that the word 'obstetrician' comes from the same Latin root as 'obstacle', are negatively referred to by Odent – although, of course, Odent is also a man, and in that sense may also reasonably be considered an obstacle. It is suggested that many obstetricians had difficult births themselves (which helps to explain their difficult behaviour) and Odent says that at the ideal birth only a midwife would be in attendance. A degree of charity is exhibited towards women as a class when Odent acknowledges that it was women with their power of 'instinctive emotional fusion' who enabled everyone else to understand what Leboyer was on about. On the other hand, one of the clearest motifs of Leboyer's theme was the mother's capacity to act as enemy to her baby.

Leboyer and indeed, Odent, are primarily advocates of babies and only secondarily advocates of women. In *Entering the World* there are several very unambiguous passages in which Odent aligns himself with a long tradition of male experts advising women in deciding to define for us the essence of a good mother. A good mother adapts herself entirely to the needs of her child, but cannot be trusted to be an 'objective' or 'reliable' informant on her child's development. Bad mothers are responsible for everything, including perforated duodenal ulcers in their adult children (a crisis of rebirth) and, needless to say, for every form of sexual difficulty in adult males, especially premature ejaculation (sexual problems in adult females are not mentioned).

Odent's world includes male obstetricians but not fathers. What he really thinks about women I do not know. But the didactic quality of his philosophy regarding mothers mars what is otherwise a wonderful sensitivity to the experiential aspects of human birth and parenthood. We can do without the new creation myth of lullabies – Eve probably knew all about them before Adam was born.

14

The China Syndrome

From time to time institutions such as the Royal College of Obstetricians and Gynaecologists invite people whom they consider to be experts to give memorial lectures. As one would expect, women are severely under-represented in this process, and so too are non-doctors. 'The China Syndrome', thus called both because it refers to the artificial reproduction dilemma, and because the day after I gave it I went to China, came under the heading of a lecture in memory of a woman called Jennifer Hallam, who was, I believe, a GP associated with the College, who is said to have died young on her way to a meeting. I was the first non-doctor to give this lecture, and it was no easy task to perform. Fortunately, my imminent visit to China provided me with an excuse to escape from listening to the rest of the day's proceedings, which were mostly concerned with new methods men had devised for women to continue exposing themselves to the dangers of sex by protecting themselves with the dangers of contraception.

Marie Stopes, the great pioneer of birth control in Britain, had a second less well-known career as a writer. In 1926, she wrote a play called *Vectia* which was about a virgin wife's desire to have a baby by her husband. The play was banned just before its first performance by the Lord Chamberlain, who said: 'You have done it beautifully, there is not a word or a thing to which I can take exception, but I cannot allow

Source: Originally given under the title 'Fertility Control – a woman's issue?' as the 10th Jennifer Hallem Memorial Lecture at the Royal College of Obstetricians and Gynaecologists, London, in October, 1983, and published in *Journal of Obstetrics and Gynaecology* 1984, **4** (Supplement 1) pp. 1–10, © John Wright and Sons.

the *theme*.'[81] The theme was, of course, taken from Marie Stopes' own life. Fifteen years previously she had married a young botanist, Reginald Gates, and in the months following the wedding had experienced a growing realization that something was not quite right with the marriage. It took a visit to the British Museum for her to find out what this was. It was the British Museum that taught her the facts of life. The marriage had not been consummated and was annulled five years later.

No wonder, one might say, that Marie Stopes was inspired throughout her life by the desire to invest women with a basic level of information about, and control over, the functions and capacities of their own bodies. Yet, in this respect Marie Stopes was not a pioneer; she was merely a more prominent and public pioneer than most. The real pioneers of fertility control have been the many women throughout history and in different cultures who have not needed a trip to the British Museum to teach them a very important fact about a woman's life – that without control over reproduction it may not be much of a life at all. In this paper I am going to ask some rather elementary questions about the concept of fertility control, beginning with the question as to where the concept comes from, moving on to why it is important to women and to men, and ending with some speculations about the social implications of modern techniques of fertility control.

HISTORICAL CONTINUITIES IN FERTILITY CONTROL

Most self-respecting fertility controllers these days are aware that they are engaged in an activity as old as recorded human history, and at the same time as new as the medical profession. By this I mean that there is well-documented historical evidence about the social importance of controlling fertility in different societies. There are also anthropological data from contemporary pre-literate cultures, showing that the impetus to devise ways of controlling fertility predates modern 'scientific' medicine.[82]

Within both the history of fertility control and its present-day medical practice lie two diametrically opposed motives: promoting and preventing birth. Thus the early fifteenth-century *Medieval Woman's Guide to Health*[83] contains both sorts of prescriptions. In order to conceive, a medicine containing 15 different herbs mixed with six gallons of water and one gallon of wine is recommended, or alternatively a woman must swallow the dried testicles of a boar. Interestingly, a third suggestion involves a plaster of raw eggs, cloves, saffron and oil of roses on which *either* the woman or the man (or perhaps both?) were supposed to lie. The manuscript recognizes that infertility may at times be incurable, and advises a rather unpleasant test in which the urine of the infertile couple is mixed with wheat bran. After nine days a terrible smell plus the presence of worms is considered absolutely diagnostic of incurable infertility.

It is easy to dismiss such remedies as magical nonsense, but in this context let me just mention the instructive example of crocodile and elephant dung. Egyptian papyri, discovered in 1889 and dating from about 1850 BC, contain a prescription for the contraceptive use of crocodile dung mixed with honey and sodium carbonate as a vaginal pessary.[84] Since greasy substances such as honey form the basis of some modern contraceptive suppositories and may inhibit the motility of sperm, the Egyptians may well have been on to something. But what about the crocodile dung? Enthusiastic biochemists in the 1920s set out to test this material for its pH value, but unfortunately could only get hold of Cuban crocodiles, whose dung showed a pH of 7.9, which did not suggest contraceptive efficacy. The mystery of the pH value of Egyptian crocodile dung remains, but what happened to the dung contraceptive was that over the centuries elephant dung came to be substituted, and there is no doubt that the pH value of elephant faeces would have had some spermicidal effect (the Indian elephant being preferable to the African elephant here).

When we look at such prophylactics we do not, of course, know who first invented them, but we do know which sex they were used by, and we can guess the answer to two further key questions, namely who controlled the availability of the remedy in question, and who was likely to have been most highly motivated to use it. Most methods of fertility control described in the historical and anthropological literature were used by women, and almost all the necessary technical resources (for example elephant dung) were readily available. As to motivation for deployment of fertility control, I would say that there are good reasons why women as a social group are *always* more likely than men to be highly motivated fertility controllers. That is, women are more likely than men to be interested in both the promotion and prevention of pregnancy. This is a most significant historical continuity, which I shall return to below.

If we compare the fertility control scene today with that obtaining in fifteenth-century England, or in Egypt in 1850 BC, we can also say that, in all probability, a second common theme is the greater number of female over male fertility control methods. Men would have practised *coitus interruptus* and used certain potions; women not only swallowed potions, used ointments and put all sorts of substances in their vaginas, but also practised abortion and relied on prolonged breastfeeding and/or sexual abstinence to protect themselves from unwanted pregnancy. Today, oral contraception is swallowed by women; the sheath, withdrawal and male sterilization are the only 'male' methods. Among contraceptive-using married populations in Britain and the USA, some 60 per cent or more use female methods.[85]

The biggest single difference between what one might call the 'traditional' and the 'modern' fertility control scenes is, therefore, not one of who wants to use, or does use, fertility control. It is that the technical and knowledge resources for practising fertility control now belong to the medical profession. Which is, of course, why a symposium such as this is being held in an institution called the Royal College of Obstetricians and Gynaecologists – I am what you could call the odd woman out. Modern 'scientific' medicine has made fertility control a medical subject, whereas before it belonged to the people. Fertility control is, in this sense, exactly like many other areas of modern life such as birth, childcare and unhappiness – now known respectively by their medical titles as obstetrics, paediatrics and depression.

WHY IS FERTILITY CONTROL IMPORTANT TO WOMEN

I am not sure how controversial it is to say that fertility control is more important to women than to men; I am also not sure how true it is. Obviously, some aspects of this question are self-evident. As Hawkins and Elder's *Human Fertility Control* puts it, 'if a woman has sexual intercourse, then she must accept a finite risk to her life – whether that risk be encountered by childbearing or by the prevention or termination of pregnancy.'[86] It is not necessary to be a militant feminist to note that when a man has sexual intercourse with a woman, he does not risk his life in the same way, and that a different formulation of this risk problematic might be 'sex with men is dangerous to women's health.' By far the most important manifestation of this danger has been maternal mortality – female deaths due to, or associated with, pregnancy – but there has also been, and still is, an enormous amount of morbidity associated with childbearing. A recent study of 900 women having babies in Berkshire revealed, for example, that three months after childbirth 20 per cent of women were troubled with varying degrees of incontinence.[87]

Taking a broad view of the risks for women of sexual activity with men also means looking at the risks associated with pregnancy prevention. Hence the concept of 'reproductive' mortality promoted by Valerie Beral, a term that includes deaths due to spontaneous or induced abortion, complications of pregnancy, delivery and the puerperium and adverse effects of female contraception and sterilization. According to Valerie Beral's calculations, for British women aged twenty-five to forty-four mortality from pregnancy alone has declined by more than 85 per cent since 1950. Among women aged thirty-five to forty-four, 85 per cent of reproductive deaths were due to the pill, and these outweighed the fall in pregnancy mortality. Overall, for these older women reproductive mortality had actually increased.[88]

Some time ago, a feminist parody of the possible hazards of modern contraception highlighted the ways in which these are handled by both a medical profession and a lay public accustomed to the idea that women probably do have to suffer in order to prevent pregnancy. Because it makes several important points well, I shall quote this parody nearly in full:

> The newest development in male contraception was unveiled recently at the American Women's Surgical Symposium held at the Ann Arbor Medical Centre. Dr Sophie Merkin. . . announced the findings of a study conducted on 763 . . . male undergraduates.
>
> The IPD (intrapenile device) resembles a tiny rolled umbrella which is inserted through the head of the penis and pushed into the scrotum with a plunger-like device. . . .
>
> Experiments on 1,000 white whales from the continental shelf proved the IPD to be 100 per cent effective in preventing the production of sperm, and eminently satisfactory to the female whale since it does not interfere with her rutting pleasure.
>
> Dr Merkin declared [the IPD]. . . to be statistically safe for the human male. She reported that of the 763 undergraduates tested with the device only 2 died of scrotal infection, only 20 developed swelling of the testicles, and 13 were too depressed to have an erection. She stated that common complaints ranged from cramping and bleeding to acute abdominal pains. She emphasized that these symptoms were merely indications that the man's body had not yet adjusted to the device. . . .
>
> One complication caused by the IPD and briefly mentioned by Dr Merkin was the incidence of massive scrotal infection necessitating the surgical removal of the testicles. 'But this is rare', said Dr Merkin, 'too rare to be statistically important.' She and other distinguished members of the Women's College of Surgeons agreed that the benefits far outweighed the risk to any individual man.[89]

This uncomfortable rewriting of the fertility control scene of course brings out the paradox that while women are the main users of modern contraceptive techniques, men are quite interested in getting them to use them. This is one of the senses in which fertility control is in men's interests as much as it is in women's. It is also a demonstration of the fact that we cannot hope to understand what fertility control is all about unless we see it in a context of social and sexual relations.

Control of fertility has been a plank in the political platform of every feminist movement. Control over one's own life and destiny, the very essence of feminism, is not possible without that first 'freedom' – freedom from unplanned and unwanted pregnancy. For this reason the feminist struggle is nowhere near won in those countries where either the Church or the state forbids contraception and where abortion is illegal. If there is one single lesson to be learnt from the history of fertility control it is that whether abortion is legal or illegal women will have abortions – it is just that they will die more often when abortion is against the law.

Defending the rights of women and advocating safe and effective fertility control have historically gone hand-in-hand, but the situation is more complex than that. In the first place, many non-feminists have argued the need for humane methods of fertility control. In the second place, from the sex equality viewpoint it is not enough to advocate safe and effective fertility control: one must ask who controls the fertility control? Thirdly, the feminist perspective on fertility control has been, until very recently, extremely one-sided. Far more attention has been paid to preventing pregnancy than to promoting it. Female biology has been defined as a burden to be off-loaded by the effective prevention of pregnancy. No particularly positive value has been attached to the achievement of motherhood. It was the American writer Adrienne Rich who some years ago in a provocative book about motherhood made a crucial distinction between the *experience* of motherhood on the one hand, and the *institution* of motherhood on the other. She says: 'The institution of motherhood is not identical with bearing and caring for children, any more than the institution of heterosexuality is identical with intimacy and sexual love. Both create the prescriptions and the conditions in which choices are made or blocked: they are not reality but they have shaped the circumstances of our lives.'[90]

What Rich means by this is that social forces beyond the control of the individual partly determine the shape of parenthood in any culture. Are children wanted? How many children are wanted? Are women needed in the labour force? What do cultural attitudes say about the role of women – what is the status of mothers and what is the status of non-mothers? Answers to these questions outline the social context within which motherhood is lived, but the actual relationship of mothers to their children – the day-to-day experience of joy, anger, labour, peace and love – may be very different. This clash between experience and institution, between the reality of motherhood on the one hand and social expectations of women-as-mothers on the other, has been, I think, one of those conflicts responsible for the very birth of feminism itself.

FERTILITY CONTROL TODAY

In comparing fertility control among the ancient Egyptians with modern fertility control I identified the key difference as one of medicalization. Today's experts on fertility control are not its users, but those who develop, market, prescribe, and thus control, fertility control. When we add the medicalization of fertility control to the medicalization of birth and childcare we have a situation in which reproduction as a human activity is increasingly divorced from sexual and social relations. Medical and technical considerations have come to dominate the management and shaping of parenthood. One example of this is the near 100 per cent hospitalization rate for childbirth, a policy which has evolved in many countries on a completely unscientific basis, since it has never been proved that the majority of women and their babies benefit from institutionalized birth.[91] More than this, the success of different ways of managing birth has been judged totally in terms of *physical* parameters – what happens to bodies, rather than what happens to minds, emotions and interpersonal relationships.

There are many other examples of how the medicalization of reproduction ignores its character as a social process, from the husband who becomes impotent whenever his infertile wife is induced to ovulate, to the new terminology for describing female unhappiness as premenstrual tension and postpartum depression, a terminology which allows us to enquire more closely into the mechanics of female body functioning and not into the social dynamics of women's situation. Consider, too, the idea of the 'perfect' contraceptive as pursued by fertility controllers and, following them, the lay public. The perfect contraceptive is one that has no practical or temporal connection to the sexual act. It is just 'there', suspending the woman's body in a 'no-risk-of-pregnancy' state, so that whenever an act of intercourse oocurs neither she nor her partner are forced to consider the necessity for contraception, or the biological and social consequences of their union. The 'perfect' contraceptive is one that encourages irresponsibility precisely because sexual intercourse is permitted to become a purely physical activity. This is the sense, of course, in which the pill has liberated women. It has encouraged them to place sexuality in one compartment of their lives and reproduction in another. Whether this was what women wanted and whether it is a good thing are ethical questions that have not been answered – I do not think there is much evidence suggesting that most women are happily able to separate childbearing and sexuality in this way. I would suggest that the separation is easier for men, who do not experience both in the same body. Certainly, the idea of the liberated woman as the 'woman-who-is-perfectly-protected-against-pregnancy' has been a new stereotype for women in the post-pill era to rail against – *sexual* liberation is not the same thing as liberation, and what is so sexually liberating anyway about a continuous medication that tends to suppress one's libido? Personally, I have always felt that women have been a great deal more liberated by the invention of tampons than by the pill – if, that is, one can somehow avoid toxic shock and frightening books such as *Everything You Must Know About Tampons*.[92]

I could produce many more examples of this divorce of reproduction from social relations, but will content myself with only one: so-called preconceptual care (an odd term: surely it should be preconceptional?). What are the implications of extending medical care backwards to the period before pregnancy has even started? Stemming from a basically sound and commonsense idea – that parental health before conception is as important as parental health after conception – the new vogue for preconceptual care nevertheless conjures up a disturbing vision. In this vision we see an epidemic of preconceptual clinics arising at which the purveyors of preconceptual care advocate a variety of dietary and vitamin packages on the basis of what is at the moment a very uncertain knowledge about which elements of diet are really needed for healthy reproduction.[93] In the end perhaps, these enthusiastic purveyors of the new preconceptual expertise will find themselves asking 'but why don't women attend for preconceptual care?' in much the same way as the protagonists of antenatal care have repeated the question about women's non-attendance for antenatal care.[94]

As a matter of fact, we may also note that the same question has been asked by birth controllers who have confronted over the years the results of population surveys showing that a significant proportion of women (and therefore of course men as well) indulge in the dangerous activity of sexual intercourse without using contraception. Why are women (and men) so silly? The two main answers to this question have been:

(1) inadequate knowledge and availability of contraception; and (2) inadequate personality. Neither of these theories has ever satisfactorily explained the fact that some couples clearly know about contraception, or do not suffer from confusions and unresolved conflicts over whether or not to have a baby, but still do not use an effective contraceptive method. In 1975, a Californian sociologist called Kristin Luker wrote a very important book called *Taking Chances*[95] which I think has not been taken nearly seriously enough by the medical profession. In this book Luker argues, firstly, that it takes two to make a baby, a point that, mysteriously, sometimes seems most apt to be forgotten by those best acquainted with the facts of life. Secondly, she proposes that if you talk to women (and men) about why they don't use contraception when they don't want a baby, you are liable to find they are actually able to give a rational account of their behaviour. Within this rational account the most significant component is the citation of the personal, social, biological and economic costs of using contraception. It may be costly in personal terms to acknowledge that one is in a sexual relationship. Getting contraception may cost time and money. Using contraception may mean putting up with side-effects in the short-term and unwanted consequences such as disturbed fertility in the long-term. The balancing of costs and benefits can only be done by the individual, but the point is that it usually is done. Not using contraception may thus be a means of exercising control over one's fertility though it challenges a basic precept behind the medicalization of fertility control – that in the struggle to avoid pregnancy some form of contraception is always better than none.

I have not yet talked about the most extreme manifestation of the divorce of reproduction from social relations, namely, artificial reproduction. This is a futuristic aspect of fertility control, which so far impinges on the lives of very few users or providers of fertility control; nevertheless it raises in a particularly blatant manner the issue of whose responsibility fertility control is, or should be.

ARTIFICIAL REPRODUCTION: WHOSE BABY?

The new techniques of *in vitro* fertilization (IVF) and embryo transfer (ET) have achieved for the beginning of pregnancy what neonatal intensive care has done for its end – they have made the participation of the mother's body redundant. About half the total span of human pregnancy can in theory be accomplished outside the body. In theory too, pregnancy can be the burden and the joy of both sexes, since an embryo could be transferred into a male abdomen rather than into a female uterus, leading the fantasy of the 1970 contraception advertisement which portrays a pregnant man to become a reality, albeit a highly uncomfortable one. If women can occasionally have successful abdominal pregnancies, why not men?

The idea of male gestation is perhaps the most advanced flight of fantasy engendered by recent advances towards artificial reproduction. Yet it illustrates how profoundly this infant scenario of new reproductive techniques is able to challenge a tradition of sex and gender roles which is itself as long as human history. People have speculated endlessly on just how far and in what ways the division of reproductive labour – female as gestator, male as inseminator – has influenced the social roles and statuses of men and women. Nobody has really come up with an answer, except to say that different cultures link reproduction and social gender roles differently, that the biological imperative of sex differences can be played up or down, that it is all a matter of what human beings decide is most important. If it is important that women be people first and women second, then all sorts of social arrangements are possible to facilitate reproduction without oppression. With the vista of artificial reproduction on the horizon, it appears that we may not need to answer these questions after all. The solution has come off the pages of science fiction into the world around us. Well, has it? It was the former US astronaut James Lovell who said, 'we will fly women into space and use them the same way we use them on earth – for the same purpose.'[96] Before taking a closer look at the present day scientific reality of artificial reproduction, let us learn another instructive lesson (the lesson of the crocodile dung reversed, as it were) from the genre of science fiction.

Science fiction writers are commonly supposed to invent fictional forms of science, to create worlds containing all sorts of exotic possibilities based on some future scientific mode. Yet what most science fiction writers actually do is subscribe to the conservative partisan (medicalized?) view that all social revolutions are a scientific product. Within that framework, the social relations of present-day society are astonishingly persistent. As science fiction writer Pamela Sargent has put it:

> There are a vast number of science fiction stories which show the impact of labour-saving devices, computers, space travel, increased communications, and new scientific ideas on men. About all such things seem to accomplish for women, however, is to give them more leisure time in which to worry about their children, lounge about their residences in

futuristic fashions, oversee robotic or computerized 'servants'. . . . and worry
about retaining the affections of their husbands. . . . On other planets
. . . they often quickly become involved primarily in childbearing.[97]

There *are* works of science fiction or futurology – Huxley's *Brave New World* is the most famous example – which *do* question the assumption that reproduction is a woman's job. Some, and Huxley's is not in this category, use the possibility of artificial reproduction completely to restructure gender roles. In Thomas M. Disch's *334*,[98] early twenty-first century New York is used as a setting for various permutations on laboratory-aided parenthood. A lesbian called Shrimp is caught up in a fantasy of childbearing by artificial insemination, and a man called Boz has a child brought to term in an artificial womb, after which he has a breast implant to enable him to breastfeed. There are a number of science fiction novels in which reproduction is not relegated to the laboratory and to the hospital, but becomes a human rather than sex-specific activity. Men and women take it in turns to have children, or there are no men and women – everyone is bisexual. Alternatively, there are no men, and the science fiction element is used to replace the male contribution in childbearing by technology.

My favourite among all these fictional diversions is a novel called *Woman on the Edge of Time* by the American writer Marge Piercy. The heroine (even science fiction has heroines) is a decayed, middle-aged and welfare-dependent Mexican American called Connie who is an inmate in a public mental hospital. She participates in an experiment involving electronic implants in the brain, and an unintended consequence of the experiment is that she finds herself intermittently in a society where sex roles are unknown. It is a very untechnological society in which everyone lives ecologically and in harmony with nature, with one exception – childbearing is done mechanically in a 'brooder' which stores genetic material and replicates the conditions of the human uterus. The inhabitants of this world explain to Connie why they have allowed the intrusion of this technology:

> It is part of women's long revolution. . . . Finally there was that one thing we had to give up too, the only power we ever had. . . . The original production: the power to give birth. [Be]cause as long as we were biologically enchained, we'd never be equal. And males never would be humanized to be loving and tender. So we all became mothers.[99]

To summarize the lesson of science fiction, it could be said, then, that the limits and possibilities of artificial reproduction are not set by the technology itself. Scientific discovery and social change do not exist in a one-to-one relationship. The kind of society we live in determines the kind of scientific progress that is made – the areas where research effort and money are concentrated, the areas where they are not, the questions within these areas that are either pursued or ignored. What this means is that, as Virginia Woolf[100] put it, science is not sexless, she is a man. I am not suggesting any sort of simple male conspiracy theory here, for that does not adequately fit the facts. For example, the lack of research on male contraceptives is sometimes pointed to as evident misogyny. Yet it may be that it is genuinely technically easier to disrupt the mechanisms responsible for ovulation and implantation in the female than to interfere with those involved with sperm production in the male.[101] In any case, the arguments about the ethical superiority of shared contraceptive responsibility must compete with the argument about fertility control being essentially a woman's issue, and thus being better in the hands, bloodstreams or at least in the reproductive apparatuses of women.

One good illustration of the two-way relationship between scientific development and social relations is the issue of sex selection. Like fertility control itself, the desire to be able to decide the sex of children is not new – what is new is the technical capacity to do so. Of course we already have that with prenatal sex chromosome analysis and selective termination of pregnancies containing the 'wrong' sexed fetus.

But have we even begun to disentangle the ethical issues involved in disposing of fetuses merely because of their sex? According to studies of parents' sex preferences, there is a sustained bias towards males and against females. This is more marked among men than women, but women sometimes follow their husbands' preferences rather than their own.[102] If parents were able to decide fetal sex now, the sex ratio would show a marked change in favour of males. This is already happening in China. Sex predetermination functions also as birth control, since 'trying for a boy' or 'trying for a girl' become unnecessary motivations for increased family size. If the 'cereal packet' norm of a boy first and a girl second become reality there would also be the 'birth order' effect to consider. Position in the family is known to affect personality and life chances, with firstborns being generally more anxious, intelligent and achievement-oriented.[103] A consistent concentration of males among the firstborn would therefore add to the gender division a further structural inequality in life chances.

The implications of changes in the sex ratio are thus enormous. Yet the social consequences of this potential transformation are much less discussed than the technical status of the field. Most of all, scientists apparently do not feel it to be part of their brief to consider *why* fetal biological sex should be regarded as so important that its manipulation is worth the expenditure of considerable amounts of time and money. At the same time, of course, most doctors probably do not feel prepared to terminate a 'wrong' sexed pregnancy or even *diagnose* the sex of a pregnancy simply because the parents want it. One American case quoted in a recent discussion of the sex predetermination issue concerned a pregnant woman and her husband who presented themselves to a paediatrician with a family history of haemophilia. Following amniocentesis, the paediatrician was glad to be able to tell the parents that the fetus was a girl and they need not worry about a sex-linked disorder, to which the parents replied that they were going off to get an abortion because they really wanted a boy and had merely made up the story about haemophilia in order to get the amniocentesis done.[104]

The new technologies for controlling reproduction take us – all of us – to the point at which it is impossible any longer to avoid confronting ethical issues. This dilemma is most clearly marked in the notion of 'the artificial family' created by the techniques of artificial insemination, *in vitro* fertilization and embryo transfer. Using these techniques, a whole scientific soap opera of parental roles can be written: an infertile woman implanted with another woman's *in vitro* fertilized egg – and fertilized with, perhaps, anonymously donated sperm: so-called surrogate motherhood – 'rent-a-womb' – in which, for payment, a woman bears a child by artificial insemination of the payer's sperm, giving up that child at birth; the insemination of women with Nobel prize sperm, or rather the sperm of Nobel prize-winners (not at all the same thing) according to the persisting science fiction fantasy that the roots of scientific achievement lie firmly in the underworld of the genes.

Within this realm of ever-expanding possibilities two stand out. The first is the possibility that the family is no longer necessary. The second is the possibility that men are no longer necessary. I am, of course, overstating the current situation a little. But the ease with which sperm may be collected and frozen for long periods of time, and the relative simplicity of the technique of artificial insemination do mean that women can in theory bear children without ever relating to men. For the time being, until the era of the artificial placenta, real female wombs are still needed. The theoretical redundancy of men is itself a challenge to the family, but there are other challenges to the family in here too, some of which are apparent in the recent report of the Royal College of

Obstetricians and Gynaecologists Ethics Committee on *in vitro* fertilization and embryo replacement or transfer.[105]

The report begins by considering the circumstances under which IVF and ER (as the Committee calls it) should be used. The first consideration of the medical profession in this field is whether technical interference in conception risks an abnormal fetus – if it does, the doctors concerned may be the subject of legal action. The second consideration is the use of the techniques of IVF and ER within 'marriage', defined generously by the committee as comprising 'a heterosexual couple cohabiting on a stable basis'. Should doctors accept for treatment all 'married' people who request it? The answer is no, for it is the 'province' of the doctor to take on for treatment only those couples who are suitable on physical, genetic, psychiatric and social grounds. The third consideration is whether IVF and ER should be used outside 'marriage', and about this the committee has 'grave reservations'. Its argument here is that

> IVF and ER differ from other forms of treatment for infertility and put extra strain not only on patients but also on doctors. The latter are not acting only as 'enablers'; with IVF and ER they are taking part in the formation of the embryo itself. That role brings a special sense of responsibility for the welfare of the child thus conceived. The committee believes that most practitioners will intuitively feel that IVF and ER should be performed in the most 'natural' of family environments.

I have always wondered why donors preferred for artificial insemination are English, middle-class medical students[106] and here, perhaps, is part of the answer. Medical students are said to be preferred because an acceptable level of intelligence, a stable personality and character as a 'good all-rounder' is thereby assured,[107] but I am not sure either that studies on medical students are quite as reassuring as one would like them to be on these matters, or that being a good all-rounder is a qualification for fatherhood which is at all important to mothers.

The point I am making in a roundabout way here is that the medical profession seems to have negotiated itself into an extremely difficult position of enormous power with respect to the new techniques of artificial reproduction. Doctors are making moral and social decisions about suitability for parenthood for which their training does not equip them. They are playing God as never before – God the Father, for as the RCOG report so succinctly puts it, doctors are now actually participating in the formation of embryos. In the face of this new role, and in view of the ability of the new techniques to liberate men and women from traditional sexual relationships, it seems a little disingenuous to fall back on that 'intuitive' notion of the 'natural' family.

CONCLUSION

In his book *The Technological Society*, Jacques Ellul called ours 'a civilization committed to the quest for continually improved means to carelessly examined ends'.[108] Perhaps this would also do as a description of the process of scientific discovery, and certainly it applies to the history of scientific development within the fertility control field, including its most recent product of artificially engineered conception.

Having acquired the technology we now have to examine the reasons why we wanted it in the first place. Obviously, these new techniques are welcomed by infertile couples. But there is an issue about the possible uncontrolled growth of a technology that benefits only a minority. As I have indicated, there are good reasons why women throughout history have needed to control the mixed blessing of motherhood. That I am standing here talking about this very subject owes something to the fact that I have spent a mere five and a half years of my life either pregnant or lactating; the capacity women have to experience themselves as persons apart from the function of reproduction is limited, first and foremost, by the choice they are able to exercise over whether, when and how they will become mothers. In this sense fertility control is not a feminist issue – though it is that as well. It is primarily a *woman's* issue.

In considering the implications of this we need to take into account not only access to the means of controlling fertility, but who owns the knowledge and the technical resources and who makes the decisions about the promotion and prevention of fertility in individual cases. Artificial insemination from a donor is a good example of a technique for which doctors *per se* are not actually needed, but which it is nevertheless argued should be under medical control. Radical feminist groups have been using AID without medical help successfully for years.[109]

In short, there are strong grounds for arguing that because fertility control is a woman's issue, doctors should be prepared to share their expertise, and particularly their decision-making power, more equally with their patients. Like shared income-earning within the family (either natural or artificial) it seems to me that this shared responsibility could only in the long run be a relief to those who so manfully now shoulder it alone. The spectre of a future in which reproduction is entirely an artificial exercise is either horrific or wonderful. Which it is will depend on our willingness from this moment on to oversee the evolution of a brave new world which is truly brave in the human and humane sense of increasing freedom and engendering good human relationships, rather than trapping us in a technology that, as a society, we did not choose and do not wholly want.

Part 3

The Health of Eve (and Adam)

If only it weren't for this dreadful fatigue. It lies on my eyelids like lead, they want to drop and stay closed. These days of menstruation are particularly dangerous...do I want to avoid something disagreeable, through sleep? But what could that be? Housekeeping? ....I want only something friendly, quiet, peaceful – and not to see some memory laughing out of every corner, and not to think on every path I take: I used to talk here with this one or that one, here we kissed, here we picked raspberies.....

The Adolescent Diaries of Karen Horney,
New York, Basic Books, 1980, p. 240

15

Beyond the Yellow Wallpaper

As no less a person than the Director-General of the World Health Organization has said, 'Health is not everything, but without health everything else is nothing.'[1] And, according to another useful aphorism, health doesn't have a price, but it does have a cost. The pieces in this section concentrate rather awkwardly on a mixture of some global concerns to do with women's health and health-care work, and some very particular ones related to the problems of doctors and patients and health-care researchers in the industrialized world today.

The opening monologue, 'Beyond the Yellow Wallpaper, or taking women seriously', tries to provide a framework for pursuing all kinds of questions – theoretical, political, practical, epidemiological – in the area of women's health. It was written for an interesting event, a conference in 1983 on Women and Health sponsored jointly by WHO and the Scottish Health Education Group (SHEG). The originator of the event, Ilona Kickbusch, a sharp and energetic social scientist in charge of health education for the European region of WHO, most unfortunately missed its materialization by giving birth the day it began. As the opening ceremonies took place in the unlikely surroundings of Edinburgh Castle, it was reported that Ilona was in the early stages of labour. Some of the Scottish officials attending seemed a little embarrassed by this reporting of intimate bodily happenings (not unconnected with the conference theme).

The conference on 'Women and Health' was held shortly before the

Source: Originally given as Keynote Address to WHO/Scottish Health Education Group Conference on Women and Health, Edinburgh, 25–7 May 1983.

British national elections in 1983, which returned a Conservative Government with an enlarged majority. I managed to draw attention to myself just before the conference opened by saying in a newspaper interview that British women should vote Labour to protect their own health – and for all sorts of other reasons. This didn't go down well with the conference organizers, who issued a press release disclaiming any identification with my personal political views. The meeting was held in the Peebles Hydro hotel, which was more accustomed to the golfing and business deliberations of grey-suited men, than to the intelligent ravings of radical women. However, the meeting itself started on a suitably patriarchal note, as the banner 'Women and Health' was slung below the heads of the three grey-suited men who formally opened the conference proceedings: Jo Asvall, from WHO, John Reid from the Scottish Home and Health Department, and Stanley Mitchell from the SHEG. My memory is that all three dignitaries departed immediately after they had made their points, presumably relieved to have got out before the temperature inside the Hydro rose too much. As a further aid to feverish temperatures, a BBC/SHEG health education pamphlet, written just before the conference for a series of television programmes on women's health, was censored by SHEG for its inclusion of the suggestion that masturbating to orgasm is effective therapy for period pains. The media all over the country got very excited about this. Angela Phillips, the author of the ill-fated pamphlet, sanely remarked that 'As orgasms don't do anyone any harm and as some people thought it might do some good, I thought it worthwhile including it.'[2] But, obviously, sexual self-help strategies for improving women's health are a deviation from the direction history in most places has taken, and are thus scarcely likely to be popular with policy-makers, except perhaps as ways of saving money (and then only when they don't offend conventional anti-women morality). All this would have struck a familiar chord with Charlotte Perkins Gilman, whose short story 'The Yellow Wallpaper', published originally in 1892, lent its title to my own inflammatory contribution to the meeting.

The very idea of a conference on 'Women and Health' challenges two central myths of the industrialized world in the twentieth century. The first of these two myths is the one that says health is a medical product, that a state of health in individuals and societies is brought about principally through the efforts of members of the medical profession: illness is prevented or cured and death avoided through the beneficence of medical science. The second myth is that inequalities between men and women are surface blemishes only, and may be removed merely by cosmetic attention to the superstructure of social relations: all we need is a few good laws and minor social changes and women will be able to look men in the eyes as equals.

These myths are powerful organizing ideas in what is commonly, if misleadingly, referred to as 'the developed world'. The enormously important role in our cultural thinking and social policy of the myths challenged by the phrase 'women and health' makes this conference even more important. It is a radical departure for two national and international organizations concerned with health issues first of all to pay serious attention to women's role in health care, secondly to confront directly the social, economic and political context of health – and thirdly to do both at the same time.

In order to set the scene for this discussion, it is perhaps useful to run through some of the main issues to be tackled under the heading 'Women and Health'. From a global perspective, what burning questions need to be asked and answered about women as users and providers of health-care? Next, what are the implications for women of the differences between these two conceptualizations – health as a medical product and health as a social product. Lastly, I will look at the implications for health-care systems of the differences between the two conceptualizations of women: the 'equal rights' view of women on the one hand, and on the other the rather more disturbing notion of women's oppression.

Women and Health: the Main Questions

Before producing a shopping list of burning questions, we need to make a basic distinction between three terms: health, health-care and medical care. The last is the easiest to define: medical care is that provided by a medical professional, with the aim of treating or preventing illness. Health-care need not be provided by a medical professional, but can be an activity of non-medical, non-professional groups and even of individuals themselves. Health, as by far the most complex of the three terms, need not have anything to do either with health-care or with medical care, and here I am, of course, referring to that substantial body of evidence demonstrating that changes in broad indicators of the health of communities are rarely brought about by changes in the provision of medical care. Although this type of evidence is limited by the indicators of health chosen (since the most oft-used indicator of health is death – which is more than strange, when you think about it), it does point in the direction of a certain definition of health which is relevant for us at this conference. The definition is that health requires, or is impossible without, a moral basis of good social relations.

The reason why we need a conference on women and health is because women are the major social providers of health and health-care, and they are also the principal users of health- and medical-care services. In these two ways, the truth of the matter negates the dominant cultural message. The dominant cultural message is that doctors, not women, ensure health and that men, not women, are biologically the more vulnerable sex, with a mortality and physical morbidity record exceeding that of women from the cradle to the grave.[3] There is therefore something acutely paradoxical about women's relationship to health and health-care which needs to be unravelled.

WOMEN AS PROVIDERS OF HEALTH, HEALTH-CARE AND MEDICAL CARE

As providers of health and health-care, women are important through their role in the division of labour. In their domestic lives they provide health-care by attending to the physical needs of those with whom they live. They obtain food, provide and dispose of the remains of meals, clean the home, buy or make and wash and repair clothing, and take personal care of those who are too young or too old, or too sick or too busy to take care of their own physical needs. These activities are known as housework, a somewhat peculiar term, since most of the work done has nothing to do with houses, but a great deal to do with maintaining the health and vitality of individuals. Incidentally, or perhaps not so incidentally, it is a matter of great importance to policy-makers as to how this health-promoting work of women is described. Mostly it is described in terms of an ideology of women's natural commitment to family welfare, an ideology which attributes to women a feminine altruism that many would prefer to have recognized as unpaid labour.

To call women's household health work by the name of 'housework' is to ignore an extremely important aspect of the domestic division of labour, and that is women's role as the chief managers of personal relations both inside and outside the family. Emotional support promotes health – there is good evidence that a person's social relationships or lack of them are crucial influences on physical and mental functioning. As family welfare workers – as mothers, mothers-in-law, wives, housewives, sisters and daughters, and often neighbours as well – women take care of personal relations.

The impact of industrial economic development, although commonly seen in terms of the work-home division, also had this other effect: that personal relationships were equated with 'the family', and women were seen as responsible for them. 'The family –' increasingly the nuclear family of parents and children, with its incorporated division of labour – became the paradigm for all female–male relationships, for the division of all labour. Thus, also, before the modern industrial era the domestic health-care provided by women extended beyond the home and out into the community. Women were recognized as the main potential healers for the bulk of the population; hence such terms as 'wisewoman' and 'old wives' tale'; and hence the traditional role of midwives purveying a set of skills derived not from formal training but from personal practical experience. With the rise of professionalized medicine, many of women's traditional healing activities acquired a new definition as dangerous to health, if not actually illegal. This did not necessarily put an end to them, since, fortunately, women have almost always been strong enough to put up some resistance to the imposition of the state's power. It is because the subculture of women's healing and midwifery was never entirely eliminated by the combined misogyny of state and medical profession that in a research project we are doing in WHO we are finding the existence of 'alternative' services for maternal and child health in most countries – a coming-out-into-the-open of a old tradition spurred on by the unresolvable dilemmas for women of the health-is-a-medical-product idea.[4]

Even within official health-care systems, women remain extremely important as providers of care. To take Britain as an example, some three-quarters of workers in the National Health Service are women. However, only about 20 per cent of British doctors are women: there is a division of labour by gender in professionalized health-care, just as there is in every other sphere of social life. As doctors, as midwives and as nurses, women health-care providers in Britain and most other so-called developed countries are concentrated in the lower status grades of health services. For example, while only some 11 per cent of British hospital nurses are male, a disproportionate 23 per cent of senior posts within the hospital nursing service are held by men.[5] When we look at the division by gender of specialties within medicine, we not surprisingly learn that women specialize in areas to do with children, mental illness, microbiology (perhaps a form of housework carried into the hospital setting?) and putting people to sleep, otherwise known as anaesthetics.[6] This pattern is not a reflection simply of choice, for research into medical careers has revealed much more dissatisfaction with existing career opportunities among female than among male doctors.[7] Individual women may struggle against the prescribed pattern, but a collective effort is needed to alter it.

There are many important questions here about the future role of women as health- and medical-care providers. The two I would like to single out as the most deserving of our attention are: (1) the family health and welfare work of women; and (2) female midwifery – women's work as managers of normal childbearing. Both family welfare and midwifery work are areas in which the rights of women are especially threatened today. In the family welfare domain they are threatened because in most ways and in most countries the necessity to the economy and prevailing moral order of women's so-called labour of love has never been eroded by a recognition of their rights as individuals. With respect to the management of childbearing, and although most of the world's babies are still delivered by midwives, recent technological growth in obstetrics has eroded the independence of the midwife's role, and indeed promises to extinguish it altogether in the future. For women as a class this, I believe, is more than a marginal retrogressive development, since, if allowed to proceed unimpeded, it will engulf motherhood in a masculine medical structure whose ideologies will, on the whole, project a different definition of health from that held by mothers themselves.

WOMEN AS USERS OF HEALTH- AND MEDICAL-CARE

The Yellow Wallpaper: Fact as Fiction

Before moving on to some of the important questions to be addressed in women's *use* of health services, I want to go back in time to a story written nearly 100 years ago by the American feminist Charlotte Perkins Gilman. The story is called 'The Yellow Wallpaper',[8] and it illustrates the historical and cross-cultural continuity marking the unsolved problems of women and health. It also highlights three of the most central of these – those relating to production, reproduction and the medicalization, in the form of mental illness, of the psychological costs of women's situation.

'The Yellow Wallpaper' describes three months in the life of a New England woman diagnosed by her husband, a physician, as suffering from nervous depression following the birth of her first child. The physician rents a house for the summer and confines his wife to bed in a large room on the top floor, a room with yellow wallpaper. He prescribes total rest for her, and expressly forbids her to do any work in the form of writing, her chosen occupation. The story describes the progression of the invalid's feelings locked up in that room; it is an account at the same time (and depending on how you look at it) of an escape into madness and a discovery of sanity. The woman becomes increasingly obsessed with the yellow wallpaper since, deprived of companionship, exercise and any intellectual stimulation, she doesn't have anything else to do but look at the walls. Finally, she becomes convinced that there is a woman in there behind the yellow wallpaper waiting to get out, a woman who creeps around the house and garden only by moonlight when no one will see her. So on their last day in the house, in an act of frenzy, she strips all the paper off the walls in order to let this other woman out, in order to free her once and for all from her prison. Her husband comes home, discovers what she has done, and faints with shock – a most undoctorly reaction – and thus apparently ends the story.

So in 'The Yellow Wallpaper' we have the following moral lessons: (1) don't put women with postnatal depression into solitary confinement; (2) avoid yellow wallpaper if possible. Actually, I think the real moral is the one summed up in that dictum of the American writer Tillie Olsen: 'Every woman who writes is a survivor',[9] which, translated into everyday language, becomes what is good for women's health is involvement in productive activity, involvement in, not withdrawal from, society. There is also a message in 'The Yellow Wallpaper' about reproduction. This is a complex message which runs as follows: childbearing, women's special biological and social contribution, may either be a source of weakness or a source of strength. Which it is depends less on the woman herself than on the social and medical context in which pregnancy, childbirth and childrearing take place. But I suppose the most profound message in 'The Yellow Wallpaper' (remember it was written nearly 100 years ago) is the one about how women's problems are constantly individualized: it is the individual woman who has the problem, and even if many individual women have the same problem, the explanation of a defective psychology rather than that of a defective social structure is usually preferred. Here we are up against not only individualization but medicalization. The medicalization of unhappiness as depression is one of the great disasters of the twentieth century, and it is a disaster that has had, and still has, a very big impact on women.

Some 20 or so years after 'The Yellow Wallpaper' came out, Gilman published a note about it in which she admitted that the story came directly from her own experience.[10] She observed that at the age of twenty-seven, married and the mother of a two-year-old, and having felt unhappy for some time, she had visited in 1887 a noted specialist in nervous diseases who put her to bed and prescribed a fate much like that of the woman in the story. The eminent man told her never to touch pen, brush, or pencil again as long as she lived. She followed his advice for three months and then, on the verge of what *she* felt to be total insanity, and with the help of a woman friend she left her husband, moved to California, and established a writing career for herself. She sent a copy of 'The Yellow Wallpaper' to the specialist in question, and, although he did not acknowledge receipt of it at the time, she learnt many years later that he had publicly said that not only had he read the story, but he had altered his treatment of nervous depression in women after reading it. I think we may be justified in concluding that (1) there is something intrinsically valid about personal experience: and (2) in coming clean about their own perspectives on health and illness, women may actually bring about the beginning of a change in those who hold powerful alternative views.

Women and Production

The first of the three burning issues I mentioned under the heading of women and health services is women's economic role, their participation in production.

Whenever we discuss women's employment we have the sense of being caught up in a circular, historical, but also timeless, debate: is women's employment a good thing or a bad thing: should women/wives/mothers work, or not? What is the effect of employment on health, both physical and mental; or, indeed, what is the effect of women's health and illness on employment? These questions cannot be given general answers. But we can easily note some important features about the employment of women. According to that oft-quoted United Nations Report, women perform two-thirds of the world's work-hours, receive one-tenth of the world's income, and own less than one-hundredth of the world's property. Thus, whatever else work may be, it is a dead end in the business sense for women – a bad deal. In undeveloped countries the reality behind the myth of the male hunter–provider has always been the woman hunter–gatherer supporting her family through her own autonomous agricultural work. Once the process of urban-industrial development sets in, what seems to happen is that women remain locked in the subsistence economy, while men become involved in the cash economy of the cities, and from then on the road is downwards, according to the rule that women's labour earns them less.[11] In industrialized countries today, women earn some 30–40 per cent less than men, and it matters not a great deal from this point of view whether the country is capitalist or socialist in character – the same kind of earnings gap exists.[12] This is because most political structures ignore the politics of gender, or tend to pay lip-service to the idea of gender equality by passing a few weak laws referring to the illegality of certain forms of sex discrimination, or exhort women already overburdened with domestic work to enter the paid labour force for their own good, when they are not really talking about women's own good at all.

The paradox of working more and earning less than men derives from the double meaning of work for women: working inside the home for love and outside it for money; maintaining the health of families through housework and by earning a wage. In Britain and other industrialized nations it now requires two incomes to maintain a family at the same standard of living provided by one income twenty years ago, [13] and many employed women are the sole breadwinners for their children or elderly parents. The notion that most of women's employment is accounted for by married women working for pin money or purely to escape the worst excesses of captivity in the home never had any real basis. It was a self-perpetuating myth rooted in the post-war sexism of social science, whose investigators found what the dominant mood of the culture told them to find, namely an apparently harmonious acceptance of the inequality model of family life. The idea of the family wage earned by a male breadwinner, with women's income as a luxury extra, is still the basis of many countries' tax, national insurance and social security systems – even though it has always been based on a fictionalized and therefore unreal middle-class view of the world. Further, the family wage presupposes an equal division of income inside the family. But the reality is income rarely divided so that women get their due share: women (and children) may well be in poverty when men are not. [14]

The relationship between the division of labour inside the family and the division of labour outside it has provided much fuel for theoretical debate. Which is the cause of which, and is it women's role in production within a capitalist economy that condemns them to relative disadvantage, or is it their role in reproduction within a patriarchal family that explains this continuing discrimination? Everywhere we see the interconnections between the two divisions of labour, and nowhere better than in the statistics of part-time employment, which the American sociologist Alice Rossi described many years ago as this century's panacea for the problems of women's disadvantaged social position. A part-time job individualized the problem by seeming to index a state of personal liberation, while actually, very often, representing further exploitation. In Britain, some 40 per cent of employed women work in part-time employment, an increase of 28 per cent since 1956. Part-time employment is a large factor in the low status and low pay of women's work. Women are not only concentrated in a small number of occupations, but in those in which both male and female workers tend to be poorly paid and poorly unionized. There is also home-working, working for pay at home, a 'solution' 'chosen' by increasing numbers of women and frequently carried out under appallingly unhealthy conditions.

A paid job may not signal liberation, but in the modern world it is an important basis for self-identity and self-esteem. The money it brings in is important and so is the kind of involvement in social relationships provided by it. That is the plus side, and supporting data come from various groups of studies on factors correlated with work satisfaction, on social factors in depression, and stress and employment. On the negative side, there is the interesting, but as yet unproven, suggestion that if women adopt male employment patterns they will lose the edge they have over men in life expectancy, and cancer and heart disease mortality – a kind of moral penalty for liberation, a reworking of the old Victorian idea that God will punish any woman who unsexes herself by doing anything except sitting or lying still with a blank mind and even blanker smile on her face.

We do not, of course, have any idea what would happen to men if they assumed women's typical double burden of unpaid domestic and poorly paid non-domestic work. Perhaps they would die less often, or perhaps their health would suffer through their not having been socialized to the role. Since domestic accidents are a leading cause of death among young and middle-aged adults, if men tried their hands at women's juggling act there would certainly be some shift in causes of death. It is an interesting reflection of the cultural trivialization of housework, that, when we think of fatal accidents, we think classically of the dramatic motorway collision, whereas the kitchen, seemingly a most innocuous place, is the place that ought to come to mind, the place we must all try to avoid if we do not wish to die in an accident.

Of the less fatal and more chronically painful effects of housework we know very little for a similar reason – that the overlap of housework and family life has underestimated the power of what happens in the home to shape life and death and public events. It is simply not the case that only the really momentous historical events and processes take place in the public power arena; this alternative truth being, of course, implicitly, if dishonestly, recognized by patriarchy in the enormous preoccupation that has grown up over the last 100 years with the impact of mothers on children's health. Mothers have been held responsible for everything bad and everything good about children, a conflating of female power that, significantly, men have hardly created a protest about. As mothers create children's personalities, so they also create adult personalities in such a manner that all conformity to, and all deviance from, social norms has been laid at women's door, from homosexuality to schizophrenia, from the stuff of which the Yorkshire Ripper or American Presidents are made, to his holiness the Pope – yes, even the Pope had a mother. This cultural fixation on mothers' ability to mould children's health and character has not been matched by any corresponding degree of concern with the impact of children on women's health. Indeed, the three questions of whether housework is good for women's health, whether motherhood is good for women's health, and whether marriage is good for women's health are three very basic questions to which we can only give partial answers because the assumption that domesticity promotes health in women has been an obstacle to serious research for a long time.

Women and Reproduction

The place of childbearing in women's lives, like the competing claims of patriarchy and capitalism as controlling structures, has been a theme of debate for feminists. Whether childbearing is good or bad for women's health of course cannot be answered without paying attention to the exact historical context in which it occurs; it is one thing to talk about maternity in Europe or North America 50 years ago or the Third World today, where maternal deaths due to childbearing were/are one or more for every 250 babies born, and another to discuss it in a context where death is rare, so rare, fortunately, that epidemiologists have been heard to mutter under their breath that they will have to find some other way than counting deaths to measure health. However, to speak of the risks to physical health and survival of pregnancy and childbirth, one must remember the contribution of induced abortion, contraception and sterilization. These aspects of women's health-care (or lack of it) have tended to make childbearing itself safer, but carry their own risks of death which need to be computed in order to get a complete picture of the impact of reproduction on the health of women.[15]

Having babies and trying not to have babies makes women sicker than men in terms of use of hospital and other medical services. But here the question arises as to whether the management of childbearing itself has fallen under a medical rubric because there is something genuinely sickening about the process of having a baby, or for some other reason. In short, whose idea was it to treat having a baby as an illness and was it a good idea? Taking the second part of the question first, there is no doubt that the rise of modern obstetric care has been accompanied by a fall in the mortalities of childbearing but (as is usual with such issues) there is little evidence on which to hang the belief that medical maternity care was what did it. This point was made, some years ago, by a British epidemiologist who observed that, whereas perinatal mortality had declined as the proportion of hospital deliveries had risen, the figures could be alternatively presented to show that childbirth got safer the shorter the length of time mothers stayed in hospital after the birth.[16]

The extent of medical surveillance over pregnancy and birth is virtually 100 per cent in most industrialized countries today – that is, all women attend for prenatal care and, in addition, the majority give birth in hospital. The extent of medical intervention in childbirth has risen exponentially over the last 20 years. In some European countries operative deliveries are now in excess of 20 per cent. The evidence as to the benefits of individual obstetric technologies such as ultrasound scanning, other prenatal screening tests, instrumental or caesarean delivery, induction of labour, etc., is equivocal, and an unexplained factor about obstetric technology policies is the enormous variation that exists between countries, between regions within countries, and even between hospitals and individual practitioners within the same region. This is a variation far greater than any 'biological' variation between different populations of women having babies.

Most of all perhaps we cannot answer from the available data three questions about reproduction and women's health. The first question is, What would have happened to the health of mothers and babies had the obstetric technology explosion not taken place: might survival and health, for example, have been even better than it presently is? The second question is, What will be the long-term effect on women and children of this level of use of technology in childbearing? Some consequences of a high level of technology are already making themselves felt: for instance caesarean section rates rise geometrically as one caesarean delivery becomes the reason for another in a woman's subsequent pregnancy. The third question, which cannot be answered so easily by an appeal to perinatal epidemiology (even an appeal to an appropriate perinatal epidemiology), is, What does it do to women to have their babies gestated and born so very much within such a closed structure of medical surveillance? It is hard to feel in control of one's body and one's destiny during 16 trips to the hospital antenatal clinic for the ritual laying on of hands by a succession of different doctors, none of them especially trained in the art of talking to the faces beyond the abdomens, or in the science of knowing about the interaction between mind and body, the connection between peace of mind and a competent cervix, or between emotional confidence and a co-ordinated uterus.

What we see involved here are issues of control and responsibility that come up again and again in looking at women's health. Who is in control of the process – of having a baby, of being ill, of determining the relative balance between housework and employment work? Who is responsible for the outcome of any choice that is made, and is it really a choice? At the present time it is not often women who are in control of matters affecting their own health, and this situation arises not only through the overall medicalization of life – a process which, after all, affects men too – but through the infantilization of women as incapable of taking responsibility for themselves. Pregnant women are especially seen as being incapable of taking responsible decisions on behalf of themselves and their fetuses. What this conference is about is women's resistance to the patronizing professionalized health-care formula that women cannot take responsibility for their own health and illness. It is, indeed, a paradox that, although women's lives are all about providing health for others, as users of formal health-care services custom decrees that they be no more than patient patients.

Turning to motherhood, we see this paradox written large. Infantilized in pregnancy, and delivered of their babies by others, women as mothers are liable to discover that the devotion of the state to the necessity of reproduction is too often a devotion in name only. Whenever the demand for out-of-home childcare among mothers is surveyed, it is found to be many times greater than its supply. Time-budget studies of the division of labour in the home are not convincing on the topic of men's willingness to share childcare and, in so far as men seem to be doing more for children than they were, they have chosen the more pleasurable aspects of childcare – playing with the baby rather than changing its dirty nappy, or playing with the baby so that mother can get the dinner ready: if more active fathering along these lines is good for health, the question remains as to whose health it is good for.

So there is a contradiction here at the heart of women's situation: women are both irresponsible and they have too much responsibility. They cannot make decision and have to make all of them. In the privacy of the home, and as mothers, women are powerful, but in public they are not, for always there is a relationship between power and responsibility. You cannot have power without responsibility, and the taking of responsibility brings power; this is why it is essential for women to resist the arbitration by anyone else on their behalf of their responsibilities in both health and health-care.

Medicalization of Women's Distress

The last of the three issues I extracted from the story of 'The Yellow Wallpaper' was the issue of the medical labelling of women's distress as mental illness.

Although women are physically healthier than men, it appears that they made up for this superiority by a certain mental instability. That is, when one looks at psychiatric admissions to hospital and at prescriptions for psychotropic drugs, women predominate over men. Hidden biases in the data are possible; thus it may be that unhappy or mentally ill men are more likely to be cared for by women at home than vice versa and/or that the greater help-seeking behaviour of women as against that of men leads them more readily to take their unhappiness to doctors. However, it does seem that when men and women present essentially the same symptoms to GPs the women are more likely to get a psychiatric diagnosis.[17] A clue to this mystery is provided by a study of doctors' attitudes to patients carried out in this country in the 1970s. In this study doctors were asked to say which types of patients caused them the most and least trouble. The least troublesome type of patient was defined as male, intelligent, employed and middle-class, with specific easily treatable organic illness. The most troublesome patient was female, not employed, working-class, described vaguely as 'inadequate', and possessing diffuse symptoms of psychiatric illness that were difficult or impossible to diagnose and treat.[18]

What this suggests to me is that a psychiatric or pseudo-psychiatric diagnosis is most likely to be dragged in when men are unable to understand the problems that women have. It is not accidental that the two main biological events placing women beyond men's understanding, namely menstruation and childbirth, have both generated psychiatric diagnoses in the form, respectively of premenstrual tension and postpartum depression. Since menstruation and childbirth are liable to make women ill, and all women menstruate and over 90 per cent of them give birth, the chances are that quite a lot of us will be out of action at any one time. The attribution to women as a class of mental instability is obviously highly consequential, since it affects one's claim to be a responsible person. Historically speaking, the evolution of these diagnoses of women's distress has gone hand-in-hand with a continuing cultural prejudice against the ability of women to hold responsible public positions.

The Catch 22 here is that, while the concepts of premenstrual tension and postpartum depression may have a particular meaning within medical discourse and in terms of the structures affecting women's health, some women do have problems in the lead-up to menstruation, and some do feel especially distressed after childbirth.[19] How do we recognize the subjective validity of the problem without enclosing it in a terminology that inhibits political insight? How do we name it in such a way that we remain interested not only in what the problem is, but in how it might be caused and in what might be done to prevent it on a social and not purely individual level?

HEALTH AS A SOCIAL PRODUCT

In an essay on 'Professions for Women', written in 1931,[20] Virginia Woolf described two particular obstacles she found had to be overcome in learning to be a writer. Although she was talking about writing, I think what she said is important for all women. Woolf described first of all a phantom with whom she had to battle in her writing. She called the phantom after the heroine of a famous poem, 'The Angel in the House'. The Angel in the House was the ideal woman – intensely sympathetic, immensely charming, very domesticated, completely un-selfish: 'if there was chicken she took the leg, if there was a draught she sat in it – in short she was so constituted that she never had a mind or a wish of her own.' This spectre of womanhood plucked the heart out of Woolf's writing, drained it of all strength, prevented her writing what she wanted to write. Many women recognize the same problem in themselves today. It is all too easy to hide behind the defence of femininity, and mask behind a facade of smiling and commendable altruism our own refusal to take ourselves seriously. The second obstacle Woolf confronted concerned something of even more obvious relevance to this conference, and that is the problem of telling the truth about the experience of one's own body. As a novelist, Woolf felt she had not beaten this problem, that no woman yet had, that the weight of convention, of male power and masculine history, was against such truth-telling.

Recognizing that health is a social product is a first task confronting women, as is to tell the truth about our own experiences. Our own experiences determine our health; they do so whether or not they are experiences which put us directly in contact with professional medical care, and whether or not professional medical care is able to provide any form of treatment which will make us feel better.

Not telling the truth about our experiences is equivalent to lying about them, and the social significance of lying is, as the American writer

Adrienne Rich,[21] reminds us, that it makes the world appear much simpler and also bleaker than it really is. Lying takes away the possibility of honour between human beings, and the possibility of growth and change. It destroys trust and contorts history.

Another challenge following from an acceptance of health as socially determined is that women take a wider degree of responsibility for their own health and health-care decision-making in the future, even if this means in part taking such responsibility away from medical professionals. In a way this is already happening with the growth of the self-help movement in health-care. What comes under the heading of self-help is, however, a mixed bag. Some of it is fairly accepting of the conventional division of labour, for example branches of the consumer movement in maternity care present themselves in terms of a defence of natural childbirth that sounds awfully like the Angel of the House; they may even worship charismatic male heroes along well-established angelic lines. But, on the other hand, other self-help groups could hardly be a more direct threat to the status quo, for example the early self-help gynaecology groups in the USA which led to women being placed under police surveillance because they had looked up their vaginas, an official response whose bizarre nature is perhaps only fully clear when one considers under what circumstances men might be subject to police surveillance for looking at their penises.[22]

HEALTH-CARE AND OPPRESSION

Finally, I want to say something about what it means for the health-care system to recognize that women are not simply prone to suffer from the last vestiges of an unequal social relationship with men, but in fact constitute an oppressed social group.

Most modern medical-care systems, whether financed on a state- or private-insurance basis, have not succeeded in distributing medical care equitably throughout the population. Class, ethnic and gender oppression are all political facts affecting health and illness and medical care. However, the oppression of women is unique among the three forms of oppression, in that women's function as guardians of the nation's health forms the central core of their oppression. Women's role in reproduction, their role as unpaid family welfare workers, the personal emotional support they provide for men and children – these activities, which are indistinguishable from the fact of being a woman in our culture, may also be said to encapsulate, to hold within them, the causes of women's ill-health. For example, a high proportion of physical problems in women (including maternity) are due to their habit of having sexual relations with men. I am thinking here not only of rape and marital violence, but of diseases such as cancer of the cervix, which are apparently associated not only with women's own sexual history, but with the sexual proclivities of the men with whom they live.[23] But, for example, most of all I return once again to the ghost of the Angel in the House. The emotional, political and financial *dependency* of women's family welfare role is perhaps their – our – greatest disablement today. In being carriers of our society's unsolved problems of dependency in human relationships – how to love one another without giving up one's autonomy as an individual – in carrying this cultural dilemma, women are not helped even to articulate, let alone put forward for serious consideration, their own interests.

When I said that health depends upon a moral basis of good social relations, I meant that the pursuit of health in a society in which one social group is systematically at a disadvantage in relation to another, is attempting the impossible. It is attempting to erect a healthy community on the basis of unhealthy, that is exploitative, human relations. Whether the exploitation is rationalized, maintained and mystified in the name of love – the phantom Angel in the House of Woolf's essay – is, in a sense, neither here nor there. In contemporary industrialized cultures female babies are not exactly thrown away, as they were in the past, but there is a painful metaphorical throwing away of women still. While this continues to be condoned, there will be no radical change. And not condoning it means combating the processes which I have been discussing: the medicalization of women's distress; the individualization of their problems; the infantilization of women. An isolated unhappy child is not a political threat to anyone. But the political energy of a socially involved adult prepared to accept conflict and contradiction as a part of life is, on the other hand, enormous.

These issues possibly matter more now than they have ever done. Economic recession combined with the cash and confidence crisis of Western medicine make women and health key words. Not all that women have gained in emancipation this century, but a good part of it, is threatened by new talk of bolstering the family, of a need to shore up the haven of community care for those who cannot care for themselves (what is community care but the work of women?) and of a need to take another look at the social costs of liberating women. All the traditional answers are the cheapest ones – of course. It is cheaper to edge women out of the paid labour force and traditional to say that nurturing others comes best to women. But we cannot say that these solutions are what women want, or what is good for the health of women. At the same time as the old answers are heard again, there is a growing and healthy recognition on the part of government of the need to curb the power of professionals to control people's lives. This offers a route even within conservative political dogmas to changing the traditional relationship between women and health-care.

None of the tasks ahead of us are easy, and all of them demand confrontation of the conflict endemic in social relations between people and professionals, women and men. In the end everyone has a stake in moving towards a more humane society where health and illness are not split off from the rest of experience, in which bodies are seen as connected to the environment, and minds and emotions are understood to shape the way bodies function; everyone also has a stake in appreciating the limits of science, and in understanding the new technologies of our brave new world. What we want *is* a brave new world, not a defunct, dispirited and depressing old one. What we want is a world in which women who ask for change are taken seriously.

16

Premenstrual Tension
The Depressed (for J. W.)

The medicalization of women's unhappiness as depression may be one of the greatest disasters of the twentieth century; but the reality is that many of us *do* feel depressed. Political awareness, like psychoanalytic understanding, doesn't automatically dispel the problem. These two poems are personal statements about these conditions. Both wrote themselves suddenly one particularly bad weekend in 1985, when I felt submerged in interminable life-events and incurable personal difficulties. And I even began to wonder what it is about some of us that encourages us persistently to attach the label of depression to our inner feelings, thus invalidating the outer world's injustices as a cause of these feelings.

Premenstrual Tension

there are pills to treat this condition
industries that make money out of it
doctors who profess authority about it
and women who menstruate

a walk in the park is good for people
and so is clean underwear and a joke in the bath
but some things are bad such as war
and also women get tense

the condition is thus a conjunction
of our genes and our jeans
bleeding is caused by chromosomes
and the garments of our culture constrain us

so periodically we erupt
in flurries of anger
breaking a few frying pans here and there
when what we should like to hear

is the pop of a champagne cork
hitting the ceiling
and letting it all out

The Depressed (for J. W.)

who hears the hardwood drill
at dawn, as the duck sing?
only us, whose eyes fill
at the mention of starlight
as green trees bend to a warm silver wind

who sees the cold early brightness
breaking over blank rooftops
cracking a sideways smile
at suburbia's silly ways?
only us, who fancy our own deaths

we are the ones who see skeletons everywhere
sharpish bones spittled with stinking flesh
they people the earth, are its only immortal souls
we fall over them in the night, find them in bookcases
or sometimes they just hit us from all sides
as things do in ghost trains, rattling through a black tunnel

our role being to live in such unlit places
smelling odours of time past
alive simply to our own childish intimations
of mortality; love, the appalling joke
standing there in its own bleached halo
like some wet angel a dog found in the park

look, see! here is the little pathway
amid the emerald fields, flashed by an opal sky
here the cornflowers and the daisies, the dewy coral roses
curled sweetly like a baby's finger
and here two figures moving hand in hand

it's all what you might call a still life
a pretty picture is a frozen crystal
it's unmeltable by anyone's tears
the world awash touches not
any really locked-up pain

pain makes the heart pound
the mind wander
gravity unreliable
touch disengaging

pain drives a fork through the heart
puts needles in the uterus
blood from the various parts is mixed
as it was anyway

dripping we know it's not us
who will clear up the mess
it's not our fault the blood is round our ankles
we are merely defenceless against it
what life has given life has taken away

look, see! the red rises in a tide beside us
outside and within it seethes to destroy us
and make us victims of our own misdirected energy

who, then, suffers their own silence
but the depressed, who weakly pleasure in it?

who understands how vacuous the sanctity
in the face of anyone, woman, man or child
but we, who wonder why the sun still rises?

17

Health-care Policy – Whose Priority?

One of the features of modern patriarchy is its rampant token feminism. Perhaps organized feminism should count among its long-term psychological effects a certain infiltration into the male ego, so that a token admission of the rights of women to be considered full human beings enters into men's vision of their own proper humanity. At any rate, what happens in academic and medical circles is that women are sometimes called upon, in preference to men, to represent the views of women as a collectivity, and this perception of gender-appropriateness causes a degree of scurrying around to locate women whose statuses as experts might be considered suitable for this role (the relevant considerers being, naturally, not the women for whom the token women speak, but members of the patriarchal order itself).

The following piece is part of this process. In order to help or hinder it on its way, the World Health Organization creates committees to consider what kinds of future health-care programmes are needed. These committees are international and interdisciplinary and are thus cumbersome procedurally, with language and other barriers obscuring the possibility of communication. For a brief time I was the European region representative on a Programme Advisory Committee concerned with maternal and child health: the reasons why I was demoted were never spelled out, but were thought by most people to be not unconnected with what I said. In fact I said rather little. My contribution, made in the

Source: Paper presented to WHO Advisory Committee in Maternal and Child Health, Geneva, 14–18 June 1982.

plushy bureaucracy of the Geneva headquarters, merely identified a few important issues in maternal and child health-care in the industrialized world. I was, and am, acutely discomforted by the disjunction between this perspective and that of Third World mothers and children, where death and not dissatisfaction is the major enemy. Representatives from Third World countries at this meeting spoke eloquently and sensibly of the basic political and social engineering needed to create a healthy environment for mothers and children. As Fritjof Capra has said, in *The Turning Point*,[24] while over 15 million people (mostly children) die of starvation each year, and 35 per cent of the world's population lacks safe drinking water, some of us have the insane temerity to be engaged in the pursuit of technologies not only irrelevant but actively injurious to health, from synthetic food additives to motor cars (causing accident death-rates 20 times higher than the death-rate in polio epidemics) to, of course, the whole monstrosity of military spending, which is now running at a level in excess of one billion dollars per day. This also means that some of us must express concern about the social and other effects of technologies that have not yet reached the stage of being the most immediately important health hazards to the majority of the population.

I am not going to attempt to deal in any systematic way with all the issues involved in determing the current health needs of mothers and children in the European region. This would take too long, but also might be ultimately unhelpful in enabling this committee to achieve its objective which is to decide which are the most important issues in the health-care needs of mothers and children today.

THE MEASUREMENT OF OUTCOME

Table 17.1 shows three alternative ways of measuring the outcome of childbirth: (1) by counting deaths; (2) by looking at physical illness and handicap; and (3) by attempting to assess what might broadly be termed 'psychological morbidity'. Counting deaths has, for some strange reason, been by far the most popular way of assessing outcome among those who have looked at the effectiveness of medical care for mothers and children. But it may not always be the most important measure of outcome for the mothers and children who use the health-care services. Thus, my main argument would be that any rational future policy for maternal and child health must pay far more attention to the second and third outcome measures.

Table 17.1
Unsuccessful childbirth: alternative outcome measures

Mother	Child
Mortality	Mortality
Physical morbidity	Physical morbidity
Psychological morbidity	Psychological morbidity

Why *should* this issue of the quality, as opposed to the quantity, of life have priority?

Death is a Relatively Rare Event

Perinatal and infant mortality rates vary a great deal within the European region, but in the industrialized countries they have reached the kind of low level that would not have been anticipated 10 or 20 years ago. We do not know what the limits are of medicine in terms of eradicating death. But we can see that if we evaluate health-care for mothers and children in terms of, say, perinatal mortality, we are saying something about the 13 or 9 or whatever, babies per 1,000 that die and *nothing* about the 990-odd per 1,000 babies that survive.

Psychosocial Considerations

Another reason for concentrating on the second and third measures of outcome *is the close relationship known to exist between the way bodies function physically on the one hand and the state of their owners' minds and emotions on the other*. Health and illness are not simply states produced or prevented by medical care. They are products of the social structure. The point I am making is a simple one: childbirth is a psychosocial event, and mothers and children are individuals and members of families rather than simply, or primarily, patients.

Consumer Protest

A third reason for assessing the effectiveness of maternal and child health programmes in terms other than mortality statistics concerns the protest that is evident in many industrialized European countries on the part of those who use the maternal and child health services. Over the last

10 years this so-called 'consumer' protest has reached a level that can no longer be ignored by the providers of care and the policy-makers. But what are the consumers protesting about? It is often said that they are complaining about the dehumanizing effect of some forms of health-care on the individual. I think that this is true, but I think it misses two very important points. The first is that, in many countries today, so-called health care increasingly has the opposite effect, that is, it makes people less, not more, healthy.

Take, for example, the relationship between the fate of the perineum during labour and breast-feeding. Table 17.2 shows that comfortable breast-feeding is not promoted by episiotomy. Indeed, in this and other ways, it is reasonable to see episiotomy as a form of genital mutilation, which is merely a new medical version of the old Third World practices of female circumcision and infibulation.

TABLE 17.2
Perineal comfort and breast-feeding

| | Pain in perineum affected breast-feeding: | | | |
	not at all %	a little %	a lot %	Total
Tear	68	23	9	100
Episiotomy/episiotomy + tear	42	40	18	100
Intact perineum	92	5	3	100

Source: S. Kitzinger, *Episiotomy* London, National Childbirth Trust, 1981.

A second theme that underlies the consumer protest in the field of maternal and child health is, thus, that many health-care procedures that mothers and children receive on a routine basis remain almost totally unevaluated; that is, their effectiveness is unproven.

If the providers of medical care for mothers and children are themselves uncertain about which procedures to use how often, it is hardly surprising that the users of care experience a certain crisis of confidence about the ability of the official health-care system to guarantee health or even physical survival. This is a major reason why there exists in most, if not all, developed countries, a network of alternative perinatal services. In some cases these services exist entirely outside the official system, for example, illegal lay midwifery in the USA, and in some cases they have been incorporated as elements *within* the system, for example, the use of 'Leboyer' birth techniques within maternity hospitals themselves. In the survey of these alternative services that is currently being undertaken by WHO, it seems that such alternative provision is most likely to arise when one or more of the following conditions are not met by the 'official' system; these conditions are: (1) attention to the *psychosocial* needs of mothers and children; (2) *continuity* of the personnel providing care; (3) some provision for mothers to feel *in control of* childbearing and childrearing; and (4) a relatively high and autonomous status for midwives as managers of normal childbirth. Thus, there has in many countries been an intimate relationship between the consumer protest and the feminist movement. The feminist movement as a whole has provided a profound critique of modern medicine, and of both the technical competence of doctors and their competence to pronounce upon women's health and illness. Feminists have used a variety of means in an attempt to repossess women's health-care, to put it back in the community of women. Because these attempts have been world-wide and because they tie in with other contemporary critiques of health-care, we cannot afford to ignore them.

This brings me to the second major issue I want to highlight in the health-care needs of mothers and children today:

THE NEED FOR HEALTH AND HEALTH-CARE

Care should be seen as the responsibility of the community as a whole rather than as the responsibility of one particular segment of it, namely the health-care, and particularly the medical, professions. This is a general statement that applies to the relationship between medicine and society in the second half of the twentieth century, but it must apply especially cogently to the field of maternal and child health for the very simple and oft-repeated reason that childbearing and childrearing are not in themselves pathologies. It is medical care and medical ideology that has defined them as such and now has to confront some of the unintended negative consequences of this definition. One such consequence is that people expect doctors to make them healthy instead of believing that they could and should keep themselves healthy.

As the medical profession in many countries has increasingly come to recognize that people will not avoid illness and unnecessary death unless they take responsibility for their own health, so it has responded overwhelmingly with one solution. This solution is a new version of the old idea that medical care is something you impose on people and it is that health education is something you also impose on people in order to make them take responsibility for their own health. It is because the magic solution of 'health education' as applied to mothers appears so rife at the moment that I want to say a word or two about it. Health education is an activity dominated by the ideologies of the professional providers of health-care. As such it is not intrinsically sensitive to the needs and perceptions of those who are being educated. Both the idea of health and the idea of education are political ideas, that is, they are embedded in the values of a particular social and economic system. Put more simply, what most programmes of health education *do not* do is begin from the baseline of how the individual in the community defines health or defines her or his responsibility for health.

One concrete example concerns smoking in pregnancy. In many industrialized countries this has been seen as a problem to which health education is appropriate, and in many – including my own – it is still seen this way. Health education programmes aimed at reducing maternal smoking rely on a particular model of individual behaviour which has been termed the knowledge-attitude-practice model. According to this model, if women are informed of the 'facts' about smoking and pregnancy their attitudes and then their practice relating to smoking will change. (Much the same model operates in other health education fields such as birth control.) But the model is based on false assumptions. We have no evidence that smoking mothers are ignorant of the so-called medical facts about smoking and pregnancy. It is assumed that *because* they smoke they are *ignorant*. It is *not* assumed that they smoke because they hold a different view of the facts, or that they have chosen for one good reason or another to take a particular health-care risk *and consider themselves fully responsible in relation to this risk*. The key issues are two: (1) a different version of the facts on the part of the mothers; and (2) maternal behaviour which is out-of-line with the medical model. It is dangerous to assume that these are evidence of maternal irresponsibility. On the contrary, what sociological studies in this area have shown is that mothers who smoke do indeed know about the medical argument that smoking is dangerous for mothers and children. However, they do not agree, and they do not agree on grounds *of evidence* – for example, that they themselves have smoked in previous pregnancies and had normal weight babies. That such evidence could be called 'personal' or 'anecdotal' does not mean it is not evidence. It is just evidence of a different kind. Perhaps more important, the moral condemnation of those who do not accept the conventional medical wisdom as *irresponsible* towards their children simply does not hold water. Again, studies of mothers' attitudes have shown that those who smoke do so precisely out of a *deep sense of responsibility*. Smoking is a way of coping with the stresses of their daily lives. A pregnant woman or a mother with a young child is a person with many roles and responsibilities. She does not just have a responsibility to that child, but a responsibility to herself, often to other children, often to her children's father, usually as a housewife and increasingly towards a paid work role as well.[25]

PSYCHOSOCIAL NEEDS AND HEALTH-CARE

So, finally, there is the theme that I think we now know to be vitally important in the domain of maternal and child health, and this is: *the desirability of considering the social position of mothers and children as a whole when defining their health-care needs*. Motherhood is an idealized state even in the sophisticated industrialized conditions of many European countries today. Childhood and children are implicitly viewed as sacred, as wonderful, as essentially good and pleasurable. But this is only one side of the coin. The other side is that motherhood is difficult and children can be a burden as well as a blessing.

Policy for maternal and child health needs to take account of both sides of motherhood and childhood. 'Health' for mothers and children is not simply a matter of providing efficient and satisfying medical maternity care, of providing a free and easily available birth control and abortion service; it is a matter also, for example, of making sure that sufficient out-of-family childcare exists for those mothers and children who need it.

The problem of day care may ironically be lessened in the short-term by growing unemployment among married women, who are seen as a dispensable reserve of labour in times of economic recession, but in the long run it can only become more acute as the financial and psychological need of mothers to work outside the home increases, and as the resources of the wider kinship network in meeting the need for childcare are further eroded in an industrial society. There is no point, in other words, in perfecting health-care services for mothers and children if these are seen in isolation from the social context in which mothers and children live, and in isolation from the need to provide for them financially and in other ways.

To summarize, I have three recommendations for future WHO policy in the field of maternal and child health: (1) to put the health-care system in its social context; (2) to pay attention to the self-expressed and self-perceived needs of mothers and children; and (3) to emphasize the urgent need for more of the right kind of research on the provision and use of health-care. The health services need to be humanized, but they also need to be rationalized. The problem, as somebody famous whose name I've forgotten once said, is not whether medicine *is* scientific, but whether it might be possible one day to make it so.

18

Adam and Eve in the Garden of Health Research

When I wrote 'Adam and Eve in the Garden of Health Research' I was particularly angry at my own local failure to get a research project on social support and pregnancy funded. (After the preliminaries, I resume this on p. 164.) This meeting, another World Health Organization exercise entitled 'Life Styles and Living Conditions and their Impact on Health', had an underlying agenda of rooting WHO policy more securely in social conditions and less in fantasies of medical omnipotence, and was sufficiently far away from home (in Höhr-Grenzhausen, Germany, a train journey up the Rhine from Frankfurt) for me to let my hair down about the inequities of British social science research funding.

Three years on, I have to say that the story had a happy ending. The unfunded project, located here in a miserable Garden of Eden, is now underway. Whether through persistence, political serendipity, a final short burst of bureaucratic imagination, simply a bit of money in the budget, or the kindness and intelligence of a few civil servants, somehow the project got funded, and a number of people became a little more optimistic about the future as a consequence. Needless to say, the poem that follows 'Adam and Eve' was written *before* this happened.

The Irish playwright George Bernard Shaw once wrote a play called 'Back to Methuselah', which is not nearly as famous as another play he wrote called 'The Doctor's Dilemma'. Medical sociologists often quote lines from 'The Doctor's Dilemma' because it is full of good lines about the proper

Source: Originally published in *European Monographs in Health Education Research* 5, 1983.

role of modern medicine. However, the Doctor's dilemma is not about lifestyles and health; the other play, 'Back to Methuselah' is more appropriate to this theme.

The play begins in the Garden of Eden, where the main characters are, not suprisingly, Adam and Eve. The first scene begins with Adam's discovery of a dead animal. Its neck is broken. Both he and Eve are upset by this warning that in the very midst of the paradise of life there is death. Eve thinks about the implications of this message for the two of them. 'You must be careful' she says to Adam, 'Promise me you will be careful'. By way of reply Adam says, 'What is the good of being careful? We have to live here for ever. Think of what forever means! Sooner or later', he goes on, 'I shall trip and fall. It may be tomorrow; it may be after as many days as there are leaves in the garden and grains of sand by the river. No matter; some day I shall forget and stumble.' And when he realises that something of this sort is bound to happen to Eve too he is even more horrified – because if she dies then he would be alone forever. 'You must never put yourself in danger of stumbling' he tells her, 'You must not move about. You must sit still. I will take care of you and bring you what you want.'

Of course Eve's response to this image of herself sitting still forever in case anything dangerous happens is to say she would soon get tired of it. She says to Adam that she doesn't really have time to worry about the risks of mortality – or immortality – because she's too busy thinking about Adam. She says to Adam, I have to think about you because 'You are lazy; you are dirty; you neglect yourself; you are always dreaming; you would eat bad food and become disgusting if I did not watch you and occupy myself with you.'[26]

What is the message of this scenario in the Garden of Eden? The first message is that the mortality of life is 100 per cent – or perhaps *more* than 100 per cent if one counts those who consider that they are born twice (and hence able to die twice). At any rate, this is a statistic not published by WHO, which is surprising because, as Adam discovered in the Garden of Eden, the prospect of living forever is absolutely *awful*. The second message is that even understanding this – that death at some stage in one's life from some cause is inevitable – does *not* mean that it's *necessarily* a good thing to live in such a manner that one's chances of survival and health are maximized. People do probably have a right to live in an unhealthy way, and even to die of this if that's what they choose. The third message is that whatever the individual decides about the best and most healthy way to live, it is quite possible that he or she will not be left alone to make this decision. Somebody else may make it on the individual's behalf – Eve on behalf of Adam, women in their capacity as lay health providers in the community or as professional health workers, governments on behalf of nations, even, ultimately WHO. The fourth message is one about control. Adam in the Garden of Eden is worried because he has no control over what is happening to him – whether he will live forever or not, whether he will die or not, *how* he might die.

These are aspects of the human condition. They are aspects of the human condition with which both social policy and health policy must deal. Since we now have this thing called 'research' which Adam and Eve did not have in the garden of Eden, one might suppose that policy would be based in a rational manner, not on guesswork, but on actually *finding out* what kind of policy is good for people – on research. This doesn't seem to happen, which is interesting. Why doesn't it happen? Is it because there is not enough research, or not enough of the right kind of research? Or is it because the people and organizations who formulate health policy and social policy do not really have the interests of all their constituents equally at heart?

I suspect that this last answer is the right one and I want to illustrate the relationship, or non-relationship, between research and policy by saying something about one particular subject, and that is the subject of lifestyles and pregnancy outcome.

LIFESTYLES AND PREGNANCY OUTCOME

The condition of pregnancy illustrates especially well the central issue with which we at this meeting are concerned, which is the interface between social life and biological functioning. What is the relationship between these two? How can we alter one, and if we do so, will it directly affect the other? What are the different models of the social –biological or mind–body relation operated by different professional and lay groups? I think we are also able to see from examining the social and medical treatment of motherhood just how social policy and health policy can quite systematically deny the importance to the individual of a sense of control over her or his fate, even in this new era of self-help health-care and personal liberation movements. Lastly, pregnancy is the major medical experience of most adult women; it is one in which they often for the first time really confront the importance of lifestyle, as opposed to (or as well as) medical care, in ensuring health.

The Puzzle of Healthy Motherhood

For something approaching 100 years it has been clear that risks of mortality in childbirth – for both mother and baby – are different in different social groups. At the end of the nineteenth century it was the socio-economic differential in *maternal* mortality that was noted; then in the early decades of this century attention in many countries shifted to *infant* mortality; why were there such big differences in the chances of infant death between countries, between different areas of the same country, and between groups with different life-circumstances within the *same* community? As infant mortality rates began to fall, makers of health policy turned once more to the problem of maternal death. Once the problem of maternal death began to be licked, a new problem – that of *perinatal* mortality was identified; perinatal fetal and infant deaths were those occurring between 28 weeks of pregnancy and the end of the first week of life. But, whatever index of obstetric mortality was taken – maternal or infant or perinatal – quite striking and unexplained differences emerged between the life- (or death-) chances of mothers and babies at different ends of the socio-economic spectrum.

The same is true today. In WHO 1978 Report *Social and Biological Effects on Perinatal Mortality*, for example, an association between perinatal mortality and socio-economic status was shown for all the countries covered by the report. There is a gradient in perinatal mortality rates by father's occupation which rises more or less continuously from the professional, technical and administrative to the agricultural and production groups. (The measure used is father's occupation, rather than mother's occupation, because of that strange constellation called social class which is assumed by statisticians to depend wholly on men's rather than women's work.)

So here we have an enduring puzzle. The puzzle is why healthy motherhood appears to be determined by the relationship that the husbands of mothers have to the occupational structure. What is the explanation? An oversimplification of the picture emerging from investigations carried out over the years would be that biologically the worst mother is one who has a low level of education, has attended no childbirth or parenthood education classes, holds a paid job, lives in crowded housing conditions on a low wage, is unmarried, sexually active, eats a diet of junk food laced with liberal amounts of poor quality alcohol and nicotine, and belongs to an ethnic minority group. By this I mean that each of these factors on its own has been shown to be associated with a raised risk of perinatal mortality.

That is what we *do* know, but it is not very much, and even a closer look at each of these associations reveals the picture to be a good deal more complex than it at first appears. For example, a working-class woman who smokes raises her chances of having a low birthweight baby, but a middle-class mother who smokes does not run the same risk of depressing her baby's birthweight.[27] Why? We don't know. In fact we do not know a great deal about which of those factors I have listed as associated with social class are the really dangerous ones in terms of posing a threat to health – either singly or together. Perhaps you can be unmarried and a heavy smoker as long as you don't have sex and you live in a four-bedroomed house, or conversely perhaps you and your baby will be alright if you sit down all day and write lectures even if you live off junk food. But even if we knew more about which factors, which aspects of lifestyle, were bad and which good, would we know *why*? How does a woman's poverty or unhappiness get translated into poor fetal growth, and why does smoking appear to affect some women's babies and not others?

HEALTH RESEARCH AND HEALTH POLICY

Perhaps the most striking thing about what we do know and what we don't know is that this lack of knowledge, this fundamental uncertainty about exactly how the social environment affects health, has apparently not been an obstacle to certainty. Individuals, institutions and funding agencies in the health field have pursued certain themes with an air of certainty about their relevance. Professional providers of health-care and makers of health-care policy have also not lacked conviction about what people or, in this case, women and children, need – about what is good for them and their health. Equipped with knowledge about how disadvantaged lifestyles predict bad maternal and infant health, many governments, policy-makers and medical professionals have pursued a policy of intensifying the *clinical* component of health-care for pregnant women. They have followed this course of action not only on the assumption that it is *not* the business of governments or doctors to eradicate social inequality, but in some places, for instance in Britain, on the assumption that high-technology medical care is actually able to *override* the adverse effects of social disadvantage.[28]

There seem to be two different competing theoretical models here. The first model, which we might call the *medical* model, makes the assumption that improvement in health requires medical care. The other model, which we could call the *social* model, makes a different assumption, namely that it is life in general that makes people ill and thus life in general that needs correction. Thus phrased, the two models are opposed, contradictory. They do not need to be seen that way, of course, but my argument is that advances in our understanding of the relevance of both models to the promotion of health are obstructed by a profound division within the culture of modern industrialized societies. To put it simply, there are people who believe in one model and people who believe in the other, and they belong to different professional groups. There are organizations and institutions for promoting one model and organizations and institutions for promoting the other, and they are different. Perhaps most crucially, the structure of research funding in many countries encourages an almost total division between research relevant to the medical model and research relevant to the social model. The World Health Organization has to be the great hope here, and I have to say that whereas I was not really clear before I came to this meeting what it was really about, I have now had my confusions sorted out. I now see very clearly just what a key role recommendation of the lifestyle concept has to play in bridging the gap between these two models, and hopefully leading to a situation in which people's health is improved because a *unification* has taken place between social policy on the one hand and health policy on the other.

So what about *research* which is policy-relevant in the sense of addressing the need to bridge the gap between social and medical models? I recently asked the British government or, rather, the Social Science Research Council (now the Economic and Social Research Council) as the body funding most social research in Britain, for £200,000 to do a piece of research which I think exactly addresses this issue. The Social Science Research Council did not react very well to my request – in fact they suggested that I should find something else to do because they didn't like the research design proposed. The reasons they didn't like it were, of course, complex. It was to be a relatively expensive piece of research on women, who in an economic recession can hardly be regarded as a 'growth' area – though maternity care itself continues to be in the news. But, more fundamentally, I suspect that the SSRC did not recognize the application as the kind of 'social' research they had been used to funding.

The basic idea of the research design was simple. The research was designed to test the hypothesis that being kind to pregnant women will result in a better outcome for them and their babies and, particularly, that it will result in the birth of *bigger* babies. Now, depending on your background and orientation (or which model you carry round in your head) you will either see this idea as brilliantly sensible or as obviously stupid. The methodology proposed for the research was that of a randomized controlled trial. What was on trial was kindness as an alternative form of antenatal care – alternative, that is, to the form of antenatal care which is currently practised in most places today. In the application to the SSRC I didn't call it kindness. I called it social support, and, of course, in defending the use of this term I refer to those many studies demonstrating that social networks and relationships supportive of the individual can be crucial factors in preventing illness and preserving health; or, to put it the other way round, the *lack* of such networks and relationships is a factor increasing an individual's vulnerability to illness. I am referring to a very wide range of studies here, from Meyer and Haggerty's documentation of stress as a factor promoting symptomatic streptococcal infection,[29] to Emile Durkheim's hypothesis, since validated, that anomie and social isolation are potentially suicidal states.[30]

The idea I had was to provide pregnant women with social support in the form of social science interviewers. Since the sample was intended to be women who had previously had a low birthweight baby, the research would also have addressed a major factor contributing to perinatal mortality and morbidity – low birthweight. In the course of the interviewing detailed information about lifestyles would have been collected – for instance, dietary information, data on 'work' hours (meaning by 'work' both employment and housework), information on housing conditions and self-perceived needs in relation to housing. Although the need for such detailed information is obvious, we have in fact very little of it because of the biases of research hitherto done in this field. Most such research has been based on the medical model, and has sought to examine the antecedent conditions of death, but only after death has happened. I forgot to mention that the main preoccupation of the medical model is with death. The Adam in George Bernard Shaw's play wasn't the only one to seize so happily on the certainty of death – clinicians, statisticians, epidemiologists and many others involved in research like death because it can be counted. Death is 'hard' data, a 'hard' outcome, not literally because rigor mortis sets in, but because there is rarely any doubt as to whether someone is dead or not. 'Soft' outcomes such as life, or the quality of life – outcomes important in the social model – are, paradoxically not so easy to measure. Mental health outcomes are, therefore, more difficult to quantify than physical health outcomes – or because of the dominance of the medical model, we tend to believe they are. The problem with research on death and lifestyles is a methodological one. Since you don't know who's going to die, you can only attempt to collect lifestyle data after the death has happened, when, for obvious reasons, it is difficult to get good quality information that is detailed and reliable. This is one main reason why we have so little lifestyle data – and it is certainly the reason why a *prospective* rather than *retrospective* approach is needed.

One more word about the measurement of outcome in either 'lifestyle' or traditional epidemiological research. How do you measure outcome – the outcome of a particular lifestyle, or medical care, or health education, or health promotion package? It seems to me that there is only one way to measure outcome, and that is in a lot of ways. It is particularly important to look at both biological and social outcomes. Thus, in my ill-fated research proposal I intended to examine the effect of the social support intervention – beneficial, hazardous or none – by looking at a wide range of outcomes, from the weight of the baby to maternal postpartum depression. Yet, paradoxically, the problem is that, rather than seeming attractive from a funding point of view because of its relevance to different perspectives, disciplines and policy interests, such research, is apparently seen in the opposite way, as awkwardly failing to fit the existing research funding framework. In Britain the three main funding bodies for health research are the Social Science Research Council, the Medical Research Council and the Department of Health and Social Security (the latter supporting specifically policy-relevant research). The same situation of a division between social and medical research funding interests exists, I suspect, in many countries.

HEALTH POLICY AND SOCIAL POLICY: THE WAY FORWARD

I would like to end by returning to two of the points I made at the beginning – the point about control and the point about the basic division of interests between those who formulate policy in the social and health fields, and those for whom it is formulated. These points are of course very closely related to one another.

Governments have an interest in the lifestyles and health of their people which is not necessarily the same as the interests of the people themselves. This is especially true of one half of the population, namely women, and it is, of course, also true of the working classes. In this sense the notion of a lifestyle is potentially dangerous, because it can be used to deny the reality of political relations – relations between classes and relations between men and women. There is no denying that the major health-related problems, even in what have been referred to as 'over-developed' countries, are those pertaining to social inequality. So far as inequality between men and women is concerned – a subject in which I have a particular interest – it is evident that, to date and with only a few exceptions, the interests of social and health policy-makers have not taken into account the personal needs of women as a collectivity, but have pursued a traditional idea of women as primarily wives and mothers locked in the family and responsible for everyone's health except their own. I am not convinced that this situation has changed a great deal recently. Women not only continue to provide much in the way of lay health-care: they are also still doing most of the childrearing, and much of the care of the elderly and handicapped. The reality of much 'community' care is an extra burden for women – it does not need to be, but that is the way it usually is. And, since we are now in the grip of an economic recession, this hard reality is unlikely to alter. Women have always constituted cheap or unpaid labour, and they still do so in the 1980s. The family is probably on the whole bad for women's health *because* it is good for men's and children's. Most social policy has incorporated a sexist formula of the family in which men are part of the public world and women relegated to a private one, and in this way most social policy has effectively been a health policy which has actually been detrimental to women's health. I am thinking here, of course, particularly of mental health. One consequence of taking on board the lifestyle concept is that no separation can be assumed between mental and physical health. However you look at it, mental health is important.

Talking about the hidden biases of social policy means talking about power. Here, there is no doubt that until there is a more even distribution of all forms of power between men and women, both social policy and health policy are likely to be subversive to women's interests. The fact that, for example, 75 per cent of workers in the British National Health Service are women, is about as relevant to the issue of who wields power as observing that 100 per cent of mothers are women. The significant variable is the low status of these two 'professional' groups – nurses and mothers.

What kind of research do we need in the future? First, we need research which links the biological and the social. What we do not need is 'research' in its literal meaning – an endless finding out of what we already know we don't know. We need, too, an imaginative rephrasing of the questions. For example, I think asking those questions which are the obverse of the ones suggested by the medical model could be quite illuminating.

Instead of asking people why they smoke, ask them why they don't smoke, for instance. This alternative approach may produce a different kind of answer, one that addresses *positive* conceptions of health.

Finally, I would like to draw your attention to the desirability of seeing enterprises such as this particular conference, and other related initiatives of WHO, within their broader cultural and historical context. The question before us is a question about the relationship between health and the way people live. It is a question about what we know and what we don't know, and a question about how to be certain in the face of uncertainty, that is, how to get health-care planners and political decision-makers on national and regional levels to take notice of the importance of people's own lifestyles when considering what kind of health-care is appropriate to them. But why are we asking these questions and setting ourselves these tasks? Why, for example, are we taking it as axiomatic that personal health is the primary definition of human wellbeing? What are the implications of such an approach for the emergence of that political consciousness that is necessary to change those social conditions that are detrimental to wellbeing – and health? Or to put it another way, if, even unintentionally, we medicalize unhappiness, do we thereby subvert the possibility of revolution?

The tension between social and biological explanations of ill-health has been evident in writing, research and practice for well over a century. In this sense the present concern with lifestyles is merely a revamping of the nineteenth-century idea of the public health, in which the main positive factor was considered to be the promotion of a 'sanitary' environment. When the British pioneer Edwin Chadwick carried out his *Inquiry into the Sanitary Condition of the Labouring Population of Great Britain* in 1842, he thought that 13 years would be added to the average expectation of life of the working classes by improving town drainage, clearing the streets and houses of refuse, and securing a better and cleaner water supply.[31] It is interesting that, in an era preoccupied with moral propriety, Chadwick saw the securing of a sanitary environment as the first priority, but one from which a heightened individual morality would necessarily follow. Perhaps this is the obverse of the idea that a new *individual* responsibility for health will lead to a political movement for a more sanitary environment. At any rate, we can be certain that there is a close relationship between private health and public health, even if, for some of the reasons I have discussed, we have so far been prevented from discovering the exact nature of the relationship.

I am going to end by quoting from one of my heroes, William Farr, who was statistician to Britain's first Registrar-General in the 1830s, and who pioneered the collection and analysis of health and population data. His aim was to promote the understanding of the causes of death with the further aim of understanding how to preserve and extend life. 'The laws of life,' wrote Farr in his 'Vital Statistics' published in 1885,

> are of the highest possible interest, even if the knowledge of those laws gave men no more power over the course of human existence than the meteorologist wields over the storms of the atmosphere or the astronomer over the revolutions of the heavens. . . . It is clear that conservative medicine [by which he meant preventive medicine], rendered more efficient by reason of social institutions, must in the long run banish transmissible and contagious diseases, as well as maladies due to climate, diet, [and] occupation. . . the hope of relief may be extended to all other diseases whose remote causes may probably be recognised. Now, is it absurd to assume that this perfectability of man will go indefinitely through endless ages? . . . The great source of the misery of mankind is not their numbers but their imperfections and their want of control over the conditions in which they live. The exact determination of evils is the first step towards the remedies.[32]

19

A Persisting Ridge of High Pressure

A Persisting Ridge of High Pressure

a persisting ridge of high pressure
hovers up there somewhere
bisects a blue sky stretched tightly under silenced stars

even the trees feel it
indolently straddling the sprawled bored houses
their branches ending in small sharp needles, a

leaf crackling in the eye of the sun
sun, sun, who tells no one
of wasted gold spilt on a sterile landscape

holding the weather
taughtly in a single beam
with a touch like a pope's lullaby

sun, designing storms and rainbows
vesuvius and hurricanes in Paris
pockets of cloud stuck on a slippery mountain

pressure packed into persisting ridges
on an unseen horizon

20

The Doctor's Problem

Like patients, doctors have many problems. However, unlike patients, doctors tend not to talk publicly about their problems – although it is reasonable to believe that their high rates of alcohol and drug addiction and suicide are not only due to their privileged access to strategies for self-destruction, but also represent some of the strains of their profession. In *Healing the Wounds*, David Hilfiker takes the unusual step of describing what it feels like to make medical mistakes. For example, a pregnancy wrongly diagnosed as 'nonviable' and scraped out of a protesting uterus: telling the fetus's parents was 'one of the hardest things I have ever been through. I described in some detail what I did and what my rationale had been. Nothing can obscure the hard reality: I killed their baby.' Such open disclosure goes against the grain of a profession-trained to hide and deny: 'Doctors hide their mistakes from patients, from other doctors, even from themselves.'[33]

One problem doctors have is securing their own job satisfaction in circumstances which frequently seem to militate against it. In the next piece I suggest that this drive towards occupational satisfaction explains some features of current maternity practice that otherwise remain inexplicable. Although this is a less contentious theme than medical mistake-making, some of what I said seemed to be greeted as an untoward indiscretion by some people in the Californian audience where the paper was first given. Preoccupied with escalating risks and costs of litigation, doctors in California support lawyers, not social scientists. In obstetrics the issue has become who owns the right to determine the destiny of

Source: Originally published under the title 'Doctors, Maternity Patients and Social Scientists' in *Birth* vol. 12, 3, 1985, pp. 161–6.

fetuses; to say that doctors may be driven to claim this right partly because they want to be happy is liable to come across as iconoclastic and irreverent, or at least bizarre. The idea that personal feelings inform professional conduct challenges the root ethic not only of medicine but of all specialized occupations.

It has been said that history proceeds by changing the subject, rather than by a rational progression from one state to the next, or by the dialectical process of 'doing, undoing, and reassembling things'.[34] In the early nineteenth century, and even the early part of the twentieth century, doctors and midwives who provided care for childbearing women made no hard-and-fast separation between clinical success and the patient's satisfaction.[35] But as time has advanced so the profession of obstetricians has turned in on itself and focused more and more exclusively on biological and clinical influences and effects. By the 1980s we even have babies described as 'the obstetrical product'. Over the horizon of this newly technological phase of perinatal medicine then came the consumer organizations, in uneasy and sometimes unspoken alliance with social scientists who wanted to change the subject and talk about the rights of women to make choices in childbirth, and other such liberal-romantic distractions. Now I think we are at a stage where it is at least possible to unravel and integrate these different points of view, rather than merely change the subject again. Let us concentrate on two closely linked themes. The first is the meaning of the current debate about hard versus soft outcomes.[36] The second is why so much is heard (on one level) about patient satisfaction and why so little is done about it, and why so little, correspondingly, is heard about the satisfaction of doctors when this is so clearly a powerful, albeit invisible, influence on patterns of obstetric care.

THE HEALTH-CARE DIVISION OF LABOUR

The most obvious division of labour in perinatal care is between people who are paid to provide obstetric care – doctors, midwives, nurses, paramedics and so forth – and those who are not paid – so-called 'patients' and their families. This division of labour is one example of a general rule observable in all health-care. This rule is that a great deal of health-care is done by people who are neither paid nor acknowledged for their performance of this task. Indeed it is a predominant myth of the modern age, an aspect of the 'theology' of medicine, to use Thomas

Szasz's term,[37] that the only people who can care for health are those who have been formally trained and licensed to do so. (And our belief about the impropriety of lay people caring for health is, of course, why we are in such a technological fix about such matters as health education and health promotion; having said health is something people get from the medical and allied professions, we are now trying to get people to supply it for themselves while at the same time keeping the professions in business.)

One of the consequences of this paid/unpaid division of labour in health care is unequal status between these two groups, both in general and in relation to specific issues such as the evaluation of care. In maternity care policy, as in medical care policy overall, a clear division holds between clinicians' autonomy to determine treatment and patients' attitudes to treatment. It is within this frame of reference that the attitudes of patients have traditionally been accommodated. To cite an accurate, although sexist, analogy used by Freidson:

> It is as if the housewife could choose the store she wished to patronize but not which of the articles in the store she could buy. The choice is made for her by those who run the store on the basis of their conception of what she 'really' needs which may be no articles at all, articles she does not want, or, if she is lucky, just what she wants.[38]

In the literature on doctor-patient interaction there are some stark illustrations of constraints on patients' freedom to influence their medical care. In a study of 2,500 general practitioner-patient consultations in England, for example, the theme of doctors resisting any challenge to their expertise is manifested thus in one interaction where a patient is dissatisfied with the diagnosis given by the doctor. The doctor reacts by saying: 'I will tell you what is wrong with you, I will tell you what your symptoms are, and I will tell you what to do. I am the doctor and you will kindly not forget that fact.'[39] Most interesting of all, when the tape recording of the consultation was played back to the doctor in question he said he could remember clearly what the patient had said but he had no recollection at all of his own reaction.

ARE DOCTORS SATISFIED?

Naturally, it is unfair to quote an isolated instance of one doctor-patient consultation that obviously got out of hand. However, such examples serve to make an important point. This point was framed by Cassell, writing on the philosophy of healing some years ago in the following terms: '. . . we, as a society, have come to associate the doctor and his technology so closely and to attribute such power to the association that we have difficulty in seeing them separately when such a separate view is necessary.'[40] Generalizing from this, it could be said that a comprehensive evaluation of medical care or of obstetric care must include both the technical efficiency and effectiveness of medicine on the one hand, and its social relations on the other. Most importantly, it must not mistake one for the other. We need to know, for instance, not only whether particular therapies work, but how important the social relations of doctor and patient are in making them work or in explaining why they do not work – an issue that is, of course, particularly well addressed in the literature on placebo effects.[41] In attempting this degree of understanding I would argue that we must be as concerned with doctors' satisfaction as we are with patients' satisfaction. In fact, I would go further than this and observe that obstetric practice as an entity cannot be understood without appreciating that doctors are motivated by personal and professional feelings, and, among these feelings, perhaps the most influential is the need to maximize her or his own job satisfaction within a framework in which the major 'quality control' over obstetrical work is exercised by the somewhat fragile brake of 'peer review'.[42]

In her national survey of induction in England and Wales in the mid-1970s, Ann Cartwright[43] collected some interesting data on obstetricians' attitudes to induction, which are buried in the last chapters of her report on the study and are not often referred to by those who use it. A sample of consultant obstetricians were asked open-ended questions about the advantages and disadvantages of induction. Nearly half said that in their view it had increased the job satisfaction of obstetricians because it had enabled more planning of deliveries, tidier departments, and *happier* mothers. At the same time some of the consultants contradicted themselves and three out of five said induction had not improved the experience of childbearing for women, or had actually made it worse. When Cartwright looked at obstetricians' views on induction according to gender, age and type of appointment (university versus National Health Service) she found women doctors and those in university appointments somewhat less in favour of induction (there was no clear trend with age). The doctors in her sample were also in favour of epidurals as increasing their own job satisfaction and were surprisingly certain about the effects on the patients of these interventions. For example, two-thirds stated that induction for non-medical reasons would have no effect on mothers' health or on the relationship between mothers and babies. Cartwright found that fewer than one in five midwives (compared to half the obstetricians) said that induction had increased their own job satisfaction.

These data belong with a wide range of others showing the importance of what could broadly be termed 'social' factors in determining the clinical behaviour of medical professionals and others engaged in providing care for sick or pregnant people. Perhaps my favourite among these studies is the one that analysed the educational background of British doctors in different medical specialties and found that those who in their youth had been to public (i.e., private) schools were more likely than others to work on living bodies rather than dead bodies, on the head rather than on the lower trunk, on male bodies rather than female bodies, and on the body surface rather than inside.[44] This raises the pertinent question of whether, and how, doctors are satisfied. What do doctors really want?

'PATIENT SATISFACTION'

What *is* satisfaction? How can it be measured? One way *not* to measure it is illustrated in a somewhat more exciting area of study, that of human sexuality. The pioneering work of Alfred Kinsey and his colleagues in the 1950s told us much that we did not know about the sexual behaviour of human beings, mostly because Kinsey and his team went into the community and replaced 'soft' speculation with 'hard' data. However the team also committed some errors. In one special research project the object was to find out which areas of the female genitals were most sensitive to sexual stimulation. To achieve this end, three male and two female gynaecologists touched more than 800 women at 16 different points, including the clitoris, labia, vaginal lining and cervix. In order to be appropriately impersonal and scientific the gynaecologists did not use their hands; they used cotton swabs. These produced a response in the clitoral area but not in the vagina, which, as we now know (and presumably some women knew then), is sensitive not to soft touch but rather to deep pressure. The researchers thus concluded, on the basis of an inappropriate methodology, that vaginas are insensitive, a myth propagated until Masters and Johnson came along with the more appropriately sensitive measuring instrument of the laboratory observation of human sexual behaviour.[45]

A broad but appropriate generalization from the 'patient satisfaction' literature would certainly be that most obstetric patients – ranging from 60 to over 90 per cent in different studies – say they are satisfied when asked somewhat unspecific questions about their satisfaction with care.[46] In this respect it is reassuring to know that obstetric patients resemble other patients of the same sex and age.[47] This is partly because most patients do not readily admit to basic dissatisfaction with their care. In an exactly parallel fashion, most people, when asked by a researcher, will say they are happy.[48] The reason is presumably the same in both cases: there is little point in admitting to dissatisfaction unless there is some hope of changing the status quo. Readiness to declare dissatisfaction rises proportionately with the personal opportunity to bring about change. And most people are not in a position, at least in the short-term, to change very much in their lives.

Patients may often feel an incentive to make the relationship work; they like the doctor; they cannot easily change doctors; they do not want to get involved in unpleasant hassles in pregnancy, and so forth. Not surprisingly, then, the highest rates of 'satisfaction' are reported in studies where patients are asked about their satisfaction in a medical setting by medical personnel or in a context which is unambiguously that of medical sponsorship.[49] At one extreme is the patient 'satisfaction' rate of 95 per cent reported by a doctor in a 'short internal study' of an antenatal clinic. In answer to the question, asked in the antenatal clinic by a staff member, 'Do you understand what your doctor has told you?' 95 per cent of women said yes.[50]

In another study, 87 working-class women were asked (at home, by a social scientist) the meaning of 13 common obstetric terms such as breech, membranes, rhesus, and so forth. A group of physicians was also asked (in hospital, by a social scientist) which of these terms they would expect such patients to understand. Results of the study indicated an 'overwhelming underestimation' by the physicians of working-class patients' ability to understand what they, the doctors, were talking about. I cannot avoid mentioning that the male physicians thought the pregnant women considerably more ignorant than did their female colleagues.

Rates of patient 'satisfaction' are considerably lower in non-medical studies.[51] In Cartwright's study of hospital care 61 per cent of patients interviewed by a social scientist in their own homes after discharge from hospital complained they had not been able to get adequate information about their treatment.[52] Direct rather than open-ended questions apparently produce more dissatisfied patients.[53]

An excellent rundown on the different data-collecting methods and their variable yields is provided by Cartwright in her recent book, *Health*

Surveys,[54] which addresses the role of small scale, more qualitative research studies as useful to provide insights and hypotheses to be tested in larger-scale work. Smaller-scale studies are especially likely to be illuminating on the difficult question of alternatives to existing forms of care. Large-scale and questionnaire surveys have an inbuilt conservatism. They do not allow people to range freely in the realm of their more utopian visions of prenatal clinics, delivery rooms, and obstetrical or midwifery bedside manners.

It is unlikely that the statistically common and personally disabling 'soft' outcome of postpartum depression, for example, will be tapped satisfactorily in a large questionnaire survey, and certainly its antecedent social and medical care factors are unlikely to be found using this approach.[55] Another criticism of large-scale quantitative work is that the global rates of patient satisfaction found in these studies may conceal a large range of different rates in different subgroups of patients. Furthermore, they are able to give us absolutely no information about what patients expect or want from their medical encounters. What patients expect has been shown significantly to affect satisfaction levels.[56] Although continuity of care is a feature of patient expectations that is predictive of high satisfaction among obstetric patients,[57] other studies demonstrate that what patients are after is good clinical care together with intelligible and unpatronizing information about what doctors are doing. This may be one explanation of an aspect of patient behaviour infrequently set alongside the patient satisfaction data which very much deserves to be. While most patients may *appear* satisfied, between 19 and 72 per cent – an average of 30 per cent – do not take the medications prescribed by their doctors. They are 'drug defaulters'[58] (though who actually is defaulting here would seem very much an open question).

Doctors, Patients and Social Scientists

In the debate about the management of childbirth over the last 20 years the spectre of 'the happy mother' has emerged to haunt hospital corridors, medical journal editors, and the hidden recesses of the obstetrical mind. The opposition between 'hard' and 'soft' outcomes is personified in the idealized objective of 'healthier babies and happier mothers'. The problem of how to achieve both at the same time or even, in some quarters, *whether* to, suggests that we are victims of a 'two culture' dilemma. Child-bearing women and their families on the one hand, and those who manage childbearing on their behalf on the other, bring different sets of cultural baggage to their mutual encounters, and these encounters are often experienced in confrontational terms for this very reason.

To what extent might social scientists offer a bridge between doctors and childbearing families? Studies of how pregnant women felt about their care have been a main strand in medical sociological work.[59] Some social scientists have observed doctors,[60] or analysed the structure and power relations of medical professions, the state and society.[61] But these professional exercises have proved quite challenging, because doctors have a certain reluctance to be studied, or to give information to 'outsiders' about their practice.[62]

Moreover, communication is not an art taught in medical school; it is, rather, one that appears to be actually bred out of medical students in the course of their training programmes. As an illustration, there is the well known tendency of doctors to present different faces to patients from different social class groups.[63] Social scientists are therefore best known for their research on obstetric patients, and most of these researchers have been women. As a result of this division of labour, social scientists have tended to play an awkward kind of marital counselling role in the difficult interplay between doctors and patients. Some of us are better marital counsellors than others. But it is an essential element in the counselling process that attention is paid to the perspectives of both partners in the communication difficulties that have developed between them.

CONCLUSION

I do not believe that a satisfactory mode of assessing and integrating soft outcomes will be found merely by co-opting into randomized controlled trials or such methodologies a few questions about what mothers think about this or that procedure. The relations between the profession of medicine and the profession of social science fortunately have a good deal more potential than that.

In the words of one social scientist, Richard Titmuss, written 30 years ago in an attempt to bridge the growing gap between medical power and social needs:

> Scientific medicine has let into clinical medicine a new spirit of criticism and questioning. . . . The danger is, however, that in the stage through which we are now passing a new authoritarianism will replace. . . the old

one . . . for the greater the expectations we place on the doctor the more may we strengthen his [sic] need to maintain his role, and, while attempting to satisfy others, satisfy himself. . . . There is a danger of medicine becoming a technology. . . . There is the problem of medical power in society; a problem which concerns much more of our national life than simply the organization of medical care. . . . The task of the future is to make medicine more 'social' in its application without losing in the process the benefits of science and specialized knowledge.[64]

21

On the Importance of Being a Nurse

Just as in the world-wide provision of health-care women are more important than men, so nurses are quite indisputably more important than doctors. But just as public opinion is moulded by the dominant reverse view, so too medical sociologists are unlikely to approach their researchers unencumbered by prevailing value-judgements and mis-conceptions. The last piece in this section of the book is a personal confession of blindness to the importance of nursing, and a serious effort at persuading nurses that the model of professionalization is not necessarily the best one to follow.

The problem for women trying to escape their cultural destiny is that the escape routes are already marked by cartographers whose own view of the perfect destination takes no particular account of women's situation. In order to stop being women in the debased feminine sense, we are tempted to become like men. We don't exactly wear suits but we do carry briefcases and wear trousers; or we find ourselves engaging in behaviour and attitudes unsympathetic to the interests of those who haven't even got round to thinking about escape routes. In other words, the fact that nursing is a low-status feminine occupation has to do with the fact that most nurses are women; and the best remedy may not be to turn it into a profession of militant careerists. This is a difficult message, and it by

Source: Originally given under the title 'On the Importance of Being a Nurse: nursing and the health-care division of labour, past, present and future' at WHO Symposium on Post-Basic and Graduate Education for Nurses, held in Helsinki, Finland, 4–8 June 1984.

no means amounts to advocacy of an economically depressed position. But challenging the ethic of professionalization is, nevertheless, an important part of the feminist challenge.

This message did not go down particularly well at this conference on 'Post Basic and Graduate Education for Nurses' in Helsinki, although the climate in which the meeting was held, the Finnish summer with days scarcely turning into nights, at least encouraged a spirited longevity in our discussions.

Illness and suffering are part of the human condition. They create dependency, for to be sick and in pain is to be dependent on, and vulnerable to, others. The very persistence of this dependency throughout history provides a motive for the rise of all forms of health-care. All health-care has a common aim, namely the relief of human suffering.

Nursing fits into this picture somewhere, though just where it fits depends on the time and the place and is, to some extent, in the eye of the beholder. Nursing needs to be looked at within two forms of the division of labour: the division of labour in health-care, and the division of labour between the sexes. In what ways are nurses different kinds of people from doctors, or patients, or other health-care workers? What is, or should be, their particular contribution to the relief of suffering in any community? The second question is contained in the first, for no one can really pursue a definition of nursing without examining the relations between the role of nurse and the general position of women.

The reason for asking these questions is not merely academic. In many countries of the world, health services are now in a state of crisis. There are two edges to the crisis. One is economic; a growing failure to match the demand for medical services with available economic resources. The other factor is a crisis of confidence in the ability of medicine to deliver the goods: adequately to prevent illness, to prevent disability and death when illness does occur, and to do so with treatments and technologies that are not more damaging than beneficial to the lives of patients.

THE INVISIBLE NURSE: A PERSONAL AND PROFESSIONAL APOLOGY

In a fifteen-year career as a medical sociologist studying medical services, I have to admit to a certain blindness with respect to the contribution nurses make to health-care. Indeed, over a period of some months spent observing health-care work in a large London hospital, I hardly noticed nurses at all. When I sat there with my notebook and tape recorder, watching doctors and patients interacting, nurses were around somewhere in these scenarios; I took their presence for granted (much as, I imagine, the doctors and patients did) – but the character of the nurse's role in no way impressed itself on me. If this sounds a bit like Florence Nightingale's definition of a good nurse – an invisible, good woman – then perhaps we should not be too surprised. In many ways, history *has* defined a good nurse as a good woman, and this can be counted as both the weakness and the strength of nursing as a profession.

Having apologized for not noticing nurses in my professional role, I shall now attempt to salvage my reputation by telling you when I did seriously begin to notice them. About seven years ago I was in hospital, in a cancer ward, as a patient. As a cancer patient – I believe that is what we are called – I suffered from the usual, well-documented inability to obtain information about my condition. Doctors tended to lapse into mystifying technical-medical language in front of me, and my 'illness' was treated as a mechanical malfunction of my body without implications for my mind, my feelings, or my life. Of course I can describe my experiences accurately now, but at the time I was in a profound state of shock. I remember silently crying in front of the consultant the day the tumour was diagnosed. All he said was, 'what are you crying about? The treatment won't affect your appearance.' My appearance was not what I was worried about.

After that, I didn't cry again until the moment when I discovered the importance of nurses. I was lying in bed with a radioactive implant stitched into my tongue, and suddenly my resolve to face with a calm equanimity the experience of having cancer deserted me, as I realized I might, simply, not survive that experience. A young nurse came into the room to fetch the remains of my lunch, and she saw that I was distressed. Instead of taking my lunch tray away, or offering me drugs for the pain I was in, she sat down on my bed and held my hand and talked to me. I told her how I felt and after a while she went away and read my notes and came back and told me everything that was in them, and that, in her, of course unmedical view, I would probably be all right. She stayed with me for nearly an hour, which she should not have done. I was radioactive and no one was meant to spend any longer than 10 minutes at a time with me. She was also, presumably, not supposed to tell me what was in my case-notes, so she was breaking at least two sets of rules. I never saw this nurse again after I left hospital, but I would like her to know that she was important to my survival.

Since then, I have read some of the literature on communication with cancer patients. I have learnt, for example, that less than 1 per cent of cancer patients' discussions with doctors concern emotional or psychological well-being.[65] Many patients see their doctors as being too busy and interested only in their physical condition.[66] Both doctors and patients tend to define a 'good' patient as one who is compliant, and superficially cheerful. A patient who is openly distressed is as much a problem patient as one who is refusing to take her pills.

The moral of this story is that medical care is only a part of health-care. Caring for someone's health means more than removing bits of disordered tissue, or bombarding the body with drugs and other 'therapeutic' influences. Above all, it means relating to the ill person as a whole person whose psyche is equally involved with her or his soma in the illness in question. This is the substance of many modern critiques of medicine. Ivan Illich, in his much-quoted *Medical Nemesis*,[67] observes that among the human experiences now 'medicalized' as the subject-matter of medical work is pain. Under the medical regime, pain becomes merely a technical problem of the body, rather than an experience with an inherent personal meaning. This is not to say that people should suffer pain, but it is to say that pain is something felt by the individual and not simply within the diseased organ or body. Thus the relief of pain involves communication with the individual who feels it. A chemical intervention at the level of the body is not enough.

NURSING IN THE HEALTH-CARE DIVISION OF LABOUR

It has, at times, been enormously difficult for medical practitioners to ignore the potent relationships between bodies on the one hand, and minds and environments on the other. In order to do so, they have had to put on one side a great deal of evidence pointing to the social causation and prevention of disease – from studies showing the connections between life-events such as family arguments and the onset of infections such as streptococcal sore throats,[68] to the presence of 'stress' chemicals in the blood and urine of unemployed men whose wives are not being especially kind to them.[69] The 'placebo' effect in medical treatments themselves has been known for a long time to be often equal to the direct therapeutic effect of medical interventions, whether the focus of the treatment is pain,[70] preterm labour,[71] or apparently technical disorders such as urinary incontinence.[72] 'Placebo' means literally 'I shall please.' As evidence emerges about the mechanisms whereby the placebo effect may cure illness, it is becoming clear that the patient's belief in the efficacy of the 'treatment' causes that 'treatment' physically to alter the body's condition. An especially vivid demonstration of the placebo effect is Norman Cousins'[73] description of how he cured his own crippling illness – ankylosing spondylitis – in 1964. He did this with two under-rated therapeutic tools: vitamin C and laughter. With large intravenous doses of vitamin C, and a few Marx brothers films, Cousins' blood sedimentation rate dropped, he no longer needed pain-killing drugs, and was eventually restored to health (although he rapidly had to move out of hospital because his laughter disturbed the other patients, who were getting more orthodox forms of medical care).

Despite this evidence as to the impact on health and happiness of what has been called 'therapeutic trust', the prevailing model of health and illness today is the one that says medical care cures illness and preserves health. This model is closely tied to the evolution of the medical profession itself: the medical profession derives its legitimacy, its claim to fame, if you like, from its promise to cure illness with those resources that it, as a profession, exclusively controls – potent drugs, surgical operations, and complex, sometimes alienating technologies. But when we come to consider the history of nursing, we do not see at all the same relationship between what nurses do, or claim to do, on the one hand, and the curative model of medicine on the other. The origins of nursing lie in a totally different model of health and illness, namely the environmental one.

Nursing began to emerge as a separate occupation in the mid-nineteenth century. At that time, it was no more and no less than a specialized form of domestic work. Middle-class people did not use hospitals when members of their households were ill, but employed private nurses at home. Hospitals were for the sick poor, and in them nurses did everything doctors didn't do, and also quite a lot of what we, in the twentieth century, are accustomed to think of as medical work (while very junior doctors also did some nursing work). Most hospital nurses were married women doing for patients what they did at home for their families. In addition, the dividing line between nurses and patients was blurred, and able-bodied convalescent patients were expected to help nurses with the domestic work of the ward. In one nineteenth-century London hospital, patients who failed to do this lost a whole day's meals for a first such offence and were abruptly discharged from hospital for a second.[74]

Having been a domestic servant was the only qualification required at this time for ordinary nursing, except that, once taken on, these women were also taught how to make poultices, an absolute neces-sity in the pre-antibiotic era. Hospital administrators of the period wondered what on earth nurses would do if they were deprived of

heavy domestic work and if they only had to administer to the sick. Even
in the early professional training schools, competence at pudding-making,
the making of bandages and the understanding of ward-ventilation were
regarded as necessary skills for nurses to have. Conditions of work for
the early nurses were poor, and nurses were expected to sleep on the
ward, and were not provided with meals when on duty. It was hardly
surprising, therefore, that some nurses were accused from time to time
of stealing the patients' meals, and that Florence Nightingale, with her
apt turn of phrase, remarked that nursing was done by those 'who were
too old, too weak, too drunken, too dirty, too stolid, or too bad to do
anything else'.[75] While food was not provided, alcohol *was* often given
as part of the nurse's wages, or in return for particularly disagreeable
work. A nineteenth-century British nurse would get a glass of gin for
laying out the dead, or two glasses of gin for one spell of night duty,
though it is not clear whether these were to be drunk at the time or
afterwards.

As with all histories, there is an official history of nursing which selects
certain kinds of developments and not others as important.[76] Hospital
nursing training in Britain, for example, was begun before Florence
Nightingale arrived on the scene, though, in the orthodox history, the
profession of nursing was created by Nightingale virtually single-handed.
Florence Nightingale's achievements on behalf of nursing were, in reality,
quite mixed. An idle daughter of the upper classes, she was drawn to
her work by visions of God, perhaps the only means available to her
for making nursing seem respectable – God said it was, and Florence
in due course proved it, with her labours in the Crimea which gave
the impression of saving the entire British army.[77] What Florence
Nightingale actually did was to wean nursing away from the cruder
aspects of domestic work and attempt to establish it as a profession
alongside the emerging profession of medicine. She saw nurses as a kind
of hospital housekeeper whose job it was to supervise the health of the
patient's environment as well as the patient's personal hygiene, and who,
in order to do this, had to be members of a highly disciplined occupation
with its own code of conduct and behavioural and ethical standards. While
medicine sought to 'cure', nursing sought to care for the patient in both
a sanitary and a moral sense.

Nightingale's efforts on behalf of nurses were aided by the growth of
the demand for nurses in many countries at the end of the nineteenth
century (in Britain the number of hospital beds tripled between 1861–91
and 1891–1911[78]), and by medicine's own insecurity about its professional credibility, and its consequent need to expand and control

hospitals as places where captive patients could be used to teach future doctors. The new, trained nurses were a particular problem for doctors, since they often came from a higher social class than the doctors themselves. This was one reason why the nurse's place in health care had to be very tightly controlled. What one could call the 'feminine' environmental model of nursing in fact changed little until the 1930s and 1940s, when nursing became clearly subordinate to medicine within a newly hierarchical technical division of labour. In the last 20 years, state intervention in health-care has, in many countries, rigidified this pattern, and nurses have become one among many groups of ancillary health workers harnessed to the promotion of the technical-curative model of medicine. In the course of these developments, some elements in the trained nurse's work have been removed from it and relabelled the work of nursing auxiliaries or domestic staff. To fill the gap, and because doctors have become increasingly occupied with specialist technologies of one kind or another, doctors have passed on to nurses some routine parts of their own work. In this manner the boundaries between different health-care occupations constantly shift, though an important question to ask is which occupation's definition of its role is the prime cause of changing occupational boundaries throughout the system. And, as with many social changes, the impetus to movement in health-care occupations comes from the top, from the highest status, highest paid, and most powerful profession, and the one with the closest link to the machinery of state power. Indeed, doctors, politicians and top civil servants are liable to share the same social background and sets of values.[79]

'A GOOD NURSE IS A GOOD WOMAN': THE HEALTH-CARE FAMILY

This historical division of labour between doctors and nurses presents today's nurse with a definite set of constraints as to what nurses are able to do for patients and for themselves. But almost an equal constraint is the gender division of labour in health-care. The details of this vary between countries, but we may make two generalizations about it. First, the vast majority of the world's health-care workers are women; many of these are nurses. Nurses thus provide more health-care than doctors. The second generalization is that the medical profession is male-dominated. In most countries it is male-dominated in a statistical sense, but, even where it is not, the stereotype of a doctor conveyed in medical training and practice owes a great deal more to cultural notions of masculinity than femininity. Doctors are rational, scientific, unemotional, and uninvolved: indeed, their very value is sometimes said to reside in their detachment from the personal needs of their patients. In talking about this gender division between medicine and nursing, we have to add that, although women may become doctors and men may become nurses, there is a tendency within both professions for men to monopolize the top jobs. While it is possible to understand why this happens in medicine – a science (or an art?) from which women were excluded so that they must now fight to be allowed back in – it is much harder to understand why nurses should allow their male colleagues to take an undue share of the top jobs. Don't women know more about nursing than men do? Of course I am being a little provocative here. But I have thought for a long time that what nurses, midwives, and women in general need is assertiveness-training. If Florence Nightingale had trained her lady pupils in assertiveness rather than obedience, perhaps nurses would be in a different place today. For nurses, like all women, have to contend with one important obstacle to change: real women are not supposed to be revolutionaries. If we complain about our situation, or the system, we are liable to be called ill, neurotic, menopausal, premenstrual, or in need of some curative relationship with a man. It is not good enough to say that there is something wrong out there, and we want to change it.

This was the iron link that Florence Nightingale did not challenge when she tried to professionalize nurses: the link between nursing and womanhood. The relationship between doctor and nurse in early nursing paralleled the husband-wife relationship in the family: *she* looked after the physical and emotional environment, while *he* decided what the really important work was, and how it should be done. 'Nursing is mothering.'[80] Or, 'To be a good nurse one must be a good woman', that is, 'attendants on the wants of the Sick – helpers in carrying out Doctors' orders.'[81] Nightingale, I want to add, was not quite as feeble as this much-quoted phrase makes her sound. She also ranted against the idea that nurses had to be nothing but devoted and subservient. 'This definition', she once said, 'would do just as well for a porter. It might even do for a horse.'[82]

But it is not just that doctor plays father and nurse plays mother: who is the child? The child is, of course, the patient. Mother and father (doctor and nurse) take care of, and make judgements about, the welfare of children (patients). Crucial to this triadic relationship is the fact that children are not asked to participate in making decisions about their own welfare; the role of children (patients) is to be passive recipients of parental (medical and nursing) treatment decisions.

THE 'CONSUMER' CRITIQUE AND THE NURSE'S ROLE

This analogy between the health-care division of labour and the family division of labour brings into focus a new social movement of our time – the movement formed by users of health-care to protest about their infantilized position within the health-care system. In many countries now there are organizations of health-care users whose agendas are very specifically asserting the rights of patients not to be treated like children. The emphasis in these organizations is that health-care users be allowed choice in the matter of who gives them health-care and how; furthermore, there is increasingly a demand that people be exposed only to treatments (whether of drugs, counselling, surgical operations or other procedures) which have been scientifically evaluated and been shown to be both effective and not unduly hazardous in either the short- or long-run.[83]

This attack on the entrenched values and practices of the health-care system comes especially, of course, from those, including oppressed social minorities, women, and childbearing women in particular, who do not feel they have totally benefited from medicine's curative claims. Indeed, the so-called 'consumer' critique is at its height in the area of maternity care, where people are able to add to all the other arguments the rejoinder that childbearing is not an illness, and therefore should not automatically be equated with a need to seek medical surveillance.

The word 'consumer' is, of course, really a misnomer in this context. People who use health-care do not 'consume' it – they are also capable of producing their own health for themselves. Self-help health-care is a mainstream development in the 'consumer' movement. Furthermore, 'consumers' of health-care do not, in most places, really have the opportunity to choose the care they want. Choice requires alternatives, information and imagination. You cannot choose something if you do not know it exists and cannot imagine it existing. Similarly, we cannot really talk about 'patients' either, since that prejudges the issue in another way. The word 'patient' comes from the latin 'patire', 'to suffer', and many people who use health services are not suffering, just as many who are suffering do not ever present themselves to health-care providers.

The inappropriateness of the terms 'consumer' and 'patient' points us in the direction of one extremely important generalization. This is that the new assertiveness on the part of users and would-be users of health-care is but one aspect of a widespread challenge to professional authority today. It is not only the profession of medicine that is being challenged, but others, including education, social welfare and the law. We in the industrialized world live in a society dominated more and more, not by industrial production, but by the production of services. Control over service production rests with professionals, whose power expands in importance as that of the older economic system declines.

What has all this to do with nurses? I think there are two main ways in which the consumer health-care movement is signalling a future for nurses of which many may be unaware. In the first place, nurses do not form a profession along the same lines as doctors or lawyers make up a profession. Nurses are not members of the professional power elite whose authority is currently being challenged. The fact that this is so provides nurses with a unique opportunity, namely to reshape their own place in health-care so that they are more closely allied with the self-stated needs of patients, rather than with the self-stated needs of the medical profession. Secondly, much of what the consumer movement in health-care is saying already has echoes in the history and ideology of nursing. Nurses need not, therefore, cover their tracks in order to map out an appropriate and successful response to the present health-care crisis. All they need to do is recover their past.

CARING VERSUS CURING

As I suggested earlier, nursing is associated not with a curative model of health and illness, but with a caring and an environmental one. The content of the first occupational training schemes for nurses emphasized not that 'patients' would be cured if their environments were clean and their personal needs were cared for, but, rather, that they would not be cured *without* this. Caring and attention to the environment were necessary, but not sufficient, conditions for restoring people's health. This ideology emerged as an accompaniment and as a support to the miracle achievements of modern medicine; the antibiotics and other chemotherapies; safe, organized blood transfusion services; new surgical and complex new diagnostic technologies. But the irony is that, after some decades of experiencing the benefits of modern medicine, it is now clear that Florence Nightingale and other like-minded women the world over had got it right. Caring about someone and their environment is normally a necessary condition for maintaining their health.

When we look at surveys of how patients feel about nurses, the importance of caring emerges very clearly. People prefer nurses to be warm, kind, sympathetic personalities.[84] Rates of 'patient-satisfaction' with nursing care are generally higher than those with medical care for two reasons. Firstly, nurses offer an emotional support service. Secondly, patients frequently have problems acquiring sufficient information about their condition and treatment from doctors, and turn to nurses to fill this gap. Most of us who have had the experience of being hospital inpatients know the usual train of events. The doctors sweep through the ward on their ward 'round', and once they have left, the patients ask the nurses what the doctors said (or meant). Surveys demonstrate that working-class patients, in particular, feel that nurses are not only good, but appropriate, givers of information, and this fits into the general picture in which nurses have higher status among lower-class patients.[85]

On the theme of emotional support, one study by Rose Coser in the USA found that patients see the nurse's essential task as giving personal reassurance and emotional support.[86] A more recent study in Britain by Evelyn Anderson had some interesting findings about how patients, nurses and doctors respectively see the role of the nurse. While both nurses and patients placed emotional support highest on the list of what a good nurse should provide, the doctors rated nurses' technical competence as most important, and were relatively uninterested in their capacity to provide emotional support.[87] Another survey with a bearing on this is that of Hughes and his co-workers in the USA. These researchers found that women in general see nurses more favourably than men do but that doctors see nurses less favourably than do men in general.[88] (In Anderson's study, 30 per cent of nurses had negative feelings towards doctors.)

Caring about, and for, the patient, is therefore an important part of the nurse's role in practice – whatever the theory. Yet, while nurses may pick up and respond to patients' needs for support and information, we have to add an important rider – that this sensitivity should not overrule nurses' perceptions of patients' physical needs. Marie Johnston's[89] study of patients and nurses in three gynaecological wards is not alone in suggesting that this sometimes happens: Johnston found nurses perceived patients to have more worries than patients said they had, at the same time as significantly underestimating patients' pain and other physical symptoms.

NURSING AND THE POSITION OF WOMEN

Alertness to the needs of others is consistently picked out as the mark of a good nurse in surveys of people's attitudes to nurses. This is also the mark of a good woman. Altruism is a social strength. But, so far as the altruistic individual is concerned, it may well be a weakness: altruism serves the community but often gets the individual nowhere. Women, in living altruistic lives, nevertheless often feel quite bad about themselves and what they are doing, and somehow end up in a position where they are not at all equal shareholders with men in the world's economic and political wealth. As Jean Baker Miller has pointed out in her *Toward a New Psychology of Women*, '"Serving others" is for losers, it is low-level stuff.'[90] But women's psychology and social roles are organized around the presumption that they *will* serve others, indeed, that from this serving of others will come the only self-enhancement that is culturally accepted as appropriate for women.

Taking care of others is a service required by every human community. Its value – good or bad, high or low – like the value of everything else human beings do, is not intrinsic to the activity itself but is given it by the culture. And the problem with caring in modern Euro-American culture is that it is one-sided. While women do it and know it to be important work, men do not do it, therefore they do not know it to be important and are likely to deny and deride its importance. But more than that, because these values are the dominant values, the dominant value is that caring is unimportant work. Women therefore are trapped. Their experience tells them caring is important, but their culture tells them it isn't.

One of the most impressive mechanisms for denying the importance of caring work is to disenfranchise and disadvantage the people who do such work. The mechanism is effective, if not exactly subtle. The most outstanding example of it is childrearing, followed as a close second by housework. Both are unpaid occupations when located in the family and in conjunction with marriage, though of course in other circumstances both can be paid. But these occupations are not only normally financially unrewarded, they disenfranchise their holders in important ways: a woman who gives up employment to rear children will generally lose out on her pension rights for those years, and, if she is in professional work, the missing years will set her permanently behind on the career ladder. Added to this is the deception of the cultural ideology about motherhood. Feminists from the eighteenth century onwards have remarked how mothers are idolized, how the sanctity and devotion of mothers is an absolutely core social value. Yet at the same time, as a real mother, one is liable to find oneself unable to go anywhere or do anything or be anyone: the shop doors which don't easily admit a pram, and the factory without a creche, are concrete illustrations of a symbolic order in which mothers and children are good only if they are controlled, confined to a limited place, prevented from infusing the rest of society with the values of nurturance, sensitivity, creativity, and thereby turning the dominant ideology on its head. For, if relating rather than alienating, altruism rather than competitiveness, emotional expressiveness rather than intellectual rigidity, become the order of the day, what on earth will the world be coming to?

The dilemmas of doing good and feeling bad apply to nurses, just as they do to women in general. In so far as caring is the signal quality and main work of nurses, they are likely to come up against two barriers: first, they will not achieve a social and financial status which underlines their inner feeling that nursing is good work – instead the external rewards of nursing are likely to undermine nurses' confidence in the performance of caring work. Secondly, it will be difficult to feel day-in day-out, and in the face of so many counter challenges, that communication with patients and acting as a midwife to patients' own articulation of their own needs is truly as valuable work as microsurgery, diagnoses with body-scanners, and intricate immunological tests. I use the word 'midwife' carefully, since that word conveys exactly the part of health-care work which nurses have historically excelled in, but which has been their downfall, for they have, I believe, facilitated patients' own abilities to cure themselves, just as midwives properly enable mothers to be their own deliverers.

NURSING – A PROFESSION?

A simple message could be extracted from all this – that nursing needs to lose its association with femaleness in order to achieve full professional status. The logic is undeniable, and it certainly appears to be the case that male nurses are more likely to emphasize the professional status of nurses than are female nurses.[91] On the other hand, and to complicate the issue, only a minority of doctors are prepared to accept male nurses at all, and two-thirds express a jocular or uncomfortable ambivalence to the whole idea. If male nurses are to be tolerated anywhere, it is apparently on violent psychiatric or urological wards.[92]

I am not in favour of simple answers, and so want to consider a few implications of this one – that the problem of nursing is that it needs more men to make it into a profession. First of all, what is a profession? Perhaps most obviously a profession is a superior type of occupation, a non-manual occupation requiring advanced education and training.

A profession thus has a specific and exclusively-owned body of knowledge and expertise. A profession organizes and to some extent controls itself by establishing standards of ethics, knowledge, and skill for its licensed practitioners. Lacking these, people will not be admitted into its ranks. A profession is also recognized as such by its members, and by society at large. This definition of a profession is extracted from the sociological literature on professions and professionalization,[93] but is arguably not very helpful. According to it, some time ago nursing was dubbed a 'semi-profession', along with others dominated by women (schoolteaching and social work). In fact, the predominance of women in these occupations was counted a reason for their lack of full professional status, women being said to be less committed to employment than men and more interested in on-the-job personal relations than in such 'masculine' attributes as long training programmes.[94]

If a profession is by definition male-dominated, then nurses might as well give up. Alternatively, nurses might ask the truly radical question as to what's so wonderful about being a profession anyway? This question is a bit like asking what's so wonderful about the family, motherhood, Father Christmas and the space programme. It is self-evident that being a professional is superior to not being one, just as living in a family or going to the moon are better than being a single parent (which would, in any case, disqualify one for training as an astronaut). The point in each case is that the world we know takes the goodness of some people, activities and objects, and the badness of others, for granted. Yet, so far as nursing and its professional or non-professional status is concerned, the current crisis of confidence in medical care should tell us that professionalization is not only not the answer, that it may indeed be positively damaging to health. It has been said that professions in the twentieth century have in general created a 'dependent, cajoled and harassed, economically deprived and physically and mentally damaged' clientele. They are more entrenched and 'international than a world church, more stable than any labour union, endowed with wider competence than any shaman, and equipped with a tighter hold over those they claim as victims than any mafia'.[95] This situation is disabling for everyone except the professionals – though Jean Baker Miller, and any decent analyst worth her salt, would say it is disabling for professionals too, since to achieve success the 'true' professional must deny at least half of humanity's needs and potential – the need and capacity for caring about oneself and others as whole people, not merely as sets of specialized and segmented skills.

Interestingly, those radical critics who attack the evils of professionalism do not mention nurses. Just as I failed to notice nurses when researching doctors and patients some years ago, so in the orchestration of the 'doctor-bashing' theme, the motif of who nurses are and how they could help to make things better is not even heard as a single tune played lightly on the woodwind above the crashing of the brass and percussion and the persistent grinding of the wind section – the motif just isn't there.

THE WORLD WE KNOW, AND THE WORLD WE DON'T KNOW

To conclude I will give a brief historical reflection, together with a pointer for the future. But first, I shall summarize my main points so far:

(1) Nurses and nursing deserve more serious attention and research from all of us than they have hitherto received. A good nurse is not invisible, nor is she a ghost from the past.

(2) Communication between those who provide, and those who use, the health services is of paramount importance in both curing and caring work.

(3) Doctors try to cure and nurses try to care. Curing isn't possible as often as doctors claim it is, and it usually isn't possible without caring. This is because emotional support is good for peoples' bodies as well as their minds.

(4) The doctor-nurse-patient relationship mirrors that of the traditional nuclear family. Neither structure is especially good for people's health, and it is damaging in particular ways for the health of nurses-wives and patients-children.

(5) Users of health-care and intellectuals who write about what is wrong with it tend to criticize the medical profession more than nurses. This suggests that nurses have got something right, even if, or even because, they are not professionals in the same way that doctors are. It also suggests that an alliance between nurses and health-care users is a strategy that could drastically improve the health-care scene.

(6) Serving others, as nurses do, and as women have traditionally done, is an enormously good capacity to have, so long as it is developed at the same time as a sense of one's own self-worth and self-identity. Thus, specifically, dedication to the occupation of nursing is never an argument for taking bad working conditions and poor financial rewards without protest. In fact it is extremely important to bring about improvements in the value attached to nursing work.[96]

The historical reflection comes from Florence Nightingale's *Notes on Nursing*, first published in 1859. She wrote:

> 'Keep clear of both the jargons now current everywhere . . . of the jargon, namely about the 'rights' of women, which urges women to do all that men do including the medical and other professions, merely because men do it, and without regard to whether this *is* the best that women can do; and of the jargon which urges women to do nothing men do, merely because they are women . . . you want to do the thing that is good whether it is suitable for a woman or not.[97]

And the pointer for the future is from Jean Baker Miller, who said that 'one of the major issues before us as a human community is the question of how to create a way of life that includes serving others without being subservient.'[98] That is the task ahead for all of us, and especially for nurses, who owe it to themselves to lift off the veil that has made them invisible, and make everyone see and understand how important they really are.

Part 4

Social Science: a Useful Masculine Paradigm?

If the struggle for academic freedom and for the social sciences is predicated upon liberation and imagination, then it may well be possible to recruit the anger that women have learned from oppression and the creativity they have developed in aiming to emerge from it. Women will not be supine. We have our own struggle anyway. The struggle to preserve and improve the social sciences and the institutions of learning is part of that same struggle. . . . Let us all continue to fight 'like a woman'. . . .

M. Stacey 'Social Sciences and the State: fighting like a woman' in *The Public and the Private* E. Gamarnikow, D. Morgan, J. Purvis and D. Taylorson (eds), London, Heinemann, 1983, p. 11

22

Feminist Sociology
– is it Possible?

To be a feminist is a destiny that conflicts in many interesting ways with others. Quite early on in my involvement with the women's movement – that is, in the early 1970s, which now feels like several millennia ago – I found myself vilified by certain sections of that movement for being a sociologist and therefore 'a servant of the bourgeois state'. I found this allegation distressing and ideologically difficult to handle. Accordingly, my work tends not to be acknowledged by Marxist feminists in this country, although the same discrimination doesn't operate elsewhere. While I understand their position, I understand my own as well, and the first piece in this section is a defence of the difficult enterprise of being a feminist sociologist. It was written again for a Scandinavian audience in the depths of winter, and seemed to go down as well, if not so warmingly, as the vodka we drank afterwards.

The two poems that follow it: 'On Visiting a Female Professor' and 'To an Academic Adviser' were written several years before and serve as a personal commentary on some of my own conflicts with academia. The 'male-identified' academic woman was someone I felt uncomfortable with, even when personified as a friend and colleague I respected and admired. The second poem articulates some of the perhaps inevitable hostility students feel towards teachers – particularly perhaps female students towards male teachers.

Source: Originally given under the title 'Is a Feminist Sociology either Possible or Desirable?' to the Department of Sociology, University of Helsinki, Finland, 26 January 1982.

When I was invited to give a seminar here, it was suggested that the basis of my talk should be my book *Subject Women*, which was published in 1982.[1] *Subject Women* was commissioned by a publisher who asked me to write a textbook for the many women's studies courses that have been created in Britain and other countries. What I set out to do in *Subject Women* was to provide a comprehensive introduction and overview of a relatively new subject. This immediately raises the question as to whether women's studies can really be considered to be a subject. It is clearly not a subject in the same sense as sociology or psychology or modern languages. Is it simply a new and revolutionary way of defining academic subjects? Or is it, rather, a *methodology* – a way of asking questions, a formulation of the problem, a mode of enquiry, that is distinctively different from all pre-existing academic methodologies? The other basic question which I confronted before and during the writing of the book is related to this first question of what kind of subject women's studies is, and it concerns the relationship between women's studies as an exercise carried out in academic institutions on the one hand, and the politics of the women's liberation movement on the other. What is the relationship between these two? Is the domain of the women's movement entirely outside that of the university, the polytechnic, the school? Or is there no real separation to be made between the politics of women's oppression and liberation on the one hand, and their partici- pation as subjects, teachers and researchers in the academic world on the other? If this second alternative obtains, just what are the implica- tions of feminist politics for women's academic work and academic work on women? Another way to put this is to be more specific and ask: is a feminist sociology either possible or desirable?

A colleague of mine, Dale Spender, who has done a lot of work both on the education of women and girls, and on the way in which language reflects and perpetuates sex inequality, wrote a piece called 'Theorising about Theorising' in an edited collection of articles by women on *Theories of Women's Studies*. In this piece Dale recalls a significant moment in her life when, walking by the River Thames in London, she realized that everything she 'knew' had been 'made up' – that is 'discovered' or 'stated' by somebody. She realized that all 'knowledge' in this sense is both artificial and arbitrary. Thus, she came eventually to the inevitable conclusion that the idea that meaning is necessary, that all of us should be leading meaningful lives, also had to be made up by somebody. Why *is* meaning necessary? Why can't we accept the idea of meaninglessness? Dale said:

If everything I know is 'wrong', that is, if there are no absolutes, no truths, only transitory meanings imposed by human beings in an attempt to make sense of the world, then 'wrong' becomes a meaningless category. Instead of being frightened that something I am arguing for as truth, as right, as logic, may in fact be wrong, I am starting from the other end and arguing that I know it is temporary and inadequate and that I am searching for the 'errors' and the 'flaws'. . . . Unlike many academics, *I have a vested interest in finding the limitations of my thesis, not in having it perpetuated.*[2]

My starting point in discussing whether women's studies is a respectable academic subject would therefore be to question the terms of the question itself. I am not particularly interested in what kind of a subject women's studies is. Why should I be? I am much more interested in *doing* women's studies than in arguing its status within the academic community. It doesn't worry me that academic women's studies can be seen as a temporary response to a political movement, that it doesn't have the same kind of claim to be a distinctive field of enquiry as other subjects pursued in academic institutions. I believe that people who practise women's studies do have a vested interest in finding the limitations of their thesis rather than endlessly defending and perpetuating it.

I adopt this view in the first place because, as a sociologist, I recognize the temporary and socially-constructed nature of everything that passes under the heading of 'knowledge'; secondly, because, as a feminist, I understand that the culture in which our contemporary academic 'knowledge' and institutions developed is a male-dominated one, and there is therefore no particular reason to believe it is relevant to women; and thirdly because what sociology itself is – has become in this culture – makes it a masculine enterprise. It could therefore be argued that to define a feminist sociology is not possible because it is not desirable. However, I would say that a feminist sociology *is* desirable for women, for women's studies and that it *is* possible, though it is neither possible nor desirable in quite the way in which it is usual to argue the justification for any particular kind of academic subject.

There are three themes in this argument. The first theme concerns the nature of university education – of the academic community. The second concerns the way in which modern sociology has constituted knowledge about women. The third theme concerns the 'doing' of feminist sociology.

What is Education?

The chapter on education in *Subject Women* begins with a quotation from *A Vindication of the Rights of Woman* written by the eighteenth-century feminist Mary Wollstonecraft and first published in 1792. In discussing the idea that education is the most important pathway to women's liberation, Wollstonecraft refers to the famous statement made by the French philosopher, Rousseau, that if you educate women in the same way as men, women will lose those forms of power they have traditionally been able to exercise over men. 'This is the very point I aim at', says Wollstonecraft, 'I do not wish them to have power over men; but over themselves.'[3] Do women gain this power over themselves from the educational institutions through which they pass in modern capitalist societies? An equal right to an equal education has always been an important element in the politics of movements for women's equality. But in practice this demand has also been a particularly difficult one to achieve. Thus, in Britain, as in many other countries, there has been disappointingly little progress towards educational sex equality over the last ten years. Some measures of this are: the fact that in 1970 41.3 per cent of full-time higher education students in the UK were women, while in 1979 this figure had only risen to 41.9 per cent. The fact that 16.7 per cent of all examination passes in Physics at Advanced level (the qualification need for university entrance) were taken by women in 1970, with an increase to only 18.2 per cent in 1978.[4]

There are two kinds of educational curriculum: the public and the private. The private or 'hidden' curriculum of educational institutions cannot be deduced from their official agendas or rules, but the differences between the educational destinies of men and women cannot be understood without reference to this second kind of curriculum, which is defined as 'those aspects of learning. . . . that are unofficial, or unintentional or undeclared consequences of the way teaching and learning are organised and performed'.[5] A capitalist society not only produces consumption goods; it produces people too. In order to achieve its economic goals, both the forces of production (workers and technology) and the relations of production (between employers and employed, between social classes, between men and women) must be constantly reproduced. It is the role of non-economic institutions, primarily those of the family and education, to ensure the continuation of labour power and social relations of production required by the capitalist economic system. Thus both the family and education can be said to function as 'ideological state apparatuses'. They transmit the ideas and practices needed for the survival of capitalism. In so far as capitalism requires, and itself gave rise to, a particular division of labour by sex – between men as workers and women as people who produce and service workers – then it will be the function of education to maintain precisely this division.

In other words, the flexibility of the educational system to accommodate itself to new definitions of gender is not very great. This does not mean that feminists should not work for a change within education; but it does mean that they cannot really hope for revolutionary change. It also means that the accommodation of women's studies within the official academic curriculum is a necessary, but not sufficient, condition for women's liberation.

In her essay 'Toward a Woman-Centred University', the American writer Adrienne Rich describes the feminist renaissance that was under way by the early 1970s within and outside the educational system in America. She points out that then and now 'immense forces in the university . . . are intrinsically opposed to anything resembling an actual feminist renaissance, wherever that process appears to be a serious undertaking and not merely a piece of decorative reformism.' Rich observes that:

> As women have gradually and reluctantly been admitted to the mainstream of higher education, they have been made participants in a system that prepares men to take up roles of power in a man-centred society, that asks questions and teaches 'facts' generated by a male intellectual tradition, and that both subtly and openly confirms men as the leaders and shapers of human destiny. . . . The exceptional women who have emerged from this system and who hold distinguished positions in it are just that: the required exceptions used by every system to justify and maintain itself.

A university education, in its methodology and values if not always in its subject-matter, is an induction into masculine thought processes, a preparation for a male career pattern. Universities are hierarchical institutions: 'At the top is a small cluster of highly paid and prestigious persons, chiefly men, whose careers entail the services of a very large base of ill-paid or unpaid persons, chiefly women.' Women within a university, whether they are the exceptional female professor, the faculty wife, the typist or the cleaning woman, most importantly do not see themselves as sharing a common destiny. As well as being a hierarchy built on exploitation, the university is a breeding ground for masculine values: of competitiveness, of status–seeking, of public accomplishment, of the supposed supremacy of so-called 'objectivity' and 'scientific neutrality'.[6]

SOCIOLOGY: A MASCULINE SUBJECT

Sociology as an enterprise carried on within male-centred universities has been historically biased against women.

Perhaps I can take for granted an understanding that some of the classic theoretical texts of sociology (such as Weber's *The Protestant Ethic and the Spirit of Capitalism* and Talcott Parsons' *The Social System*) are sexist either directly in contending that social arrangements oppressive to women are 'natural' and/or 'necessary' to society, or indirectly by supposing that when we look at the world of men we look at the world. Although sociology is defined as the 'scientific' study of society, it has for most of its history been a male science of male society. Its highest status practitioners have been men, and in content areas, values and research methodologies, it has reflected the patriarchal structure, relations and ideology of capitalist society. For example, with regard to content areas, emphasis is put on such concerns as the analysis of competition and strategies of status aggressiveness; there is a preoccupation with power, men's work and conflict, all of which are concerns of society as a whole only if women – and other social minorities – are excluded. The point at which women are 'let in' to this analysis is the point at which they are over-represented in social life – which is in marriage and the family, in their roles as wives and mothers. Even here the perspective adopted has generally been a male-oriented one. The best-known instance of this is probably Talcott Parsons' functionalist distinction between the 'instrumental' role of the man in marriage as opposed to the 'expressive' role of the woman. As anybody who has ever washed a floor, emptied the rubbish or cleaned a lavatory has known, there is nothing particularly 'expressive' about housework. Another example would be the sociological literature on women's employment which, until quite late in the history of sociology, did not exist, and, when it did, focused almost entirely on the so-called 'social problem' of the employment of married women and the hazards this might pose to the satisfactory functioning of marriage as an institution, and to the physical and psychological welfare of husbands and children.

The feminist critique of sociology identifies three main ways in which sociology has not treated women fairly: (1) much of sociology has totally ignored women; (2) when it has not ignored women its concern has not been based in the subjective experiences of the women themselves; (3) the lack of attention paid to women and their experiences cannot be remedied merely by adding them to a formula or agenda that is systematically and fundamentally biased against them.

A good example of this last criticism is the observation made by Arlie Russell Hochschild that there is no subject area within sociology devoted to the study of feelings and emotions.[7] This, as Hochschild says, is not because people do not feel, nor because there is no relationship between the kind of feelings a person has and his or her social circumstances. The data are there, and they are definitely sociological in character. But male society defines cognitive, intellectual and rational dimensions of experience as superior to emotional or sentimental forms of experience – indeed the word 'sentimental' has come to be used as a form of abuse. There would be nothing intrinsically unscientific about a sociology of emotion. But such a statement misses the main point, which is that social science, like science in general, is not a value-neutral activity somehow raised above ordinary cultural concerns. The cognitive and technical domain of science is a social product. That is one reason why all science, including sociology, needs a conceptual apparatus, a language such as the one about roles, norms, systems and structures, because it is only by channelling their thought and activity into such language that sociologists have been able to pretend that they, and their own social relations, are no part of what they are studying, of the scientific enterprise in which they are engaged.

Even if a new subject area within sociology could be set up to represent traditional 'feminine' concerns, such as why people experience certain emotions under certain circumstances, this subject area would certainly not equal in status those relating to such concerns as the sociology of occupations, education, deviance and so forth. Indeed, this is the sort of fate that has befallen women's studies; it has been seen by the sociological establishment predominantly as a low-status and trivial activity in part, of course, because its practitioners are women and because many of them do not hold tenured positions and are employed on a part-time basis.

Being a Feminist Sociologist

I am not suggesting that women should not fight for the acceptance of women's studies as an academic subject. What I am saying is that they should not be over-impressed by the significance of winning this battle. The basic problem is not how to get women's studies accepted in departments of sociology (or anywhere else), but how it is possible, and what it means, to be a feminist sociologist and practise an activity which one believes can accurately be called feminist sociology.

One of the main difficulties here has been described by the American sociologist, Dorothy Smith, in an essay entitled 'A Sociology for Women':

> In attempting to develop a sociology from the standpoint of women, we find a persistent difficulty that does not yield to the critique of standard themes and topics. In any one of the many ways we might do a sociology of women, women remain the objects of the study. . . . By insisting that women be entered into sociology as its subjects, we find that we cannot escape how its practices transform us into its objects.[8]

Thus, what we need, argues Smith, is not a sociology *of* women, but a sociology *for* women. The aim of such a sociology would be to develop *for* women analyses, descriptions and understandings of their situation in their everyday world and the broader socioeconomic organization of which it is part. A sociology *for* women, by beginning with women's experiences in the everyday world, would not confine itself to these experiences. Although its objective would be to explain to women the social organization of their experienced world, it is essential to this objective that the everyday world is seen as organized by social relations that are not observable within it.

One example that I think constitutes a sociology *of* women, but not a sociology *for* women, in exactly this sense, is a large research project carried out in London in the 1970s and concerned with depression in women. The book describing this research is called *Social Origins of Depression*[9] and the research findings are, I believe, very important and relevant to women's experiences of the everyday world.

Yet, while this analysis can be read into the research findings and into the book, the framework within which the research was carried out and the data analysed and written up, lacks any articulated connection between women's depression and their oppression. Depression, even when proven to have social origins, is not seen to be a political phenomenon rooted in a sexist and classist society. One reason why it is not seen in this way is because the researchers were not concerned with whether or how women defined themselves as depressed, but how the state of women's mental health could be exposed and fitted into a system of classification developed by a profession of 'experts' on mental health – psychiatrists. Another reason why such research is the kind of sociology that tends to make women merely objects of enquiry is because these particular researchers did not begin with a desire to study the situation of women. They did not set out to give women a chance to understand their everyday experience as determined by its location in a particular type of society. The primary aim of the research was to study depression, and women were selected as subjects because women are easier and therefore cheaper to interview, being more likely than men to be at home and available for interview during the day.

It is easy to criticize and much more difficult to be constructive: how in practice can a sociology for women be achieved? I did not find this objective at all easy to attain in writing *Subject Women*. I did, however, make certain decisions about how to put together what was supposed to be a 'women's studies' textbook in ways which I thought might be compatible with the doing of a feminist sociology. In the first place, I tried to use women's own accounts of their experiences as much as possible throughout the book. Although I was already aware of this particular problem of history – that the experiences of women have been made invisible through the concentration on historical events and processes which are not of special importance to women – I did come out at the end of writing the book with a heightened consciousness of how few women have written down their life-experiences, both in the distant and much more recent past, in the way that is necessary for people like me to locate sociology in a women's world. A second approach I followed in writing the book was to choose a way of organizing the material that reflected themes important to women, rather than the conventional subject-divisions of sociology. Thus, there is in the book, for instance, no chapter on marriage and the family. The third section of the book, which is called 'Labour' includes a chapter on domestic work and one on reproduction. The fourth section, which is called 'Relationships' includes a chapter on children, one on men, and one on relationships with other women. The fifth section, called 'Power' begins with a chapter on class and looks at what conventional definitions of social class (based on male occupation) mean to women, at what happens to women who lack such an attachment to men, and at the whole complex question of the relationship between what could be called 'economic class', and what is for women a very important opposed concept, that of 'gender class'.

One problem I faced in drawing together material on these various aspects of women's lives was that, while I disapproved of some of the ways in which, and reasons why, certain pieces of research have been done, I nevertheless found the conclusions of some of this research of great significance in interpreting women's situation. (The work on depression I quoted just now is one example.) This, I think, illustrates a general precept to be followed in the practice of a feminist sociology which is, to use a popular English phrase, the rule that one should not 'throw the baby out with the bathwater'. While discarding what is not relevant or simply obviously rubbish, it is no use pretending that there is nothing of value in the entire field of male-oriented sociology as it has developed: it is essential to preserve, and redefine, what is good. There are some ideas that grew up originally without any reference to women's experience which I personally have found extremely helpful in my own research and writing. One early one was the concept of 'alienation' as describing a certain mode of relation between the worker on the one hand and the work process and product on the other. In my study of women's attitudes to housework, I took this concept out of the factory and into the home and used it as one way of providing what I saw as a necessary basis of comparison between women's experiences of unpaid domestic labour and the experiences of labourers outside the home.[10]

Another example from my own work of not throwing the baby out with the bathwater, is the use I made in the analysis of women's experiences in becoming mothers of certain well-established sociological ideas. These included the work of Arnold van Gennep, and that of Glaser and Strauss, on status passage; sociological studies of workers' responses to retirement and to occupational career changes; the work of medical sociologists on the nature of medical patienthood and on depressive and other responses to surgery; research on people's reactions to natural and human-made disasters (earthquakes, wars, etc.); and Goffman's work on institutionalization. I found all of these approaches useful in making sense of women's accounts of how they felt during the transition to motherhood, and in locating these feelings within the specific material context in which they occurred.[11] For while the predominant cultural myth of women and motherhood states that giving birth to, and being able to look after, a baby, is an achievement of a peculiarly feminine and beneficial kind, it was obvious from what women in the study said that childbearing and childrearing commonly possess quite profound qualities of loss for the woman herself. In interpreting the nature of this loss I argued what is not an original or especially daring thesis – that it is necessary to see women as human-beings and childbirth as a life-event – and through this perception the potential usefulness of other sociological work on the responses of human-beings to life-events became clear.

So far I have talked about data analysis: what about the research process itself? It is in this area that I believe the greatest contradiction between sociology and feminism lies. For sociology has traditionally postulated the notion of value-free research and the idea of neutrality and indifference towards the research objects – those individuals who are asked to give information about themselves and their lives that will constitute the raw data of the research. The trouble with this is that, in the first place, no research is value-free because no human activity is initiated or carried out in a medium that is culture-free. Whatever research is done, the people who do it have their own personal–historical reasons for engaging in that particular research at that particular time, and they do it in the way that they do it because of the people that they are. It is just that the masculine mystique of science has bred the pretence that no such reasons or personal influences in the research process exist. Since a feminist sociology, in taking a position on the link between academic women's studies and the politics of feminism, does not subscribe to this myth, it must be an important part of the feminist sociological enterprise to expose the link between personal life and academic work.

A second fault in the notion of value-free research concerns its inbuilt insistence on using people as research objects. What is to be avoided at all costs is subjectivity, personal involvement and the so-called 'fiction' of equality between the researcher and the researched; only objectivity, detachment and hierarchy are venerated. In other words, the whole notion of research and its methodology within sociology is derived from a masculine world view.

TOWARDS A FEMINIST SOCIOLOGY

One requirement for a feminist sociology is, then, that the postulate of value-free research has to be replaced by that of conscious *partiality*, which is to be achieved through an identification with the so-called 'objects' of research. Such a suggestion often leads to the conventional objection of bias, but this has to be countered by asking those who make such an objection to defend the charge that any research is really *not* biased in some way.

One of the issues here is the distinction between quantitative and qualitative data – the first of which is conventionally considered to be 'hard' and 'good' and the second of which is, by comparison, 'soft' and 'inferior'. The American sociologist Jessie Bernard was the first to point out the double meaning in these descriptions; for what are men and women characterized as being in our culture, if not 'hard' and 'soft' respectively? As Bernard went on to say, this invidious distinction has been one of the factors leading to a need for women's studies. A very large amount of research has been invested in the sociology of sex as a quantifiable variable, and very little in a sociology of, or for, women as a collectivity. 'A great deal of research focuses on men with no reference at all to women; but when research is focused on women, it is almost always with reference to men. If comparisons are not to be made with men the research is viewed as incomplete.'[12] A feminist sociology must therefore challenge what is hidden within, and because of, this traditional justaposition of the quantitative and qualitative in sociology.

One final question is why a feminist should bother with sociology at all. The answer I would give to this might seem to contradict almost everything else I have said, since my answer would be that the sociological perspective, in its most basic elements, is an inherently feminist perspective. Sociology as the study of society, of social life as a whole, of social institutions and processes, is concerned first and foremost with the *relations between people*. Human relations have historically been women's most important domain of labour, and it is women's labour and interests with which feminism as a political ideology and movement is associated. Another way in which the sociological approach is sympathetic to feminism is that it is capable of supplying an understanding of the social construction of individual identity. While it can be argued that we all need such an understanding, it can also be argued that feminists have a specially urgent need for it, since they begin with the often painful discovery of a point of rupture between their *actual* experiences as women and what they are *supposed* to experience as women. In Dale Spender's essay, quoted earlier, she said that two factors had been particularly important in structuring the framework within which she worked. One was the women's movement, and the other was being socialized in one culture and then living as a member of another; both these factors pose elements of challenging what was previously taken for granted and of exposing ways in which the individual is shaped by social processes.

To summarize, then: I believe in sociology partly because I am a feminist, and I am optimistic about the chances of using sociology to improve the situation of women. I put it in these terms deliberately, for as the German feminist, Maria Mies, has argued, women who are committed to the causes of women's liberation cannot be satisfied with challenging existing definitions of sociological theory, disciplines, methods, etc., or with giving to sociology better, more authentic and more relevant data. 'Only if women's studies is deliberately made part of the struggle against women's oppression...can women prevent the misuse of their theoretical and methodological innovations.'[13] Indeed, the real challenge *is* to innovate, and in producing new theoretical understandings and ways of working, liberate sociology from its own oppression as a didactic and chauvinistic science.

23

On Visiting a Female Professor
To an Academic Adviser

On Visiting a Female Professor

what a triumph
your chiselled face hides
in this unnatural habitat

your sunday game
of tea and tennis
meriting another prize

you must be the envy of all women

the first I knew of you my friend said
disgraceful, she's pregnant and only a student
her baby has red hair
is looked after by a mother-in-law
what is the world coming to

babies get in your way? never
oh I'm sure you loved them
but you climbed over them
onwards and upwards to the corridors of power

a cold and cutting path
trail-blazing you could call it (and you did)
an ascent against the laws of gravity and men

our hands in our cluttered pockets
we watched you go
chirruping in amazement – she's won
just imagine what she's done

she's made her mark and carved a place
hold on tight, we'll follow
the land is bright and beckoning
white-lined and sharp like the moon
our future home

the point is we don't want to go there

it doesn't feel right
you can keep your cure
the treatment's worse

than the pain
let us muddle along
it's a trip we prefer

To an Academic Adviser

keep your papers and your scientific head
I come home to the bravery of child-played Bach
to a cottonwool chaos bound by a baby's smile
and a chemistry of recognition you can't count
this is my fenced pond of smooth water
your welcome is the gross grey turbulence of the unowned sea

who would want a history of articles
typed and dissected, lost and uncredited
who even could envy that slumped precise man
his caught moments of imagination
ecliptic pathways in a midday world

hands map out the tired pattern of my face
lit eyes examine my bereft spaces
faith brewed in the kitchen holds me up
straight and unschooled in my frantic faith
now I see through the dark glass clearly
I am grateful for your labour and your example

24

Reflections on the Study of Household Labour

Housework wasn't a serious academic subject when I began to tackle it both personally and professionally in the late 1960s. But in this respect the world has changed during the adulthood of women of my generation, and it is now permissible to cite housework as a topic of theoretical and empirical importance within sociology. Other disciplines have also seen some light: for instance economics now takes housework more seriously than it used to, and epidemiology is beginning to take to heart the truth of the observation made by a woman doctor more than 60 years ago:

> The more children a woman has the heavier will her household tasks become, the greater the strain upon health and strength, and the less her chance of passing through pregnancy without ill results. Heavy domestic work, including especially the household washing, is often far more fatiguing and liable to cause injury than an industrial occupation.[14]

To untangle the causes of women's poor health, and of the reproductive mortalities, we need to know not only what work women are doing that they are paid for, but also the work they do that is not dignified by the title 'labour' because it is done in the name of love and in the closeted confines of the household.

I had great fun writing this piece, which serves as a prelude to an

Source: Published 1980 as 'Prologue' to *Women and Household Labor* S. Fenstermaker Berk (ed.). Reprinted by permission of Sage Publications, Inc.

American book on housework. In it I compare studying housework to the writing of science fiction, because both constitute a reversal of the usual world-view. Unfortunately, however, housework is not fictional, and the doing of it continues to explain a large part of the structured inequalities between men and women in the world outside the home.[15] As I write this, my efforts to concentrate must contend with the alternative knowledge of the washing to be done and the meal waiting to be cooked, and I am uneasily aware, as I have always been, that my 'professional' work would be better if my time and energy were not depleted by the work of the household. Yet I defend the dignity of that labour, and have socialized myself into not only an acceptance but an enjoyment of that dual role. Those who juggle the benefits and hazards of two worlds are, after all, in the best position to judge the value and importance of science fiction.

In Charlotte Perkins Gilman's utopian novel *Herland* (first published in book form in 1979), three men representing the higher echelons of early twentieth-century American society (a playboy, a doctor, and a sociologist) chance, during a scientific expedition, on an all-female culture where for two thousand years women have given birth to daughters unaided by men. The three men are shattered by, and indeed ultimately unable to grasp, the fact that for the citizens of Herland civilization itself is a female concept. The problem is not only one of crediting women with the achievement of creating a truly civilized society (no wars, poverty, illness, crime, or dogs; population and economic resources neatly balanced; government by co-operation and mutual goodwill). Basically the issue is one of how people, and men especially, are able to break out of and move beyond that system of thought whose conceptual content and structure presupposes the necessity and desirability of pro-masculine gender differentiation.

This is the reason why many so-called utopias are not so for women, and why feminist utopias are not merely fictional but outside the limits of conventional fiction as a genre, which can only question the status quo with the status quo's own terminology and assumptions. And it is the reason why women in the 1970s are writing more science fiction. It offers them the opportunity to dispute the current conditions of gender and to envisage what a society with really liberated women might be like.

The study of housework is like the exercise of writing feminist science fiction: it constitutes an attempt to reverse the accepted order of concepts and values. The task has to be set in its historical context. Capitalist society is pervaded by two historically new divisions between work and the family and between the family and personal life.[16] The 'solution' of women becoming managers of the family and of personal life was facilitated in the late eighteenth and nineteenth centuries by the collective weight of specific circumstances: the absence of effective fertility control and a safe technology for the artificial feeding of infants; the constriction of employment opportunities with the move toward capital-intensive industry; a masculine hegemony in positions of public power (government, administration, the Church, and the legal, medical, and academic professions); and the creation of childhood as a legally protected and distinct state. These circumstances suggested a construction of women as private, non-productive, domesticated, expressive, and nurturant. Cultural convenience was called natural necessity, and such a typification of women became institutionalized as the division of labour by gender, as the 'position of women'.

Central to the position of women today is the interpretation of female labour as an inferior version of male labour. In relation to male labour, female labour is characterized as unproductive, marginal, trivial, temporary, intermittent, dispensable, less valuable, less skilled, and less physically demanding. These stereotypes apply both to female household labour and to women's labour in paid occupations. Thus, it is normative to regard the employment work of women as an activity interrupted by domesticity, and to view housework as an intermittent (and interruptable) rather than continuous activity; to reinforce the poverty (in relation to the male norm) of women's monetary rewards for paid work by the total lack of remuneration attached to housework; to see both housework and women's paid work as marginal contributions to the national economy. It is a definition which endows women with the status of a labour reserve to be drawn on during periods of national need (such as wartime) and dispensed with during periods of economic recession. As employed women are legally 'protected' from the requirement of certain sorts of physically demanding work, so housework is categorized as essentially undemanding of the houseworker's physical energy. Since housework is preindustrial in nature it must be less skilled, as is women's other work. Most fundamental of all, since only those who are economically productive do 'real' work, housework is not real work at all: in its unreality it is either not-work or an intrinsically trivial work activity.

Any academic study of household labour must challenge at least the last of these assumptions by saying that housework is important enough to be studied. Many of those who have researched and discussed household labour in recent years have challenged much more of the stereotype than this and have exposed other important dimensions of what could be termed the 'official morality' of housework. The importance of doing this, and of going beyond it to research and make accessible the process of household labour, can hardly be overstated. In the first place, it is simply amazing that an activity which consumes a large proportion of the daily energy of 85 per cent of the adult female population as housewives, and of a majority of the total population in one form or another, should have been ignored so completely for so long. But, second, it is obvious that any understanding of the social position of women cannot proceed without a revelation of their role as houseworkers. Since stereotypes of housework apply to women's paid work as well, they, in an important sense, portray the attributed psychology of women in a capitalist society. There is, in fact, no clear demarcation between production and the other structures of women's oppression, because the social construction of femininity mediates and pervades them all.

In talking about gender differentiation it is important to make a distinction between two types of differentiation: those identified by Rogers[17] as 'behavioural' and 'ideological'. The first refers to the performance by the two sexes of different social roles; the second refers to the perceptions males and females have of themselves. Differentiation by gender does not amount to discrimination against women except where behavioural and ideological differentiation are out of step, so that women's own view of themselves and their sphere in society undergoes a basic revision. From perceiving their own interests and activities as valued and valuable, as capable of conferring status and promoting self-esteem, women move to an altogether different valuation, in which their image of themselves is derived from masculine ideology and becomes crucially self-derogating. Rogers suggests that this disturbance of balance between the two systems of differentiation is what happens when industrialization intrudes into the domestic and social relations of the sexes. The resulting transformation of female values is connected with shifts in the distribution of power between men and women.

Changes in the valuation of household labour are at the core of this transformation. In the gender ideology of capitalist society the masculine stereotype of 'women's work' has a prominent place, a highly significant fact which was not noted by academics discussing household work until the early 1970s. Sociology, in particular, demonstrated an uncritical adherence to the masculine stereotype of women and their work, dividing its subject areas and conceptual schemes so that women were relegated to the 'expressive' area of family relations, and men, in the generic and misleading sense of Man, constituted the subjects of the main and important part of sociological work. Functionalism, a dominant sociological paradigm, adopted the Victorian domestic mythology and said that what women did in the home was pre-eminently to manage personal relations, to symbolize the sanctity of order and domestic retreat in the harshly competitive world of capitalist business and industry. This was a good thing for women because it was a biological imperative, for men because it freed them of this burdensome responsibility, and for society because it provided a fully serviced and mobile workforce.[18] From the 1950s until the early 1970s, housework was only studied in empirical sociology as a component in female kinship, under the rubric of the euphemistic title the 'division of labour' (a pre-feminist or even anti-feminist conception, as Glazer-Malbin[19] notes), or as the projection of a 'social problem' concern with the rising trend in the employment of married women. Most studies of the family proceeded with a taken-for-granted view that the documentation of family life amounted to a description of the entire field of women's lives. Elizabeth Bott's germinal work *Family and Social Network*,[20] which initiated a subsequently much relied-on distinction between 'joint' and 'segregated' conjugal role-relationships, illustrates the hidden relevance of the established stereotype. Describing two ways in which the couples in her sample organized their roles, Bott called these 'joint' and 'segregated', even though joint-role couples divided their responsibilities so that housework was hers and earning the money was his. Furthermore, because housework was 'her' responsibility, Bott did not consider it important to spell out its character as a work activity – this despite the fact that her hypothesis about the relationship between family roles and the connectedness of families' social networks was a fertile ground for the investigation of the collective social definition of norms of housework behaviour.

Community studies in the 1950s and 1960s did more than any other category of sociological work to represent the reality of women's household labour, 'the industrial sociology of the housewife'.[21] But even they did so, for the most part, in the context of a preoccupation with the conditions of male labour and family life, and imbued by a presumption that the labour of women is trivial and not worthy of serious documentation. The dominant conception was one of housework as an aspect of the marital relationship, a view which of course precluded the articulation of housework from the houseworker's point of view, and prejudged the issue of the interaction between housework and marriage on the one hand, and between housework and other work on the other.

In 1974 I published a study[22] which aimed to look at women's attitudes to housework in the same way as other workers' attitudes to their work had been examined by sociologists. I did not see the book as a study of women and the family, but as a study of women's work. The original conception in its working out required the writing of a companion volume which analysed the historical evolution of the female-houseworker/male-breadwinner formula and its validating ideology.[23] The project evolved out of my personal experience of the contradiction between the male ideology of housework (non-productive, expressive, fulfilling, and so on) and its reality as lived by me, a middle-class mother of two young children in urban Britain in the late 1960s. I was shocked to discover that housework was time-consuming, exhausting, and (in the social setting in which I was doing it) deeply alienating. I had been led in the course of both my formal and informal education to think that it would be otherwise. Reading Gavron's *The Captive Wife*,[24] the only remotely relevant study of which I knew, I discerned that other women, academic and otherwise, shared my disillusionment. The emergence of women's liberation groups in my area of London in 1969–70 enabled me to state the problem with greater clarity. It is of historical interest now that my request to register a thesis entitled 'Work Attitudes and Work Satisfaction of Housewives' at the University of London in 1969 met with either frank disbelief or patronizing jocularity. The only person I could find who was willing to supervise such a work spent the next three years trying to convince me that women's sexual satisfaction and adjustment were at the heart of the problem. Similarly, I am now mildly amused, though I was at the time outraged, by the fact that two major British publishers turned down the book I produced on the grounds that everything that needed to be said about housework had already been said, and was I really serious in being serious about such a boring subject?

Since those days attitudes have changed somewhat (at least among publishers and thesis supervisors), and the study of household labour has expanded, especially in the last five years. One area of development has been the revision of the traditional Marxist approach to household work via its reinterpretation as a form of productive labour, and of the family as a system of productive relations. Delphy states the situation thus: 'Marriage is the institution by which gratuitous work is exhorted from a particular category of the population, women–wives.'[25] Marxists disagree as to whether it is technically correct to term this labour 'productive';[26] at any rate, what they are saying is that it is important, and that its importance and function are concealed by the mystification of the dominant ideology.

In the 1970s sociological studies of the family appear to have lapsed, and in their place has been a plethora of studies of particular aspects of marriage, reproduction, and the 'division of labour'. So far as this latter theme is concerned, there is now more recognition among sociologists of the distinction between *responsibility* for, and *participation* in ('helping' with), household tasks. The interaction between women's paid work and their unpaid domestic work has been seen without the obfuscation of 'social problem' definitions. The importance of considering domestic work responsibilities in tandem with occupational and other opportunities in debates about sex equality is now receiving more than lip service, and is indeed a major and persisting reason for studying women's household labour. Time–budget studies have proliferated and become more sophisticated, the evolution of domestic work over the life cycle is becoming a more prominent theme, and the relevance of socialization to domestic work-orientation is being more thoroughly explored. The effect of these contributions has been to explode myth, question stereotypes, and demonstrate how central domesticity remains as a defining feature of women's situation in the last years of the twentieth century.

Although the study of household labour has expanded in the last five years, it has not done so nearly as much as I hoped it would. There has, in my view, been too much emphasis on the theoretical role of housework in the Marxist schema, and too little in the way of empirical work exposing that much-needed corrective of established values, the attitudes, perceptions, satisfactions, and work-styles of houseworkers themselves. Moreover, the extent to which the study of housework has been integrated with the main concerns of sociology (and other disciplines) has been disappointing. The growth of 'women's studies' could in part be responsible for this, but I suspect both the spread of such courses and the failure of integration within disciplines stem from the same underlying cause: an ideological predisposition to segregate women. I hope that household labour will continue to be seen as a serious and central social and academic concern. There is no reason why those who research household labour should not, like science fiction writers, be able to effect a transformation of values; there is, however, every reason to suppose that we are, as yet, only at the beginning of this process.

25

General Smuts Pub
Evaporation

Coming back from work one afternoon my car broke down, and I was stranded in White City, an area of London considerably less pure than its name. It was the night of a big football match, and the pub where I waited to be retrieved from this mechanical disaster (hence the title of the poem) was full of men fuelling themselves for the evening's entertainment. I was surprisingly frightened by the sense in the air of uncivilized male aggression, signified by the multiple presence of police communicating electronically with one another.

'Evaporation', the second poem, is about a woman doing housework under male surveillance. I don't know the identity of the man who watched me cook carrots, but I have a much clearer idea of his effect on me. It was quite a relief to find he'd finally disappeared.

General Smuts Pub

a broken-down car
being the reason for being here
I sit defensively reading a paper
called 'Are Feminists Afraid to Leave Home?'

sipping my gin and tonic
I fight with the words on the page
to make them make sense
not only to me but here in this place
as foreign to me and all feminists as outer space

here for the football are you, love?
no, but that's why the streets are ringed with police
chatting cheerily on their radios
at the same time feeding seeds of violence in the damp night air

there are men everywhere
I cannot afford to look at them
for looking is dangerous to the psyche
and seeing even more so

Evaporation

I was stirring the soup
gold carrots, brown lentils, steam rising
when I felt this gentleman
behind me
with icy eyes and a bow tie
just looking

I went on stirring
swan lake pouring out of the radio
he went on standing
his breath like acid rain
on my meek neck domestic

as the carrots cooked
so the cookies crumble
you know what happens to wine if you cool it
the fizz enters the air
what could have made you drunk
hits the fan

when I turned round the third time
the gentleman had gone
straight out of the window

26

Marx as Colleague and Father

Many men who have 'made history' have led unremarkable private lives. What has been unremarkable about these private lives has been their addiction to conventionality, for the family, that repository of sexist and ageist values, has often kept men afloat on tides of public acclaim while the women and children have, if not exactly sunk, then at least suffered from permanently wet feet. Anchored by the dripping garments of domestic discomfort, women have alternately supported and protested, and many have not been able to see any possible different scenarios.

Whatever women have thought and felt, it hasn't been regarded as acceptable in public political, scientific, academic or literary circles to mention famous men's treatment of women in the same breath as their public achievements. The public–private divide reigns supreme, and not even a giant can span the two – indeed, it takes a rebellious woman to point out the connections between personal behaviour and public missions, and to observe that a poor record in the first is not automatically redeemed by a galaxy of gold stars in the second. It is, of course, men, stubbornly defending their private lives from scrutiny, who are liable to tie successful women up in the knots of their own intimate bliss – or otherwise: Margaret Thatcher's twins, Indira Gandhi's weaknesses as a mother, the divorces and hair dyes of female professionals, the necessary assumption of unmet heterosexual longings in the female revolutionary.

The following comments on the personal life of Karl Marx emerged as a review of two collections of letters[27] written within and between the

Source: Published in *The New York Times Book Review* 2 May 1982. Copyright © 1982 by the New York Times Company. Reprinted by permission.

Marx–Engels households. Aside from the revealed vulgarity of the relationship between Marx and Engels themselves, some of these letters are shockingly poignant on a woman's lot under the aegis of the master of materialist history; as Engels said at Mrs Marx's graveside, 'If ever woman found her highest happiness in rendering others happy, that woman was she.'[28] I hope she did, and that they did; and the letters in which Jenny senior, Jenny junior, Laura and Eleanor talk of the political struggle and the domestic domain contain wisdom, sincerity, intelligence and love, if not quite that peaceful happiness we are all supposed to find in our havens from a heartless world.

The usurpation of letter writing by the transient cadences of the telephone is probably one of the sadder developments of our time. It certainly must be one that future historians will bemoan. But what *do* collections of letters reveal about the people who wrote them?

Before deciding that, one must consider the process of selective editing. The volume of Marx and Engels's correspondence between 1844 and 1877, edited by Fritz Raddatz, represents only 150 pages out of a total of some 4,000 in their collected works. And in order to avoid any disclosure of the human side of Marx, the German socialist leaders August Bebel and Eduard Bernstein had *already* severely pruned the Marx–Engels personal correspondence for its first publication in 1913. The aim of Fritz Raddatz's collection seems, in fact, to be almost the obverse of this earlier canonization. It is hard at times to remember when scanning the evidence of these pages the enormous and lasting contribution the two men made to the political philosophy, history and action of the world – not so much in their lifetimes, perhaps, as afterward (it being a prime historical law that 'great' contributions are not recognized while their donors are alive).

Instead of two intellectual giants, we see two often infantile minds (the 'Moor' and the 'General') exchanging neurotic demands and promises and making snide, even outrageously rude remarks (sexist, classist and racist, to boot) about others in their circle. 'Are you studying physiology on Mary Burns' asks Marx of Engels, 'or elsewhere?' Or: 'My wife has unfortunately given birth to a girl and not to a boy.' 'I now feel a need...for money', writes Engels from Berne. 'If on receipt of this you have not yet sent me anything then do it at once for...you can't get anything on tick in this lousy town.'

Of course, Marx was usually the demander of money, and the twin evils of poverty and sickness, which in turn ruled the Marx household, dominate the correspondence. It is most remarkable that the Marx family never seemed to have any money, despite the fact that Marx asked for it from practically everyone he knew. Perhaps even more remarkable is the fact that Engels nearly always responded. He did, in a multitude of ways, take care of his friend's needs – from giving advice about how to treat the carbuncles that prevented Marx from sitting down, and thus from working, to writing manuscripts with Marx's name on them, to declaring himself the father of Marx's illegitimate son by the faithful Marx family servant, Helen Demuth, in order to divert the wrath of Marx's wife and daughters. (This latter act of generosity led to the contortion in which the Marx family made charitable payments to the boy, Freddy Demuth, out of the money Engels gave them, a fact they concealed from Engels himself.)

Engels, the younger of the two, does seem to have had a filial regard for Marx, which enabled him to bear this harsh treatment. Living with his working class mistress, Mary Burns, and her sister Lizzie, Engels appears to have liberated himself from the constraints of the bourgeois family, only to replace them with those of Marx's own. The rift that most threatened the solidarity Marx and Engels felt with one another came about, most significantly, when Mary Burns died and Marx did not react with appropriate regret. ('She was very kindhearted, witty and clung to you firmly', notes Marx, moving rapidly on to his latest money troubles.) But then neither Marx nor Engels was anxious to avoid eccentricity of feeling, thought or practice. In order to achieve their political goals, they recognized that they had to outdo the revolutionary in everyone else.

It is quite impossible to get beyond these surface impressions of Marx and Engels in the Raddatz volume – and not a great deal easier in *The Daughters of Karl Marx*. (The title is slightly misleading, since the volume includes some other letters, for instance from Marx's son-in-law Paul Lafargue.) The three Marx daughters were Jenny, born in 1844, Laura, born in 1845, and Eleanor (Tussy), born in 1855. There were four other children who died; of Marx's grandchildren, only four out of nine survived. Such a rate of infant mortality was surely characteristic of the time, but to read in the intimate mode of a family correspondence of the births and subsequent deaths of babies is sufficient to make the reader want to parcel up 'a few babycare books, antibiotics and baby clinics' and take them back into the past, as Sheila Rowbotham observes in her introduction.

One of the clearest messages that emerges from these letters is the intense and lifelong participation of the three women in an international political movement. Politics was integral to their lives, and they switched effortlessly in their letters from the wakefulness of children to the Fenians in Ireland, the Paris Commune, the Second International; thus, Jenny writes Laura in 1881 to ask for soap, and in the next line refers to the second Land Act and the death of Disraeli by enquiring, 'What do you think of the Land Bill and Dizzy's exit?' They were also multilingual and appeared to experience no difficulty in moving from one part of Europe to another. Eleanor provided English, French and German translations for the International Socialist Labour Congress in Paris in 1889, was the first to translate *Madame Bovary* into English and also rendered Ibsen into English for Havelock Ellis.

Competing with the three women's immersion in the international world was their situation *as women*. There is no doubt that, like other women of their day and age, they were the ones who both profited and lost from a sexual dependence of men. They took care of the housework, the men and the childrearing in order for their men to be free for higher activities. Many of the Marx daughters' letters to one another are constructed around tales of domestic events, but the tone is almost apologetic, as though nursing babies and so on should *not* occupy so much of one's time.

While Marx acknowledged that the human social condition, which is materially produced, has common psychological effects on people, his insight – breathed into all three girls in childhood – was in no way expanded by them in their lifetimes to include women. Women's problems were personal, men's political. The axiom that the personal *is* the political had to wait for another revolutionary movement a century later. Indeed, despite the occasional burst of intellectual protest ('I do believe', wrote Jenny to Laura in 1882, 'That even the dull routine of factory work is not more killing than are the endless duties of the *ménage*'), the Marx sisters hardly ever seemed to complain.

Again entirely in line with the psychology of women then and now, not Jenny nor Laura nor Eleanor saw women as *important*. Their own mother, their feelings about her, her significance to them – these things are scarcely mentioned. Their father exerts by far the most potent influence, to such an extent that all three women played out aspects of him in their subsequent relations with men. Jenny and Laura made political marriages, and Eleanor set up house with Edward Aveling, a philanderer and squanderer of other people's money. It was she who suffered most from the patriarchal robbing of women's self-identity that characterized Marx's relations with his daughters. 'Jenny is most like me', said Marx, 'but Tussy is me.' She suffered from 'mental' trouble all her life, from anorexia nervosa during her mother's terminal illness in 1881, and from what was virtually manic depression after Marx's death in 1883, and Jenny's in the same year of bladder cancer at the age of thirty-eight. On discovering the extent of Aveling's infidelity to her, Eleanor killed herself with prussic acid at the age of forty-three in 1898. (Laura also committed suicide some years later.)

Such vulnerability to emotion is often the lot of women. It is also, of course, one main reason why the second volume of letters appears to reveal more of the inner fires of their authors than the first. However, the expression of emotion – in letter writing and in life – may ultimately be just as distoring as its repression. The contrast between these two styles of communication is a good example of the extreme positions occupied by the two sexes in a capitalist society, positions that Marx and Engels were not able to see as the central division, because they did not themselves think women important enough to take seriously.

27

'Il Duomo'

An isolated poem about conferences, containing a minor insight into
the humanity of great men, and a few observations about the ritual
aspects of conference-attending, as merely one duty (or sin) among many
performed on the way to the confessional.

'Il Duomo'

out of the heavy white sky grows
an excrescence
grey and gothic
il duomo

every cathedral considers itself
the centre of the universe
but this one
more than most

makes a weighty statement
containing many long words
about the necessity
of its own pointed structures

love, pouring out of liquid candles
into lemon shadows creeping up the walls
the priest, important in his dark dress
aiming to hear confessions and not be affected by them
the woman with her head bowed over her shopping bag
silenzio! but the offensive crashes of the workmen
riding the scaffolding of God's holy house

what God has never built
no woman may put asunder

we may therefore make a case
for this conference living out its brief life
round the corner from il duomo
being actually about nothing

on the one hand there's enough rabid language
to make a dog mad
enough concepts are tangled with
ideas remarked upon
conclusions excoriated
percentages preened at

judged by the verbal barometer
the weather is getting better all the time

but on the other hand I in the pink dress
seriously survey the acres of faces
upturned like artichokes to the microphones

in their very expectancy
the code is cracked
their waiting dark eyes
subjugate a kingdom of emptiness

what the hell are they hoping for?

everything we know is known from within
experts cannot tell you what knowledge is
Galileo, Copernicus, Newton, Harvey
were little men who picked their noses
like the rest of us
and like mice scrabbling away in the cellars
of il duomo
hoped to find a crumb or two on their way to the confessional

28

Interviewing Women: a Contradiction in Terms?

One curious characteristic dominating the twentieth-century is the discrepancy between theory and practice. On the one hand, there are statements, arguments, ideas and suppositions about how the world is, and how people fit into and construct it, and, on the other, there are the lived realities of individual lives. Yet theory and practice are always liable to contradict each other. Experience is too messy to be reduced to neat philosophical or mathematical expressions; alternatively, it could be said that, since the whole aim of theory is to tidy up the world, it is unlikely ever to succeed in this aim.

The best way out of this conundrum is to regard the tension between theory and practice as creative: out of its dialectics will arise a new theory and a new practice. This is true, but must be squared with the politically uncomfortable fact that certain historical circumstances breed the greatest tension between the rigid arrogance of theory and the reflexive domesticity of practice. In an unequal society, where one social group imposes itself on others, major contradictions between theory and practice are going to be revealed. So it was, and is, with women, and so it is too, whenever the difficult relationship between theory and practice in any particular disciplinary niche is exposed to the critical scrutiny of the new feminist, or at least feminine, world-view.

'Interviewing Women: a contradiction in terms?' came out of my own

Source: Originally published in H. Roberts (ed.) *Doing Feminist Research* London, Routledge & Kegan Paul, 1981.

experience of trying to research issues of concern to women from a basis in masculinist social science. 'Interviewing Women' develops the themes raised in the first piece in this section on the possibility of feminist social science by examining carefully one crucial area in which theory has traditionally been highly unresponsive to practice, simply because it has ignored the social and personal relations of the research process. The male sociologist's cover is blown, and with it the idea that personal identity can be wrapped up into a Galilean world of discrete and different objects.

Interviewing is rather like marriage: everybody knows what it is, an awful lot of people do it, and yet behind each closed front door there is a world of secrets. Despite the fact that much of modern sociology could justifiably be considered 'the science of the interview',[29] very few sociologists who employ interview data actually bother to describe in detail the process of interviewing itself. The conventions of research reporting require them to offer such information as how many interviews were done and how many were not done; the length of time the interviews lasted; whether the questions were asked following some standardized format or not; and how the information was recorded. Some issues on which research reports do not usually comment are: social/personal characteristics of those doing the interviewing; interviewees' feelings about being interviewed and about the interview; interviewers' feelings about interviewees; and quality of interviewer–interviewee interaction; hospitality offered by interviewees to interviewers; attempts by interviewees to use interviewers as sources of information; and the extension of interviewer–interviewee encounters into more broadly-based social relationships.

I shall argue in this chapter that social science researchers' awareness of those aspects of interviewing which are 'legitimate' and 'illegitimate' from the viewpoint of inclusion in research reports reflect their embeddedness in a particular research protocol. This protocol assumes a predominantly masculine model of sociology and society. The relative undervaluation of women's models has led to an unreal theoretical characterization of the interview as a means of gathering sociological data which cannot and does not work in practice. This lack of fit between the theory and practice of interviewing is especially likely to come to the fore when a feminist interviewer is interviewing women (who may or may not be feminists).

INTERVIEWING: A MASCULINE PARADIGM?

Let us consider first what the methodology textbooks say about interviewing. First, and most obviously, an interview is a way of finding out about people. 'If you want an answer, ask a question. . . . The asking of questions is the main source of social scientific information about everyday behaviour.'[30] According to Johan Galtung:

> The survey method. . .has been indispensable in gaining information about the human condition and new insights in social theory.
> The reasons for the success of the survey method seem to be two: (1) *theoretically relevant* data are obtained (2) they are amenable to *statistical treatment*, which means (a) the use of the powerful tools of correlation analysis and multi-variate analysis to test substantive relationships, and (b) the tools of statistical tests of hypotheses about generalizability from samples to universes.[31]

Interviewing, which is one means of conducting a survey, is essentially a conversation, 'merely one of the many ways in which two people talk to one another',[32] but it is also, significantly, an *instrument* of data collection: 'the interviewer is really a tool or an instrument.'[33] As Benny and Hughes express it:

> Regarded as an information-gathering tool, the interview is designed to minimise the local concrete, immediate circumstances of the particular encounter – including the respective personalities of the participants – and to emphasise only those aspects that can be kept general enough and demonstrable enough to be counted. As an encounter between these two particular people the typical interview has no meaning; it is conceived in a framework of other, comparable meetings between other couples, each recorded in such fashion that elements of communication in common can be easily isolated from more idiosyncratic qualities.[34]

Thus an interview is 'not simply a conversation. It is, rather, a pseudo-conversation. In order to be successful, it must have all the warmth and personality exchange of a conversation with the clarity and guidelines of scientific searching.'[35] This requirement means that the interview must be seen as 'a specialised pattern of verbal interaction – initiated for a specific purpose, and focussed on some specific content areas, with consequent elimination of extraneous material.'[36]

The motif of successful interviewing is 'be friendly but not too friendly'.

For the contradiction at the heart of the textbook paradigm is that interviewing necessitates the manipulation of interviewees as objects of study/sources of data, but this can only be achieved via a certain amount of humane treatment. If the interviewee doesn't believe he/she is being kindly and sympathetically treated by the interviewer, then he/she will not consent to be studied and will not come up with the desired information. A balance must then be struck between the warmth required to generate 'rapport' and the detachment necessary to see the interviewee as an object under surveillance; walking this tightrope means, not surprisingly, that 'interviewing is not easy',[37] although mostly the textbooks do support the idea that it *is* possible to be a perfect interviewer and both to get reliable and valid data and make interviewees believe they are not simple statistics-to-be. It is just a matter of following the rules.

A major preoccupation in the spelling out of the rules is to counsel potential interviewers about where necessary friendliness ends and unwarranted involvement begins. Goode and Hatt's statement on this topic quoted earlier, for example continues:

> Consequently, the interviewer cannot merely lose himself in being friendly. He must introduce himself as though beginning a conversation but from the beginning the additional element of respect, of professional competence, should be maintained. Even the beginning student will make this attempt, else he will find himself merely 'maintaining rapport', while failing to penetrate the cliches of contradictions of the respondent. Further he will find that his own confidence is lessened, if his only goal is to maintain friendliness. He is a professional researcher in this situation and he must demand and obtain respect for the task he is trying to perform.[38]

Claire Selltiz and her colleagues give a more explicit recipe. They say:

> The interviewer's manner should be friendly, courteous, conversational and unbiased. He should be neither too grim nor too effusive; neither too talkative nor too timid. The idea should be to put the respondent at ease, so that he[39] will talk freely and fully. . . . [Hence] A brief remark about the weather, the family pets, flowers or children will often serve to break the ice. Above all, an informal, conversational interview is dependent upon a thorough mastery by the interviewer of the actual questions in his schedule. He should be familiar enough with them to ask them conversationally, rather than read them stiffly; and he should know what questions are coming next, so there will be no awkward pauses while he studies the questionnaire.[40]

C. A. Moser, in an earlier text, advises of the dangers of 'overrapport':

> Some interviewers are no doubt better than others at establishing what
> the psychologists call 'rapport' and some may even be too good at it –
> the National Opinion Research Centre Studies found slightly less satisfac-
> tory results from the...sociable interviewers who are 'fascinated by
> people...there is something to be said for the interviewer who, while
> friendly and interested, does not get too emotionally involved with the
> respondent and his problems. Interviewing on most surveys is a fairly
> straightforward job, not one calling for exceptional industry, charm or
> tact. What one asks is that the interviewer's personality should be neither
> over-aggressive nor over-sociable. Pleasantness and a business-like nature
> is the ideal combination.[41]

'Rapport', a commonly used but ill-defined term, does not mean in
this context what the dictionary says it does ('a sympathetic relationship')[42] but the acceptance by the interviewee of the interviewer's
research goals, and the interviewee's active search to help the interviewer
in providing the relevant information. The person who is interviewed
has a passive role in adapting to the definition of the situation offered
by the person doing the interviewing. The person doing the interviewing
must actively and continually construct the 'respondent' (a telling name)
as passive. Another way to phrase this is to say that both interviewer
and interviewee must be 'socialized' into the correct interviewing
behaviour:

> it is essential not only to train scientists to construct carefully worded
> questions and draw representative samples but also to educate the public
> to respond to questions on matters of interest to scientists and to do so
> in a manner advantageous for scientific analysis. To the extent that such
> is achieved, a common bond is established between interviewer and
> interviewee. [However] It is not enough for the scientist to understand
> the world of meaning of his informants; if he is to secure valid data via
> the structured interview, respondents must be socialised into answering
> questions in proper fashion.[43]

One piece of behaviour that properly socialized respondents do not
engage in is asking questions back. Although the textbooks do not present
any evidence about the extent to which interviewers do find in practice
that this happens, they warn of its dangers and in the process suggest
some possible strategies of avoidance: 'Never provide the interviewee
with any formal indication of the interviewer's beliefs and values. If the

informant poses a question...parry it'.[44] When asked what you mean and think, tell them you are here to learn, not to pass any judgement, that the situation is very complex.'[45] 'If he (the interviewer) should be asked for his views, he should laugh off the request with the remark that his job at the moment is to get opinions, not to have them'[46] and so on. Goode and Hatt offer the most detailed advice on this issue:

> What is the interviewer to do, however, if the respondent really wants information? Suppose the interviewee does answer the question but then asks for the opinions of the interviewer. Should he give his honest opinion, or an opinion which he thinks the interviewee wants? In most cases, the rule remains that he is there to obtain information and to focus on the respondent, not himself. Usually, a few simple phrases will shift the emphasis back to the respondent. Some which have been fairly successful are 'I guess I haven't thought enough about it to give a good answer right now', 'Well, right now, your opinions are more important than mine', and 'If you really want to know what I think, I'll be honest and tell you in a moment, after we've finished the interview.' Sometimes the diversion can be accomplished by a headshaking gesture which suggests 'That's a hard one!' while continuing with the interview. In short, the interviewer must avoid the temptation to express his own views, even if given the opportunity.[47]

Of course the reason why the interviewer must pretend not to have opinions (or to be possessed of information the interviewee wants) is because behaving otherwise might 'bias' the interview. 'Bias' occurs when there are systematic differences between interviewers in the way interviews are conducted, with resulting differences in the data produced. Such bias clearly invalidates the scientific claims of the research, since the question of which information might be coloured by interviewees' responses to interviewers' attitudinal stances and which is independent of this 'contamination' cannot be settled in any decisive way.

The paradigm of the social research interview prompted in the methodology textbooks does, then, emphasize

(1) its status as a mechanical instrument of data-collection;
(2) its function as a specialized form of conversation in which one person asks the questions and another gives the answers;
(3) its characterization of interviewees as essentially passive individuals, and
(4) its reduction of interviewers to a question-asking and rapport-promoting role.

Actually, two separate typifications of the interviewer are prominent in the literature, though the disjunction between the two is never commented on. In one the interviewer is 'a combined phonograph and recording system';[48] the job of the interviewer 'is fundamentally that of a reporter not an evangelist, a curiosity-seeker, or a debater'.[49] It is important to note that while the interviewer must treat the interviewee as an object or data-producing machine which, when handled correctly will function properly, the interviewer herself/himself has the same status from the point of view of the person/people, institution or corporation conducting the research. Both interviewer and interviewee are thus depersonalized participants in the research process.

The second typification of interviewers in the methodology literature is that of the interviewer as psychoanalyst. The interviewer's relationship to the interviewee is hierarchical and it is the body of expertise possessed by the interviewer that allows the interview to be successfully conducted. Most crucial in this exercise is the interviewer's use of non-directive comments and probes to encourage a free association of ideas which reveals whatever truth the research has been set up to uncover. Indeed, the term 'non-directive interview' is derived directly from the language of psychotherapy and carries the logic of interviewer-impersonality to its extreme:

> Perhaps the most typical remarks made by the interviewer in a non-directive interview are: 'You feel that...' or 'Tell me more' or 'Why?' or 'Isn't that interesting?' or simply 'Uh huh'. The nondirective interviewer's function is primarily to serve as a catalyst to a comprehensive expression of the subject's feelings and beliefs and of the frame of reference within which his feelings and beliefs take on personal significance. To achieve this result, the interviewer must create a completely permissive atmosphere, in which the subject is free to express himself without fear of disapproval, admonition or dispute and without advice from the interviewer.[50]

Sjoberg and Nett spell out the premises of the free association method:

> the actor's [interviewee's] mental condition [is]...confused and difficult to grasp. Frequently the actor himself does not know what he believes; he may be so 'immature' that he cannot perceive or cope with his own subconscious thought patterns...the interviewer must be prepared to follow the interviewee through a jungle of meandering thought ways if he is to arrive at the person's true self.[51]

It seems clear that both psychoanalytic and mechanical typifications of the interviewer and, indeed, the entire paradigmatic representation of 'proper' interviews in the methodology textbooks, owe a great deal more to a masculine social and sociological vantage point than to a feminine one. For example, the paradigm of the 'proper' interview appeals to such values as objectivity, detachment, hierarchy and 'science' as an important cultural activity which takes priority over people's more individualized concerns. Thus the errors of poor interviewing comprise subjectivity, involvement, the 'fiction' of equality and an undue concern with the ways in which people are not statistically comparable. This polarity of 'proper' and 'improper' interviewing is an almost classical representation of the widespread gender stereotyping which has been shown, in countless studies, to occur in modern industrial civilizations. Women are characterized as sensitive, intuitive, incapable of objectivity and emotional detachment and as immersed in the business of making and sustaining personal relationships. Men are thought superior through their own capacity for rationality and scientific objectivity and are thus seen to be possessed of an instrumental orientation in their relationships with others. Women are the exploited, the abused; they are unable to exploit others through the 'natural' weakness of altruism – a quality which is also their strength as wives, mothers and housewives. Conversely, men find it easy to exploit, although it is most important that any exploitation be justified in the name of some broad political or economic ideology ('the end justifies the means').

Feminine and masculine psychology in patriarchal societies is the psychology of subordinate and dominant social groups. The tie between women's irrationality and heightened sensibility on the one hand, and their materially disadvantaged position on the other is, for example, also to be found in the case of ethnic minorities. The psychological characteristics of subordinates

> form a certain familiar cluster: submissiveness, passivity, docility, dependency, lack of initiative, inability to act, to decide, to think and the like. In general, this cluster includes qualities more characteristic of children than adults – immaturity, weakness and helplessness. If subordinates adopt these characteristics, they are considered well adjusted.[52]

It is no accident that the methodology textbooks refer to the interviewer as male. Although not all interviewees are referred to as female, there are a number of references to 'housewives' as the kind of people interviewers are most likely to meet in the course of their work.[53] Some of what Jean Baker Miller has to say about the relationship between dominant and subordinate groups would appear to be relevant to this paradigmatic interviewer–interviewee relationship:

> A dominant group, inevitably, has the greatest influence in determining a culture's overall outlook – its philosophy, morality, social theory and even its science. The dominant group, thus, legitimizes the unequal relationship and incorporates it into society's guiding concepts. . . .
>
> Inevitably the dominant group is the model for 'normal human relationships'. It then becomes 'normal' to treat others destructively and to derogate them, to obscure the truth of what you are doing by creating false explanations and to oppose actions toward equality. In short, if one's identification is with the dominant group, it is 'normal' to continue in this pattern. . . .
>
> It follows from this that dominant groups generally do not like to be told about or even quietly reminded of the existence of inequality. 'Normally' they can avoid awareness because their explanation of the relationship becomes so well integrated *in other terms*; they can even believe that both they and the subordinate group share the same interests and, to some extent, a common experience. . . .
>
> Clearly, inequality has created a state of conflict. Yet dominant groups will tend to suppress conflict. They will see any questioning of the 'normal' situation as threatening; activities by subordinates in this direction will be perceived with alarm. Dominants are usually convinced that the way things are is right and good, not only for them but especially for the subordinates. All morality confirms this view and all social structure sustains it.[54]

To paraphrase the relevance of this to the interviewer–interviewee relationship we could say that: interviewers define the role of interviewees as subordinates; extracting information is more to be valued than yielding it; the convention of interviewer–interviewee hierarchy is a rationalization of inequality; what is good for interviewers is not necessarily good for interviewees.

Another way to approach this question of the masculinity of the 'proper' interview is to observe that a sociology of feelings and emotion does not exist. Sociology mirrors society in not looking at social interaction from the viewpoint of women. While everyone has feelings, 'Our society defines being cognitive, intellectual or rational dimensions of experience as superior to being emotional or sentimental. (Significantly, the terms "emotional" and "sentimental" have come to connote excessive or degenerate forms of feeling.) Through the prism of our technological and rationalistic culture, we are led to perceive and feel emotions as some irrelevancy or impediment to getting things done.' Hence their role in interviewing. But 'Another reason for sociologists' neglect of emotions may be the discipline's attempt to be recognized as a "real science" and the consequent need to focus on the most objective and measurable features of social life. This coincides with the values of the traditional "male culture"'.[55]

Getting involved with the people you interview is doubly bad: it jeopardizes the hard-won status of sociology as a science and it is indicative of a form of personal degeneracy.

WOMEN INTERVIEWING WOMEN:
OR OBJECTIFYING YOUR SISTER

Before I became an interviewer I had read what the textbooks said interviewing ought to be. However, I found it very difficult to realize the prescription in practice, in a number of ways which I describe below. It was these practical difficulties which led me to take a new look at the textbook paradigm. In the rest of this chapter the case I want to make is that when a feminist interviews women:

(1) use of prescribed interviewing practice is morally indefensible;
(2) general and irreconcilable contradictions at the heart of the textbook paradigm are exposed; and
(3) it becomes clear that, in most cases, the goal of finding out about people through interviewing is best achieved when the relationship of interviewer and interviewee is non-hierarchical and when the interviewer is prepared to invest his or her own personal identity in the relationship.

Before arguing the general case I will briefly mention some relevant aspects of my own interviewing experience. I have interviewed several hundred women over a period of some ten years, but it was the most recent research project, one concerned with the transition to motherhood, that particularly highlighted problems in the conventional interviewing recipe. Salient features of this research were that it involved repeated interviewing of a sample of women during a critical phase in their lives (in fact 55 women were interviewed four times; twice in pregnancy and twice afterwards and the average total period of interviewing was 9.4 hours). It included, for some, my attendance at the most critical point in this phase: the birth of the baby. The research was preceded by nine months of participant observation chiefly in the hospital setting of interactions between mothers or mothers-to-be and medical people. Although I had a research assistant to help me, I myself did the bulk of the interviewing – 178 interviews over a period of some 12 months. The project was my idea and the analysis and writing up of the data was entirely my responsibility.

My difficulties in interviewing women were of two main kinds. First, they asked me a great many questions. Second, repeated interviewing over this kind of period and involving the intensely personal experiences of pregnancy, birth and motherhood, established a rationale of personal involvement I found it problematic and ultimately unhelpful to avoid.

Asking Questions Back

Analysing the tape-recorded interviews I had conducted, I listed 878 questions that interviewees had asked me at some point in the interviewing process. Three-quarters of these (see Table 28.1) were requests for information (e.g. 'Who will deliver my baby?' 'How do you cook an egg for a baby?') Fifteen per cent were questions about me, my experiences or attitudes in the area of reproduction ('Have you got any children?'

TABLE 28.1
Questions interviewees asked (total 878),
Transition to Motherhood Project (%)

Information requests	76
Personal questions	15
Questions about the research	6
Advice questions	4

'Did you breastfeed?'); 6 per cent were questions about the research ('Are you going to write a book?' 'Who pays you for doing this?'), and 4 per cent were more directly requests for advice on a particular matter ('How long should you wait for sex after childbirth?' 'Do you think my baby's got too many clothes on?'). Table 28.2 goes into more detail about the topics on which interviewees wanted information. The largest category of questions concerned medical procedures: for example, how induction of labour is done, and whether all women attending a particular hospital are given episiotomies. The second largest category related to infant care or development: for example, 'How do you clean a baby's nails?' 'When do babies sleep through the night?' Third, there were questions about organizational procedures in the institutional settings where antenatal or delivery care was done; typical questions were concerned with who exactly would be doing antenatal care and what the rules are for husbands' attendance at delivery. Last, there were questions about the physiology of reproduction; for example 'Why do some women need caesareans?' and (from one very frightened mother-to-be) 'Is it right that the baby doesn't come out of the same hole you pass water out of?'

TABLE 28.2
Interviewees' requests for information (total 664),
Transition to Motherhood Project (%)

Medical procedures	31
Organizational procedures	19
Physiology of reproduction	15
Baby care/development/feeding	21
Other	15

It would be the understatement of all time to say that I found it very difficult to avoid answering these questions as honestly and fully as I could. I was faced, typically, with a woman who was quite anxious about the fate of herself and her baby, who found it either impossible or extremely difficult to ask questions and receive satisfactory answers from the medical staff with whom she came into contact, and who saw me as someone who could not only reassure but inform. I felt that I was asking a great deal from these women in the way of time, co-operation and hospitality at a stage in their lives when they had every reason to exclude strangers altogether in order to concentrate on the momentous character of the experiences being lived through. Indeed, I *was* asking a great deal – not only 9.4 hours of interviewing time but confidences on highly personal matters such as sex and money and 'real' (i.e. possibly negative or ambivalent) feelings about babies, husbands, etc. I was, in addition, asking some of the women to allow me to witness them in the highly personal act of giving birth. Although the pregnancy interviews did not have to compete with the demands of motherhood for time, 90 per cent of the women were employed when first interviewed and 76 per cent of the first interviews had to take place in the evenings. Although

I had timed the first postnatal interview (at about five weeks postpartum) to occur after the disturbances of very early motherhood, for many women it was nevertheless a stressful and busy time. And all this in the interests of 'science' or for some book that might possibly materialize out of the research – a book which many of the women interviewed would not read and none would profit from directly (though they hoped that they would not lose too much).

THE TRANSITION TO FRIENDSHIP?

In a paper on 'Collaborative Interviewing and Interactive Research', Laslett and Rapoport[56] discuss the advantages and disadvantages of repeated interviewing. They say that the gain in terms of collecting more information in greater depth than would otherwise be possible is partly made by 'being responsive to, rather than seeking to avoid, respondent reactions to the interview situation and experience'. This sort of research is deemed by them 'interactive'. The principle of a hierarchical relationship between interviewer and interviewee is not adhered to and 'an attempt is made to generate a collaborative approach to the research which engages both the interviewer and respondent in a joint enterprise.' Such an approach explicitly does not seek to minimize the personal involvement of the interviewer, but, as Rapoport and Rapoport put it, relies 'very much on the formulation of a relationship between interviewer and interviewee as an important element in achieving the quality of the information . . . required'.[57]

As Laslett and Rapoport note, repeated interviewing is not much discussed in the methodological literature: the paradigm is of an interview as a 'one-off' affair. Common sense would suggest that an ethic of detachment on the interviewer's part is much easier to maintain where there is only one meeting with the interviewee (and the idea of a 'one-off' affair rather than a longer-term relationship is undoubtedly closer to the traditional masculine world-view I discussed earlier).

In terms of my experience in the childbirth project, I found that interviewees very often took the initiative in defining the interviewer–interviewee relationship as something which existed beyond the limits of question-asking and answering. For example, they did not only offer the minimum hospitality of accommodating me in their homes for the duration of the interview: at 92 per cent of the interviews I was offered tea, coffee or some other drink; 14 per cent of the women also offered me a meal on at least one occasion. As Table 28.1 suggests, there was also a certain amount of interest in my own situation. What sort of person was I and how did I come to be interested in this subject?

In some cases these kind of 'respondent' reactions were evident at the first interview. More often they were generated after the second interview and an important factor here was probably the timing of the interviews. There was an average of 20 weeks between interviews 1 and 2, an average of 11 weeks between interviews 2 and 3 and an average of 15 weeks between interviews 3 and 4. Between the first two interviews most of the women were very busy. Most were still employed and had the extra work of preparing equipment/clothes/a room for the baby – which sometimes meant moving house. Between interviews 2 and 3 most were not out at work and, sensitized by the questions I had asked in the first two interviews to my interest in their birth experiences, probably began to associate me in a more direct way with their experiences of the transition to motherhood. At interview 2 I gave them all a stamped addressed postcard on which I asked them to write the date of their baby's birth so I would know when to re-contact them for the first postnatal interview. I noticed that this was usually placed in a prominent position (for example on the mantelpiece), to remind the woman or her partner to complete it and it probably served in this way as a reminder of my intrusion into their lives. One illustration of this awareness comes from the third interview with Mary Rosen, a twenty-five year-old exhibition organizer: 'I thought of you after he was born, I thought she'll *never* believe it – a six-hour labour, a 9lb 6oz baby and *no* forceps – and all without an epidural, although I had said to you that I wanted one.' Sixty-two per cent of the women expressed a sustained and quite detailed interest in the research; they wanted to know its goals, any proposed methods for disseminating its findings, how I had come to think of it in the first place, what the attitudes of doctors I had met, or collaborated with, were to it and so forth. Some of the women took the initiative in contacting me to arrange the second or a subsequent interview, although I had made it clear that I would get in touch with them. Several rang up to report particularly important pieces of information about their antenatal care – in one case a distressing encounter with a doctor who told a woman keen on natural childbirth that this was 'for animals: in this hospital we give epidurals'; in another case to tell me of an ultrasound result that changed the expected date of delivery. Several also got in touch to correct or add to things they had said during an interview – for instance, one contacted me several weeks after the fourth interview to explain that she had had an emergency appendicectomy five days after my visit and that her physical symptoms at the time could have affected some of her responses to the questions I asked.

Arguably, these signs of interviewees' involvement indicated their acceptance of the goals of the research project rather than any desire to feel themselves participating in a personal relationship with me. Yet the research was presented to them as *my* research in which I had a personal interest, so it is not likely that a hard and fast dividing line between the two was drawn. One index of their and my reactions to our joint participation in the repeated interviewing situation is that some four years after the final interview I am still in touch with more than a third of the women I interviewed. Four have become close friends, several others I visit occasionally, and the rest write or telephone when they have something salient to report such as the birth of another child.

A FEMINIST INTERVIEWS WOMEN

Such responses as I have described on the part of the interviewees to participation in research, particularly that involving repeated interviewing, are not unknown, although they are almost certainly under-reported. It could be suggested that the reasons why they were so pronounced in the research project discussed here is because of the attitudes of the interviewer – that is, the women were reacting to my own evident wish for a relatively intimate and non-hierarchical relationship. While I was careful not to take direct initiatives in this direction, I certainly set out to convey to the people whose co-operation I was seeking, the fact that I did not intend to exploit either them or the information they gave me. For instance, if the interview clashed with the demands of housework and motherhood I offered to, and often did, help with the work that had to be done. When asking the women's permission to record the interview, I said that no one but I would ever listen to the tapes; in mentioning the possibility of publications arising out of the research I told them that their names and personal details would be changed and I would, if they wished, send them details of any such publications, and so forth. The attitude I conveyed could have had some influence in encouraging the women to regard me as a friend rather than purely as a data-gatherer.

The pilot interviews, together with my previous experience of interviewing women, led me to decide that when I was asked questions I would answer them. The practice I followed was to answer all personal questions and questions about the research as fully as was required. For example, when two women asked if I had read their hospital case notes

I said I had, and when one of them went on to ask what reason was given in these notes for her forceps delivery, I told her what the notes said. On the emotive issue of whether I experienced childbirth as painful (a common topic of conversation) I told them that I did find it so, but that in my view it was worth it to get a baby at the end. Advice questions I also answered fully but made it clear when I was using my own experiences of motherhood as the basis for advice. I also referred women requesting advice to the antenatal and childbearing advice literature or to health visitors, GPs, etc. when appropriate – though the women usually made it clear that it was my opinion in particular they were soliciting. When asked for information I gave it if I could or, again, referred the questioner to an appropriate medical or non-medical authority. Again, the way I responded to interviewee's questions probably encouraged them to regard me as more than an instrument of data-collection.

Dissecting my practice of interviewing further, there were three principal reasons why I decided not to follow the textbook code of ethics with regard to interviewing women. First, I did not regard it as reasonable to adopt a purely exploitative attitude to interviewees as sources of data. My involvement in the women's movement in the early 1970s and the rebirth of feminism in an academic context had led me, along with many others, to reassess society and sociology as masculine paradigms and to want to bring about change in the traditional cultural and academic treatment of women. 'Sisterhood', a somewhat nebulous and problematic, but nevertheless important, concept, certainly demanded that women re-evaluate the basis of their relationships with one another.

The dilemma of a feminist interviewer interviewing women could be summarized by considering the practical application of some of the strategies recommended in the textbooks for meeting interviewee's questions. For example, these advise that such questions as 'Which hole does the baby come out of?' 'Does an epidural ever paralyse women?' and 'Why is it dangerous to leave a small baby alone in the house?' should be met with such responses from the interviewer as 'I guess I haven't thought enough about it to give a good answer right now,' or 'a head-shaking gesture which suggests "that's a hard one."'[58] Also recommended is laughing off the request with the remark that 'my job at the moment is to get opinions, not to have them.'[59]

A second reason for departing from conventional interviewing ethics was that I regarded sociological research as an essential way of giving the subjective situation of women greater visibility not only in sociology, but, more importantly, in society, than it has traditionally had. Interviewing women was, then, a strategy for documenting women's own accounts of their lives. What *was* important was not taken-for-granted sociological assumptions about the role of the interviewer, but a new awareness of the interviewer as an instrument for promoting a sociology for women, that is, as a tool for making possible the articulated and recorded commentary of women on the very personal business of being female in a patriarchal capitalist society. Note that the formulation of the interviewer role has changed dramatically from being a data-collecting instrument for researchers to being a data-collecting instrument for those whose lives are being researched. Such a reformulation is enhanced where the interviewer is also the researcher. It is not coincidental that in the methodological literature the paradigm of the research process is essentially disjunctive, that is, researcher and interviewer functions are typically performed by different individuals.

A third reason why I undertook the childbirth research with a degree of scepticism about how far traditional percepts of interviewing could, or should, be applied in practice was because I had found, in my previous interviewing experiences, that an attitude of refusing to answer questions or offer any kind of personal feedback was not helpful in terms of the traditional goal of promoting 'rapport'. A different role, that could be termed 'no intimacy without reciprocity', seemed especially important in longitudinal in-depth interviewing. Without feeling that the interviewing process offered some personal satisfaction to them, interviewees would not be prepared to continue after the first interview. This involves being sensitive not only to those questions that are asked (by either party) but to those that are not asked. The interviewee's definition of the interview is important.

The success of this method cannot, of course, be judged from the evidence I have given so far. On the question of the rapport established in the Transition to Motherhood research I offer the following cameo:

> AO: 'Did you have any questions you wanted to ask but didn't when you last went to the hospital?'
>
> MC: 'Er, I don't know how to put this really. After sexual intercourse I had some bleeding, three times, only a few drops and I didn't tell the hospital because I didn't know how to put it to them. It worried me first off, as soon as I saw it I cried. I don't know if I'd be able to tell them. You see, I've also got a sore down there and a discharge and you know I wash there lots of times a day. You think I should tell the hospital; I could never speak to my own doctor about it. You see I feel like this but I can talk to you about it and I can talk to my sister about it.'

More generally the quality and depth of the information given to me by the women I interviewed can be assessed in *Becoming a Mother*,[60] the book arising out of the research which is based almost exclusively on interviewee accounts.

So far as interviewees' reactions to being interviewed are concerned, I asked them at the end of the last interview the question, 'Do you feel that being involved in this research – my coming to see you – has affected your experience of becoming a mother in any way?' Table 28.3 shows the answers.

TABLE 28.3
'Has the research affected your experience
of becoming a mother?' (%)

No	27
Yes:	73
Thought about it more	30
Found it reassuring	25
A relief to talk	25
Changed attitudes/behaviour	7

(Percentages do not add up to 100 per cent because some women gave more than one answer.)

Nearly three-quarters of the women said that being interviewed had affected them and the three most common forms this influence took were in leading them to reflect on their experiences more than they would otherwise have done; in reducing the level of their anxiety and/or in reassuring them of their normality; and in giving a valuable outlet for the verbalization of feelings. None of those who thought being interviewed had affected them regarded this effect as negative. There were many references to the 'therapeutic' effect of talking: 'getting it out of your system'. (It was generally felt that husbands, mothers, friends, etc., did not provide a sufficiently sympathetic or interested audience for a detailed recounting of the experiences and difficulties of becoming a mother.) It is perhaps important to note here that one of the main conclusions of the research was that there is a considerable discrepancy between the expectations and the reality of the different aspects of motherhood – pregnancy, childbirth, the emotional relationship of mother and child, the work of childrearing. A dominant metaphor used by interviewees to describe their reactions to this hiatus was 'shock'. In this sense, a process of emotional recovery is endemic in the normal transition to motherhood and there is a general need for some kind of 'therapeutic listener' that is not met within the usual circle of family and friends.

On the issue of co-operation, only two out of 82 women contacted initially about the research actually refused to take part in it, making a refusal rate of 2 per cent which is extremely low. Once the interviewing was under way only one woman voluntarily dropped out (because of marital problems); an attrition from 66 at interview 1 to 55 at interview 4 was otherwise accounted for by miscarriage, moves, etc. All the women who were asked if they would mind me attending the birth said they didn't mind and all got in touch either directly or indirectly through their husbands when they started labour. The postcards left after interview 2, for interviewees to return after the birth, were all completed and returned.

IS A 'PROPER' INTERVIEW EVER POSSIBLE?

Hidden amongst the admonitions on how to be a perfect interviewer in the social research methods manuals is the covert recognition that the goal of perfection is actually unattainable: the contradiction between the need for 'rapport' and the requirement of between-interview comparability cannot be solved. For example, Dexter, following Paul,[61] observes that the pretence of neutrality on the interviewer's part is counterproductive: participation demands alignment. Selltiz et al. say that 'Much of what we call interviewer bias can more correctly be described as interviewer *differences*, which are inherent in the fact that interviewers are human beings and not machines and that they do not work identically.'[62] Richardson and his colleagues in their popular textbook on interviewing note that:

> Although gaining and maintaining satisfactory participation is never the primary objective of the interviewer, it is so intimately related to the quality and quantity of the information sought that the interviewer must always maintain a dual concern: for the quality of his respondent's participation and for the quality of the information being sought. Often . . . these qualities are independent of each other and occasionally they may be mutually exclusive.[63]

It is not hard to find echoes of this point of view in the few accounts of the actual process of interviewing that do exist. For example, Zweig, in his study of *Labour, Life and Poverty,*

> dropped the idea of a questionnaire or formal verbal questions . . . instead I had casual talks with working-class men on an absolutely equal footing . . . .

I made many friends and some of them paid me a visit afterwards or expressed a wish to keep in touch with me. Some of them confided their troubles to me and I often heard the remark: 'Strangely enough, I have never talked about that to anybody else.' They regarded my interest in their way of life as a sign of sympathy and understanding rarely shown to them even in the inner circle of their family. I never posed as somebody superior to them or as a judge of their actions but as one of them.[64]

Zweig defended his method on the grounds that telling people they were objects of study met with 'an icy reception' and that finding out about other peoples' lives is much more readily done on a basis of friendship than in a formal interview.

More typically and recently, Marie Corbin, the interviewer for the Pahls' study of *Managers and their Wives*, commented in an Appendix to the book of that name:

Obviously the exact type of relationship that is formed between an interviewer and the people being interviewed is something that the interviewer cannot control entirely, even though the nature of this relationship and how the interviewees classify the interviewer will affect the kinds of information given. . . simply because I am a woman and a wife I shared interests with the other wives and this helped to make the relationship a relaxed one.

Corbin goes on:

In these particular interviews I was conscious of the need to establish some kind of confidence with the couples if the sorts of information required were to be forthcoming. . . . In theory it should be possible to establish confidence simply by courtesy towards and interest in the interviewees. In practice it can be difficult to spend eight hours in a person's home, share their meals and listen to their problems and at the same time remain polite, detached and largely uncommunicative. I found the balance between prejudicing the answers to questions which covered almost every aspect of the couples' lives, establishing a relationship that would allow the interviews to be successful and holding a civilized conversation over dinner to be a very precarious one.[65]

Discussing research on copper-mining on Bougainville Island, Papua New Guinea, Alexander Mamak describes his growing consciousness of the political context in which research is done:

as I became increasingly aware of the unequal relationship existing between management and the union, I found myself becoming more and more emotionally involved in the proceedings. I do not believe this reaction is unusual since, in the words of the wellknown black sociologist Nathan Hare, 'If one is truly cognizant of adverse circumstances, he would be expected, through the process of reason, to experience some emotional response.'[66]

And, a third illustration of this point, Dorothy Hobson's account of her research on housewives' experiences of social isolation contains the following remarks:

> The method of interviewing in a one-to-one situation requires some comment. What I find most difficult is to resist commenting in a way which may direct the answers which the women give to my questions. However, when the taped interview ends we usually talk and then the women ask me questions about my life and family. These questions often reflect areas where they have experienced ambivalent feelings in their own replies. For example, one woman who said during the interview that she did not like being married, asked me how long I had been married and if I liked it. When I told her how long I had been married she said, 'Well I suppose you get used to it in time, I suppose I will.' In fact the informal talk after the interview often continues what the women have said during the interview.
>
> It is impossible to tell exactly how the women perceive me but I do not think they see me as too far removed from themselves. This may partly be because I have to arrange the interviews when my own son is at school and leave in time to collect him.[67]

As Bell and Newby note 'accounts of doing sociological research are at least as valuable, both to students of sociology and its practitioners, as the exhortations to be found in the much more common textbooks on methodology'.[68] All research is political, 'from the micropolitics of interpersonal relationships, through the politics of research units, institutions and universities, to those of government departments and finally to the state' – which is one reason why social research is not 'like it is presented and prescribed in those texts. It is infinitely more complex, messy, various and much more interesting.'[69] The 'cookbooks' of research methods largely ignore the political context of research, although some make asides about its 'ethical dilemmas': 'Since we are all human we are all involved in what we are studying when we try to study any aspect of social relations';[70] 'frequently researchers, in the course of their interviewing, establish rapport not as scientists but as human beings; yet they proceed to use this humanistically gained knowledge for scientific ends, usually without the informants' knowledge.'[71]

These ethical dilemmas are generic to all research involving interviewing, for reasons I have already discussed. But they are greatest where there is least social distance between the interviewer and interviewee. Where both share the same gender socialization and critical life-experiences, social distance can be minimal. Where both interviewer and interviewee share membership of the same minority group, the basis for equality may impress itself even more urgently on the interviewer's consciousness. Mamak's comments apply equally to a feminist interviewing women:

> I found that my academic training in the methodological views of Western social science and its emphasis on 'scientific objectivity' conflicted with the experiences of my colonial past. The traditional way in which social science research is conducted proved inadequate for an understanding of the reality, needs and desires of the people I was researching.[72]

Some of the reasons why a 'proper' interview is a masculine fiction are illustrated by observations from another field in which individuals try to find out about other individuals – anthropology. Evans-Pritchard reported this conversation during his early research with the Nuers of East Africa:

I: 'Who are you?'
Cuol: 'A man.'
I: 'What is your name?'
Cuol: 'Do you want to know my *name*?'
I: 'Yes.'
Cuol: 'You want to know *my* name?'
I: 'Yes, you have come to visit me in my tent and I would like to know who you are.'
Cuol: 'All right, I am Cuol. What is your name?'
I: 'My name is Pritchard.'
Cuol: 'What is your father's name?'
I: 'My father's name is also Pritchard.'
Cuol: 'No, that cannot be true, you cannot have the same name as your father.'
I: 'It is the name of my lineage. What is the name of your lineage?'
Cuol: 'Do you want to know the name of my lineage?'

I: 'Yes.'

Cuol: 'What will you do with it if I tell you? Will you take it to your country?'

I: 'I don't want to do anything with it. I just want to know it since I am living at your camp.'

Cuol: 'Oh well, we are Lou.'

I: 'I did not ask you the name of your tribe. I know that. I am asking you the name of your lineage.'

Cuol: 'Why do you want to know the name of my lineage?'

I: 'I don't want to know it.'

Cuol: 'Then why do you ask me for it? Give me some tobacco.'

I defy the most patient ethnologist to make headway against this kind of opposition [concluded Evans-Pritchard].[73]

Interviewees are people with considerable potential for sabotaging the attempt to research them. Where, as in the case of anthropology or repeated interviewing in sociology, the research cannot proceed without a relationship of mutual trust being established between interviewer and interviewee the prospects are particularly dismal. This inevitably changes the interviewer/anthropologist's attitude to the people he/she is studying. A poignant example is the incident related in Elenore Smith Bowen's *Return to Laughter* when the anthropologist witnesses one of her most trusted informants dying in childbirth:

> I stood over Amara. She tried to smile at me. She was very ill. I was convinced these women could not help her. She would die. She was my friend but my epitaph for her would be impersonal observations scribbled in my notebook, her memory preserved in an anthropologist's file: 'Death (in childbirth)/Cause: witchcraft/Case of Amara.' A lecture from the past reproached me: 'The anthropologist cannot, like the chemist or biologist, arrange controlled experiments. Like the astronomer, his mere presence produces changes in the data he is trying to observe. He himself is a disturbing influence which he must endeavour to keep to the minimum. His claim to science must therefore rest on a meticulous accuracy of observations and on a cool, objective approach to his data.'
>
> A cool, objective approach to Amara's death?
>
> One can, perhaps, be cool when dealing with questionnaires or when interviewing strangers. But what is one to do when one can collect one's data only by forming personal friendships? It is hard enough to think of a friend as a case history. Was I to stand aloof, observing the course of events?[74]

Professional hesitation meant that Bowen might never see the ceremonies connected with death in childbirth. But, on the other hand, she would see her friend die. Bowen's difficult decision to plead with Amara's kin and the midwives in charge of her case to allow her access to Western medicine did not pay off and Amara did eventually die.

An anthropologist has to 'get inside the culture'; participant observations means 'that. . . the observer participates in the daily life of the people under study, either openly in the role of researcher or covertly in some disguised role.'[75] A feminist interviewing women is by definition both 'inside' the culture and participating in that which she is observing. However, in these respects the behaviour of a feminist interviewer/researcher is not extraordinary. Although:

> Descriptions of the research process in the social sciences often suggest that the motivation for carrying out substantive work lies in theoretical concerns. . . the research process appears a very orderly and coherent process indeed. . . . The personal tends to be carefully removed from public statements; these are full of rational argument [and] careful discussion of academic points. [It can equally easily be seen that] all research is 'grounded', because no researcher can separate herself from personhood and thus from deriving second order constructs from experience.[76]

A feminist methodology of social science requires that this rationale of research be described and discussed not only in feminist research but in social science research in general. It requires, further, that the mythology of 'hygienic' research with its accompanying mystification of the researcher and the researched as objective instruments of data production be replaced by the recognition that personal involvement is more than dangerous bias – it is the condition under which people come to know each other and to admit others into their lives.

29

Telling the Truth about Jerusalem

Telling the truth is simple but not easy. It's simpler to speak what one knows and feels, because actions and words and even attitudes are not then clouded by the desire to deceive, or pretend, or exaggerate, or manipulate. Yet, perversely, the truth isn't easy to live with. The consequences, personal and public, of telling the truth are frequently experienced as extremely difficult, as one attempts to undo the hurt unintentionally done, or tries to persuade people to live comfortably with those contradictory perspectives that arise out of the dilemma of being human.

The truths that women have been specially responsible for generating have been of two kinds. First, there is the domestic contact with matters of life and death, dirt and disease, hopelessness and optimism, caring, preserving and loving, as well as hating, repudiating, excising and ruthlessly remaindering. Second, women have repeatedly laid bare the dishonesties of power. They have been in perpetual revolt against a writing of history that has said the truth is what the powerful say it is.

To validate the powerless is to discover a different Jerusalem, as the article of the book's title, originally published in the magazine *New Society*, explains. The origin of the species isn't always what most of us learn to think it is; and the sparkling promise of a Jerusalem is, of all things, what we most need to speak the truth about. The vision, any vision, carries us on, although the particular symbolism comes and goes: as long

Source: Originally published in *New Society*, 25 October 1984.

as we can see with the mind's eye, any temporary physical astigmatism can be survived. But, as well as the importance of a unifying vision, it must be said that every woman's Jerusalem is different. My utopia is sharper at the edges than yours; yours has a harder centre:

> I stood with her on the cold pebbled beach. The stones cut into our feet, her hand lay in mine like a pearly starfish at the sea's edge. Watching the sea, the division between cloud, sky and water, we saw the sun in its volcanic trajectory from white cloud to cosmic illumination; across the stretched surface of the sea the sun pointed out the contours of the waves, their peaks and falls, their troubled line of descent into the reservoir from which they always came.
>
> Behind us, scaffolding marked the ravages of the bomb that had been made to destroy a government, and had succeeded in destroying both much more and much less. So nothing was the same, although the sea was still there and the sun still nourished its uneven mirror, although the piers still reached out tremulously towards the horizon, although the seagulls still called and hopped and interfered with the passage of light through the universe. Nothing was the same, but everything was; for at least we were still there on the beach looking out to sea.

If men (embracing women, as the phrase goes) learn anything from history, it must surely be how to repeat themselves. And if women as a class learn anything, it must be that the impetus to improve their condition is not born out of this or that 'need', in the context of this or that political movement. Rather, feminism is contained as a possibility, a promise and a threat, within the very structure of a social order that is based on the intact foundations of commercial profit and masculine power.

What this means is a rephrasing of the usual repertoire of questions. Instead of asking: Why do we have a women's movement now, why are we seeing changes in one or another sphere of women's social existence? – we should ask: Where has feminism gone, and why are things getting worse not better, and why do people suppose they can still get away with putting women down?

The first set of questions takes us back to the sterile journey through creation myths: sex versus gender, nature versus nurture, what did Adam really do to Eve? – the issues which dominated the mood of feminism 15 years ago. But the second group of questions emerges out of an impatience with theorizing, and with the inventing and dissecting of a variety of philosophies about women's condition that achieve little more than feeding the profits of the publishing houses, fuelling the media's perfidious compulsion to caricature feminists from their underwear up, and giving the so-called political parties a cast-iron excuse to put the real issues in the cupboard along with their many other skeletons.

Theorizing may occasionally convince, but forms of words always affect the psyche. Defensiveness – explaining why women should be taken seriously – doesn't create a sense of self-worth; nor is it, on the whole, a harbinger of power.

The world is getting demonstrably worse for women in the 1980s. Not only do we have the cyclical reaction against women's claims to human rights, but we in Britain have the misfortune to be saddled with a government, ironically female-led, that is impressed by the economies to be made by treating women as a dependent reserve labour force. (This devalues a core conservative value, the sanctity of 'the family'. But the social side-effect is artfully concealed in a brazen political sentimentality.)

In such a situation, women's first task must be a psychological one. The 'equal worth' arguments have had centuries to run. The origin of the species isn't relevant any more. Forget the ideology and the intellectual window-dressing; don't bother to marshall convincing evidence of women's worth to convert the listless or the unlistening: let's just get on with the work. (Or, as Marx's mother once said: 'if only Karl had made *Capital* instead of just writing about it.')

Aside from the vote, arguably the two greatest advances improving the lives of British women this century have been the creation of the National Health Service and the passing of the Abortion Act, 1967. By comparison with these, the sex discrimination and equal pay legislation was a good idea that didn't quite come off, and certainly didn't match the utopian scenarios of those of us who said (in our ideological youth) that the force of the law could radicalize parts that the inspirations of feminism couldn't reach.

In all our grand theories of women's condition, reproduction was in there, somewhere – as an opportunity to be missed or not, as the power behind or in front of women, preventing them ever leaving the haven–prison of the home. But even in a country like Britain, reproduction, and its avoidance, kills. The Abortion Act brought about a wonderful decline in the needless deaths of women, although the persistingly uneven implementation of the Act (according to the strictures of the gynaeco-logical 'conscience') is one of those many pockmarks on the face of the NHS that the present Government is trying hard to turn into craters.

There are two reasons why the NHS is especially important to women. One is that women's role as contraceptors and conceivers requires health-care resources, which many of them – in an era of increasingly privatized medical care, combined with economic recession – would be unable to afford (One in 20 hospital patients, one in five in the professional classes, paid for their hospital care in 1982.) Deaths due to childbearing have declined. But they are still more common among working-class women, and three times more common among women born in the New Commonwealth or Pakistan, than among other women.

The second reason why the NHS matters to women is because women provide much more health-care than men. Within the NHS, three-quarters of workers are women. Outside it, women are the main carers for the young, the old and the disabled – not to mention the able-bodied, who by now ought to have learnt how to look after themselves. The present and threatened cuts to the NHS are sometimes disguised under the romantic fictional heading of 'community care'. Community care is a reasonable concept as long as this means everyone, and not just women.

The true impact of the NHS on women's health is best gauged by reading one of the pre-war accounts of women's health, such as the classic *Working Class Wives*, by Margery Spring Rice. The anaemic desperation of Spring Rice's 1,250 women is matched only by the prematurely defeated and pallid postures of today's young mothers, as they grapple with the poverty line, at least three jobs, an unequal division of labour and resources in the family, and the unwillingness of the public transport system and local shopping centre to cope with the realities of motherhood.

In so far as the usefulness to women of the NHS today is limited, it is because of the escalating power and patronage of the medical profession. Many doctors are over-impressed with their own status and therapeutic potential. They commit two errors. First, they make more and more judgements about what is in people's best interests without bothering to find out about them, and they are particularly likely to do this for women. Secondly, doctors' mystic faith in medical therapy blurs their vision of the social causes of disease and the social implications of medical treatment. For example, for some 30 years, about 7 per cent of British babies have been born weighing less than 5½ lb, with increased chances of death, illness and handicap. Low birthweight is not medically preventable, but it may be socially preventable – through improved housing, better long-term nutrition and less stress.

The issue of women and health signposts a more fundamental ecological challenge – and that is the pace and direction of technological change. Such change has always existed. What is new is the amount that is taking place, and the capacity of new technologies to affect social relations; most basically, of course, by annihilating them altogether.

There is a spectrum of protest. At one extreme there are those who wonder about the possible reproductive hazards of working airport baggage X-ray machines. At the other, there are the brave, bedraggled women of Greenham Common. In between, some still small voices may be heard querying the bizarre lack of scientific application to everyday problems of domestic technology. Why do we have washing machines with 20 different programmes but put out children in *white* nappies which have to be *washed*? Answer, because science is a rich capitalist who needs to fill her washing machines with something so that they will wear out in time to justify the commercial propagation of the next, equally silly model. Any sane society would provide state-subsidized disposable nappies along with child benefits (and of course suitably ecological methods of disposing of them).

A culture's attitudes towards housework and childbearing are inseparable from its attitudes towards women. In China last year I had the privilege of watching cadres of two-year-olds crap through the slit in their trousers at six in the morning while daylight came to the blue-uniformed genderless adults performing their exercises under the trees. Of course, there is much wrong with China. The restriction of women's reproductive choices under the one-child policy goes far beyond that threatened by the infant industry of artificial reproduction in the West. (The new technologies of fertility control do, however, facilitate sex preselection schemes, which have truly *international* implications for women.) Yet China is a marvellously non-sexist place. It is also a society which has visibly achieved a basic level of health, nutrition and welfare for the whole population – including women – in the space of one generation.

When the world changes, women change too. They either benefit or lose out, depending on whether increasing their freedom and happiness was, or was not, a directed part of the change in question. Sometimes it is hard to know if women have won or lost.

For example, the divorce rate in Britain in 1980 was six times that in 1961. 'No family' households, one in six in 1961, had become one in four by 1978. Since 1971, the number of single-parent families has risen by 56 per cent, and eight out of nine single parents are women. Out of such facts, two different kinds of interpretation may be harvested.

The first is that these official statistics confirm a syndrome of misery with conventional family life, which can now be resolved into alternative lifestyles. We all know that marriage is bad for women's mental health and good for men's. However, we know less about why, and we know very little about the relationship between health and alternative ways of living. We also know that work – paid work, in the capitalist sense – gives not only money but a sense of well-being. So women must fight for it, fight even to be counted as real statistics among the unemployed. The other interpretation that looks at us out of the statistics is one in which women's share of poverty is now significantly greater than it was. Society has finally renegued on the well-worn assumptions of Lord Beveridge about women caring for the family, and the family, obviously, no longer cares so much for women.

Perhaps there has always been a tension between the welfare of women and the welfare of human beings generally. Certainly this tension has been an insurmountable dilemma for feminist theorists and activists alike. The trials women undergo on behalf of the human 'race' are hardly good for women's pursuit of their own needs. Yet, conversely, women are so much better than men at representing the interests of life on earth. And without life on earth, where are women anyway?

The peace movement is an invigorating pragmatic representation of a problem that has given many a thinking feminist (not to mention other kinds of people) a good dose of insomnia from time to time. We live in a world divided uncomfortably and unevenly between public and private domains. Women and children; humming hoovers, lavender-scented polish and community care, *Coronation Street* and *Dynasty*; leaking roofs and empty purses; toilet-training, table manners and marital violence: these make up the complex fabric of privacy. The public sphere of factories, board rooms, hierarchical offices, smart clothes, business lunches and financial favours often seems as different as another planet. Yet the twain must meet. They do meet, and women are their inter-locutors – symbolizing and signifying the strain of living in two worlds, sensing the advantages of each and reaping, fully, those of neither.

The time has come, as the Walrus said, to talk of many things. All that glossy literature of the 1960s – the how working mothers manage, a briefcase in one hand, the key to a freezer full of home-baked casseroles in another, the women's two (only two?) roles manuals; the superwoman advice books, how to curl your hair, run your own business, manage the au-pair girl and still not overcook the brussels sprouts – all those deceitful texts belong with the media mystifications of women's libera-tion . . . in the wastepaper basket (but not burning). None of us really managed. It was a lie.

And the worst aspect of lying is that eventually the truth isn't known any more. It becomes impossible to speak it, either to oneself or to others. So let us now familiarize ourselves and others with the truth. Let us now praise, not famous men, but ordinary women, whose massive achievements in making ends meet will never get them into *Who's Who* or the officially sanctioned corridors of power.

There is a generation of young women in our midst who don't know what the struggle is all about. It is our job to tell them. Not so they don't make their own mistakes – for that is what each generation must do – but so they can at least recognize when the world makes them into pawns; so that they can protest and survive, having the confidence and the language to tell the truth about their own experiences; and so give themselves a chance to do what Marx's mother said he never did.

The point is not to change the world (though that would be nice as well). The point is to know what you think, say what you mean, and believe that your own bit of the world is listening to you.

Notes

PART 1

1 T. Solantaus, M. Rimtelä and V. Taípale 'The Threat of War in the Minds of 12-18 year olds in Finland' *Lancet* 8380, 1984, pp. 784–5.
2 Minerva *British Medical Journal* 8 November 1980, p. 1290.
3 P. Barss and K. Wallace 'Grass-Skirt Burns in Papua New Guinea' *Lancet* 2 April 1983, p. 733.
4 I. L. C. Ferguson, R. W. Taylor and J. M. Watson *Records and Curiosities in Obstetrics and Gynaecology* London, Baillière Tindall, 1982.
5 A. Oakley *Taking it Like a Woman* London, Jonathan Cape, 1984.
6 V. Woolf 'The Moment: summer's night' in *The Moment and Other Essays* New York, Harcourt Brace Jovanovich, 1948, p. 3.
7 L. B. Tolstoy *Complete Works* vol. XVIII London, Dent, 1904.
8 S. Sontag *Illness as Metaphor* New York, Farrar, Strauss and Giroux, 1977.
9 Quoted in C. Rover *Women's Suffrage and Party Politics in Britain 1866–1914* London, Routledge & Kegan Paul, 1967, p. 2.
10 Letter, quoted in R. Strachey *Millicent Garrett Fawcett* London, John Murray, 1931, p. 240.
11 Strachey, *Millicent Garrett Fawcett* 1931, p. 321.
12 Ibid., p. 317.
13 M. Garrett Fawcett, Introduction to M. Wollstonecraft *A Vindication of the Rights of Woman*, London, T. Fisher Unwin, 1891, p. 2.
14 Born Louise Dunnell; neither Millicent's autobiography nor the Strachey biography name her.
15 M. G. Fawcett *What I Remember* London, T. Fisher Unwin, 1924, p. 10.
16 M. G. Fawcett *Five Famous French Women* London, Cassell, 1905, p. 16.
17 R. Strachey *The Cause* London, Bell, 1928, p. 101.

18 Fawcett *What I Remember* p. 64.
19 Ibid., p. 73.
20 *Westminster Gazette* 9 June 1890.
21 Quoted in Strachey *Millicent Garrett Fawcett* pp. 43–44.
22 Ibid., pp. 106–7.
23 Fawcett *What I Remember* p. 117.
24 Ibid., p. 62.
25 Letter from M. G. Fawcett to Edmund Garrett, 21 February 1885 (Fawcett Library collection).
26 H. Fawcett and M. G. Fawcett *Essays and Lectures on Social and Political Subjects* London, Macmillan, 1872, pp. 64–5.
27 Ibid., p. 245.
28 M. G. Fawcett 'Women's Suffrage', address delivered to the Women's Debating Society, the Owen's College, Manchester, 13 February 1899.
29 M. G. Fawcett *The Women's Victory – and After; personal reminiscences* London, Sidgwick and Jackson, 1920, p. 157.
30 Fawcett and Fawcett *Essays and Lectures* pp. 200–03.
31 M. G. Fawcett 'Women's Suffrage', address delivered at the Junior Constitutional Club, Piccadilly, London, 1897, McCorquodale and Co., pp. 6–7.
32 Letter, quoted in Strachey *Millicent Garrett Fawcett* p. 163.
33 M. G. Fawcett *Women's Suffrage* London, T. C. and E. C. Jack, n.d., p. 57.
34 M. G. Fawcett and E. M. Turner *Josephine Butler* London, Association for Moral and Social Hygiene, 1927, p. 151.
35 M. G. Fawcett, Introduction to *A Vindication*, 1891, p. 23.
36 Letter from Thomas Hardy to M. G. Fawcett, 14 April 1892, Fawcett Library collection.
37 Statement made by M. G. Fawcett to A. J. Balfour 19 March 1894, Fawcett Library Archives.
38 Letter quoted in Strachey *Millicent Garrett Fawcett* p. 301.
39 M. G. Fawcett 'Women's Suffrage', Manchester Speech, 1899.
40 Concentration Camps Commission *Report on the Concentration Camps in South Africa by the Committee of Ladies Appointed by the Secretary of State for War* 1902, London, HMSO, p. 16.
41 Strachey *Millicent Garrett Fawcett* p. 276.
42 S. Pankhurst *The Suffragette Movement* London, Virago, 1977 (originally published 1931), p. 523.
43 Ibid., p. 182.
44 Ibid., p. 239.
45 Letter from M. G. Fawcett to Lady Frances Balfour, 30 June 1909, Fawcett Library collection.
46 Fawcett *What I Remember* p. 195.
47 Ibid., p. 185.

48 *Daily Telegraph* 6 August 1929.
49 Strachey *Millicent Garrett Fawcett* p. 212.
50 Ibid., p. 100.
51 Ibid., p. 229.
52 Ibid., p. 46.
53 Rover *Women's Suffrage* p. 58.
54 *Time and Tide* 16 August 1929.
55 *Northern Mail* 5 August 1929.
56 Fawcett *What I Remember* p. 40.
57 Letter M. G. Fawcett to 'Miss Ward' 18 June 1929, Fawcett Library collection.
58 Strachey *Millicent Garrett Fawcett* p. 138.
59 A good short summary is M. Pugh *Women's Suffrage in Britain 1867–1929* London, Historical Association Pamphlet, 1980.
60 *Manchester Guardian* 6 August 1929.
61 *Daily Telegraph* 6 August 1929.
62 Strachey *Millicent Garrett Fawcett* 1931, p. 349.
63 *Manchester Guardian* 8 August 1929.
64 F. Alberoni *Falling in Love* New York, Random House, 1983.
65 J. Joyce *Ulysses*.
66 T. Carlyle *Heroes and Hero-Worship*.
67 E. Gibbon *Decline and Fall of the Roman Empire*, chapter 2.
68 H. Ford, reported to have been said in the witness box when suing the *Chicago Tribune*, July 1919.
69 G. W. Hegel cited in G. B. Shaw *The Revolutionists' Handbook*.
70 For example H. R. Spencer *The History of British Midwifery from 1650 to 1800* London, John Bale Sons and Danielsson Ltd, 1927.
71 References for statements made in this paper, unless otherwise indicated, are to be found in A. Oakley *The Captured Womb* Oxford, Basil Blackwell, 1984.
72 C. W. Hohler and L. D. Platt, American College of Obstetrics and Gynecology Office Ultrasound Survey. Personal Communication. Quoted in National Institutes of Health, *Consensus Development Conference* 'The Use of Diagnostic Ultrasound Imaging in Pregnancy' 6–8 February 1984, Washington, DC, USA.
73 J. W. Wladimiroff and L. Laar 'Ultrasonic Measurement of the Fetal Body Size: a randomized controlled trial' *Acta Obstetrica et Gynaecologica Scandinavica* 1980, **59**, pp. 177–9.
74 J. B. McKinlay 'From "Promising Report" to "Standard Procedure": seven stages in the career of a medical innovation' *Milbank Memorial Fund Quarterly* 1981, **59**, 3, pp. 374–411.
75 L. N. Reece 'The Estimation of Foetal Maturity by a New Method of X-Ray Cephalometry: its bearing on clinical midwifery' *Proceedings of the Royal Society of Medicine* 18 January 1938, p. 489.

76 S. N. Hassani *Ultrasound in Gynecology and Obstetrics* New York, Springer Verlag, 1978, p. vii.

77 S. Campbell and D. J. Little 'Clinical Potential of Real-Time Ultrasound' in M. J. Bennett and S. Campbell (eds) *Real-Time Ultrasound in Obstetrics* Oxford, Basil Blackwell, 1980.

78 McKinlay, 'From "Promising Report"', p. 398.

79 W. A. N. Dorland and M. J. Huberry *The X-Ray in Embryology and Obstetrics* London, Henry Kimpton, 1926, p. viii.

80 E. Reinold 'Fetal Movements in Early Pregnancy' in A. Kurjak (ed.) *Progress in Medical Ultrasound* I, Amsterdam, Excerpta Medica, 1980, pp. 64–6.

81 R. W. A. Salmond 'The Uses and Value of Radiology in Obstetrics' in F. J. Browne (ed.) *Antenatal and Postnatal Care* 2nd edn London, J. and A. Churchill, 1937, p. 497.

82 J. Chassar Moir 'The Uses and Value of Radiology in Obstetrics' in F. J. Browne and J. C. McClure-Browne (eds) *Antenatal and Postnatal Care* 9th edn London, J. and A. Churchill, 1960, p. 389.

83 A. Stewart, J. Webb, D. Giles and D. Hewitt 'Malignant Disease in Childhood and Diagnostic Irradiation in Utero' *Lancet* **2**, 1956, p. 447.

84 S. N. Hassani *Ultrasound in Gynecology and Obstetrics* New York, Springer Verlag, 1978, p. vii.

85 I. Donald 'Sonar – Its Present Status in Medicine' in A. Kurjak (ed.) *Progress in Medical Ultrasound* **I**, 1980, Amsterdam, Excerpta Medica, p. I.

86 S. T. Coleridge 18 December 1831, quoted in McKinlay, 'From "Promising Report"'.

PART 2

1 A. W. Grogono, M. M. Johnson, M. S. Jastremsta and R. F. Russell 'Educational Graffiti: better use of the lavatory wall' *Lancet* 22 May 1982, pp. 1175–6.

2 M. Mead *Blackberry Winter* New York, Pocket Books, 1975, p. 225.

3 Quoted in A. Davin 'Imperialism and Motherhood' *History Workshop Journal* Spring 1978, p. 17.

4 E. Key *The Century of the Child* New York, G. P. Putman, 1909, pp. 100–1.

5 Cited in B. Ehrenreich and D. English *For Her Own Good* London, Pluto Press, 1979, p. 171.

6 C. P. Gilman 'The Home: its Work and Influence', 1903, in R. Salper *Female Liberation* New York, Knopf, 1972, p. 113.

7 A. Oakley *Women Confined: Towards a sociology of childbirth* Oxford, Martin Robertson, 1980.

8 G. W. Brown and T. Harris *Social Origins of Depression* London, Tavistock, 1978.

9 D. C. Skegg, R. Doll and J. Perry 'Use of Medicines in General Practice' *British Medical Journal* 18 June, 1977, pp. 1501–3.

10 H. Graham and L. McKee 'The First Months of Motherhood', unpublished report, London, Health Education Council, 1980.

11 J. B. Miller *Toward a New Psychology of Women* Boston, Beacon Press, 1976.

12 N. Chodorow *The Reproduction of Mothering* Berkeley, California, University of California Press, 1978.

13 L. W. Hoffman and F. I. Nye (eds) *Working Mothers: An Evaluative Review of the Consequences for Wife, Husband and Child* San Francisco, Jossey-Bass, 1974.

14 A. Rossi 'Transition to Parenthood' *Journal of Marriage and the Family* February, 1968, pp. 26–39.

15 D. Levy *Maternal Overprotection* New York, Columbia University Press, 1943, p. 3–4.

16 M. Mead *Blackberry Winter* p. 269.

17 J. F. Bernal and M. P. M. Richards 'Why Some Babies Don't Sleep' *New Society* 28 February 1974, p. 509.

18 For example, D. Breen *The Birth of a First Child* London, Tavistock, 1975.

19 Simone de Beauvoir *The Second Sex* London, Four Square Books, 1960, p. 233.

20 Central Policy Review Staff *Services for Young Children with Working Mothers* London, HMSO, 1978.

21 A. Rich *On Lies, Secrets, Silence* London, Virago, 1980, pp. 263–4.

22 I. Illich *Medical Nemesis* London, Calder and Boyars, 1975.

23 T. McKeown *The Role of Medicine* Oxford, Basil Blackwell, 1979.

24 M. P. M. Richards 'Innovation in Medical Practice: obstetricians and the induction of labour in Britain' *Social Science and Medicine* 9, 1975, p. 598.

25 Figure cited by the Dutch obstetrician G. J. Kloosterman.

26 I have discussed this fully in 'Normal Motherhood: An Exercise in Self Control?' in B. Hutter and G. Williams (eds) *Controlling Women* Croom Helm, 1981.

27 British Medical Association, Family Doctor Publication 'From Pregnancy to Birth' *You and Your Baby, Part 1* 1977, p. 22.

28 R. Cooperstock and H. L. Lennard 'Some Social Meanings of Tranquiliser Use' *Sociology of Health and Illness* 1979, 1, 3, pp. 331–47.

29 I. Broverman et al. 'Sex-role Stereotypes and Clinical Judgements of Mental Health' *Journal of Consulting and Clinical Psychology* 1970, pp. 341–7.

30 See the discussion in A. Oakley and G. Chamberlain 'Medical and Social Factors in Postpartum Depression' *Journal of Obstetrics and Gynaecology* 1, 1981, pp. 182–7.

31 For a fuller discussion of these themes and references to the literature, see A. Oakley *Women Confined: Towards a sociology of childbirth* Oxford, Martin Robertson 1980, chapter 2, 'Psychological Constructs'.

32 S. Wolkind 'Prenatal Emotional Stress – Effects on the Fetus' in S. Wolkind and E. Kajicek (eds) *Pregnancy: A Psychological and Social Study* London, Academic Press, 1981.

33 For example, W. S. Kroger and S. T. DeLee 'The Psychosomatic Treatment

of Hyperemesis Gravidarum by Hypnosis' *American Journal of Obstetrics and Gynecology* 1946, p. 51.

34 For example A Nilsson 'Perinatal Emotional Adjustment' in N. Morris (ed.) *Psychosomatic Medicine in Obstetrics and Gynaecology* 3rd International Congress, London 1971, Basel, Karger, 1972.

35 A. Milinski 'Different Behaviour of Women in Labour as a Symptom of Different Psychic Patterns' in H. Hirsch (ed.) *The Family*, 4th International Congress of Psychosomatic Obstetrics and Gynaecology Basel, Karger, 1975.

36 M. Heiman 'Psychiatric Complications: a psychoanalytic view of pregnancy' in J. J. Rovinsky and A. F. Guttmacher (eds) *Medical, Surgical and Gynecological Complications of Pregnancy* Baltimore, Williams and Wilkins, 1965.

37 Ibid.

38 L. Chertok *Motherhood and Personality* London, Tavistock, 1969.

39 D. Breen *The Birth of the First Child* London, Tavistock, 1975, p. 193.

40 M. B. Parlee 'Psychology' *Signs: Journal of Women in Culture and Society* 1975, 1, Autumn, pp. 119–35.

41 T. Parsons and R. F. Bales *Family: Socialisation and Interaction Process* London, Routledge & Kegan Paul, 1956.

42 S. Macintyre 'The Management of Childbirth: a review of sociological research issues' *Social Science and Medicine* 11, 1977, pp. 477–84.

43 J. L. Halliday 'Epidemiology and the Psychosomatic Affections' *Lancet* 10 August 1946, p. 185.

44 Ibid., p. 186.

45 A. E. Roberts 'Feeding and Mortality in the Early Months of Life; Changes in Medical Opinion and Popular Feeding Practice 1850–1900', unpublished PhD thesis, University of Hull, 1973.

46 National Conference on Infantile Mortality *Report of the Proceedings of the National Conference on Infantile Mortality* London, P. S. King and Son, 1906, p. 15.

47 D. B. Jelliffe and E. F. P. Jelliffe *Human Milk in the Modern World* Oxford, Oxford University Press, 1978, p. 188.

48 E. Shorter *A History of Women's Bodies* New York, Basic Books, 1982.

49 F. Falkner (ed.) *Prevention in Childhood of Health Problems in Adult Life* Geneva, WHO, 1980.

50 J. Martin and J. Monk *Infant Feeding 1980* OPCS, Social Survey Division, London, HMSO, 1982.

51 J. P. Elliot and J. F. Flaherty 'The Use of Breast Stimulation to Ripen the Cervix in Term Pregnancies' *American Journal of Obstetrics and Gynecology* 1 March, 1983, pp. 553–6.

52 J. Martin *Infant Feeding 1975: attitudes and practice in England and Wales* OPCS, Social Survey Division, London, HMSO, 1978.

53 L. B. Rubin *Intimate Strangers* New York, Harper and Row, 1983.

54 M. Wagner *Having a Baby in Europe* WHO, Copenhagen, 1985.

55 See, for a general discussion, S. Romalis (ed.) *Childbirth: alternatives to medical control* Austin, University of Texas Press, 1981.

56 See for a review and references A. Oakley, I. Chalmers and A. Macfarlane 'Social Class, Stress and Reproduction' in A. R. Rees and H. Purcell (eds) *Disease and Environment* Chichester, John Wiley, 1982.

57 G. W. Brown and T. Harris *Social Origins of Depression* London, Tavistock, 1978.

58 World Health Organization, *Report on Social and Biological Effects on Perinatal Mortality* 1, Budapest, 1978.

59 R. Illsley *Professional or Public Health?* London, Nuffield Provincial Hospitals Trust, 1980.

60 D. Baird, 'Environment and Reproduction' *British Journal of Obstetrics and Gynaecology* 87, 1980, pp. 1057-67.

61 See for a review L. S. Bakketeig, H. G. Hoffman and A. Oakley 'Perinatal Mortality' in M. B. Bracken (ed.) *Perinatal Epidemiology* New York, Oxford University Press, 1984.

62 J. Tudor Hart 'The Inverse Care Law' *Lancet* 27 February 1971, pp. 405-12.

63 WHO, *Report on Social and Biological Effects*.

64 For a review see L. S. Bakketeig et al. 'Perinatal Mortality'.

65 See A. Oakley et al. 'Social Class, Stress & Reproduction' for references.

66 K. B. Nuckolls, J. Cassel and J. H. Kaplan 'Psychosocial Assets, Life Crises and the Prognosis of Pregnancy' *American Journal of Epidemiology* 95, 1972, p. 431.

67 J. S. Norbeck and V. P. Tilden 'Life Stress, Social Support and Emotional Disequilibrium' in 'Complications of Pregnancy: a prospective multivariate study' *Journal of Health and Social Behaviour* 24, 1, 1983, p. 30.

68 G. S. Berkowitz and S. V. Kasl 'The Role of Psychosocial Factors in Spontaneous Preterm Delivery' *Journal of Psychosomatic Research* 27, 4, 1983, p. 283.

69 R. Sosa, J. Kennell, M. Klaus, S. Robertson and J. Urruta 'The Effect of a Supportive Companion on Perinatal Problems, Length of Labour and Mother–Infant Interaction' 303, 11, 1980, p. 597.

70 M. A. Herron, M. Katz and R. K. Creasy 'Evaluation of Preterm Birth Prevention Programme: a preliminary report' *Obstetrics and Gynecology* 59, 4, 1982, p. 452.

71 M. D. Peoples, R. C. Grimson and A. B. Daughty 'Evaluation of the Effects of the North Carolina Improved Pregnancy Outcome Project: implications for state-level decision making' *American Journal of Health* 74, 6, 1984, p. 549.

72 R. J. Sokol, R. B. Woolf, M. G. Rosen and K. Weiggarden 'Risk, Antepartem Care and Outcome: impact of a maternity and infant care project' *Obstetrics and Gynecology* 56, 2, 1980, p. 159.

73 L. R. Runnerstrom 'The Effectiveness of Nurse-Midwifery in a Supervised Hospital Environment' *American College of Nurse Midwives Bulletin* 14, 2, 1969, p. 40.

74 M. Sexton and J. R. Hebel 'A Clinical Trial of Change in Maternal Smoking and its Effects on Birthweight' *Journal of the American Medical Association* **251**, 7, 1984, p. 911.

75 For further references see A. Oakley, D. Elbourne and I. Chalmers 'The Effects of Social Interventions in Pregnancy', Paper given at Conference on Prevention de la Naissance Prematurée: nouveaux objectifs et nouvelles practiques des soins preventaux. Evian, France 19–22 May, 1985.

76 S. Cobb 'Social Support as a Moderator of Life Stress' *Psychosomatic Medicine* **38**, 5, 1976, p. 300.

77 D. Rush 'Effects of Changes in Protein and Calorie Intake During Pregnancy on the Fetus and Developing Child' in D. M. Campbell and M. D. G. Gillmer (eds) *Nutrition in Pregnancy* RCOG, London, 1983.

78 D. Rush, Z. Stein and M. Susser 'A Randomised Controlled Trial of Prenatal Nutritional Supplementation in New York City' *Pediatrics* **65**, 4, 1980, p. 583.

79 N. Spira, F. Andras, A. Chapel, E. Debuisson, J. Jacquelin, C. Kirchoffer, C. Lebrun and C. Prudent, 'Surveillance à Domicile des Grossesses Pathologiques' *Journal of Gynaecology, Obstetrics and Biological Reproduction* **10**, 1981, p. 543.

80 A. Oakley et al., 'Social Interventions', 1985.

81 M. C. Stopes *A Banned Play and a Preface on the Censorship* London, 1926, p. 15.

82 M. Mead and N. Newton 'Cultural Patterning of Perinatal Behaviour' in S. Richardson and A. F. Guttmacher (eds) *Childbearing – Its Social and Psychological Aspects* Baltimore, Williams and Wilkins, 1967.

83 B. Rowland *Medieval Woman's Guide to Health* London, Croom Helm, 1981.

84 N. E. Himes *Medical History of Contraception* New York, Gamut Press, 1963.

85 K. Dunnell *Family Formation* London, Office of Population Census and Surveys, 1979; National Center for Health Statistics *Contraceptive Utilization* US Department of Health Education and Welfare, 1978.

86 D. F. Hawkins and M. Elder *Human Fertility Control* London, Butterworth, 1979, p. 129.

87 J. Sleep, A. Grant, J. Garcia, D. Elbourne, J. Spencer and I. Chalmers 'The West Berkshire Perineal Management Trial' Paper presented at the 23rd British Congress of Obstetrics and Gynaecology, Birmingham, 23 July 1983.

88 V. Beral 'Reproductive Mortality' *British Medical Journal* II, 1979, pp. 632–4.

89 The East Bay Men's Center Newsletter, (Undated) USA.

90 A. Rich *Of Woman Born* London, Virago, 1977, p. 42.

91 M. P. M. Richards 'A Place of Safety? An examination of the risks of hospital delivery' in S. Kitzinger and J. A. Davis (eds), *The Place of Birth* Oxford, Oxford University Press, 1978.

92 N. Friedman *Everything you Must Know about Tampons* New York, Berkeley, 1981.

93 D. Rush 'Effects of Changes in Protein and Calorie Intake During Preg-
    nancy on the Growth of the Human Fetus' in M. Enkin and I. Chalmers
    (eds) *Effectiveness and Satisfaction in Antenatal Care* London, Spastics Inter-
    national Medical Publications, 1982.
94 A. Oakley *The Captured Womb* Oxford, Basil Blackwell, 1984.
95 K. Luker *Taking Chances: abortion and the decision not to contracept* Berkeley,
    University of California Press, 1975.
96 J. Zimmerman 'Technology and the Future of Women: haven't we met
    somewhere before?' *Women's Studies International Quarterly* **4**, 1981,
    pp. 335–67.
97 P. Sargent (ed.) *More Women of Wonder*, Harmondsworth, Penguin, 1979,
    p. 30.
98 T. Disch *334* New York, Avon Books, 1970.
99 M. Piercy *Woman on the Edge of Time* London, The Women's Press, 1979,
    p. 105.
100 V. Woolf *Three Guineas* Harmondsworth, Penguin, Reprinted 1977.
101 W. J. Bremner and D. M. de Kretser 'Contraceptives for Males' *Signs:
    Journal of Women in Culture and Society*, **1**, 1975, pp. 387–96.
102 R. Steinbacher 'Futuristic Implications of Sex Preselection' in H. B.
    Holmes, B. B. Hoskins and M. Gross (eds) *The Custom-Made Child?* Clifton,
    New Jersey, The Humana Press, 1981; N. E. Williamson 'Sex Preferences,
    Sex Control and the Effects on Women' *Signs: Journal of Women in Culture
    and Society* **1**, 1976, pp. 847–62.
103 L. Belmont and F. Marolla 'Birth Order, Family Size and Intelligence'
    Science **182**, 1973, pp. 1096–1101.
104 M. R. Nentwig 'Technical Aspects of Sex Preselection' in Holmes, Hoskins
    and Gross (eds) *The Custom-Made Child?*.
105 Royal College of Obstetricians and Gynaecologists *Report of the RCOG Ethics
    Committee on In Vitro Fertilization and Embryo Replacement or Transfer*, London,
    RCOG, 1983.
106 R. Snowden and G. D. Mitchell *The Artificial Family* London, Unwin, 1983.
107 E. Philipp *Childlessness* London, Arrow Books, 1975.
108 J. Ellul *The Technological Society* New York, Alfred Knopf, 1964, p. vi.
109 Feminist Self Insemination Group *Self Insemination* London, 1980.

PART 3

1 H. Mahler, Director-General of WHO, cited in *Health and Population*
   pamphlet, WHO, Geneva, 1984.
2 'Scots Find Orgasm Advice to Relieve Pain "offensive"' *Medical News* 24
   February 1983.
3 For a summary of the evidence, see A. Oakley *Subject Women* Oxford, Martin
   Robertson, 1981, chapter 3.

4 S. Houd and A. Oakley 'Alternative Perinatal Services in the European Region and North America: a pilot survey', unpublished paper, WHO, Copenhagen, 1983.

5 J. MacGuire, 'Nursing: none is held in higher esteem' in R. Silverstone and A. Ward (eds) *Careers of Professional Women* London, Croom Helm, 1980.

6 Department of Health and Social Security, Statistics and Research Division, Hospital Medical Staff, England and Wales, National Tables, 30 September 1977 (February 1978).

7 M. A. Elston 'Medicine: half our future doctors?' in R. Silverstone and A. Ward (eds) *Careers of Professional Women* London, Croom Helm, 1980.

8 C. P. Gilman 'The Yellow Wallpaper', *The New England Magazine* January 1892. Reprinted in *The Charlotte Perkins Gilman Reader: the Yellow Wallpaper and Other Fiction* London, The Women's Press, 1981.

9 T. Olsen *Silences* London, Virago, 1980.

10 C. P. Gilman 'Why I Wrote the Yellow Wallpaper' *The Forerunner* October, 1913. Reprinted in *The Charlotte Perkins Gilman Reader: the Yellow Wallpaper and Other Fiction* London, The Women's Press, 1981.

11 E. Boulding *Women in the Twentieth Century World* New York, Sage Publications, 1977.

12 B. Chiplin and P. J. Sloane *Tackling Discrimination at the Workplace* Cambridge, Cambridge University Press, 1982.

13 L. Hamill *Wives as Sole and Joint Breadwinners*, Government Economic Service Working Papers no. 13, London, HMSO, 1978.

14 H. Land 'The Family Wage' *Feminist Review* **6**, 1980, pp. 55–77.

15 V. Beral 'Reproductive Mortality' *British Medical Journal* 15 September 1979, pp. 632–4.

16 A. Cochrane *Effectiveness and Efficiency* The Nuffield Provincial Hospitals Trust, 1971, p. 64.

17 M. Shepherd, B. Cooper, A. C. Brown and G. W. Kalton *Psychiatric Illness in General Practice* London, Oxford University Press, 1966.

18 G. V. Stimson 'GPs, "Trouble" and Types of Patient' in M. Stacey (ed.) *The Sociology of the National Health Service* Sociological Review Monograph 22, University of Keele, Staffordshire, 1976.

19 For a discussion of this dilemma in relation to premenstrual tension, see S. Laws 'The Sexual Politics of Premenstrual Tension' *Women's Studies International Forum* **6**, 1983, pp. 19–31.

20 V. Woolf 'Professions for Women', reprinted in V. Woolf *Women and Writing* London, The Women's Press, 1979.

21 A. Rich 'Women and Honor: some notes on lying' *On Lies, Secrets, Silence* London, Virago, 1980.

22 A point made by J. Hirsch and cited in S. B. Rusek *The Women's Health Movement* New York, Praeger, 1979, p. 58.

23 J. Robinson 'Cervical Cancer: a feminist critique' *Times Health Supplement* 1981, 5, p. 16.

24 F. Capra *The Turning Point* New York, Bantam Books, 1983.

25 H. Graham 'Smoking in Pregnancy: the attitudes of expectant mothers' *Social Science and Medicine*, 1976, 10, pp. 399–405.

26 G. B. Shaw 'Back to Methuselah' *The Complete Plays of Bernard Shaw* London, Odhams' Press, 1934.

27 P. Rantakallio 'Social Background of Mothers who Smoke During Pregnancy and Influence of these Factors on the Offspring' *Social Science and Medicine* **13A**, 1979, pp. 423–9.

28 Social Services Committee *Perinatal and Neonatal Mortality Volume I* Report, London, HMSO, 1980.

29 R. J. Meyer and R. J. Haggerty 'Streptococcal Infections in Families' *Pediatrics* **29**, 1962, pp. 539–49.

30 E. Durkheim *Suicide* London, Routledge & Kegan Paul, 1952.

31 *Report from the Poor Law Commissioners on an Inquiry into the Sanitary Condition of the Labouring Population of Great Britain* London, HMSO, 1842.

32 W. Farr *Vital Statistics* London, Edward Stanford, 1885.

33 D. Hilfiker *Healing the Wounds* New York, Pantheon, 1985.

34 R. Dahrendorf *The Listener* 92, 1974, p. 624.

35 A. Oakley *The Captured Womb: a history of medical care for pregnant women* Oxford, Basil Blackwell, 1984.

36 A. Oakley 'Social Consequences of Obstetric Technology: the importance of measuring "soft" outcomes' *Birth* **10**, 2, 1983, pp. 99–108.

37 T. Szasz *The Theology of Medicine* Baton Rouge, Louisiana State University Press, 1977.

38 E. Freidson *Profession of Medicine: a study of the sociology of applied knowledge* New York, Dodd, Mead and Co., 1972.

39 P. S. Byrne and B. E. L. Long *Doctors Talking to Patients* London, HMSO, 1976.

40 E. J. Cassell *The Healer's Art: a new approach to the doctor-patient relationship* Philadelphia, J. B. Lippincott, 1976, p. 18.

41 H. Brody *Placebos and the Philosophy of Medicine* Chicago, Chicago University Press, 1980.

42 M. P. M. Richards 'Innovation in Medical Practice: obstetricians and the induction of labour in Britain' *Social Science and Medicine* **93**, 1975, pp. 595–602.

43 A. Cartwright *The Dignity of Labour?* London, Tavistock, 1979.

44 L. Hudson and B. Jacot 'Education and Eminence in British Medicine' *British Medical Journal* **2**, 1971, pp. 162–3.

45 A. K. Ladas, B. Whipple and J. D. Perry *The G Spot and Other Recent Discoveries about Human Sexuality* London, Corgi Books, 1983.

46 E. D. M. Riley '"What Do Women Want?" – The question of choice in the conduct of labour' in T. Chard and M. P. M. Richards (eds) *Benefits and Hazards of the New Obstetrics*, London, Spastics International Medical Publications, 1977.

47 A. Cartwright *Human Relations and Hospital Care* London, Routledge & Kegan Paul, 1964.

48 W. Wilson 'Correlates of Avowed Happiness' *Psychological Bulletin* **67**, 4, 1967.

49 P. R. Kaim-Caudle and G. N. Marsh 'Patient Satisfaction Survey in General Practice' *British Medical Journal* **1**, 1975, pp. 262–4.

50 R. S. Ledward 'Communication in Hospital' *British Medical Journal* **2**, 1978, p. 505 (letter).

51 A. Oakley *Becoming a Mother* Oxford, Martin Robertson, 1979; H. Graham and L. McKee *The First Months of Motherhood*, London, Health Education Council, 1980.

52 Cartwright *Human Relations*.

53 D. Locker and D. Dunt 'Theoretical and Methodological Issues in Sociological Studies of Consumer Satisfaction with Medical Care' *Social Science and Medicine* **12**, 1978, pp. 283–92.

54 A. Cartwright *Health Surveys in Practice and in Potential: a critical review of their scope and methods* London, King's Fund, 1983.

55 A. Oakley *Women Confined: Towards a sociology of childbirth* Oxford, Martin Robertson, 1980.

56 J. Y. Green, M. Weinberger and J. J. Mamlin 'Patient Attitudes Towards Health Care: expectations of primary care in a clinic setting' *Social Science and Medicine* **14**, 1980, pp. 133–8.

57 C. L. Shear, B. T. Gipe, J. K. Mattheis and M. Riery 'Provider Continuity and Quality of Medical Care' *Medical Care* **21**, 12, 1983, pp. 1204–10.

58 G. V. Stimson 'Obeying Doctor's Orders: a view from the other side' *Social Science and Medicine* **8**, 1974, pp. 97–104.

59 S. Macintyre 'The Management of Childbirth: a review of sociological research issues' *Social Science and Medicine* **11**, 1977, pp. 477–84.

60 M. Millman *The Unkindest Cut: life in the backrooms of medicine* New York, William Morrow, 1977; S. Danziger 'On Doctor Watching: field work in medical settings' *Urban Life* **7**, 4, 1979, pp. 513–32.

61 W. R. Arney *Power and the Profession of Obstetrics* Chicago, University of Chicago Press, 1982; D. Scully *Men Who Control Women's Health* Boston, Houghton Mifflin, 1980.

62 A. Cartwright 'Professsionals as Responders; variations in and effects of response rates to questionnaires 1961–77' *British Medical Journal* **2**, 1978, pp. 1419–21.

63 J. B. McKinlay 'Who is Really Ignorant – Physician or Patient?' *Journal of Health and Social Behaviour* **16**, 1, 1975, pp. 3–11.

64 R. M. Titmuss *Essays on the Welfare State* London, Allen and Unwin, 1958, pp. 200–2.

65 T. B. Brewin 'The Cancer Patient: communication and morale' *British Medical Journal* **2**, 1977, pp. 1623–7.

66 G. P. Maguire, E. G. Lee, D. J. Bevington et al, 'Psychiatric Problems in the First Year After Mastectomy' *British Medical Journal* **1**, 1978, pp. 963–5.

67 I. Illich *Medical Nemesis* London, Calder and Boyars, 1975.

68 R. J. Haggerty 'Life Stress, Illness and Social Supports' *Developmental Medicine and Child Neurology* **22**, 1980, pp. 391–400.
69 S. Cobb 'Physiologic Changes in Men Whose Jobs Were Abolished' *Journal of Psychosomatic Research* **18**, 1974, pp. 245–258.
70 H. R. Bourne 'The Placebo – a Poorly Understood and Neglected Therapeutic Agent' *Rational Drug Therapy* November 1971, pp. 1–6.
71 A. Anderson and A. Turnbull 'Effect of Oestrogens, Progestogens and Betamimetics in Pregnancy' in M. Enkin and I. Chalmers (eds) *Effectiveness and Satisfaction in Antenatal Care* London, Spastics International Medical Publications, 1982.
72 H. H. Meyhoff, T. C. Gerstenberg and J. Nordling 'Placebo – the Drug of Choice in Female Motor Urge Incontinence' *British Journal of Urology* **55**, 1983, 34–7.
73 N. Cousins *Anatomy of an Illness as Perceived by the Patient* New York, W. W. Norton, 1979.
74 Cited in B. Abel-Smith *A History of the Nursing Profession* London, Heinemann, 1960.
75 Ibid., p. 5.
76 See C. Davies (ed.) *Rewriting Nursing History* London, Croom Helm, 1980.
77 C. Woodham-Smith *Florence Nightingale 1820–1910* London, Constable, 1950.
78 C. Magges 'Nurse Recruitment to Four Provincial Hospitals 1881–1921' in Davies *Rewriting Nursing History*.
79 R. Lewis and A. Maude *Professional People* London, Phoenix House, 1952.
80 1905 comment, cited in E. Gamarnikow 'Sexual Division of Labour: the case of nursing' in A. Kuhn and A. Wolpe (eds) *Feminism and Materialism* London, Routledge & Kegan Paul, 1978, p. 105.
81 Nightingale, 1881, ibid., p. 115.
82 Cited in Woodham-Smith *Florence Nightingale*, p. 340.
83 See, for example, S. B. Ruzek *The Women's Health Movement* New York, Praeger, 1978.
84 J. M. MacGuire *From Student to Nurse* Oxford Area Nurse Training Committee, 1966.
85 E. Hughes, H. Hughes and I. Deutscher *Twenty Thousand Nurses Tell Their Story* Philadelphia, J. B. Lippincott, 1958.
86 R. L. Coser *Life in the Ward* East Lansing, Michigan, Michigan State University Press, 1962.
87 E. R. Anderson, *The Role of the Nurse* Royal College of Nursing of the United Kingdom, 1973.
88 Hughes *Twenty Thousand Nurses*.
89 M. Johnston 'Communication of Patients' Feelings in Hospital' in A. E. Bennett (ed.) *Communication between Doctors and Patients* Oxford, Oxford University Press, 1976.
90 J. B. Miller *Toward a New Psychology of Women* Boston, Beacon Press, 1977.
91 J. G. Rosen and K. Jones 'The Male Nurse' *New Society* 9 March 1972, pp. 493–4.

92 Anderson *The Role of the Nurse*, pp. 90–1.
93 See, for example, A. M. Carr-Saunders and P. A. Wilson *The Professions* Oxford, Clarendon Press, 1933; E. Freidson *Profession of Medicine* New York, Dodd, Mead and Co., 1972.
94 A. Etzioni (ed.) *The Semi-Professions and Their Organization; Teachers, Nurses and Social Workers* New York, The Free Press, 1969.
95 I. Illich 'Disabling Professions' in I. Illich, I. K. Zola, J. McNight, J. Caplan and H. Shaiken *Disabling Professions* London, Marion Boyars, 1977, p. 15.
96 J. A. Ashley *Hospitals, Paternalism, and the Role of the Nurse* New York, Teachers College Press, 1976.
97 Cited in Woodham-Smith *Florence Nightingale*, p. 341.
98 Miller *Toward a New Psychology of Woman*, p. 71.

PART 4

1 A. Oakley *Subject Women* London, Fontana, 1982.
2 D. Spender 'Theorizing about Theorizing' in G. Bowles and R. Duelli-Klein (eds) *Theories of Women's Studies* London, Routledge & Kegan Paul, 1983, p. 28.
3 M. Wollstonecraft *Vindication of the Rights of Woman* London, Everyman, 1929 (first published 1792, p. 69).
4 Central Statistical Office *Social Trends 1982* London, HMSO.
5 R. Meighan 'The Pupils' Point of View' in R. Meighan, I. Skelton and T. Marks (eds) *Perspectives on Society: an introductory reader in sociology* London, Thomas Nelson, 1979, p. 102.
6 A. Rich 'Toward a Woman-Centered University' in *On Lies, Secrets, Silence* London, Virago, 1980.
7 A. R. Hochschild 'The Sociology of Feeling and Emotion: selected possibilities' in M. Millman and R. M. Kanter (eds) *Another Voice* New York, Anchor Books, 1975.
8 D. Smith 'A Sociology for Women' in J. A. Sherman and E. T. Beck (eds) *The Prism of Sex* Madison, University of Wisconsin Press, 1979, p. 159.
9 G. W. Brown and T. Harris *Social Origins of Depression* London, Tavistock, 1978.
10 A. Oakley *The Sociology of Housework* London, Martin Robertson, 1974 (reprinted Basil Blackwell, Oxford, 1985).
11 A. Oakley *Women Confined* Oxford, Martin Robertson, 1980.
12 J. Bernard *Women, Wives, Mothers* Chicago, Aldine, 1975.
13 M. Mies 'Towards a Methodology for Feminist Research' in Bowles and Duelli-Klein (eds) *Theories of Women's Studies* pp. 123–4.
14 J. Campbell *Maternal Mortality* Reports on Public Health and Medical Subjects No. 25 Ministry of Health, London, HMSO, 1924, p. 38.

15 B. Chiplin and P. J. Sloane *Tackling Discrimination at the Workplace* Cambridge, Cambridge University Press, 1983.

16 E. Zaretsky *Capitalism, the Family and Personal Life* London, Pluto Press, 1976.

17 S. C. Rogers, 'Woman's Place: a critical review of anthropological theory' *Comparative Studies in Society and History* **20**, 1, 1978, pp. 123–62.

18 V. Beechey 'Women and Production: a critical analysis of some sociological theories of women's work' in A. Kuhn and A. Wolpe (eds) *Feminism and Materialism: women and modes of production* London, Routledge & Kegan Paul, 1978.

19 N. Glazer-Malbin 'Housework' *Signs: Journal of Women in Culture and Society* **1**, 4, 1976, pp. 905–22.

20 E. Bott *Family and Social Network* London, Tavistock, 1957.

21 R. Frankenberg 'In the Production of Their Lives, Men...Sex and Gender in British Community Studies' in D. L. Barker and S. Allen (eds) *Sexual Divisions and Society* London, Tavistock, 1976.

22 A. Oakley *The Sociology of Housework* London, Martin Robertson, 1974 (reprinted 1985).

23 A. Oakley *Housewife* London, Allen Lane, 1974.

24 H. Gavron *The Captive Wife* Harmondsworth, Penguin, 1966.

25 C. Delphy 'Continuities and Discontinuities in Marriage and Divorce' in D. L. Barker and S. Allen (eds) *Sexual Divisions and Society* London, Tavistock, 1976.

26 M. Benston 'The Political Economy of Women's Liberation' *Monthly Review* **21**, 4, 1969, pp. 13–27; M. Dalla Costa 'Women and The Subversion of the Community' *Radical America* **6** (January/February 1972) pp. 67–102; W. Secombe 'The Housewife and her Labour Under Capitalism' *New Left Review* **83** (January/February 1974), pp. 3–24.

27 F. J. Raddatz (ed.) *Karl Marx-Friedrich Engels Selected Letters. The Personal Correspondence 1844–77* Boston, Little, Brown and Co.; *The Daughters of Karl Marx Family Correspondence 1866–98* Commentary and Notes by O. Meier New York, Harcourt Brace Jovanovich.

28 *The Daughters of Karl Marx*, p. 277.

29 M. Benney and E. C. Hughes 'Of Sociology and The Interview' in N. C. Denzin (ed.) *Sociological Methods: a source book* London, Butterworth, 1970, p. 190.

30 M. D. Shipman *The Limitations of Social Research* London, Longman, 1972, p. 76.

31 J. Galtung *Theory and Methods of Social Research* London, Allen and Unwin, 1967, p. 149.

32 Benney and Hughes in *Sociological Methods* p. 191.

33 W. J. Goode and P. K. Hatt *Methods in Social Research* New York, McGraw-Hill, 1952, p. 185.

34 Benney and Hughes, in *Sociological Methods* pp. 196–7.

35 Goode and Hatt *Methods in Social Research* p. 191.

36 R. L. Kahn and L. F. Cannell *The Dynamics of Interviewing* New York, John Wiley, 1957, p. 16.
37 N. K. Denzin (ed.) *Sociological Methods: a source book* London, Butterworth, 1970, p. 186.
38 Goode and Hatt *Methods in Social Research* p. 191.
39 Most respondents appear to be female.
40 C. Selltiz, M. Jahoda, M. Deutsch and S. W. Cook *Research Methods in Social Relations* London, Methuen, 1965.
41 C. A. Moser *Survey Methods in Social Investigation* London, Heinemann, 1958, pp. 187–8, p. 195.
42 *Oxford English Dictionary*.
43 G. Sjoberg and R. Nett *A Methodology for Social Research* New York, Harper and Row, 1968, p. 210.
44 Ibid., p. 212.
45 Galtung, *Theory and Methods of Social Research*, p. 161.
46 Selltiz et al. *Research Methods* p. 576.
47 Goode and Hatt *Methods in Social Reseach* p. 198.
48 A. M. Rose 'A Research Note on Experimentation in Interviewing' *American Journal of Sociology* **51**, 1945, p. 143.
49 Selltiz et al. *Research Methods* p. 576.
50 Ibid., p. 268.
51 Sjoberg and Nett *A Methodology for Social Research* p. 211.
52 J. B. Miller *Toward a New Psychology of Women* Boston, Beacon Press, 1967, p. 7.
53 For example Goode and Hatt *Methods in Social Research* p. 189.
54 Miller *Toward a New Psychology of Women* pp. 6–8.
55 A. R. Hochschild 'The Sociology of Feeling and Emotion: selected possibilities' in M. Millman and R. M. Kanter (eds) *Another Voice: Feminist Perspectives on Social Life and Social Science* New York, Anchor Books, 1975, p. 281.
56 B. Laslett and R. Rapoport 'Collaborative Interviewing and Interactive Research' *Journal of Marriage and the Family* November 1975, p. 968.
57 R. Rapoport and R. Rapoport *Dual Career Families Re-examined* London, Martin Robertson, 1976, p. 31.
58 Goode and Hatt, *Methods in Social Research*, p. 189.
59 Selltiz et al., *Research Methods*, p. 576.
60 A. Oakley *Becoming a Mother* Oxford, Martin Robertson, 1979.
61 L. A. Dexter 'Role Relationships and Conceptions of Neutrality in Interviewing' *American Journal of Sociology* LXI, 4, 1956, p. 156; B. Paul 'Interview Techniques and Field Relationships' in A. L. Kroeber (ed.) *Anthropology Today* University of Chicago Press, 1954.
62 Selltiz et al., *Research Methods* p. 583.
63 S. A. Richardson et al., *Interviewing: its forms and functions* New York, Basic Books, 1965, p. 129.

64 F. Zweig *Labour, Life and Poverty* London, Gollancz, 1949.
65 M. Corbin 'Appendix 3' in J. M. and R. E. Pahl *Managers and Their Wives* London, Allen Lane, 1971, pp. 303–5.
66 A. F. Mamak 'Nationalism, Race-Class Consciousness and Social Research on Bougainville Island, Papua New Guinea' in C. Bell and S. Encel (eds) *Inside the Whale* Oxford, Pergamon Press, 1978, p. 176.
67 D. Hobson 'Housewives: isolation as oppression' in Women's Studies Group, Centre for Contemporary Cultural Studies, *Women Take Issue* London, Hutchinson, 1975.
68 C. Bell and H. Newby *Doing Sociological Research* London, Allen and Unwin, 1977, pp. 9–10.
69 C. Bell and S. Encel (eds) *Inside the Whale* p. 4.
70 M. Stacey *Methods of Social Research* Oxford, Pergamon Press, 1969, p. 2.
71 Sjoberg and Nett *A Methodology for Social Research* pp. 215–6.
72 Mamak, 'Nationalism', p. 168.
73 E. E. Evans-Pritchard *The Nuer* London, Oxford University Press, 1940, pp. 12–13.
74 E. S. Bowen *Return to Laughter* London, Gollancz, 1956, p. 163.
75 H. S. Becker and B. Geer 'Participant Observation and Interviewing: a comparison' *Human Organization* XVI, 1957, p. 28.
76 L. Stanley and S. Wise 'Feminist Research, Feminist Consciousness and Experiences of Sexism' *Women's Studies International Quarterly* 2, 3, 1979, pp. 359–79.

Index

Index by Fiona Barr